THE FORGOTTEN

DAVID BALDACCI

THE FORGOTTEN

DOUBLEDAY LARGE PRINT HOME LIBRARY EDITION

GRAND CENTRAL
PUBLISHING

NEW YORK   BOSTON

Grand Central Publishing
Hachette Book Group
237 Park Avenue
New York, NY 10017

Printed in the United States of America

Grand Central Publishing is a division of Hachette Book Group, Inc.
The Grand Central Publishing name and logo is a trademark of Hachette Book Group, Inc.

ISBN 978-1-62090-578-4

*To Aunt Peggy, an angel on earth
if ever there was one*

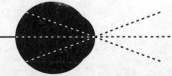

This Large Print Book carries the
Seal of Approval of N.A.V.H.

THE
FORGOTTEN

CHAPTER

1

He had the look of a man who was afraid that tonight would be his last on earth. And he had good reason to think so. The odds were fifty-fifty that it might be, and the percentage could go higher depending on how the next hour turned out.

The margin of error was that small.

The roar of the twin-engine boat moving at near full throttle wiped away the nighttime quiet on calm ocean waters. At this time of year the Gulf of Mexico was usually not so peaceful. This was typically the most active period of the hurricane season. While several storms were brewing out in the open Atlantic, none as yet had formed a firm center and entered the Gulf. Everyone on the coast was crossing his fingers and praying it would remain that way.

The fiberglass hull cut cleanly through the dense, salty water. The boat could hold about twenty people comfortably, but there were thirty folks on board. They were desperately gripping anything they could to keep from being bounced overboard. Despite the smooth waters, a boat carrying far too many people and moving at high speed was never very stable.

The captain piloting the boat did not care about the comfort of his passengers. His top priority was staying alive. He kept one hand on the wheel and the other on the dual throttles. He eyed the speed gauge with a worried look.

Come on. Come on. You can do this. You can make it.

Forty miles per hour. He pushed the throttles ahead and crept the speed stick up to forty-five. He was almost topped out now. Even with the twin stern-drive engines he wouldn't be able to muster more speed without unduly depleting his fuel. And there were no marinas around here to provide more gas.

Even with the breeze created by the boat's movement it was still hot out here. At least one did not have to worry about mosquitoes, not at this speed and this far from land. The man eyed the passengers one by one. It was not an idle observation. He was counting heads, although he already knew the answer. He had four crewmen with him. They were all armed, all watching the "passengers." In a mutiny it would be five against one. But the passengers did not have submachine guns. One clip could take out every one of them with bullets to spare. And the majority were women and children, because that was where the real demand was.

No, he was not worried about a mutiny. He was worried about timing.

The captain checked his illuminated watch. It would be close. They had been late leaving the last outpost. Then their chart plotter had gone haywire for thirty nerve-racking minutes, sending them in completely the wrong direction. This was vast ocean. Every bit of it looked the same. No landmass to aid in navigation. They were not in well-marked shipping channels. Without their electronic guidepost they would be screwed, like flying a plane without instrumentation in thick fog. The only outcome would be disaster.

But they had gotten the plotter straightened out, corrected course, and he had immediately pushed the stern-drives hard. Then he had pushed them some more. His gaze continued to flit to his dash, checking the oil, fuel, and engine temperature gauges. A break-down out here would be catastrophic. They couldn't exactly call the Coast Guard for assistance.

He futilely looked to the skies for eyes watching from up there. Un-manned eyes that would send back gigs of digital data about what they were seeing. He would never hear the response team until it was too late. The Coast Guard cutters would be on them before he could do anything. They would board, know immediately what was going on, and he would go to prison for a very long time, perhaps the rest of his life.

But he was not as scared of the Coast Guard as he was of certain other people.

He pushed the boat's speed up to forty-seven and said a silent prayer that a vital engine part would not blow. He looked at his watch again. He counted the minutes in his head as he scanned the water ahead of them.

"They'll feed me to the sharks," he muttered.

Not for the first time, he regretted agreeing to this business venture. Yet the money was so good he could not turn it down, despite the risks. He had done fifteen of these runs and figured with a similar number in the future he could retire to a nice, quiet spot in the Florida Keys and live like a king. It beat the hell out of driving his boat for pasty tourists from the North looking to land a tuna or marlin but more often simply puking all over his boat in rough seas.

But first I have to get this boat and these people where they need to go.

He eyed the red and green navigation lights on the bow. They gave a solemn glow to an otherwise moonless night. He counted more minutes in his head at the same time as he scanned the boat's gauges.

His heart sank.

His fuel was running low. The stick was dipping perilously close to reserve status. He felt his gut tighten. They had too much weight. And the problem with the navigation system had cost them over an hour, many nautical miles, and precious fuel. He always added a fuel buffer of ten percent to be sure, but even this surplus might not be enough. He scanned the passengers again. Most were women and teenagers, but some were beefy men, easily over two hundred pounds each. And there was one man who was a true giant. But dumping passengers as a solution to his fuel issue was beyond problematic. He might as well put a gun to his own head and pull the trigger.

He swiftly redid the calculations in

his head, just as airline pilots did after getting a full passenger and cargo manifest. It was the same question regardless of whether your ride was in the water or thirty thousand feet above it.

Do I have enough fuel to get there?

He caught the eye of one of his men and beckoned him over.

The man listened to his boss's problem and did his own calculations. "It's gonna be tight," he said worriedly.

"And it's not like we can start throwing people overboard," said the captain.

"Right. They have the manifest. They know how many we're carrying. We start throwing them overboard, we might as well jump in too."

"Tell me some shit I don't know," the captain snapped.

He made a decision and eased off the throttles, cutting their speed back to forty miles per hour. The dual props started spinning more slowly. The boat was still fully up on plane. To the naked eye there wasn't a big difference between forty and forty-seven miles per hour on the water, but with the reduced fuel burn it could be the difference between running dry or making it. They would fuel up, and the return trip, with only five of them on board, would be no problem.

"Better to be a little late than not get there at all," said the captain.

There was a hollow ring to his statement and the other man did not miss it. He clenched his weapon tighter. The captain looked away from him, his throat constricting as a cold dread gripped him.

To the people who'd hired him, timing was important. And being late, even by a few minutes, was never a good thing.

Right now the insane profit margin did not really seem worth it. You couldn't spend money if you were dead.

But thirty minutes later, with his engines starting to suck on air instead of fuel, the captain saw his destination straight ahead. It rose out of the ocean like a throne for Neptune.

They were here. They were very late, but at least they'd made it.

He looked at the passengers. They too were staring at the structure, their eyes bugged out. He couldn't blame them. Even though this was not the first such structure they had seen it was still a monstrous sight, especially at night. Hell, it still freaked him out, even after all the similar trips he'd made. He just wanted to dump his load, fuel up, and get his ass back to where he'd come from. As soon as the twenty-five passengers stepped off his boat they were someone else's problem.

He slowed his engines and took his time docking alongside a floating metal platform tethered to the larger structure. After the ropes were secured, hands reached across and started pulling the passengers onto the platform, which bobbed up and down from the light chop created by the docking process.

He didn't see the larger ship that was normally waiting to take passengers onward. It must have already left with a load.

As the captain signed off on some documents and received his pay in plastic bundles taped down, he looked at the passengers as they were herded up a long metal stairway. They all looked terrified.

They should be, he thought. The unknown was not nearly as terrifying as the known. And he understood quite clearly that these people were well aware of what was about to happen to them. And they also knew that no one else cared.

They were not rich.

They were not powerful.

They were truly the forgotten.

And their numbers were growing exponentially as the world was settling swiftly into a permanent state of the rich and thus powerful and then everyone else. And what the rich and powerful wanted, they usually got.

He opened one of the plastic bundles. His mind did not immediately register what he was seeing. When it became apparent that what he was holding was cut-up newspaper and not money, he looked up.

The muzzle of the MP5 was pointed directly at him, less than ten feet away, held by a man standing on Neptune's Seat. The MP was an awesome killing weapon at close quarters. It would prove so tonight.

The captain had time to put up his hand, as though flesh and bone would block shaped ordnance coming at him far faster than a jumbo jet could fly. When it hit him it did so with thousands of foot-pounds of kinetic energy. Twenty such rounds slammed into him at roughly the same time, shredding his body.

The impact of the spray of slugs knocked him off his feet and then over the gunwale. Before he sank beneath the waves the four other men on board joined him in the water. All shredded, all dead, they disappeared into the depths. The sharks would have a buffet tonight.

Punctuality was not only a virtue, it seemed, but also an absolute necessity.

CHAPTER

2

The vessel was immediately drained of its fuel, oil, and other fluids and then scuttled. Oil and gas created a large sheen on the water's surface that could be seen from above by patrolling Coast Guard and DEA planes.

During the day the abandoned oil platform would look, well, abandoned. Not a prisoner in sight. They would all be inside the main structure safely away from view. Shipments of fresh product moved in and out only at night. During the day the operation shut down. The risk of being seen was too great.

There were thousands of shuttered oil platforms in the Gulf awaiting either demolition or else transformation into artificial reefs. Though laws required that the demolition or transformation take place typically within a year of abandonment, the actual time for that to happen could be much longer. And all the while these platforms, large enough to comfortably house hundreds, just sat there well out to sea. They were empty and ripe for exploitation by certain ambitious folks who needed a series of landing sites as they shepherded their precious cargo across broad waters.

As the vessel slowly sank into the deep Gulf, the passengers were herded up steel steps. They had been roped together and spaced a foot apart. The younger ones had a hard time keeping in step with the adults. When they fell, they were immediately jerked back into line and then beaten around the shoulders and arms. Their faces, however, were not touched.

One man, far bigger than the rest, kept his gaze downcast as he marched up the metal steps. He was over six-six and rock-solid, with broad shoulders and narrow hips, and thighs and calves easily the girth of a professional athlete's. He also possessed the hard, bony musculature and near-gaunt features of a man who had grown up with not enough to eat. He would fetch a good price, but not as high as the girls, for obvious reasons. Everything was based on profit margins, and the girls, particularly the younger ones, had the highest margins of all. And that could be extended over at least ten years. By that time they would have collectively earned millions of dollars for their owners.

By contrast, his life would be relatively short as he was literally worked to death, or so his captors believed. "LMP," or "low-margin product," he would be called. The girls, on the other hand, were simply referred to as "gold."

He seemed to be mumbling to himself, but not in a language that anyone around him could understand. He missed a step and stumbled. Batons immediately rained down on his shoulders and the back of his legs. One struck him in the face, bloodying his nose. They were apparently not worried about *his* looks.

He rose and kept going. And kept mumbling. The blows did not seem to have affected him.

There was a young girl in front of him who glanced back at him once, but he didn't return her gaze. An older woman in line behind him shook her head and said a prayer in her native Spanish and then made the sign of the cross.

The man stumbled again, and again the beating took place. The guards jabbered at him, slapped him with their roughened hands. He took the punishment, rose, and kept going. And kept mumbling.

A shaft of heat lightning to the east illuminated the sky for about a second. Whether or not the man interpreted this event as some divine signal to act was unclear. His actions, however, were crystal clear.

He bulled past one guard, slamming into the man so hard that the guard pitched over the rail and plummeted down more than thirty feet, hitting and bouncing off the steel platform. His neck broke on impact and he lay still.

What was unnoticed was the sharp knife that the mumbling man had taken from the guard's belt. It was his sole reason for attacking him. As the other gunmen lined up their shots, the man cut through his bindings, grabbed a life jacket hanging on a hook on the stair rail, slipped it on, and dove off on the opposite side from where the guard had gone over.

When he landed he did not hit steel. He slammed into the warm waters of the Gulf.

He broke the surface awkwardly and went under.

Seconds later a barrage of MP5 rounds ripped the surface of the water, creating hundreds of tiny whitecaps. A boat was sent out a few minutes later to look for him. But there was no sign. In the dark, he could have gone in any direction, and it was a lot of surface water to cover. The boat finally returned. The Gulf waters grew calm once more. He was probably dead, they thought.

If not he soon would be.

The remaining prisoners, twenty-four of them now, continued their slow ascent to the cells where they would be kept until another boat came to take them onward. They were placed mostly five to a cage. There they joined other prisoners who were also awaiting rides to the mainland. They were young, older, and in between. They were all foreigners, all poor or otherwise not part of any mainstream society. Some had been targeted and captured. Others had merely been unlucky.

As bad as that luck had been, it would only get worse once they left here.

The guards, mostly foreigners themselves, never made eye contact and did not even acknowledge the existence of their captives, other than when they slid plates of food and jugs of water inside the cages.

The captives were just nameless, meaningless bits of particle temporarily residing in the Gulf of Mexico. They sat on their haunches. Some stared out between the bars of the cages; most kept their gazes on the floor. They were defeated, resigned, unwilling to attempt a fight, or find a path to freedom. They seemed to have stoically accepted their fate.

The older woman who had been behind the large man would occasionally direct her gaze far down to the ocean's surface. It would have been impossible for her to see anything in the water from the enclosed space. But once or twice she imagined that she had seen something. When the food and water came she ate and drank her small allotted share and pondered the man who had attempted an escape. She silently admired his bravery, even if it had cost him his life. At least he was free, if dead. That was far better than what awaited her.

Yes, maybe he was the lucky one, she thought. She put a bit of bread in her mouth and took a sip of warm water from the plastic jug and forgot all about the man.

A half mile from Neptune's Seat the man swam through the water. He looked back in the direction of the structure, now invisible to him. He had never intended to swim to shore from an oil platform. This was solely improvisation on his part. He had planned to take a plane from Texas to Florida. His current dilemma was the result of carelessness on his part that had resulted in his becoming a victim. But he had to get to land, and swimming there seemed to be the only way.

He adjusted the life jacket—which was too small for him but provided some needed buoyancy—and treaded water for a bit, trying to move as little as possible. Next he turned and started to float on his back. Darkness was when the sharks came out. Eventually, though, he would have to swim. Nighttime was the best time to do that, despite the dangers from the finned predators. Daylight would leave him exposed to many hazards, many of them man-made. Aided by the stars, which provided some needed navigational guidance, he set out in the direction that he believed to be toward land. He would occasionally look back at the platform, trying hard to solidify in his mind its location in the vastness of the Gulf. It was unlikely, he knew, but he might one day have to find it again.

His strokes were compact, seemingly effortless. With the buoyancy of the life jacket he could keep this pace up for hours. And he would have to, to get where he needed to go. He had decided to turn a possible catastrophe into an advantage.

He would head in the same direction another fast boat would have taken him at a later point in time. Perhaps he would beat his fellow captives to the final destination, if the sharks didn't disrupt his plans by shearing off a limb or two and leaving him to bleed out alone.

His strokes became automatic, his breathing the same. This allowed his mind to wander and then focus on what lay ahead. The swim would be long and exhausting and fraught with peril. He could die at many points along the way. But he had survived much to get to this point. He would simply will himself to live.

He had to hope it would be enough.

It usually had been in a life marked more by tragedy and pain than by anything remotely approaching normalcy.

He stoically accepted it as his lot in life.

And he swam on.

CHAPTER

3

The old woman was tall but bent. Her spine had curved itself over the last decade, and that had reduced her height by three inches. Her hair was cut short and in severe lines around her face, which had all the wrinkles and sun damage one would expect after more than eight decades of living, two of them in coastal Florida. She navigated with the aid of a walker, two tennis balls stuck onto the bottoms of the front legs for stability.

Her large hands clutched the top bar of the walker. Over her shoulder was her purse. It was large and bulky and rode awkwardly against her body. Her gait was steady and purposeful. She looked neither right nor left, nor over her shoulder. She was a woman on a mission and the passersby on the street voluntarily moved out of her way. Some smiled at what they no doubt believed was a dotty old woman who no longer cared what anyone thought about her behavior. It was true she no longer cared what others thought. But she was far from dotty.

Her destination was just up ahead.

A mailbox.

She ran her walker right up to it, using a free hand to balance herself against the stout property of the U.S. Postal Service. With her other hand she reached into her purse and pulled out the letter. She paused and looked at the address one last time.

She had spent considerable time writing the letter. The younger generation, with all of its tweets and Facebook and cryptic texts and emails where no actual language or grammar were involved, would never have understood taking the time to compose a handwritten missive such as this one. But she had wanted to get the words just right, because what she was writing about was so extraordinary. At least to her way of thinking.

The addressee's name was written in block letters to make it as clear as possible. She did not want this piece of mail to go astray.

General John Puller, Senior (Ret.).

She was sending it in care of the VA hospital where she knew he was staying. She knew his health was not good, but she also knew that he was a man who could make things happen. He had risen nearly as high in the military as it was possible to go.

And he was also her brother. Her younger brother.

Big sisters were special to their little brothers. While they were growing up he had done his best to make her life miserable, playing an endless series of practical jokes on her, embarrassing her in front of her boyfriends, competing with her for their parents' affections.

It was different when they became adults. Then it was like the grown man was desperately trying to make up for all the hardship he had caused his older sister.

She could count on him to sort this out. More to the point, he had a son, her nephew, who was very good at figuring things out. She reckoned this letter would eventually end up in his capable hands. And she hoped he came down here. It had been a long time since she had seen her nephew.

Too long.

She opened the lid of the mailbox and watched the letter slide down the metal gullet. She closed the lid and then opened it twice more just to make sure the letter was in the belly of the box.

She turned her walker around and made her way back to the cabstand. She had a favorite taxi driver who had picked her up from her home and now would drive her back there. She could still drive but chose not to tonight.

The mailbox was situated at the end

of a one-way street. It was easier for him to park where he had, leaving her with only a short walk to the mailbox. He had offered to post the letter for her, but she had declined. She needed to do it herself, and she also needed the exercise.

He was a youngster to her, only in his late fifties. He wore an old-fashioned chauffeur's hat, although the rest of his outfit was decidedly more casual: khaki shorts, blue polo shirt, and canvas boat shoes on his feet. His tan was so uniformly dark that it looked like the product of a UV bed or spray-on tan.

"Thank you, Jerry," she said, as she climbed, with his assistance, into the backseat of the Prius. Jerry folded up her walker and put it in the rear of the car before getting into the driver's seat.

"Everything good to go, Ms. Simon?" he asked.

"I hope so," she replied. For the first time she looked and felt truly nervous.

"You want to go back home now?"

"Yes, please. I'm tired."

Jerry turned around in his seat and

scrutinized her. "You look pale. Maybe you should go see a doctor. Got enough of them in Florida."

"Maybe I will. But not right now. I just need some rest."

He drove her back to her little community on the beach. They passed a pair of soaring palm trees and a sign set on a brick wall that read, "Sunset by the Sea."

The sign had always irritated her, because she lived by an ocean, not a sea. Technically, she actually lived on the coast of the Gulf of Mexico in the Panhandle of Florida. She had always thought that "Sunset Coast" or "Sunset Gulf" sounded better than "Sunset by the Sea." But the name was official and there was no changing it.

Jerry drove her to her house on Orion Street and saw her inside. A typical residence for this part of Florida, it was a two-story structure with cinderblock walls covered in beige stucco with a red terra-cotta roof and a two-car garage. The house had three bedrooms, with hers right off the kitchen. It was thirty-one hundred square feet in an efficient footprint, far larger than she needed, but she had no interest in moving. This would be her last home. She had known that for a long time.

She had a palm tree out front and some grass and decorative rocks in the yard. In the back a privacy fence ran along the property line, and she had a small reflecting pool along with a bench and a table where she could sit, drink her coffee, and enjoy both the cooler mornings and the final rays of the evening light. On either side of her house was another house pretty much exactly the same. All of Sunset by the Sea was pretty much the same, as though the builder had some large machine to spit the houses out off-site to later be transported and erected here.

The beach was behind her house, just a short drive or long walk to the sugar-white sand of the Emerald Coast.

It was summer and the temperature was in the low seventies at nearly six in the evening. That was about twenty degrees cooler than the high for the day, which was about average for Paradise, Florida, at this time of the year.

Paradise, she thought. A silly, conceited name, but she also couldn't say it didn't fit. It was beautiful here most of the time.

She would take heat over cold any day. That's why they had invented Florida, she assumed. And perhaps Paradise in particular.

And why the snowbirds flocked here every winter.

She sat in her living room and gazed around at the memories of a lifetime. On the walls and shelves were photos of friends and family. Her gaze rested longest on a picture of her husband, Lloyd, a natural-born salesman. She had fallen in love with him after World War II. He had sold her a bill of goods, too, she supposed. He always claimed to be more successful than he was. He was a good salesman but a bigger spendthrift, she had found. But he was funny, made her laugh, didn't have a violent bone in his body, never drank to excess, and he loved her. He never cheated on her, though with his job and the traveling involved, he certainly had had chances to wander from his marriage vows.

Yes, she missed her Lloyd. After he'd passed away, she'd discovered he had a sizable life insurance policy he'd kept in force. She'd taken the whole of it and bought two stocks. Apple and Amazon. This had been way back. The two A's on her report card, she liked to call them. The investment return had been enough to allow her to pay off the mortgage on this house and live very comfortably on far more money than Social Security alone would have allowed her.

She had a light supper and some iced tea. Her appetite wasn't nearly what it once was. Then she watched some TV, falling asleep in front of the screen. When she awoke she felt disoriented. Shaking her head to clear it, she decided it was time to go to bed. She rose with the aid of her walker and headed toward her bedroom. She would sleep for a few hours and then get back up, start her day over again. That was her life now.

She noticed a shadow of movement

behind her, but had no chance to feel alarmed about it.

That was to be Betsy Puller Simon's last memory.

A shadow behind her.

A few minutes later there was a splash from the backyard.

CHAPTER

4

The timing was as good as it would ever get. He performed a few more strokes in the water until he finally felt the earth beneath his feet.

He had lucked out and been picked up by a small fishing boat about two hours after his escape from the platform. The men had asked no questions. They gave him some food and water. They told him their location, and by reversing that course he got a better fix on the platform out in the Gulf. He could not forget all the prisoners housed there. They would be gone before he would ever return there. But there would be others to replace them.

The fishing boat could not take him all the way to shore, they told him, but they would get him close enough. They chugged along slowly for what seemed a long time and he helped them with their work as part repayment for their helping him. They could not make a beeline for his destination. They were out here to work, and work they would.

His great strength was marveled at by the fishermen, and they seemed sorry to see him go.

They pointed in the direction of land when they got to the place where he needed to get off. They gave him a better-fitted life jacket and he slipped over the side of the boat and started swimming toward land.

As he turned back he saw one of the men make the sign of the cross over his chest. Then his sole focus became reaching something he could stand on.

By the time he arrived on shore his muscles were tight, knotted, and he was once more dehydrated. Water had been all around him for such a long time and yet he had not been able to drink even a drop of it. Fish had nipped at him. Singly that was not a problem. Cumulatively, his legs and arms were covered in tiny cuts and welts. And his head and shoulders hurt from the beating he'd taken from the guards and from his plunge off the platform. He could feel the bruises and cuts on his face from these impacts.

But he was alive.

And on land.

Finally.

The darkness covered his high-stepping through the last few breakers until he reached the sugar-white sand of the Emerald Coast in Florida's Panhandle. He looked right and left up the beach for any late-night beachcombers. Seeing none, he dropped to his knees, rolled onto his back, and drew in long deep breaths as he stared at a sky so clear there seemed to be no space between the billions of visible stars. Paradise was a small town with long beaches, but its downtown area was built right along the sand. The central business district was farther down and to the west. And luckily it was so late that there was no one out on the board-walk that ran parallel to the beach where he was.

He thanked God for allowing him to live. So many hours of swimming, and then being picked up by the boat. In the vastness of the Gulf, what were the odds of that without divine interven-tion? The sharks had also miraculously left him alone. He had to attribute that to his prayers as well.

His captors had not come after him. Prayer again.

Thankfully, the beach was deserted.

Well, not quite.

God must have missed that one.

He hunkered down in the sand as he heard the people coming.

Then he flattened himself to the beach and burrowed in, allowing his over six-foot-six-inch, 290-pound frame to blend into the white grit that people from around the world came to lie on during the course of a year.

It was two people. He could tell by the different voices.

One man. One woman.

He lifted his head a bare inch and stared in their direction. They were not walking a dog. Prayer, again. A dog would have found his scent by now.

He would not act unless they spotted him. And even then, they might just assume he was simply lying on the beach enjoying the evening. He hoped they would not see him, and that if they did they would not panic. He knew that after his long journey at sea he must look pretty bad.

He tensed his body, waited for them to pass by.

They were within forty feet of him. The woman looked in his direction. The moonlight was not strong, but not weak either.

He heard her exclaim and then say something to her companion.

But then he realized that she was not actually looking in his direction.

As he watched, a lithe figure came out from behind the cover of sand dunes.

There was one pop and the man fell.

The woman turned to run, but there was another pop and she fell too, hitting the compacted sand with a thud.

The figure put the gun away, gripped the woman's hands, and dragged her into the water a good ten feet. The tide took over from there and the body quickly sank beneath the water and was swept out.

This same process was repeated on the man.

The figure stood on the sand a few inches from the water and scanned the breakers, probably making sure the bodies were not going to be swept back to shore. Then the figure turned and was gone the way it had come.

He kept his body flat to the stretch of beach even as he felt shame for not coming to the couple's assistance. But it had happened so quickly that he doubted he could have prevented their deaths.

And sometimes God was busy with other things. This he knew to be true. God had often been busy when he had needed him. But then many people needed God. He was just one of billions who asked for divine assistance from time to time.

He waited until he was certain the shooter was gone. He had no idea why the couple had been killed. He had no idea who had killed them. It was not any of his business.

He could not remain on the beach now. He made his way to the boardwalk, and spotted a bicycle chained to a post. He ripped the post out of the ground, freeing the chain. He wound the chain around the frame, climbed onto the bike, and set off.

He had the city's streets mostly memorized. He had a place to go, to stay, where he could change his clothes, rest, eat, hydrate, and then he could begin his quest, the real reason he had come here.

As he disappeared into the night, he began to mumble again, to pray for forgiveness for not helping the couple by killing their attacker. He was good at killing, perhaps the best. But that did not mean that he liked it, because he did not.

He was a giant, but actually a gentle man.

But even gentle giants could be moved to violence for the right reasons.

He had such reasons.

He had them in abundance.

He was no longer going to be gentle. Not while he was here.

It was the sole thing driving him. Indeed, it was the only thing really keeping him alive.

He rode on as the two corpses were pulled slowly out to sea.

CHAPTER

5

John Puller took a sharp left-hand turn and drove down the narrow two-lane road. In the backseat of the car was his cat, AWOL, who had wandered into his life one day and would probably leave him just as unexpectedly. Puller was in the Army, formerly a Ranger, and currently a CID, or Criminal Investigation Division, special agent. He was not investigating any cases at the moment. Right now he was just returning from a protracted road trip with his cat, allowing himself a bit of R&R after a hellish experience in a small West Virginia coal-mining town that had nearly ended with him and many other people dead.

He pulled into the parking lot of his apartment complex. It was near Quantico, Virginia, where the Army's CID headquarters was located along with the 701st M.P. Group (CID), the unit to which Puller was attached. This made for an easy work commute, although he rarely spent much time at Quantico. He was more often on the road investigating crimes that involved a person who wore the uniform of the United States Army and yet was doing bad things. And unfortunately, there were a lot of cases to work.

He parked his car, a trim Army-issued Malibu, grabbed his rucksack from the trunk, opened the back door, and waited patiently for AWOL, a fat orange-and-brown tabby, to mosey out. The cat followed him up to his apartment. Puller lived in six hundred square feet of rigid lines and minimal clutter. He had been in the Army for most of his adult life and now, in his mid-thirties, his personal aversion to junk and clutter was irreversibly established.

He got food and water out for AWOL, snagged a beer from the fridge, sat down in his leather recliner, put his feet up, and closed his eyes. He couldn't remember the last time he'd actually gotten a full night's sleep. He decided to do something about it right now.

The last few weeks had not been especially kind to Puller, who was nearly six feet four and a normally solid 232 pounds. He had not gotten any shorter, but he had lost about ten pounds because his appetite had abandoned him. Physically, he was still doing okay. He could beat any test the military might offer related to strength, endurance, or speed. Mentally, however, he was not doing very well. He wasn't sure he ever would be doing well mentally again. Some days he thought he would, others not. This was one of the other days.

Puller had gone on the road trip to try to get his head back on straight after the ordeal in West Virginia.

It had not worked. If anything, he was even worse. The time away, the miles driven had only provided him with far too much time to think. Sometimes that was not good. He didn't want to think anymore. He just wanted to be doing something that would carry him into the future instead of transporting him to the past.

His phone buzzed. He looked at the readout on the screen.

USDB. That stood for the United States Disciplinary Barracks. It was located in Fort Leavenworth, Kansas. It was the Army's prison for its most important—that is, dangerous—criminals.

Puller knew it well. He had visited there often.

His older brother and only sibling, Robert Puller, would be stationed there for the rest of his natural life, and maybe even beyond, if the Pentagon had its way.

"Hello?"

"Please hold," an efficient-sounding female voice said.

The next moment a familiar voice came on the line.

It was his brother, formerly a major in the Air Force before being convicted at court-martial for treason against his country for reasons that Puller neither was privy to nor would probably ever understand for as long as he lived.

"Hey, Bobby," said Puller dully. His head was starting to ache.

"Where are you?"

He said irritably, "Just got back. Just put my feet up. What's going on?"

"How was your road trip? Get things figured out?"

"I'm good."

"Which means you didn't and you're just blowing me off. That's okay. I can take it."

Normally, Puller looked forward to talking to his brother. Their calls and visits were infrequent. But not this time. He just wanted to sit in his recliner with his beer and think of exactly nothing.

"What's going on?" he said again, a little more firmly.

"Okay, I read you loud and clear. 'Get the hell off the phone, I don't want to talk.' I wouldn't be bothering you except for the call I got."

Puller sat up in his recliner and put his beer down.

"What call? The Old Man?"

There was only one "Old Man" in the Puller brothers' lives.

That would be John Puller Sr., a retired three-star and a fighting legend. He was an old bastard from the Patton Kicking Ass and Taking No Names School of Combat. However, the former commander of the legendary 101st Airborne was now in a veterans' hospital suffering from short but intense bouts of dementia and long and even more intense episodes of depression. The dementia was probably because of age. The depression was because he no longer wore the uniform, no longer commanded a single soldier, and thus felt he had no more reason left to live. Puller Sr. had been put on earth for one reason only: to lead soldiers into combat.

More to the point, he had been put on this earth to lead soldiers to *victory* in combat. At least that's what he believed. And most days both his sons would have agreed with that assessment.

"People on behalf of the Old Man

from the hospital. They couldn't reach you, so they tried me. I can't exactly up and visit the Old Man."

"What did they call about? Is he failing mentally again? Did he fall down and break a hip?"

"No on both counts. I don't think it has to do with him personally. They weren't entirely clear what the issue was, probably because Dad wasn't entirely clear with them. I believe that it involved a letter that he received, but I can't swear to that. But that's what it seemed to be about."

"A letter. Who from?"

"Again, can't answer that. I thought with you being pretty much right there you could go over and find out what's going on. They said he was really upset."

"But they didn't know what was in the letter? How can that be?"

"You know how that can be," replied Robert. "I don't care how old or out of it Dad is. If he doesn't want you to read a letter he has, you ain't reading it. He can still kick ass even at his age. There's not a doctor in the VA system who could take him or would ever want to try."

"Okay, Bobby, I'll head over now."

"John, all bullshit aside, you okay?"

"All bullshit aside, no, Bobby, I'm not okay."

"What are you going to do about it?"

"I'm in the Army."

"Meaning what exactly?"

"Meaning I'm going to soldier on."

"You can always talk to somebody. The Army has lots of specialists who do just that. You went through a lot of shit in West Virginia. It would screw anybody up. Like PTSD."

"I don't need to talk to anybody."

"I wouldn't be too sure about that."

"Puller men don't talk about their troubles."

Puller could imagine his brother shaking his head in disappointment.

"Is that family rule number three or four?"

Puller said, "For me, right now, it's rule number one."

CHAPTER

6

As he walked down the hall at the VA hospital Puller wondered whether he would end up in one himself when he got older. As he looked around at the elderly sick and disabled former soldiers his spirits dropped even more.

Maybe a shot to the head when the time comes would be better.

He knew where his father's room was and so bypassed the nurse's desk. He actually heard his old man long before he saw him. John Puller Sr. had always possessed a voice like a bullhorn, and age and his other infirmities had done nothing to lessen its power. Indeed, in some ways, it seemed even more strident than before.

As Puller approached the door to his father's room it opened and a frazzled-looking nurse stepped out.

"God, am I glad you're here," she said, staring up at Puller. He was not in uniform but she apparently had easily recognized him.

"What's the problem?" asked Puller.

"*He's* the problem," she replied. "He's been asking for you for the last twenty-four hours. He won't let it go."

Puller put his hand on the knob. "He was a three-star. It's always personal and they never let anything go. It's in their DNA."

"Good luck," said the nurse.

"It'll have nothing to do with luck," said Puller as he walked into the room and shut the door behind him.

Inside the room he put his broad back to the door and gazed around. The place was small, maybe ten by ten, like a prison cell. Actually, it was about the same size as the place his brother would be calling home at USDB for the rest of his life.

The room was furnished with a hospital bed, a laminated wood nightstand, a curtain for privacy, and a chair that did not look comfortable and felt just how it looked.

Then there was one window, a tiny closet, and a bathroom with support bars and panic buttons all over the place.

And then, lastly, his old man, John Puller Sr., the former commander of arguably the Army's most famous division, the 101st Airborne Screaming Eagles.

"XO, where the hell you been?" said Puller Sr., staring at his son like he had him lined up over iron gunsights.

"On assignment, just got back. Hear there's something up, sir."

"Damn right there is."

Puller moved forward and stood at ease by the side of the bed where his father lay, wearing a white T-shirt and loose-fitting blue scrub pants. Once nearly as tall as his son, the old man had been shrunken by age to a little over six-one—still tall, but not the near giant he had once been. A white fringe of cottony hair ran around the rim of his head, with nothing else on top. His eyes were ice blue and went from flashing fire to vacant, sometimes in the span of a few seconds.

The doctors weren't quite sure what was going on with Puller Sr. They wouldn't officially call it Alzheimer's or even dementia. They had begun to say simply that he was "getting old."

Puller just hoped his father had enough lucidity left today to tell him about the letter. Or at least to allow him to see it.

"You received a letter?" he prompted. "Top-secret communication? Maybe from SecArm?" he added, referring to the Secretary of the Army.

Although his father had been out of the Army for nearly two decades, he didn't seem to realize that was so. Puller had found it better to keep the military subterfuge going, in order to put his father at ease, and also to move conversations forward. He felt silly doing it, but the doctors had persuaded him that this was a preferable course, at least in the short term. And maybe the short term was all his father had left.

His father nodded and looked grim. "Not bullshit, at least I don't think so. Got me concerned, XO."

"Can I get read in, sir?"

His father hesitated, stared up at him, his expression that of a man who was not quite sure what or who he was looking at.

"Think I can get read in, General?" Puller asked again, his voice quieter but also firmer.

His father pointed to his pillow. "Under there. Had me concerned."

"Yes, sir. May I, sir?"

Puller indicated the pillow and his father nodded and sat up.

Puller stepped forward and pulled up the pillow. Underneath was an envelope that had been torn open. Puller picked it up and gazed at it. The address was written in block letters. His dad. At this VA hospital. Postmarked from a place called Paradise, Florida. The place sounded vaguely familiar. He looked at the name in the top left-hand corner of the envelope.

Betsy Puller Simon. That's why it sounded familiar.

That was his aunt and his father's sister. She was older than her brother by nearly ten years. Lloyd Simon had been her husband. He'd died many years ago. Puller had been on deployment in Afghanistan back then. He remembered getting a note from his father about it. He hadn't thought about his aunt very often since then and suddenly wondered why. Well, now he was totally focused on her.

She'd written to her brother. The brother was upset. Puller was about to find out why, he supposed. He hoped it wasn't about a missing pet, or an unpaid bill, or that his elderly aunt was getting remarried and maybe wanted her younger brother to give her away.

There was no way that was happening.

He slid the single sheet of paper out of the envelope and unfolded it. It was heavy stock with a nice watermark. In five years they probably wouldn't even make this stuff anymore. Who wrote letters by hand these days?

He focused on the spidery handwriting sprawled across the page. It was written in blue ink, which made it jump off the cream-colored paper.

There were three paragraphs in the letter. Puller read all three, twice. His aunt had ended by writing, "Love to you, Johnny. Betsy."

Johnny and Betsy?

It made his father seem almost human.

Almost.

Puller could now understand why his father had been upset after reading the letter. His aunt had clearly been upset while writing it.

Something was going on down in Paradise, Florida, that she didn't like. She didn't go into detail in the letter, but what she had written was enough to get Puller interested. Mysterious happenings at night. People not being who they seemed. A general air of something not being right. She had named no names. But she had ended the letter by asking for help not from her brother.

She asked specifically for my help.

His aunt must've known that he was an Army investigator. Perhaps his father had told her. Perhaps she had found out on her own. What he did for a living was not a secret.

He folded the letter back up and put it in his pocket. He looked at his father, who was now gazing across at the little TV set connected to the wall by way of a hinged arm. On the screen was *The Price Is Right*. His father seemed intrigued by the goings-on. This was a man who, in addition to having led the 101st, had commanded an entire corps composed of up to five divisions, totaling nearly a hundred thousand highly trained soldiers, in combat. And he was now intently watching a TV show where people guessed the prices of everyday stuff in an attempt to win more stuff.

"Can I keep the letter, sir?" he asked.

Now that Puller had been summoned and had the letter and matter seemingly in hand, his father no longer seemed interested or upset. He waved his hand in a vague symbol of dismissal.

"Take care of it, XO. Report back when the matter is resolved."

"Thank you, sir, I'll do my best, sir."

Even though his father wasn't looking at him, he performed a crisp salute, spun on his heel, and exited. He did this because the last time he'd seen his father he'd walked out on him in both disgust and frustration, leaving the old man to scream after him. Apparently that memory no longer resided in his father's mind. Along with a lot of other things. But it had remained in Puller's mind, stark and fierce.

However, as his hand hit the door pull his father said, "Take care of Betsy, XO, she's the real deal."

Puller looked back at his father. The old man had turned and was staring at him. His ice blue eyes appeared to hold as much lucidity as they ever had. He was no longer in *Price Is Right* land.

"I will, sir. Count on me."

On the way out Puller ran into his father's primary-care physician. Balding and slight of build, he was a good doctor and labored here for far less money than his medical degree from Yale could have earned him elsewhere.

"So how's he doing?" asked Puller.

"As good as can be expected. Physically, he's still an amazing specimen. I wouldn't want to arm-wrestle him. But up top things seem to be continuing to slip."

"Anything that can be done?"

"He's on the meds typically prescribed for his condition. There is no cure, of course. We can't reverse things now, though the future holds some promise for that. I just think it's going to be a long downward spiral, John. And it might speed up as time goes on. Sorry it's not better news."

Puller thanked the doctor and headed on. He knew all of this, but still asked each time he was here. Maybe part of him thought the answer might one day turn out to be different.

He left the hospital and walked to his car. On the way he took the letter back out of his pocket. His aunt had helpfully written in her phone number in Paradise. He reached his car, sat on the hood, slid out his phone, and punched in the digits.

Puller was not someone who liked to put off to the next minute what he could do in the current one.

The phone rang four times and then went to voice mail. Puller left a message for his aunt and then clicked off and put the phone away.

He gazed at the letter again as he sat there on the hood of his Malibu. Well, it actually belonged to the United States Army, but Puller *was* the United States Army, so maybe it was the same thing.

A letter with troubling concerns. But then again he'd only tried to call her once. Maybe she was simply at the doctor's. Elderly people spent much of their time at doctors' offices. He had certainly seen that with his father.

Puller sighed. In many important ways this was not his problem. His father had probably forgotten all about the letter. Puller hadn't seen his aunt in a long time. She had not been a part of his life as an adult. But she had been when he was a young boy. Sort of a substitute for a mother who was not there because she couldn't be.

All these years later Puller still could recall vividly moments spent with Betsy Simon. She had been there for him when he needed something that he simply did not have in life. Things that little boys needed. Things that fathers could not supply, even if they happened to be around, which his father had not. He'd been too busy commanding thousands of men to do things not just the Army way, but also *his* way. Betsy Simon had filled that void. She was so important to him back then. He had talked to her about everything, both troubles and triumphs. She had been a wonderful listener. And Puller had come to realize that the advice she dispensed to him growing up had been couched so artfully that it seemed to be his own ideas.

He had leave time still remaining. No one had expected him back this early. He could not walk away from this.

Or her. And it wasn't entirely altruism. A part of Puller wondered whether his aunt could once more help him through troubling times. And not just with his father. He had never really talked about what had happened in West Virginia with anyone, not even his brother. Yet, despite what he'd told his brother, Puller had things he needed to talk about. What he didn't have was someone he felt comfortable doing that with.

Maybe his aunt could be that person. Again.

It looked like he was headed to Paradise.

CHAPTER

7

There were many avenues, it seemed, to get to Paradise. Puller chose a Delta flight connecting through Atlanta that got him into the Northwest Florida Regional Airport four and a half hours after he left Washington. The airport was actually on land owned by the United States government. Eglin Air Force Base was one of the biggest Air Force bases in the world, and one the Army grunt Puller had visited while in Ranger School.

This part of Florida was on central daylight saving time, so when Puller walked to the Hertz rental car counter he took a few moments to change the time on his watch. It was now ten-thirty hours CDST. He had gained an hour. The temperature was already in the eighties.

"Welcome to the Emerald Coast," the woman behind the Hertz counter told him. She was short and stout with frizzy hair dyed brown from its normal gray.

"I thought the spiel would be 'Welcome to Paradise,'" said Puller.

She looked up at him and smiled. "Well, that's about forty minutes or so from here. And I try to mix it up. But I probably say 'Welcome to Paradise' about twenty percent of the time."

"I guess even Paradise can get a little old."

"You want a convertible?" she asked. "Everyone does when they come here. Got a beautiful Corvette that was just turned in."

"I don't know, how much is it?"

When she said the per diem price he shook his head. "Army doesn't pay me enough to afford that."

"You're in the Army?"

"Ever since college."

"So is my son. He's a Ranger."

"I was an instructor with the Ranger Training Brigade and then went across the street to the 75th out of Fort Benning for two years before I deployed to the Middle East.

"Rangers lead the way."

"It's what I've always thought despite what the Marines and the SEALs say," replied Puller.

She paused. "You still want that Corvette?"

"Like I said, ma'am, it's not in my budget."

"How much can you afford?"

Puller told her.

"Then it *is* in your budget." She started clicking computer keys.

"Can you do that?" he asked.

"I just did," she replied. "And the GPS is thrown in for no charge."

"I appreciate it."

"No, I appreciate *you*."

The Corvette was a gold color, and Puller pulled out onto the road feeling pretty golden himself. He took Highway 85 south and passed places named

Shalimar, Cinco Bayou, and Fort Walton Beach. Then he merged onto the Miracle Strip Parkway, crossed over Okaloosa Island, which was also part of the massive footprint of Eglin AFB, zoomed across a bridge, drove through the town of Destin, continued east, and a short while later arrived in Paradise.

As he looked around he could see why it was named Paradise. Everything was relatively new, distinctively upscale, and clean, with postcard ocean views. There were high-rise condo buildings right on the water, a picturesque harbor with fishing boats that looked right out of a Hollywood film, chic-looking restaurants, Gucci-level shopping, beautiful women wearing very little, cars that made his Corvette look cheap, and a general air of "this is as good as it gets, people."

He parked in a free spot, climbed out of the low-slung car—no small feat for someone his size—and looked around. He wore jeans, a loose-fitting untucked long-sleeved white shirt, and loafers sans socks. His M11 pistol was tucked into a belt holster at the small of his back and covered by the shirt. As an Army CID agent he was required to carry his sidearm with him at all times. And even if it hadn't been required he would have done it anyway.

Multiple tours in the Middle East just did that to a guy. You gunned up as naturally as you drew a breath. Because without guns the odds were someone would try to stop you from breathing.

The sun was climbing high in the sky. It was hot but the breeze was nice, managing to evaporate several beads of perspiration off his forehead. Several young, curvy, and barely clothed ladies gave him long, interested looks as they passed by clutching their Kate Spade and Hermès bags and teetering in their Jimmy Choos.

He didn't reciprocate. He was still on leave, but this was no vacation. He was here on a mission, albeit a personal one.

He slipped off his shoes and walked to the beach just a few steps away. It was some of the whitest sand he could remember seeing, and it was soft. Middle East sand was different, grittier. But that might have been because on that sand people had been doing their best to kill him by gun, IED, knife, or simply using their bare hands. That sort of marred the perception one had of a place.

The water too was unique. He could now understand the appellation "Emerald Coast." The water did look like a huge pan of luminous green stones. The breakers were calm today. The wooden board displaying the water conditions indicated yellow, which meant light surf and medium hazard. But he wasn't here for a swim.

When he'd done his third and last phase in Ranger school it had been conducted in Florida. But not Paradise. It was in the swamps of the Sunshine State, filled with gators, moccasins, rattlers, and coral snakes. Puller couldn't remember a bikini-clad hottie or Gucci bag within a hundred miles. And even worse than that were the Ranger instructors, who had kicked his ass from one end of the Florida muck to the other.

He watched as sunbathers sat under blue umbrellas or lay on towels. He had never seen so many mostly naked asses and top-down ladies in his life. And more than a few were not in the best of shape. It would have been far preferable for them to dress a lot more modestly. He observed a tanned male lifeguard sitting high up in his tower, scanning the waters for trouble. Down below another tanned and buff lifeguard on a three-wheeler sped down the sand.

Nice life if you could get it.

Puller looked up toward the sun, snatched a few rays, and then decided his tanning time was over. The Army did not encourage loitering, whether he was on leave or not.

He walked back to the car, rubbed sand off his feet, and slipped his loafers back on. He watched as a cop car with "Paradise PD" and palm trees airbrushed across the doors rolled by. There were two cops inside.

The driver was a burly guy with a

shaved head, wearing reflector shades. He slowed the car, checked out Puller's ride, then gazed up at the tall man.

He nodded.

Puller nodded back, having no idea what the man was trying to communicate, if anything. But it was always a good idea to stay on the good side of the local police, even if they had foliage painted on their vehicles.

Behind her shades the lady cop eyed Puller too. She was blonde and looked to be in her early thirties. Unlike her partner, she didn't nod at him. When she looked away she said something to her partner and the cruiser sped off.

Puller stared after them for a few moments, climbed into his Corvette, and drove off. He had plugged his aunt's address into the car's GPS. It said he was only five minutes away.

Five minutes to go with no idea what he would be facing.

It was a lot like combat.

But in combat you usually had support, backup.

Here he was solo.

After going it alone in West Virginia

he was beginning to find this strategy a little annoying.

If he were lucky Betsy Simon would answer the door and invite him in for iced tea.

CHAPTER

8

He was a welcome addition to the landscaping company because he was as
strong as three men and could outwork
all of them, which he had proven beyond doubt his first day on the job.

After fleeing the beach as the bodies
of the two people slowly drifted out into
the Gulf with the tide, he had ridden
the stolen bike to a part of Paradise
that was not as picturesque as the rest.
This was a prearranged place for him
to stay, rented for one month and
stocked with food. It was a twelve-by-
twelve room with a hot plate, yet was

more living space than he had ever had before. He felt fortunate to have it. He had rested for several hours, hydrated, eaten, nursed his injuries, and contemplated his next moves.

It was the sort of neighborhood where everyone either drove decades-old pickup trucks and cars with bald tires and smoking engines or else rode bikes or hitched rides with more affluent friends to get where they needed to go. At night, the area was not safe to go out in unless you had the protection of one of the gangs that controlled this small corner of Paradise. It was not near the water, and no one would ever come here to take tourist photos. But it was where most of the men and women lived who cut the lawns, cleaned the pools, washed the clothes, and cleaned the houses for the wealthier folks who called Paradise home.

He had ventured out at night, but only to confirm his employment with one of the larger landscape companies. One look at his size and physique was all that the company foreman needed to pronounce him up to the task. On the walk back to his apartment he had encountered four young men who were street-level members of a gang that called themselves *dueños de la calle*, or the street kings.

They had encircled him on a quiet side avenue, gazing up at his great size. It was like the bull elephant surrounded by a pack of lionesses. They were trying to decide if they could collectively take him. He could see the gun bulges under their shirts and in the streetlight the glints of homemade shivs and store-bought blades resting in their hands.

He did not wonder if they could take him.

He knew they would fail, armed or not.

He had already decided how he would kill each of them if they attacked. It was not his first choice, because it would complicate his reason for being here. But he obviously couldn't let them kill him either.

He kept walking and they kept encircling him like a moving bubble of flesh and bone. Finally, he stopped, looked at them. They spoke to him in Spanish.

He shook his head, told them in broken Spanish that he didn't really speak it, though he did, fluently. He only did this to throw them off, make it harder for them to communicate with him. Frustration messed with the mind.

Then he spoke in his native tongue, and this seemed to catch them off guard, which had been his intent.

The largest gangbanger, probably in an attempt to show he was not cowed by the big man, strode closer and asked him in English where he was from.

In answer he pointed in the direction of the water.

This did not seem to please them.

The smallest of them shot forward, using more courage and adrenaline than common sense, and tried to stick a knife in his gut. The man moved with a speed that was surprising for someone his size. He disarmed the smaller man and lifted him off the pavement with one arm as though he were a child. He placed the blade against his throat, where it tickled the little man's trembling carotid. Then with a flash of movement he threw the knife and it buried point-first in a wooden door twenty feet across the street.

He dropped the man and the gang melted away into the night.

They were young, but obviously their stupidity had limits.

He walked on.

The next day had been spent in twelve hours of labor for which he received eight dollars per hour. This was paid in cash at the end of the day, but he was docked five dollars for food that consisted of a bottle of water, a sandwich, and chips. And another dollar per hour was deducted because of rising gas prices, he was told. The money was meaningless to him. He simply took it, stuffed it into his pocket, and rode in the back of a battered truck to a location near where he was staying.

The temperature had reached ninety-eight that day, and he had been out in the sun for all of it. While even the most veteran of the company's workers had wilted quickly in the heat and humidity and sought frequent breaks in whatever shade was available, he had worked away, as oblivious to the heat as he had been to swimming all those hours through the Gulf.

When one had been to hell, anything less did not intimidate.

He had sat on his bed early the next morning. Sweat dripped down his back because his rent did not include air-conditioning that actually worked. Part of what had been left for him in the room had included a cell phone, with certain numbers and information on it that would prove useful in completing his task.

He moved through the phone's screens every day going over what he needed to and deleting certain things he wouldn't want anyone to possibly discover. Finished, he sat back on his bed and lifted a glass of cold water to his lips. He stared around the close confines of his room: four plain walls and a solitary window overlooking the street where the sounds of late-night partiers could be heard coming from the waterside, a long way from here. The closer one drew to the beach, the more it cost.

He was supposed to have traveled

here by plane. Instead, he had taken a tranquilizer dart strike to his chest when he was on the street of a Mexican border town just across the line from Brownsville, Texas, one of the most dangerous places on earth. He had been fortunate to have just been tranquilized. He had woken on a vessel at sea trussed up like a shark in a net. Shifted from boat to boat, abandoned oil platform to abandoned oil platform, he had been successful at his first real chance at escape.

He took in a long breath and sat up against the wall as the frail bedframe squeaked and groaned trying to support his weight. His door was locked, a bureau in front of it. If someone came for him in the night he would not be surprised. He had slept palming a serrated knife. If someone came for him he would kill him. It was just his life, as he had always known it to be.

He got up to go to work.

CHAPTER

9

Puller eased the Corvette to the curb and gazed across the street at his aunt's house. Sunset by the Sea was the name of the community, and Puller decided it was appropriate. The place *was* near the water and the sun *did* set every day just like clockwork.

His aunt's house was a nice, sturdy-looking two-story with a garage. He had never visited her here. She had been mostly out of his life long before he'd joined the Army. She had originally lived in Pennsylvania with her husband, Lloyd. Puller recalled that the move to

Florida had come about twenty years ago, when Lloyd retired.

There had been a few points of correspondence with his aunt over the years. His brother had been better at keeping up with Betsy Simon than he had. But then Bobby had gone to prison, their father had mostly lost his mind, and Puller had lost all contact with a woman who had been central to him as a little boy.

That was what life did to you, he supposed. Wiped out important things and replaced them with other important things.

He spent a few minutes sizing up the area. Nice, upscale, palm trees. No mansions here, though. He had passed a whole spate of those on the way here. They tended to be close to or right on the water, big as condo buildings— huge pools, high gates, and Bugattis and McLarens parked in circular drives with towering fountains as focal points. That sort of lifestyle was as foreign to Puller as living in Pyongyang, North Korea, would have been. And for him probably just as distasteful.

He would never make much money. After all, the only thing he did was continually risk life and limb to keep America safe. That apparently wasn't as important or as valued as making billions on Wall Street at the expense of the average citizen, who was often left holding the bag of empty promises that seemed to be about all that remained of the American dream.

But his aunt had apparently done okay. Her house was fairly large and immaculate, and the yard watered and well tended. She apparently had not outlived her money.

He didn't see anyone outside or passing down the street, either on foot or by car. The heat was really miserable, and maybe people took their siestas around now. He gazed at his watch. It was closing in on one p.m. He climbed out of the car, crossed the street, strode up the sidewalk to his aunt's front door, and knocked.

There was no answer.

He knocked again, his gaze sliding left and then right, checking to see if her immediate neighbors had their curiosity antennae out. He didn't see any prying eyes and he knocked once more.

He heard no footsteps.

He walked to the garage door and peered through the glass. Parked inside was a Toyota Camry. It looked relatively new. He wondered if his aunt still drove. He tried to lift the garage door, but it was locked down. Probably on an automatic door lift, he thought. No way elderly people were going to bend down and constantly jack up heavy overhead doors simply because they wanted to go for a drive.

He walked to the side yard and his height allowed him to peer over the privacy fence. He saw a fountain in the middle of the small backyard.

He tried the gate. It was locked. It was a simple latch, though; a bit of jiggling and it opened. He stepped into the backyard and walked over to the fountain. The first thing he noticed was the gouge in the dirt just outside of the stone surround that held the water in. He knelt down and studied the gouge and found another one parallel to it and about three feet away. He looked at the fountain. Someone had pulled the plug on the pump, because the water, designed to flow from the top of the fountain and into the lower pool, was not operating.

He leaned over and studied the floor of the pool. There were loose decorative stones laid there, but something had disturbed them. Some of the stones had been pushed around to such a degree that the concrete floor of the pool was revealed. As he leaned closer he saw where one of the rocks from the stone surround had been partially dislodged and was lying on the ground. There was a mark on this stone. He looked at it more closely.

Is that blood?

He knelt down and studied the topography in relation to the back of the house. He noted the gouges in the dirt once more. Could they be from a walker? There were no footprints that he could see. The grass was wiry and pretty dry, so he wouldn't have expected any discernible impressions. He leaned in closer and studied the pool. Maybe two feet deep, about six feet in diameter, with the water kept in by the low stone wall.

His gaze swept around the rocks looking for any other marks. He saw no blood, no human tissue, and no hairs. He moved closer, peered down into the clear water, and once more observed the places where the stones had been disturbed.

Puller stood and pantomimed falling into the pool, hands out to break his fall. One there, one there. Knees impacting the decorative stones too. He adjusted things a bit to account for a possible walker. He compared his pantomime with what he was seeing. Not an exact fit, but something had disturbed the stones.

But unless she were unconscious his aunt could have rolled herself to the side and gotten her face out of the water. So, unconscious for some reason, facedown in the water. Two feet of it would easily cover her head. Death would have been quick.

Then Puller shook his head.

I see felonies everywhere. Dial it back, Puller.

He had no proof that his aunt was dead, or hurt in any way. He might have been crawling around her backyard in the heat looking for evidence of a crime that had not even been committed. That's what he got for investigating crimes for a living. He could also make them up out of whole cloth if necessary.

Or even unnecessarily.

Then he took a step back and received confirmation that something out of the ordinary had indeed happened back here.

There were two parallel lines visible in the grass, like miniature train tracks where the grass had been pushed down. When he looked at another spot in the lawn, he saw another pair of parallel tracks. Puller knew what that meant. He had seen it many times before.

He walked swiftly to the back door and tried the knob. Locked. At least his aunt was security-minded. But the lock was just a single bolt. It took Puller all of fifteen seconds to beat it. He stepped inside, closed the door behind him.

The interior layout of the house seemed relatively simple. Straight hall from front to back, rooms off that. Stairs leading up, fore and aft, with bedrooms no doubt on the second floor. With his aunt's advanced age he figured she might have a master suite on the main level. Puller had heard that concept was very popular in retirement communities.

He passed a laundry room, small den, and the kitchen and found the master suite off that. He finally arrived at a large family room that opened off the foyer and was visible from the kitchen over a waist-high wall. The furnishings were heavy on tropical motifs. There was a gas fireplace surrounded by stacked slate on one wall. Puller had checked out the Panhandle region and discovered that the lows in the middle of winter rarely crept down into the thirties, but he could understand his aunt, who hailed from the snowy Keystone State, wanting to warm her bones with a cozy fire that didn't require chopping wood.

He noted the alarm panel next to the

front door. The green light showed that it was not on, a fact he already knew because the alarm had not gone off when he had opened the back door.

There was an abundance of photos—mostly old ones—on shelves, consoles, and occasional tables set around the family room. Puller studied them one by one and found several of his old man, and him and his brother in their respective uniforms with their aunt Betsy. The last of these was from when Puller had joined the Army. He wondered now where the break in the family had come but couldn't quite put a finger on it. There were also quite a few photos of Betsy's husband, Lloyd. He'd been a little shorter than his wife, his face was full of life, and there was one picture of the two of them in which Lloyd was wearing his Army greens from World War II. Betsy was in her WAC, or Women's Army Corps, uniform. The way they were gazing at each other in the photo it looked like love at first sight, if there was such a thing.

Puller heard it before he had a chance to see it.

He stepped to the window and drew the curtain back just a fraction of an inch. Ever since his tours in the Middle East he never revealed more of him-self—physically or emotionally—than was absolutely necessary.

The police cruiser pulled to the curb and the driver killed the engine.

No sirens, no lights; the two cops in-side were obviously in stealth mode. They climbed out and drew their guns, looked around, their gazes inching to the front of the house.

Someone had seen Puller in the yard, maybe going into the house, and had called the cops.

The male officer was bald and burly, the same one he had seen earlier. Next to him was his female partner. She was two inches taller and looked in better shape. He was thick and muscular up top but light in the legs. Too many bench presses and not enough squats. He looked, to Puller, like a washout from the military, but he obviously couldn't be certain about that. Maybe it was just the condescending nod the man had given him earlier.

The guy held his nine-millimeter awkwardly, even unprofessionally, as if he had learned how to do it by watching TV or by sitting on his butt at a theater to see how action stars handled their weapons. She carried hers with perfect control and ease, her weight balanced equally between both legs, her knees slightly bent, her silhouette angled to the side to lower her target profile. It was like a Pro-Am tournament pairing, thought Puller.

If his aunt was dead and there had been an investigation, he sure as hell hoped bald and burly hadn't been heading it up. That had screwup written all over it.

Puller decided to cut to the chase, mainly because he didn't want the guy to accidentally shoot himself. He slipped a photo from its frame and slid it into his shirt pocket. Then he walked to the front door, opened it, and stepped out into the brilliant sunshine of Paradise.

CHAPTER

10

"Freeze!"

The order came from the woman.

Puller obeyed the command.

"Hands over your head," added her partner.

"Do you want me to freeze or put my hands over my head?" asked Puller. "Because I can't do both. And I'm not looking to get shot over a misunderstanding."

The two cops moved closer, one to his right, one to his left.

Puller noted that the woman watched his hands, while the guy was glued to his eyes. The woman was right. Puller couldn't kill with his eyes. But his hand could pull a weapon and open fire within a second without his eyes moving an inch.

She said, "Put your hands over your head, fingers interlocked. Then down on your stomach, legs spread, face-down."

"I have an M11 in a rear belt holster. And my Army creds and badge are inside my front pants pocket."

The two cops made the mistake of glancing at each other. Puller could have shot them both dead in the two seconds they took to do that. But he didn't and so they would get to live another day.

"What the hell is an M11?" asked the male officer.

Before Puller could answer the woman said, "Army's version of the Sig P228."

Puller eyed her with interest. She was about five-seven, with blonde hair pinned up tight with a clamp at the back. Her build was slender, compact, but she moved with a dancer's grace and her hands looked strong.

He said, "If I could reach very slowly in my front pants pocket I'll show you my creds and badge."

This time the woman didn't look at her partner. "What unit?"

"The 701st out of Quantico, Virginia," he answered promptly.

"CID or MP?" she asked.

"CID. I'm a CWO."

Before her partner could ask she translated: "Chief warrant officer."

Puller looked at her curiously. "You former military?"

"My brother."

Puller said, "Can I get my pack out?"

"Do it really slowly," said the guy, tightening the grip on his gun.

Puller knew that was the exact wrong thing to do. An overly tight grip meant you would increase your error rate about thirty percent or more. But he was more concerned that the guy would mess up and accidentally shoot him.

"Two fingers in the pocket, that's all," said the woman. "And keep your other hand on the top of your head." Her voice was firm, direct, even. He liked that. Her nerves were definitely not running away with her senses, unlike her partner.

Puller two-fingered out his cred pack and held it up, ID card first, badge second. The CID's one-eyed eagle symbol was unique.

The two drew close enough for Puller to simply hand the pack to the woman while the man kept his drawdown on him. He actually wished it had been the other way around, because the guy looked wound tight enough to shoot all three of them dead.

She lifted her gaze from the cred pack, checking the photo on there with the man himself, and said, "Okay, but I'm going to have to take your sidearm as a precaution until we sort this out."

"Small of my back, belt holster."

She moved behind him while her partner took a step back and lined Puller up in his iron sights.

She gave him a quick but efficient patdown, her hands flitting over his backside, then down and up the insides of his legs. Puller felt his shirt being lifted up. Then she slid the pistol out of the holster and a moment later she stood in front of him, gripping his pistol by the muzzle and pointing it downward.

She said, "We got a call about a break-in. What are you doing here?"

"This is my aunt Betsy Simon's place. I came down here to pay her a visit. No one answered the door, so I went in through the back."

"Long way to come, from Virginia," said the man, with his gun still aimed at Puller's head.

Puller didn't look at him but spoke to the woman. "Can you ask your partner to holster? Accidents can happen."

"The cred pack's legit, Barry, and he's unarmed now. You can stand down."

"John Puller," said the woman. "And your aunt was Betsy Simon?"

He nodded. "And you are?" He had glanced at her nametag, but the sun's glare made it impossible to read.

"Officer Landry, Cheryl Landry. That's Officer Barry Hooper."

She handed him back his cred pack.

"Any idea where my aunt is?" asked Puller.

Landry looked at her partner nervously.

Puller caught the look. "I saw some interesting things in the backyard. Did something happen back there?"

"Why do you think that?" she asked suspiciously.

"Clues around the fountain. And I saw tracks in the grass back there where a gurney had been wheeled in and out. I'm assuming that gurney was carrying someone. Was that someone my aunt?"

"We were first responders," said Landry quietly.

"To what exactly?"

"The lady who lived here drowned in the little pool back there," interjected Hooper.

His partner shot him a reproachful glance and said, "It seemed to be an accident. I'm sorry, Agent Puller."

Puller stood there trying to take it all in. In a way, he was not surprised. In another way he was flummoxed. He had been hoping that the victim was someone other than his aunt.

He asked, "Can you walk me through what happened?"

Hooper snapped, "We're responding to a B and E right now and you're it. We're not standing here jawing with you. We should be cuffing you and reading you your rights."

Landry looked at him. "He's right. We don't know if your aunt was Betsy Simon. And we don't know what you were doing in her house."

"Photo in my shirt pocket. I took it from the house."

Landry slid the photo out, looked at it.

"It's quite a few years old, but if you saw my aunt I don't think she's changed that much. And I look pretty much the same, with a few more lines. And our names are listed on the back."

Landry studied the picture and the reverse side and then let Hooper look at it.

"It's him, Barry," said Landry.

"Still not conclusive to me," retorted Hooper.

Puller shrugged and took the photo back. "Okay, so let's go down to the station and straighten it out. I was heading there anyway after I finished looking around here."

"Like I said, the lady fell and drowned in her little pool," said Hooper. "Accident all the way."

"Medical examiner confirm that?"

Landry said, "Haven't heard. Autopsy should be done by now."

Hooper said, "It was an accident. Lady fell and drowned. We checked the scene out thoroughly."

"Yeah, that's what you keep saying. What, are you trying to convince yourself it's true?"

Landry added, "That's what it looked like all right, Agent Puller. I can understand it's hard to accept a tragedy like that, but it happens. Especially with older folks."

"And Florida has more than most," added Hooper. "Dropping like flies every minute of every day."

Puller turned to look at him and took a step closer to the man to accentuate their differences in vertical prominence. "Except they're not."

"Not what?" said Hooper, looked confused.

"Flies. And in case you didn't know, autopsies reveal about twenty-five per-cent of the time a different cause of death than the one everybody thought it was."

"We can go down to the station," said Landry in a placating tone. "And straighten things out, like you said."

"You want me to follow you or go in your car?" asked Puller.

"It's not a choice. You go in our ride," said Hooper, before Landry could speak. "With your hands cuffed and your rights read."

"You're really going to arrest me?" asked Puller.

"Did you break into that house?" Hooper shot back.

"I went in to check on my aunt."

"Why didn't you call the police if you were concerned?" asked Landry. "We could have filled you in."

"Maybe I could have, but it's not my way of doing things," replied Puller.

"Army have the luxury of letting its guys just bop around the country doing their own stuff?" said Hooper. "No wonder our taxes are so damn high."

"Even the Army lets its guys have some R and R time, Officer Hooper."

"We'll leave your car here," broke in Landry. "You ride with us, but without the cuffs or the rights read."

"Thanks," said Puller, as Hooper eyed his partner darkly.

"But if your story doesn't check out," she warned, "that all changes."

"Fair enough," said Puller. "But after you find out I'm legit, I'll need to see my aunt's body."

He walked toward their cruiser. "Let's roll," he called back over his shoulder.

The two cops slowly followed.

CHAPTER

11

The Paradise police station was located two blocks off the beach in a two-story stone and stucco structure that had an orange terra-cotta roof and a pair of palm trees out front. It sat next to a Ritz-Carlton hotel and looked more like a country club than a place where cops went to get their patrol assignments and cruisers to go hunt criminals.

As Puller climbed out of the police car and looked around he said to Hooper, "Did you purposely locate in the high-crime area to keep watch over the criminal element?"

Hooper ignored him, but placed an arm on Puller's elbow to shepherd him into the building. Apparently Hooper was under the impression that Puller was in custody and the only things missing were the cuffs over his wrists and a Miranda warning ringing in his ears.

The place inside looked much like the place outside. High-dollar, clean, orderly. In fact it was the cleanest, most orderly police station Puller had ever seen. The personnel working inside pristinely delineated office spaces barely looked up as the trio came in. Their clothes were starched, spotless, and looked to have been fitted by a veteran tailor. No phones were ringing. No one was screaming for his lawyer or declaring that he was innocent of all trumped-up charges. No uncooperative prisoners were puking on the floor. No fat, sweaty cops with major B.O. and pissed-off attitudes were waddling down the halls in search of a myocardial infarction in the form of a vending machine stuffed with chocolate and sodium.

It was such a total disconnect for
Puller that he looked around for a camera, seriously wondering for a few moments whether he was being punked.

He glanced at Landry, who was walking next to him. "I've never seen a police station quite like this one."

"What's so different about it?" she
asked.

"You been in any others?"

"A few."

"Trust me, it's different. I was looking
around for a valet outside and a place
to order a drink in here before I teed off
for a quick round of nine holes. And I
don't even play golf."

Hooper nudged his elbow harder.
"So we've got a strong tax base. That's
a problem somehow?"

"Didn't say it was a problem. Just
said it was different."

"Then maybe everybody else should
follow our example," retorted Hooper.
"Because I think we've got it right.
Money equals a better life all around."

"Yeah, next time I'm in Kabul, I'll let
them know your thoughts."

"I was talking the United States of

America, not dipshit land where they talk funny and think their pissant god is better than our real God."

"I think I'll keep that one to myself," replied Puller.

"Like I give a crap what you do."

Puller tried to remove his elbow from Hooper's grip but the man kept it there, as if he were a magnet and Puller were a block of metal. The guy was doing it just to piss him off. That was clear. And Puller could do nothing about it unless he wanted to end up in a jail cell, which would seriously crimp the investigation of his aunt's death.

Hooper directed him to a chair outside of a frosted glass–enclosed office with the name *Henry Bullock, Chief of Police* stenciled on the door. Landry knocked twice and Puller heard a gruff voice say, "Enter."

Hooper stood next to him as Landry disappeared inside the office.

Puller had nothing else to do so he looked around. His attention was captured by a man and a woman in their early forties because they appeared distraught in a sea of otherwise complete calm. They were seated at the desk of a man dressed in black slacks, white-collared shirt with the sleeves rolled to the elbows, and a muted tie. A plastic lanyard with a badge on it hung from his reedy neck.

Puller could catch only snatches of the conversation, but he heard the words "late-night walk," then the names "Nancy and Fred Storrow."

The woman dabbed at her nose with a tissue while the man looked down at his hands. The guy behind the desk hit keys on his computer and uttered sympathetic noises.

Puller drew his attention away from this exchange when the door to Bullock's office opened and Landry and another man whom Puller assumed was the chief of police stepped out.

Henry Bullock was a fraction under six feet with thick shoulders and hammy arms that pulled tight against his regulation uniform. His gut was widening and offered even greater strain against the fabric than did his muscles. His body was better balanced than Hooper's because the man's legs were thick but tapered down to unusually small feet. He looked to be in his late fifties, with thinning gray hair, thick eyebrows, a bulbous nose, and skin that had seen too much sun and wind. The furrows on his brow were deep and permanent and left him with a perpetual scowl.

If he'd been in a different uniform Puller would have sworn the man was his former drill sergeant.

"Puller?" he said, staring down at him.

"That's me."

"Come on in. You too, Landry. Hoop, you can wait outside."

"But Chief," said Hooper. "I was in on the bust too."

Bullock turned to look at him. "There is no bust, Hoop. Not yet. If there is, I'll let you know."

And in those few words Puller could tell that Bullock was a savvy man and knew exactly the limits of Officer Hooper.

Hooper stood there sullenly, his gaze on Puller as though this slight was somehow his fault. Puller stood and walked past the man, his elbow finally free.

"Just hang tight, *Hoop*," he said. "We'll get back to you."

CHAPTER

12

Puller walked into the office, trailed by Landry. She shut the door behind her.

The office was a twelve-foot-wide, eight-foot-deep rectangle of space. It was furnished in a spartan, no-nonsense way, which, Puller assumed, precisely paralleled the personality of the occupant.

Bullock sat down behind his wooden desk and motioned for Puller to take the lone chair opposite. Landry stood at semi-attention diagonally off Puller's left shoulder.

Puller sat, looking expectantly at Bullock.

The police chief fiddled with the fingernail of his right index finger for a few moments before breaking the silence.

"We're verifying you are who you say you are."

"And after you do can I check out the crime scene?"

Bullock flicked an annoyed gaze at him. "There is no crime scene."

"Technically, maybe not, but that could change."

"Your aunt was how old?"

"Eighty-six."

"And used a walker, the report said. She fell, hit her head, and drowned. I'm very sorry it happened. Lost my grandmother to a drowning accident. Had a seizure in the bathtub. She was old too. It just happened. Nothing anyone could do. Looks to be the same here. You shouldn't feel guilty about it," he added.

"Has it been confirmed that she drowned?" asked Puller, ignoring this last barb.

When neither of them said anything, he said, "Unless Florida is really different, there has to be something written on the death certificate in the 'cause of death' box or people get a little nervous."

"Water in the lungs, so yes, she drowned," said Bullock. "Medical examiner completed the autopsy last night. Technically I believe the term is—"

Puller finished for him, "Yeah, asphyxiation. Can I see the report?"

"No, you can't. They don't go out to anyone except next of kin and those with a court order."

"I'm her nephew."

"So you say, but even so, I've always interpreted the definition of next of kin to be immediate family."

"She doesn't have any. Her husband's dead, and her only sibling is back in Virginia at a VA hospital and lacks the mental capacity to handle this. And she had no kids."

"I'm sorry. There's really nothing I can do about that," said Bullock. "The privacy of the deceased is not something I take lightly."

"But you do take lightly that someone might have murdered her?"

Bullock snapped, "I don't care for
what you're insinuating."

"Weren't you going to contact her
next of kin?" Puller asked.

"We were in the process of doing
that. We did a preliminary search of her
home, but didn't find any helpful info.
And you have to understand, this is
Florida. Lots of elderly, lots of deaths.
We have four others we're running down
next of kin on and I have limited manpower."

"The ME listing drowning as the
cause of death tells us what killed her.
It doesn't tell us how she got in the water in the first place."

"She fell."

"That's a guess, not a fact."

Landry stirred, seemingly about to
say something, but then apparently
thought better of it and remained silent.

Puller noticed this but didn't react.
He figured he could have a chat with
her later, outside the presence of her
boss.

"It's an educated, professional assumption based on the facts on the ground," corrected Bullock.

"An educated assumption is really just a guess in sheep's clothing. The real reason I'm down here is because of a letter she sent." He pulled it from his pocket and handed it to Bullock. Landry moved around and read it over her supervisor's shoulder.

Bullock finished reading, folded the letter, and handed it back. "Proves nothing. If I had a dollar for every time some old woman thought something weird was going on, I'd retire a rich man."

"Really? That would take like over a million old crazy ladies, wouldn't it? The population of Paradise is 11,457. I checked before coming down. You're going to have to recruit a lot more old crazy ladies if you want to retire."

Before Bullock could respond to this a fax machine on a credenza behind him zinged to life. A paper came down the chute. Bullock picked it up, alternated reading it and gazing at Puller.

"Okay, you are who you say you are."

"Nice to have it confirmed."

"Landry here tells me you're Army CID."

"That's right. About six years. Before that I was in the ranks carrying a rifle."

"Well, I've been chief of police of this little hamlet for fifteen, and fifteen years before that I was a cop pounding the streets. Saw my share of murders and accidents. This is the latter, not the former."

"Am I missing something here?" asked Puller. "Is there some reason you don't want to check this out more thoroughly? If it's a question of manpower I'm here to volunteer my services. And I've been around a lot of accidents and murders too. The Army unfortunately has an abundance of both. And I've handled cases that started out looking like an accident that turned into something else and vice versa."

"Well, maybe you're just not as good as we are," shot back Bullock.

"Maybe I'm not. But why don't we find out for sure? We have a little question of justice to be answered."

Bullock rubbed his face with his hand

like he was working off some fine grit, and shook his head.

"Okay, I think we're done here. I'm sorry for your loss, if she is your aunt. But I would not advise going near her property again unless you have appropriate authorization. Next time we will arrest you."

"And how exactly do I get authorization?"

"Talk to her lawyer. Maybe he can help. Probably just charge you a few thousand dollars."

"I don't know who her lawyer is. Maybe if I could go back to her house and check?"

"What part of appropriate authorization don't you get?" said Bullock.

"So it's a chicken and egg problem?"

"Hell, she's *your* family, or so you say."

Puller slipped out the picture. "I've got this."

Bullock waved his hand dismissively. "Yeah, yeah, Landry told me about that. It's not conclusive proof of anything."

"So that's it? That's all you'll do?"

"What I'm doing is my job. To serve and protect."

"Well, if Betsy Simon was killed, you didn't do a really good job on either one, did you?"

Bullock rose and stared down at Puller. For an instant Puller thought the man was going to pull his gun, but he simply said, "You have a good day, Mr. Puller." He nodded at Landry, who said, "You can follow me out, Agent Puller."

After the door closed behind them Hooper was next to Puller in an instant, his hand on his elbow again, like a sheepdog to a sheep. Only Puller would never be classified as a sheep. He firmly removed Hooper's hand from his elbow and said, "Thanks. But unlike my aunt, I can walk unaided."

Before Hooper could say anything Puller walked off, retracing his steps from the way in. Landry fell in behind him.

"I need my gun back," said Puller.

"It's in the police cruiser. We can drop you off at your car."

"Thanks, I'd rather walk," said Puller.

"It's a long walk."

Puller turned to look at her. "I have a lot to think about. And I've never been in Paradise before. I'd like to see every inch of it. Might never get another chance. Most folks who know me have me down for heading to the other place."

At this Landry cracked a smile.

They reached the cruiser and Landry handed him back his M11 as Hooper hovered in the background, still looking upset that Puller wasn't behind bars.

Landry handed Puller a card. "If you need any help," she said, her gaze searching his for an instant before looking away. "Personal cell phone number's on the back."

Puller slid his M11 into the belt holster and her card into his shirt pocket.

"Appreciate that. Might take you up on it, Officer Landry."

He glanced over her shoulder at Hooper. "He always so friendly?"

"He's a good cop," she said in a low voice.

"Never said he wasn't. But tell him to lay off the elbow intimidation thing. Gets old after about thirty seconds."

She edged closer. "Try Bailey's Funeral Home. It's over off Atlantic Avenue. Where the ME does her work. We don't have a formal medical examiner's office in Paradise. She's a doctor in practice who helps us out."

"Thanks."

He turned and strode off.

Hooper called after him, "Next time you won't get off so easy."

Puller just kept walking.

CHAPTER

13

Puller called Bailey's Funeral Home on the walk back to his car. The woman on the phone would not confirm that Betsy Simon's body was on the premises.

"Well, if you do have her body, I'm her nephew. And if you want to get paid for the funeral service then I really need confirmation that you have her. Otherwise you can just foot the bill yourselves."

This approach seemed to stimulate the woman's memory.

"Well, without giving out any private

information, we did receive an elderly female's body whose clothes were damp and who lived on Orion Street."

"I'll be over later today to make arrangements. I know the ME performed an autopsy. I'm assuming he's released the body. But I would appreciate if nothing else is done to the remains before I get there. Are we clear on that?"

"Until the contract is signed and the deposit made, I can assure you that nothing will be done," the woman said primly.

Puller clicked off and thought, *Paradise just keeps getting better and better.*

He drove his car to an outdoor café near the beach. He had chosen this spot because it afforded a nice vantage point of a major swath of the town. He ordered a turkey sandwich, fries, and iced tea. It was too hot for his normal pop of max-caffeinated coffee. And he was thinking about giving it up anyway. He was afraid it would start to impede his aim.

As he ate and drank he took mental pictures of all that was going on around him. He saw a pristine convertible Porsche driving next to an old Ford pickup truck with barely any tread on the tires or metal on the frame. A few moments later a large truck chugged by with a landscaping company's name on its side. It stopped at the traffic light.

Puller studied the five men in dirty work pants and soaked-in-sweat matching green T-shirts with the company name on them standing up in the back of the truck. They were all short, stocky Latinos, except for the biggest one, who looked like a parent surrounded by kindergartners. He was easily two inches taller and more than fifty pounds heavier than Puller with not an ounce of fat on him. Guys that size tended to be bulky and slow-looking. This guy seemed almost gaunt. His hands were long gristly bones that looked strong enough to choke an elephant. The men's gazes locked for a brief instant and then the truck and the giant were gone.

Puller saw a police cruiser pass by. He half expected to see Landry and

Hooper inside, but it was another pair of cops who barely looked at him.

Puller paid his bill, finished off his iced tea, and phoned the VA hospital back in Virginia. He asked for his father's doctor and was put on hold several different times before a woman's voice said, "Dr. Murphy is tied up, can I help you?"

Puller explained who he was and what he wanted.

"Mr. Puller, I can put you right in to talk to your father. Perhaps you can calm him down."

Doubtful, thought Puller. But he said, "I can try."

His old man's voice boomed through the phone. "XO? That you, XO?"

"It's me, sir."

"Mission brief," said his father tersely.

"I'm on the ground in Florida. I did a recon of the area, interfaced with the locals. Later I plan to assess the casualties and will report back in at that time, sir."

"Somebody took my top-secret communication, XO. From my personal safe."

"You gave it to me, sir, need to know only. You must have other things on your mind, sir. Takes a lot of thinking to run the 101st."

"Hell yes it does."

"So I've got the communication, sir. Not to worry. Report back twenty hundred hours."

"Roger that. Good luck, XO."

Puller clicked off and felt ashamed, as he did every time he played this subterfuge with his father. But what was the alternative?

One he didn't want to face, he supposed.

He next phoned USDB in Kansas and made arrangements to talk to his brother that night. After that, he put the phone away. It was time to see his aunt.

Despite their separation, once he had become an adult a part of Puller had always thought he would see Betsy Simon again.

Just not like this.

CHAPTER

14

Bailey's Funeral Home was a three-story brick building three blocks off the water and set on a half acre of mostly asphalt with a narrow perimeter of sun-baked grass. Puller parked his car near the front door, got out, and a few moments later entered the building. The air-conditioning hit him in a wave as he closed the door behind him. The place must have been at least twenty-five degrees cooler than outside and Puller was glad he was not paying the electric bill here. But then it occurred to him that every funeral home he'd ever been in had felt abnormally cold, even in New England in the middle of winter. It was like they didn't have heat, only air-conditioning. Maybe that's what you were taught in the funeral home business—keep everyone as cold as the clients in the coffins.

There was a small reception desk set a few yards from the front door. A young woman attired all in black—perhaps another funeral home tactic to show perpetual mourning—rose to greet him.

"I'm John Puller. I called before. My aunt Betsy Puller Simon is here?"

"Yes, Mr. Puller. What can we do for you?"

"I'd like to see her body, please."

The young woman's smile disappeared. "See her body?"

"Yes."

She was only about five feet tall and even in her clunky heels Puller was about a mile higher than she was. He could see her dark roots among all the blonde strands.

"We would need to see some proof of your relationship."

"She kept her maiden name as part

of her married one. Do you have that as part of her records?"

The woman sat back down and clicked some computer keys. "We just have her listed as Betsy Simon."

"Who identified the body?"

"I'm not sure about that."

"Your records have to show that the body had been identified. The ME would have required that too. You can't bury someone without confirming they are who you think they are. That might get your operating license pulled."

"I can assure you that we strictly follow all applicable laws and regulations to the letter," she said in an offended tone.

"I'm sure you do." Puller took out his creds and showed her his badge and ID card.

"You're with the Army?"

"That's what it says. You want to kick me to someone higher in authority? You probably don't want to make this call on your own."

The woman looked relieved by this suggestion. She lifted the phone, spoke some words. After a few minutes a man, dressed all in black with a white shirt that was so stiff with starch that it had left his neck permanently red, came out from behind a door with his hand extended.

"Mr. Puller? I'm Carl Brown, how can I help you?"

Puller showed Brown his cred pack and explained his situation. Brown looked suitably sympathetic. Puller figured that was taught in funeral home school as well.

Brown led him off to a side room where there were empty caskets set on long tables. "It's just that we have so many rules and regulations governing our industry," said Brown. "We have to maintain the privacy and dignity of the people who entrust their loved ones to us."

"Well, her loved ones didn't entrust Betsy Simon to you. I didn't even know she was dead until a little while ago. And I didn't request that her remains be brought here. Who did?"

"The local police asked that we pick up her body. There are many retirees down here, and many live alone. Their families may be scattered around the country or even the world. It takes time to contact them. But leaving the body in a tropical climate such as Florida's is not exactly, how shall I say, a respectful avenue to pursue for the deceased."

"I understand that an autopsy has been performed on her remains?"

"That is correct."

"And the ME has released the body?"

Brown nodded. "This morning. Apparently, she found no evidence of a crime or anything like that."

"Have you seen the autopsy report?"

Brown said hastily, "Oh, no. That's not something that would be shared with us."

"You have her contact information."

"I can get it, yes."

"Has anyone officially identified her body?" asked Puller.

"Our records indicate that that was done by people on the scene who knew her. Probably a neighbor if she didn't have family in town. But we would always prefer that family members come and confirm that."

"Well, here I am."

"Again, without—"

Puller slipped the photo from his pocket and showed it to him. "I'm on the far right, Betsy is two over from me. It was taken years ago, but I don't think she's changed all that much. Look on the back of the photo. It lists all of our names. Is that good enough? I don't see what other reason I would've come all this way to look at a body that didn't have anything to do with me. The Army pays me to do better things with my time."

Brown looked ashamed by this last comment. "Absolutely. I'm sure they do." He looked around, apparently to see if anyone was in earshot. "All right, if you'll just follow me."

CHAPTER

15

This room was even colder than the other spaces here, and there was a good reason for this. Dead bodies needed cold for preservation. Otherwise, the process of decomposition made human mortal remains extremely unpleasant to be around.

Puller gazed down at the long figure on the marble slab. A sheet covered everything except her head. Puller was alone in the room; Brown was waiting just outside to give him some privacy. His aunt's features were obviously very pale, but they were easily recognizable.

He had had no doubt that she was actually dead, but at least now he had confirmation of it.

Her hair had been tidied up and it lay flat against her head. Puller reached out and touched several of the white strands. They felt bristly, harsh. He took his hand back. He had seen many dead bodies in various states of decay, many far worse than his aunt's condition. But she had been family. He had sat on this woman's knee, listened to her stories, eaten her cooking. She had helped him learn the alphabet, come to love books, let him play in her house, make noise at all hours. But she also had instilled in him discipline, purpose, and loyalty.

His old man had earned the three stars, but his older sister could very well have done the same, Puller thought, if she'd been given the chance.

He estimated her height. About five-nine. She had seemed like a giant to him when he was a boy. Age had probably shrunken her as it had her brother. But she was still tall for a woman, as her brother was for a man. He had not seen her in a long time. He had not really regretted that in adulthood, as there were many other things to occupy his time. Like fighting wars. And finding killers.

But now he did regret it, losing that connection with a woman who had meant so much to him growing up. And now it was too late to do anything about it.

And if he had kept in touch with her would she be lying here on a slab? Maybe she would have contacted him sooner, let him know directly of her concerns.

You can only play the guilt card so much, John. The fact is I couldn't have saved her, no matter how much I might have wanted to.

But maybe I can avenge her, if she was murdered. No, I *will* avenge her.

He examined her remains in a more professional manner. This included a meticulous probing of her head. It didn't take long to find it. An abrasion, a bruise really, over her right ear. It was covered by her hair, but clearly visible when he lifted the strands out of the way.

Her scalp had been cut open and her facial skin pulled down during the autopsy to provide access to the brain. He knew this from the sutures on the back of her head. Puller also knew that a Stryker saw had been used to open her cranium so the brain could be taken out, examined, and weighed. A Y-incision had opened her chest. He could see a few of the sutures resulting from this. All major organs contained therein would have received this same processing and scrutiny.

Puller looked back at the abrasion. A blunt force trauma possibly inflicted by a third party, or it could be from where she had fallen and hit her head on the stone border of the fountain. There was a small cut, but he doubted it would have bled much. It was not in the area of the scalp, which had a superhighway of small blood vessels, all of which bled like a bitch from even a small slicing of the skin. He had seen one possible blood mark on the stone surround. But any blood that might have leached into the water would have quickly dissolved.

The ME must have concluded that the bruising had been caused by the fall and impact with the stone. Blunt force trauma, particularly to the head, almost always led to a finding of death by homicide, but apparently not in this case.

He wondered why.

Bullock had said that the official cause of death was asphyxiation. Naturally that could occur from many things, such as diseases like emphysema or illnesses such as pneumonia or accidents like drowning. Criminally, death by asphyxiation only could be caused by three things, Puller knew.

They were: strangulation, drowning caused by another party, and smothering.

He gazed closely at her neck, looking for any signs of ligature marks. But the skin there was unblemished. And there was no venous engorgement— enlarged veins that would occur around the injury site due to the pressure and constriction of the blood vessels. When you squeezed something, it swelled.

The other indicator of strangulation

was not something Puller could see: an enlarged heart, particularly the right ventricle. He checked her lips for cyanosis, a blue discoloration around the lips that occurred with strangulation. There was no sign.

Next he lifted the sheet and checked her hands. There was no evidence of cyanosis on her fingertips. And there were no defensive wounds or marks. If someone had attacked her, it did not seem that she had fought back. If she had been immobilized quickly she might not have had the opportunity to do so.

He next checked her eyes and the area around them for petechial hemorrhaging, pinpoint reddish spots caused by the pressure on blood vessels. He found none.

So smothering and strangulation were probably out. That left drowning, which was what the ME had cited as her cause of death. But was it an accident, or did she have help?

Drowning had a number of different stages and left some forensic residue.

When a person found himself in trouble in the water he typically panicked and flailed about, using up precious energy and causing lost buoyancy, resulting in the person going under. Then the person inhaled more water, which increased the panic level. They would hold their breath. Then pink foam would be exhaled when they had to take a breath and took in even more water. Respiratory arrest would ensue, and then would come the final battle, a few quick breaths to find air, and then it was over.

Is that what happened, Aunt Betsy? thought Puller.

If she had hit her head and been knocked unconscious before going into the water she would not have felt any panic. But if she had been conscious, but unable to lift her head out of the water because she was either too weak or disoriented, or because someone was holding her head under, it would have been a terrifying way to die.

It would have been like waterboarding, only with the finale tacked on.

He glanced at the doorway behind which Brown was waiting. He wanted to do a complete examination of his aunt's body, but if Brown walked in and found the sheet off and Puller poking and prying around the woman's naked body, things might get a little weird. And Puller might find his butt in a jail cell accused of all sorts of perverse behavior.

He would just have to take it as faith that his octogenarian aunt had not been raped. But he did slide the sheet partially off her and performed a cursory examination of her arms and legs. At the base of her right calf he found another bruise, maybe from her fall. If so, that supported the theory of an accident. He put the sheet back and looked down at her.

He drew out his phone and used the embedded camera to take pictures of his aunt's covered body from various angles. Not exactly up to crime scene protocol standards, but he had to work with what he had.

He could learn no more here, but

Puller found himself unable to look away from his aunt, unable to leave her just yet.

It had long been a family rule that Puller men did not cry under any circumstances. Puller always had adhered to that rule when fighting in the Middle East, where he'd had the opportunity to weep over dozens of lost comrades in arms. Yet he had broken the cardinal rule back in West Virginia when he'd watched someone he'd grown close to die. Maybe it was a sign of weakness. Or maybe it was a sign of his becoming less of a machine and more of a human.

At this point he didn't know which.

As he continued to stare down at his aunt, he felt the creep of moistness around his eyes. But he did not allow it to build. There might be time to grieve later. Right now he had to figure out what had happened to Betsy. Until he had conclusive proof that said otherwise, the letter she had sent had convinced Puller that her death was not an accident.

His aunt had been murdered.

He left the dead behind and walked back to the living.

But he would not forget her. And he would not fail her in death, as perhaps he had in life.

CHAPTER

16

Puller got the name of the medical examiner, Louise Timmins, from Carl Brown, and then left Bailey's Funeral Home. As soon as he stepped outside the heat and humidity hit him like a DU round from an Abrams tank. After the frigid interior of the funeral home it was quite a shock. He took a breath, shrugged it off, and kept moving.

He had a number of leads to run down. First, the medical examiner, where he hoped he could get a copy of the final autopsy report. Second, he had to try to track down whether his

aunt had a lawyer and whether there
was a last will and testament. And he
had to talk to her neighbors, in particular the one who had identified her body.
The neighbors in fact might know the
name of Betsy's lawyer, if she had one.
And the methodical way his aunt had
led her life told Puller that she probably
did.

He put the address of the medical
examiner into his GPS and found it
would take him past his aunt's house.
He put the Corvette in gear and drove
off. He liked the way the car rode, although getting his tall body in and out
of the low-slung vehicle was proving to
be more difficult than he had thought.

Maybe I'm just getting old.

Twenty minutes later he pulled the
car to a stop at the curb across from
Betsy's house. He took a few moments
to look up and down the street for
Hooper and Landry lurking but saw no
sign of them. He unwound his long legs
and got out. As he did so he saw a
short, big-bellied man walk by on the
other side of the street. He had a tiny
dog on a long leash. It looked like a

round ball of flesh with fuzzy cowlicks all over, riding on twigs masquerading as legs.

When the man headed to the house next door to Betsy's, Puller hurried across the street and caught up to him as he was putting his key in the lock.

The man turned and looked startled. Puller could understand that, but there was something more in the man's features.

Real fear.

Well, Puller was a big guy and a stranger and he had busted in on the man's personal space. But Puller thought he knew why the guy seemed to be shivering in ninety-plus-degree heat.

He was the one who called the cops on me.

Puller whipped out his cred pack and showed his ID card and badge. "I'm with the Army's Criminal Investigation Division," he said, and the man immediately stopped shaking. "My aunt was Betsy Simon. I was told of her death and came down to check into things."

The man's face showed his full level

of relief. "Oh my goodness. Then you're John Puller Jr. She talked about you all the time. Called you Little Johnny. Pretty ironic considering your size."

The innocuous comments deepened the guilt Puller was still feeling. "That's right. Her death was quite a shock."

"It was to me too. I found her body. It really was awful." He looked down at the dog that sat quietly next to its master. "This is Sadie. Sadie, say hello to Mr. Puller."

Sadie gave a little yap and lifted her right paw.

Puller smiled, bent down, and shook it.

"I'm Stanley Fitzsimmons," said the man. "But my friends call me Cookie."

"Why's that?"

"I used to be in the bakery business. Desserts specifically." He pointed to his belly. "And as you can see, I sampled everything I made. Would you like to come in? It's the hottest part of the day and neither Sadie nor I are really heat people. I only had her out because she had to use the bathroom and I needed a bit of exercise too."

"If you're not a heat person, why move to Florida? I'm assuming you came from somewhere else."

"I did. Michigan, Upper Peninsula. After fifty years of nine-foot snowdrifts and half of each year spent seemingly in darkness and with temperatures in the teens, I'm less of a cold person than I am a heat person. And the spring, fall, and winter are spectacular here. Three out of four ain't bad. I've got some fresh lemonade. I have my own lemon tree. And I can answer any questions you might have."

"Thanks, I appreciate it."

CHAPTER

17

Cookie took Sadie off her leash and the tiny dog immediately went to her water bowl and lapped at it for what seemed a very long time. Cookie bustled around the kitchen, getting out glasses and little plates. Puller watched as a pitcher of lemonade appeared along with a platter of cookies, pastries, and other assorted goodies.

Puller looked around the house. It was expensively decorated, with heavy, solid furnishings, all with a Caribbean theme, window treatments that were sturdy enough to keep out the afternoon light and heat, and carpet that your feet sank into.

Cookie must have been an awfully good baker.

In one glass cabinet there was a display of a dozen vintage watches. Puller drew closer and examined them.

"Started collecting them years ago," Cookie said over Puller's shoulder. "Some are very valuable."

"Will you ever sell them?"

"My kids can after I'm dead. I like them too much."

Puller could hear the air conditioner running full out and wondered what a monthly electrical bill would be for this place.

As if in answer to his thoughts Cookie said, "I put solar panels in two years ago. They work wonders. I not only get my electricity for free, I have a surplus that I sell back to the city of Paradise. Not that I need the money, but I won't turn it down either. And it's totally green. I'm into that."

They sat and drank their lemonade. It was tart and cold and had a nice aftertaste. Cookie helped himself to several chocolate fudge bars and urged Puller to try the coconut-filled pastries.

Puller bit into one and came away impressed. "This is really good."

Cookie flushed with pleasure at his words. "You would think over the years that I'd get sick of baking, but the truth is I love it more than ever. See, now I get to bake for myself and my friends. It's not a job anymore."

"Did you bake for Betsy?"

"Oh yes. And for Lloyd when he was alive."

"So you've been here a while?"

"Moved in three years after Betsy and Lloyd did. So yes, a good long time."

He set his glass of lemonade down. "And I want you to know how so very sad I was when she passed. She was a wonderful person, she really was. A good friend to me. Just very caring. And when something needed to be done in the community, you could always count on Betsy to pitch in. And Lloyd too when he was alive."

"That was how she was wired. Very can-do," replied Puller.

"She told me a lot about your father, her brother. A three-star. Army legend."

Puller nodded. "Yeah." He never liked to talk about his father. "Do you know whether she had a lawyer?"

"Yes, same one I used. His name is Griffin Mason. Everyone calls him Grif. He's an excellent attorney."

"Does he handle wills?"

"Every lawyer in Florida handles trusts and estate work," said Cookie. "Sort of their bread and butter, what with the elderly population."

"You have his contact info?"

Cookie opened the drawer of a built-in desk next to the refrigerator, drew out a business card, and handed it to him.

Puller eyed it briefly and slipped it into his pocket. "So you said you found her body? Can you run me through the details on that?"

Cookie sat back and his plump face assumed a sad expression. Puller could even see tears clustering in the corners of his eyes.

"I don't get up that early. I'm more of a night owl. And at age seventy-nine, four or five hours a night are plenty for me. At some point down the road I'll have a lot longer time to sleep. Anyway, I have a little morning routine. I let Sadie out in the backyard while I sit on the back deck and drink my first cup of coffee and read the newspaper. I still get the actual paper, most of the old folks around here do. I'm online a lot and consider myself pretty tech-savvy for an old fart, but I still like to hold the news, as it were."

"What time was that?"

"About eleven or so. This was several days ago now, you understand. So I was sitting on my deck and I noticed that Betsy's back door was open. From the deck I could see it over my fence-line. I thought that was odd because as a rule Betsy didn't really get going until around noon or so. Her osteoporosis had done a real number on her spine. It was getting difficult for her to even get around with her walker. And I knew it was difficult for her to get out of bed."

"I can see that," replied Puller. "Did she have a caregiver?"

"Yes. Jane Ryon, lovely girl. She

would come three days a week, starting around nine in the morning. She
would do some tidying up around the
house and then help Betsy get up, get
her clothes on, stuff like that."

"Why only three days a week?"

"Betsy wanted to retain her independence, I guess. And a full-time caregiver isn't cheap. And Medicare really
doesn't cover that unless you're in far
worse shape than Betsy was, and even
then they don't cover the entire expense. Betsy never seemed to be hurt-
ing for money, but folks of our generation, we're frugal. Jane also helps me
as well. Twice a week."

"You look pretty independent."

"She runs errands, takes care of Sadie when I'm gone. She's a great physical therapist and all those years of
baking left me a permanent pretzel,
particularly in my hands."

"You have her contact info?"

Cookie presented him with another
business card. "I have hundreds of
them. People in Florida pass them out
like candy. The elderly are a service industry's best customers. We all have

stuff that we can't do ourselves anymore, but that still needs doing."

"Okay, so back to that morning?"

"I walked to the fence between our
properties and called out her name. I
didn't get an answer, so I left my backyard, walked over, and knocked on her
front door. I didn't expect her to get up
and race to the door if she was in bed,
but I thought maybe she might call out.
Her bedroom is on the first floor."

"I know," said Puller. "Go on."

"Well, there was no answer at the
front door, so I decided to go into her
backyard and get into the house that
way. I was hoping nothing had happened to her, but in our neighborhood
we've had people die before and they
haven't been found for some time. At
our ages, your ticker can just stop and
down you go."

"I guess that's true," said Puller. He
kept his gaze on the man, willing him to
pick up the pace and get to what he
really needed to know.

"I managed to open the gate latch
and stepped into the backyard. I was
looking at the door as I came around

the corner of the house. I almost didn't look in the direction of her little fountain pool, but luckily I did. I couldn't see it from where my deck is situated, you see. But now I could."

Puller stopped him there. "Okay, if you could just take it one step at a time. Tell me everything you saw, smelled, heard."

Puller had taken out a notebook and Cookie looked at it anxiously. "The police told me it was an accident."

"The police might be right. Then again, they might be wrong."

"So you came down to investigate?"

"I came down to see my aunt. When I found out she was dead, I paid my respects. Then I switched to investigation mode to make sure she didn't leave this world against her wishes."

Cookie gave a little shudder and continued. "I saw her lying in the fountain pool. It's only about two feet deep. You'd think no one could drown in it. But she was facedown, her entire head was underwater."

"Which way was she facing?"

"Her head was pointed toward the house."

"Arms outstretched or by her side?"

Cookie considered this for a few moments, obviously trying to picture the scene in his mind. "Right arm outstretched and over top of the stone surround. Her left arm was by her side."

"Her legs?"

"Splayed."

"Her walker?"

"On the ground on the right side of the pool."

"What did you do next?"

"I ran over to her. At that point I didn't know if she was dead or alive. I kicked off my sandals and walked directly into the water. I grabbed her by the shoulders and lifted her head out of the water."

Puller thought about this. Cookie had wrecked the crime scene. He had to do it, because like he'd said, he didn't know if Betsy was still alive. Crime scenes could be legitimately tainted by first responders trying to save lives. That trumped even preserving evidence. In this case, unfortunately, it had been for naught.

"But she wasn't?"

Cookie shook his head. "I've seen a few dead people in my life. Not just at funerals and such. Smoke inhalation killed my little sister over fifty years ago. One of my best friends drowned in a pond when we were teenagers. Betsy's face was deathly white. Her eyes were open, her mouth hung loosely. There was no pulse, no sign of life."

"Foam around the mouth?"

"Yes, that's right."

"Were her limbs stiff or supple?"

"They seemed a little stiff."

"But just a little?"

"Yes."

"Upper arms stiff or supple?"

"Stiff. But her hands seemed normal, if cold."

"What did you do then?"

"I set her back down exactly as I had found her. I watch a lot of *CSI* and *NCIS*. I know you're not supposed to mess with the area where a body is found. Then I went back to my house and called the police. They showed up about five minutes later. A man and a woman."

"Landry and Hooper?"

"Yes, that's right. How did you know that?"

"Long story. Were you around when they went over the scene?"

"No. They took my statement and then asked me to go back to my house, and to stay there in case they had any other questions. Other police cars showed up and then I saw a woman with a medical bag drive up, get out, and go into the backyard."

"Medical examiner," said Puller.

"Right. Then a black hearse arrived a few hours later. I watched them bring Betsy out on a gurney with a white sheet over her. They put her in the hearse and it drove off."

Cookie sat back, obviously exhausted and saddened by retelling the story. "I'm really going to miss her."

"Did she still drive? I saw the car in the garage."

"Not really. I mean, I hadn't seen her out in the car in a while."

"But she was still capable of driving?"

"I would say no. Her legs were weak and her reflexes were shot. Her spine was bent. I'm not sure how she dealt with the pain." He paused. "Come to think of it, she did go out the day before I found her. I saw Jerry drive up."

"Jerry?"

"Jerry Evans. He has a car service. I've used him. He picked Betsy up around six in the evening and she was back around thirty minutes later."

"Short trip. Any idea where she went?"

"Yep. I asked Jerry. He said to mail a letter."

Puller knew it was *the* letter. "Why not just put it in the mailbox out front?"

"Our mail comes early here. Jerry said the box she used had a later pickup. It would go out that night."

Puller thought, *She mailed a letter. And a bit later she was dead.*

Before Puller could even ask, Cookie handed him a business card with Jerry's name and number on it.

"Thanks. Did she often go into the backyard at night by herself?"

"She liked to sit on the bench by the fountain pool. Usually during the day. To catch the sunlight. I'm not the best person to ask about what she did later at night. She normally went to bed long before I did. I like to get out and about. I know it's hard for you to believe, but anyone in their seventies is considered a 'young'un' down here. We're supposed to go out at night and party hearty."

"Did you notice anything suspicious the night before you found her? People, sounds, anything?"

"I was out visiting friends across town so I probably wouldn't have seen anything. I got home late. Everything seemed normal."

"Was she dressed in her pajamas or regular clothes?"

"Regular clothes."

"So the probability was she died the night before. She hadn't been to bed."

Cookie nodded. "That makes sense."

"Over the last few days leading up to my aunt's death, did she talk to you about anything she was concerned about?"

"Like what?" Cookie asked, looking curious.

"Anything out of the ordinary. Did she mention a person? An event? Something she'd seen, perhaps at night?"

"No, nothing like that. *Was* she worried about something?"

"Yeah, I think she was," said Puller. "And it looks like she might have had good reason to be."

CHAPTER

18

Puller sat in his rental and called the medical examiner, Louise Timmins, and after that the attorney, Grif Mason. Timmins was a practicing physician busy with patients until six that evening. Mason was out of the office at a meeting. Puller arranged to meet Timmins at seven at a nearby café and he left a message with Mason's office to call him back when he returned.

He called Jerry, the driver, who confirmed what Cookie had already told him but added, "She looked tired, and worried about something."

Puller thanked him, clicked off, and thought back to Cookie's commentary. Upper arms stiff, hands normal. Rigor started in the upper extremities before moving outward. Then it went away in the reverse order. She had not been dead long enough for the process to start reversing.

Puller thought through the possible timetable. She had mailed a letter at six p.m. and her body was found at eleven a.m. the next day. Puller didn't think she had died the moment she had returned from the mailbox but probably later that evening. So stiff upper arms told Puller that rigor was just beginning on his aunt's body. That meant that when Cookie found her she had been dead probably about twelve to fourteen hours. That number could be skewed by the Florida heat and humidity, which would speed up a body's decomposition, but it at least gave Puller a range to work with. If Cookie found her shortly after eleven her death might have occurred around ten the previous night, give or take. Or about four hours after she mailed the letter.

Puller checked his watch. It was past three in the afternoon and he didn't yet have a place to stay. Now it was time to find a bed.

Right as he put the car in gear he spotted it. A vehicle parked at the curb four car lengths down from him and on the other side. It was a tan Chrysler sedan, Florida plates that began ZAT. He couldn't see the rest because the plate was dirty. Perhaps intentionally so, he thought. The reason this was significant was that Puller had seen this very same car parked across the street from the funeral home.

He eased the Corvette from the curb and slowly drove off. He checked his rearview mirror. The tan Chrysler started up and pulled out.

Okay, that was progress. Someone was interested in him. He took out his phone and snapped a picture of the Chrysler's reflection in his rearview mirror. There looked to be two people inside, but the sun's glare made it difficult to see much detail.

He drove up and down the main strip right off the water but easily gauged that all of these places would be far beyond his budget. He began driving off water, block by block. He checked prices at the second and third blocks and found them to be so high he wondered how anybody could afford the places on the water.

He finally got on his cell phone and did a search of lodgings in the area by price. On the fifth block from the water was one that landed in his sweet spot, a residence inn called the Sierra, where one could rent by the day or week. Eighty bucks a night, breakfast included, or you could get it down to four-fifty for the full seven days paid in advance. Actually it wasn't all that sweet for a guy whose salary was paid by Uncle Sam, but it was going to have to do.

The three-story building was a block of ragged stucco with an orange terra-cotta roof, which was in as bad shape as the stucco. It was sandwiched between a gas station on one side and a building undergoing renovation on the other. The narrow street it was on had nary a palm tree. What the streets did have in abundance were old cars and trucks, some on cinderblocks, others looking as though they were close to being so. It didn't seem to Puller that any of the rusted vehicles were from later than the 1980s.

He looked in his rearview for the Chrysler but didn't see it.

A group of barefoot kids in shorts and no shirts was running up and down the street, kicking a soccer ball with great skill. They all stopped playing and stared when Puller pulled up in front of the Sierra in his Corvette. When he got out, they stared even harder and drew closer.

He grabbed his bag from the passenger seat, shut and beeped the doors locked with his key fob, and strode up to the kids.

One of the boys looked up at him and asked in Spanish if that was his car.

Puller answered in Spanish that it was actually being rented by a friend of his named Uncle Sam.

The boy asked if Uncle Sam was rich.

"Not as rich as he used to be," answered Puller as he walked toward the Sierra's little front office.

Puller paid for two nights, got his room key and instructions on where and when breakfast was served. The woman behind the desk told him where he could park his car. She gave him a key card to access the garage.

"I can't leave it on the street?" said Puller

She was a small Latina with straight dark hair. "You can, but it might not be there in the morning."

"Right," said Puller. "I'll put it in the garage."

When he got back to the car the gang of boys had surrounded it, touching it and whispering.

"You like cars?" Puller asked them.

They all nodded their heads.

"I'll let you hear the engine."

He got in and fired it up and revved the engine. They all jumped back at the sound, looked at each other and started laughing.

Puller drove to the garage area that was on a side street next to the Sierra.

He put his key card in an electronic reader and the large metal door rose, revealing a large space beyond. He pulled through and the door automatically closed. He parked the car, exited via a side door of the garage, and walked back to the Sierra.

At the corner he saw one of the boys who had been admiring his car. He had brown curly hair and looked about ten or eleven. Puller noted the skinny, undernourished frame. But he also saw that the boy's muscles were hard and his features determined. His gaze was wary, but then Puller figured around here one had to be careful.

"You live around here?" asked Puller in English.

The boy nodded. "*Sí.*" He pointed to his left. "*Mi casa.*"

"What's your name?"

"Diego."

"Okay, Diego, I'm Puller." They shook hands. "You know Paradise really well?"

Diego nodded. "Very good. I live here all the time."

"You live with your mom and dad."

He shook his head. "*Mi abuela.*"

So his grandmother was raising him, thought Puller.

"You want to earn some money?"

Diego nodded so vigorously that his soft brown curls bounced up and down. "*Sí. Me gusta el dinero.*"

Puller handed him a five-dollar bill and then took out his cell phone. He showed him the picture of the Chrysler.

"Keep an eye out for this car," he said. "Don't go near it, don't talk to the people in it, don't let them see you watching, but get the rest of the license plate for me if you can, and what the people inside look like. *Entiendes*?"

"*Sí.*"

Puller held out his hand for the boy to shake. He did so. Puller noticed the ring on the boy's finger. It was silver with a lion's head engraved on it.

"Nice ring."

"*Mi padre* gave it to me."

"I'll be seeing you, Diego."

"But how will I find you?" asked Diego.

"You won't have to. I'll find you."

CHAPTER

19

The home was one of the largest on the Emerald Coast, ten acres on prime waterfront on its own point with sweeping views of the Gulf across an infinite horizon. Its total cost was far more than a thousand middle-class folks collectively would earn in a year.

He pushed lawnmowers and hefted bags of yard debris and loaded them onto trucks parked in the service area behind the mansion. The landscape trucks were not allowed to come through the front entrance with its fine cobblestone drive. They were relegated to the asphalt in the rear.

There were two pools in the rear grounds, one an infinity pool and the other an Olympic-sized oval. The grandeur of the grounds was matched only by the beauty of the interior of the thirty-five-thousand-square-foot home with an additional twenty thousand square feet in various other buildings, including a pool house, guesthouse, gymnasium, theater, and security quarters.

He had seen one of the indoor maids venture outside to receive a package from a FedEx driver, who also was relegated to the service entrance. She was a Latina dressed in an old-fashioned maid's uniform complete with white apron and black cap. Her body was slim but curvy. Her face was pretty. Her hair was dark and luxurious-looking.

At the end of the dock that ran straight out into the Gulf was a 250-foot yacht with a chopper resting on top of an aft helipad.

He labored hard, the sweat running down his back and into his eyes. While other workers stopped for water or shade breaks he continued to push on. Yet his tasks had a purpose. They allowed him to circumnavigate the grounds. In his mind he placed all of the buildings onto a chessboard, moving pieces in accordance with various scenarios.

What he focused on most of all was the deployment of the security forces. There were six on duty during the day. All seemed professional, worked as a team, were well armed, observant, and loyal to their employer. In sum, there didn't seem to be many weaknesses.

He assumed there were at least a fresh half dozen deployed at night and maybe more, since the darkness was a more apt time for an attack.

He drew near enough to the main gate coming in to see the alarm pad and surveillance camera mounted there. The gates were wrought iron and massive. They looked like the ones in front of the White House main entrance. The walls surrounding the front of the estate were stucco and over six feet high.

The homeowner obviously wanted privacy.

He dropped to one knee and was performing some pruning tasks around a mound of bushes when he saw a Maserati convertible pull up to the gate. Inside were a man and a woman. They were both in their early thirties and had the well-nourished and pleased looks of folks for whom life had held no hardships.

They punched in the code and the gates swung open.

As they passed by him neither of them even looked at him. But he looked at them, memorizing every detail of their faces.

And now he also had the six-digit security code to the front gate, beacuse he'd seen the man input it. The only remaining problem was the surveillance camera.

He drew closer to the gate and worked on trimming back a bush. His gaze ran up the pole to which the camera was attached. The power line was enclosed in the metal pole, a standard practice, he knew. But once the pole was set in the ground the power lines had to go somewhere.

He stepped through the gate before it closed all the way and started to work on a patch of lawn running back from the camera post to the fenceline. As he got down on his hands and knees and clipped at weeds and picked up an errant leaf that had had the effrontery to land on the lush grass, he studied the slight hump in the ground. This was where the trench had been dug for the electrical line running to the gate, which also powered the camera, voice box and security pad.

He eyed the rumpled contour of the lawn to where it disappeared under the fence. If one had not been looking for it, the evidence of the trench would have been almost invisible. But not to him.

He had to assume that the power line would be encased in a hardened pipe, but maybe not.

He rose and walked around the perimeter of the property. He could not go back through the gate without revealing that he now knew the code. He also wondered how often it was changed. They were in the middle of the month and also the middle of the week. If they changed the code at the end of seven or thirty days, which was probable, he still had time.

He reached the rear of the grounds and saw the vastness of the Gulf spread out before him. Seagulls swooped and dove. Boats either flew across the water or slowly puttered along. People were fishing, sailing, motorboating. That was during the day.

At night they were moving other kinds of product. The kind he had once been. But luckily he had escaped. Others had not been so fortunate.

He put his bag of lawn debris in one of the trucks and paused to drink from a cup of water he had filled from one of the large orange water coolers. He glanced at two other men who were working on a tree just inside the fenceline. They were Latinos. There was also one white man, two blacks, and then there was him. He was of indeterminate origin. Technically, he was Caucasian. Technically.

He had never categorized himself that way. He belonged to an ethnic group, a strong one, judging by his features. There had not been many people looking to come to his country and breed with the ones already there. It was remote, it was harsh, outsiders were welcomed not with open arms, but only with suspicion. His people were proud, and they did not take kindly to insult or injury. Well, that was putting it mildly. They never turned the other cheek.

He crumpled up the paper cup and threw it into the garbage bin on the back of the truck. He walked through the rear gate and made his way over near the infinity pool area.

The Maserati was parked nearby. Lounging next to the pool was the woman who'd been in the car. The man was not there. She had slipped off her sundress and high heels, which sat next to her as she lay back on the chaise. Her bathing suit was tiny, a strip of fabric up top, a thong below. As she rolled over on her stomach he could see nearly all of her revealed buttocks.

They were mostly firm, but still soft enough in places to be intensely feminine. She undid the straps on her top and let them fall to the side. Her legs were long, smooth, and toned. Her light blonde hair, done up in a ponytail while in the car, now cascaded along her freckled shoulders.

She was a very beautiful woman. He could understand why the man in the Maserati had been smiling so smugly, as if she were his property.

His musings stopped when he realized he'd made a mistake.

He had watched the woman a few seconds too long. He heard footsteps behind him and felt the tug on his arm.

The voice said, "Move your ass. Now!"

He turned to see one of the security men there, earwig inserted, squiggly cord running down to the power pack hidden in his waistband behind his jacket. Though it was hot, they all wore jackets. And under the jackets were their guns.

"Now!" the man said again, staring

up at him. "You're not here to admire the view, lawn boy."

He moved off at once. He could have killed the man with one strike to his neck, but there would have been no point. His plan would have been ruined. But his time would come.

He looked back once more at the woman to find her turned slightly to her side—not enough to reveal her breasts, but nearly so.

She seemed to be watching him. Behind the sunglasses he could not be sure. He wondered why someone like her would take notice of someone like him.

The answer to that question could not be good for him.

CHAPTER

20

Puller sat on the bed in his room and looked around. Nothing special. A floor, a door, a window, a bed, and a toilet. There was a double connecting door with the room next to his. He'd stayed in some better places and many far worse ones.

The walls were thin. He could hear the sounds coming from adjacent rooms, not clearly enough to recognize words, but certainly raised voices. On his way up to the room he'd passed several people, presumably residents here, who'd gazed at him suspiciously.

He apparently was one of the few whites here. Maybe the only one.

By the glances and the whispers that had accompanied them, Puller assumed that some folks might vocalize their disapproval of his presence here in terms that would require him to take action. He didn't want that to happen and would prefer if it didn't. But he would be prepared if it did.

He unpacked the few clothes that he'd brought and checked his watch. He had some time before he was to meet Louise Timmins. Mason had not called back yet. Puller decided to do some more recon of the area and then meet Timmins. He did not like sitting in hotel rooms, whether they be a place like this or the Ritz—not that he would ever see the inside of a Ritz. Not on Uncle Sam's pay.

He locked his door on the way out. He had left nothing behind that he could not afford to lose. He walked down the hall and reached the elevator, but he passed by this and walked to the stairwell. The building wasn't in the best repair and he figured the elevator wouldn't be either. Being trapped on one for several hours was not part of his plan.

He heard it before he could see anything. A man. A woman. And what sounded like a child.

He opened the door and stepped through. It was actually three grown men, a teenage girl about sixteen, and a boy who looked about five. One man was a Latino, one black, and the other had skin color the same as Puller's. He appreciated diversity in prickish felons.

The girl—clearly against her will—was being held against the wall by the Latino. The black man had hold of the crying boy, restraining him. The kid was swinging his arms and trying to strike out. The white man was standing in front of the girl, a smile on his face. He had loosened his belt and was in the middle of unbuttoning his pants. His intent was as obvious as such intent had been for thousands of years.

Men forcing themselves on women.

When the door opened, the white guy, without even looking to see who it was, snarled, "Get the hell out of here. Now!"

Puller let the door shut behind him and noted the buige in the back pocket of the white guy's pants. Stupid place to keep your gun, but then White looked pretty dumb.

"Don't think so. And you might as well cinch your belt back up. This is not going to go according to your plan."

The three men turned to look at him. The girl shrank back and clutched at the boy.

White said, "You really want to do this, shithead?"

"Name's Puller. First name John. And you are?"

White looked at his buddies and smiled. But there was nervousness behind the smile, Puller noted. The black man was the biggest, but Puller had him by four inches and forty pounds. White was five-nine and a pudgy one-ninety. The Latino was five-six, a buck fifty, and had no demonstrable muscle.

Puller towered over them all. The width of his shoulders nearly spanned the doorway. He edged forward, his gaze directly on White, but his peripheral radar keeping his buddies in view.

White buckled his belt.

"You looking to get your ass killed?" said the black guy.

"No. Same way I'm sure she wasn't looking to get assaulted by three jerk-offs."

White slightly turned his head, his right hand dipping to his back pocket in a move that was as obvious as it would prove to be futile.

Puller sighed. Not how he wanted it to go down, but he didn't have much choice now. He struck before the gun was halfway out of the man's back pocket. He slammed his elbow into White's neck and followed that by whipping a knee into his left kidney. As White dropped screaming to the floor, Puller sent a crushing right cross to his jaw. White lay on the floor, blood coming from his mouth along with a few of his teeth.

Half of Puller wanted to give the other two guys a way out, but the looks on their faces indicated that their combined presence was puffing up each other's courage beyond all reason. Two against one, they were thinking. Easy pickings.

Too bad for them.

He hooked Latino around the head and, using him as a weapon, swung him off his feet and into Black, knocking him down the flight of stairs. He came to rest at the bottom, both the fight and his consciousness gone from him.

Puller kept swinging Latino until the latter's head met the wall with crunching impact. He slumped down, joining Black in the land of involuntary sleep.

Puller stood there for a moment, not even out of breath, and more than a little pissed off that all this had come to pass.

He looked at the girl. "You okay?"

She nodded. She was pretty, with soft curves and a large bosom. She looked older than she probably was. He doubted that this was the first time this kind of an assault had happened to her.

Puller eyed the little boy. "He your brother?"

She nodded again.

"What're your names?"

"I'm Isabel. He's Mateo," she said in a tiny, scared voice.

"You want to call the cops?"

Puller thought he knew the answer to this, but felt compelled to ask it anyway. She was shaking her head before he'd even finished the question.

"Do you want *me* to call the cops?"

"No. Please don't do that."

He looked at the fallen men. They had buzz cuts and tats all over. He didn't think it was possible, but one never knew.

"They in the military?" he asked her.

She shook her head. "No."

So no jurisdiction for me, thought Puller. Other than as a concerned citizen.

He said, "They won't stop. I just made them a lot madder, in fact. They might take it out on you."

She grabbed her brother's hand and they both ran off through the door.

Puller could hear their footsteps for a few seconds and then they were gone.

He did a quick check of the three guys. All breathing. All pulses strong. He didn't care if bones were broken or skulls fractured. That was the price one paid for being pieces of shit that preyed on others. Especially three grown men against a girl and her five-year-old brother.

When White moaned and moved a bit, Puller kicked him in the head, sending him back to sleep.

"Prick."

He debated whether to call the cops or not, but without the girl's statement he'd have nothing except his own account. And if she didn't back him up, which she wouldn't, Puller might be looking at being charged with assault, the lies of the three men stacked against him.

He decided just to keep on going. He'd have to deal with the fallout later. He went back to his room, grabbed his bag, and walked out to retrieve his car.

He still had a recon to do. He was

here to find out what had happened to his aunt. Nothing was going to detour him from that.

He could not have been more wrong.

CHAPTER

21

As Puller walked out of the building another man was walking in. When they
crossed paths Puller did something he
almost never had to do to when meeting another person.

He looked up.

It was the same guy from the back
of the truck he'd seen earlier while eating lunch on the waterfront.

Up close the man looked even larger
and more intimidating. Puller had never
before seen a more perfectly propor-
tioned physique. He could have been a
poster boy for a superhero recruiting

ad. As the two men went by each other, they both did the up-down, side-side checkout of the other. Practiced, smooth, looking for things that would not be obvious to the uninformed, meaning just about every other person on the planet.

Puller came away impressed not just with the other man's physique but also with the preciseness of the observation of those intense eyes. It was obvious to Puller that the man recognized him from earlier in the day, even though it had only been a seconds-long glance. You had to be trained to achieve that sort of recognition skill.

Puller again ran his eye up and down the man. He wore a landscaping company uniform. Dark green T-shirt soaked in sweat and dark blue pants. New-looking work shoes that must have been a size sixteen.

So the guy either had gotten a new pair of shoes, which seemed unlikely, or he had just started this job. The shirt was stretched too tight across his torso. Every muscle was revealed through the flimsy fabric. He looked like the musculature chart one saw in a doctor's office.

They probably didn't have a shirt to fit him, reasoned Puller. The pants too were a little short. Most companies didn't keep in stock uniforms to fit gents who topped six and a half feet in height. As they passed by one another Puller instinctively looked back; he wasn't completely surprised when he found the other man doing the very same thing. The look was not threatening, just watchful, curious, appraising.

Puller walked to the garage, retrieved his car, and drove off.

He took Paradise grid by grid, memorizing as many details as he could. He finally pulled into a parking lot, shut the car off, sat back, and wondered about the contents of his aunt's letter.

People not being what they seemed.

Mysterious happenings in the night.

Something just not being right.

As he drove he broke things down logically, something the military had spent years drilling into him. It was now how he approached everything in life, even the things to which logic didn't necessarily pertain.

Like families.

Emotions.

Relationships.

Applying logic to any of them was a recipe for a lifetime of heartache.

Pretty much the story of his life.

He thought about the first of his aunt's observations:

People not being what they seemed.

He didn't know who his aunt's friends were other than Cookie, who seemed innocuous and certainly exactly what he appeared to be. But that was based on only one interview, and thus to Puller the jury was still out on it.

There could be other neighbors to whom she was referring. Puller would have to check them all out. There was Jane Ryon, the caregiver. He would definitely check her out. Then the lawyer, Mason. Possibly others.

He moved on to the second observation in the letter:

Mysterious happenings in the night.

Happenings, plural. In the night. Did she mean mysterious happenings in

her neighborhood? If so, did they involve one of her neighbors? To Puller
the area had seemed like a normal sub-
urb where mysterious happenings
probably were at a minimum. But his
aunt was dead and that obviously
shined a new light on things.

Finally he considered his aunt's third
observation:

Something just not being right.

That was open to lots of interpreta-
tions. What Puller could fall back on
was his experience with his aunt. One
of the most no-nonsense people he'd
ever known, if she said it or wrote it
she believed it. She did not reach knee-
jerk conclusions. There was the possibility that old age had changed those
personality traits, but somehow Puller
didn't think so. They were too ingrained
in his family's genes.

He had to work from the assumption
that everything in his aunt's letter was
true. And if she had stumbled onto
something and the people involved in
that something had found out, it was a
prime motive to remove Betsy Simon
from this earth. And if that had hap-

pened, Puller would welcome the opportunity to repay the folks who had
done it. He would provide either a long
prison sentence or their own early exit
from the living.

Having exhausted the possibilities
based on his limited investigation so
far, he got out of the car, walked down
a wooden boardwalk, and reached the
beach. It was nearly six-thirty, and the
café where he was meeting Timmins
was close by. He decided to walk along
the sand both to relax a bit and to think
some more while the waves pounded
the shore.

There were a number of people on
the beach. Some were power walking
with exaggerated motions of their legs
and arms. Others strolled arm in arm.
Still others had their dogs with them
and were tossing tennis balls and Fris-
bees for their canine companions to
run down.

Puller moved on, letting his gaze
sweep from the ocean to the boardwalk
and beyond. There were parts of Paradise that definitely fit the name. However, having been here only a relatively

short period of time, Puller had seen other parts that did not remotely belong.

An interesting place, he thought.

When he saw what was going on up ahead, he picked up his pace. He didn't know if it would have anything to do with his aunt's death, but right now anything in Paradise that seemed unusual interested him.

CHAPTER

22

Puller saw Officer Landry first, then Bullock. Hooper was nowhere to be seen.

What he saw next made him slow down to a leisurely walk. A barrier formed from metal stands and blue tarp had been erected to shield something from view. When police were around, the thing to be shielded from view typically was a human body.

Puller drew to within a hundred feet and stopped, taking it all in. Landry was standing near a couple whom Puller recognized. He had seen them at the police station earlier, looking worried and upset. The names they had mentioned came back to his mind.

Nancy and Fred Storrow.

They went out and never came back. There seemed to be a lot of that going around in Paradise. Puller wondered if either or both of them were behind the shield.

He looked out toward the water. The tide was coming in. Had it brought the body or bodies along with it?

He couldn't imagine that two bodies had been dumped on the beach and were just now being found. You didn't dump bodies in public places in broad daylight. It was now nearing seven in the evening. He looked out toward the water again.

Tide. Had to be. He doubted the corpses were in very good shape. Prolonged time in the water did awful things to bodies.

He glanced over at the couple again. The woman was weeping, leaning in against the shoulder of the man, while Landry stood awkwardly next to them, her official notebook dangling in one hand.

Bullock was standing over near the shield shaking his head and tapping his fingers against his gun belt like he was sending out an SOS signal.

They hadn't set up a perimeter, but people were keeping their distance.

Puller walked toward Bullock until the man looked up and saw him.

He at first put up his hands to ward Puller off, but then recognized him. He strode forward, his black shoes slipping in the sand.

When Bullock got to within a foot of Puller he said, "What are you doing here?"

"Just going for a walk on the beach. What do you have here?"

"What we have is an ongoing investigation that I am not at liberty to disclose to a civilian."

"I'm not a civilian."

"To me you are."

"One body or two?"

"Excuse me?" Bullock took a step back and looked suspicious.

"Behind the shield. Did the tide bring it or them in?"

"What the hell do you know about it?"

"Nothing. But you put up a shield on a beach and you got a woman sobbing over there—a woman I saw at the station earlier today probably filing a missing persons report—and the dominos begin to fall into place. Was it an accident?"

"Look, Puller, my best advice to you is to turn yourself around, get back on a plane, and fly home."

"Appreciate the advice, but Paradise is growing on me. I can see why you like it down here so much."

Bullock turned on his heel and walked off, his shoes rooster-tailing streams of sand behind him.

Another officer came and took charge of the couple, allowing Landry to break free and walk over to him.

"What did Chief Bullock say to you?" she asked.

"He wanted me to join the investigation and lend my expertise in helping solve the crime. He also invited me over for a beer later at his house."

She smiled. "He doesn't drink beer. But I didn't believe you anyway."

Puller nodded at the blue tarp. "You called the ME yet?"

"She'll be here as soon as she can."

Puller nodded. It seemed that his seven o'clock meeting with Timmins was going to be postponed.

"I won't ask you for details, because I don't want you to get in trouble with Bullock."

"Thanks."

"Where's your partner?"

Landry looked uncomfortable. "He, uh, he ran into a little problem."

"Did he puke and pass out when he saw the body?"

She looked away, but something in her features told Puller he had nailed that one.

"I've got a lot of experience with bodies coming out of the ocean."

"Why? I thought you were Army, not Navy."

"Oh, you wouldn't believe what goes

on in the infantry. And lots of Army bases are next to bodies of water."

"I doubt Chief Bullock would approve of that."

"I know he wouldn't. But I thought I'd offer anyway. And if you ever want to run anything by me, unofficially of course, feel free."

"I appreciate that. We don't have a traditional plainclothes detective division. Uniforms do it all. If we get in over our heads we can call in help from the county or the state police."

"Sounds like a plan."

"You been busy following up on things with your aunt's death?"

"A little."

"If you find out anything that shows it wasn't an accident will you bring it to me?"

"I will."

"And you won't play vigilante?"

"I never go looking for trouble."

"But somehow it finds you?"

"Sometimes. I'm staying over at a place called the Sierra."

"Not exactly a great part of town."

"It is if you can't afford the really great parts. And for the record, eighty bucks a night is not exactly cheap in my mind. Even with breakfast thrown in."

"What can I say, it's Paradise."

"Can you tell me more about the area?"

"Like what?"

"I'm sure you have the typical problems. But do you have any gangs?"

"Officially no. In reality yes."

"What do you mean officially no, then?"

"Paradise is a tourist destination. Of the millions of people who come to the Panhandle every year, lots of them come to Paradise. So officially we don't have a gang problem."

"Okay, so what does your unofficial gang problem consist of?"

"An unusual hybrid. We don't have the typical ethnic and racial divides here. No Bloods and Crips versus Latino gangs versus skinheads."

"Meaning you have diversity in your gangs. Very commendable."

She looked at him funny. "Why do you ask? Did something happen?"

"Nothing worth mentioning. Crime limited to the poorer areas?"

"People crimes, yeah, for the most part. Gang on gang. But the property crimes leach into the higher-dollar communities, for obvious reasons."

"Go where the good stuff to steal is?"

"Exactly. The really rich places around here have their own security. Either behind community walls with rent-a-cops or behind their own gates with professional types."

"I'm seeing a whole other side of Paradise."

"Hey, this stuff happens where you have money bumping up against poverty."

"Meaning America basically."

"Don't know about that."

"So who's assigned to investigate this?" asked Puller.

"Chief Bullock is going to personally handle it. He knows the family."

"Is he good at investigative work?"

"He's the chief!"

"You didn't answer the question."

She let out a sigh. "I guess we'll find out."

"I guess you will," said Puller.

CHAPTER

23

Puller sat down on a beach chair and watched as Landry and another uniformed officer strung up yellow police tape around the scene using long metal poles driven into the sand to support it.

What Puller expected to happen did occur about twenty minutes later. A Volvo pulled up and a woman got out. She was in her fifties, with graying hair cut short, a white sleeveless blouse, a blue skirt that hit right below the knees, and sandals. She wore bifocals that rode on a chain. She carried a black medical bag.

Louise Timmins, the medical examiner, had arrived. She looked harried
and upset. She walked directly to the
police tape and was admitted by
Landry. Timmins ducked under the tape
and marched to the blue tarp, where
she was met by Bullock. After a brief
conversation Timmins slipped inside
the makeshift enclosure. It would not
be a pleasant sight or smell within such
close, heated quarters, Puller knew.

You just had to keep breathing and
pretty soon your sense of smell would
fail, and fortunately so.

By his watch it was half an hour before Timmins reemerged into the sunlight. To Puller's eye she looked a little
queasy and more than a little upset. He
wondered if she might have known the
deceased, if there was only one body
in there.

She spoke for some minutes to Bullock, who nodded and wrote things
down on a spiral notepad.

When Timmins cleared the tape and
headed for her car, Puller approached.

"Dr. Timmins?"

She looked up at him. She was only

about five-two and thus had to crane her neck back some to fully take him in.

"Yes?"

"John Puller. We talked before?"

"Right, your aunt." She did not seem pleased to have encountered him here. "I meant to call you to say that I would be delayed when I found out about this, but time got away from me."

He said, "That's okay. We can reschedule. I know you weren't expecting this thing on the beach."

He studied her more closely while she pulled her car keys from her purse. Up close she looked pale, drawn, and jumpy.

"No, I wasn't expecting it. I was totally floored by it in fact."

"Anyone you knew?"

She looked at him sharply. "What makes you ask that?"

"You look more upset than is warranted by seeing a dead body, even one pulled out of the water."

"Looking at death is never easy."

"But you're a doctor and a medical examiner. You see it all the time, under

all conditions. And since this is an
oceanside town, I doubt that's the first
drowning victim you've seen."

"'I really can't talk to you about this."

"I know. And I'd much prefer not to
waste your time. Can we meet about
my aunt?"

She looked at her watch.

He said, "I'd be glad to buy you dinner. If you have an appetite."

She glanced back at the blue tarp.
"No food, but maybe a little ginger ale
on my stomach might help."

"Okay. The café we were going to
meet at is a few blocks over. You want
to walk or drive?"

"Let's drive. My legs are a little wobbly right now."

As they walked to their cars, Puller
turned around and saw both Bullock
and Landry watching them. The police
chief looked pissed. Landry seemed
merely curious.

They drove separately to the café
and found parking on the street. The
place was crowded but they were able
to snag a table near the front.

Timmins ordered a glass of ginger

ale and Puller a Coke. It was after seven and the temperature was still in the mid-eighties and the ocean breeze had fallen away.

"Feels more like Hell than Paradise, doesn't it?" said Timmins after they had gotten their drinks. She took a long sip of her ginger ale and sat back, looking a bit better.

"I take it you're a transplant here?"

"Why do you say that?"

"Your skin is too pale and you're not used to wearing sandals, which for women down here are probably a daily accessory."

She glanced down at her feet where the sandal straps had made several red marks against her skin.

He continued, "The longer you wear sandals the more your skin will toughen up."

"You're very observant."

"The Army pays me to be."

"I'm from Minnesota originally. Moved down here about six months ago. My first summer here. Minnesota can get hot in the summer, but nothing like this."

"So why'd you come down?"

"My husband died. I'd never been out of the state. I was tired of long winters. A doctor I'd met was selling his practice and I've always had an interest in forensic pathology. When I found out the job also included being the district ME, I jumped on it."

"And the place being named Paradise probably didn't hurt."

"The brochures were very attractive," she replied, with a weary smile.

"So will you be heading back north?"

"I doubt it. Place grows on you. June through August it gets crowded and the heat and humidity are pretty bad, but the rest of the year is quite nice. I could never take a walk in shorts in February in St. Paul."

Puller leaned forward, officially ending the chitchat session. "My aunt?"

"You saw the body."

"How do you know that?"

"Carl Brown over at Bailey's told me. We're friends. Local doctor and the funeral home in Florida get very close. Lots of my patients die. Old age catches up with everyone at some point."

"I saw the body."

"And?"

"And what?"

"I checked you out, Agent Puller. I have some contacts at the Pentagon. My brother is in the Air Force. I was informed that you are absolutely terrific at what you do and that tenacity doesn't come close to describing your intensity when on the hunt."

Puller sat back, gauging the woman in a different light now. "There was a bruise on her right temple."

"I saw that. There was also a slight bloodstain on the stone surround at the fountain."

"So cause and effect. But what made her fall? Did she stumble or did she have a heart attack or stroke or did an aneurysm pop?"

"None of the above. She was in re-markably good shape, at least inter-nally. Heart, lungs, other organs dis-ease-free. She had bad osteoporosis and a curved spine but that was about it. She died from water in the lungs. Asphyxiation, technically."

"So what made her fall?"

"She was using a walker, the ground

might have been slick from some of the water from the fountain falling there. She goes down, hits her head, becomes unconscious, and drowns in twenty-four inches of water. It happens."

"I wonder how often?"

"Once is enough in this case."

"Nothing else suspicious on the body?"

"No defensive wounds, no ligature marks, no other bruising that would indicate someone had attacked her."

Puller nodded. That corresponded to what he'd found. "Tox screens?"

"Won't be back for a while. But I saw no signs of poisoning, if that's where you're going. And there were no indications of abuse of alcohol or drugs."

"I think the most my aunt ever had was a glass of wine. At least that I remember."

"The post bore that out. As I said, except for the spinal issues, she was in remarkable shape for someone her age. She had quite a few years left to go."

"My aunt wrote a letter. In that letter she was concerned about something in

Paradise. Any idea what she could have meant?"

"What sort of concerns did she have?"

"People not being who they seemed. Mysterious happenings at night."

"Like I said, I just got here six months ago. I don't know enough people to be aware if they are who they are or not. And mysterious happenings? If she counts parties of drunk guys and gals parading half-naked down the main strip at two a.m. as being mysterious then she's got my vote."

"So nothing else you can tell me?"

"Afraid not. I know it seems senseless, Agent Puller. But accidents do happen."

"Yeah, they do."

But what Puller was thinking was, *If it was an accident, why are people in a Chrysler following me?*

He wasn't just spontaneously thinking this. He had just seen the car pass by the front of the café and stop near his Corvette. The window came down and he was pretty sure he saw a flash. They had taken a picture. Before he could even think of racing after them, the Chrysler drove away.

"Agent Puller, is everything all right?"

He refocused on her. "Everything's cool."

"I hope I was able to allay your concerns about your aunt."

"I think my concerns are right where they should be."

CHAPTER

24

As Puller was leaving the café his phone buzzed.

"Puller," he said.

"Mr. Puller, this is Griffin Mason, you called my office about your aunt?"

Puller said, "That's right. Can we meet tonight or is it too late?"

"I'm still at my office if you'd care to come by. You know the address?"

"I'll be there in twenty minutes."

Puller got in the Corvette and was at the lawyer's office two minutes early. It was in a former residential area where the homes had been turned into small businesses. It was two blocks off the water and Puller assumed the land was worth more than the houses. But then again maybe that applied to pretty much all the homes on this narrow strip of earth with bay water on the north side and warm Gulf water to the south. A late-model Infiniti coupe was parked in the concrete driveway.

The front door was unlocked and Puller walked into a small reception area. There was no one there. Puller assumed the hired help had long since departed.

"Mr. Mason?" he called out.

A door off the reception area opened and a short, flabby man stood there. He had on gray pinstriped pants, braces to hold them up, although his ample belly probably needed no help to do that, and a white starched dress shirt with the sleeves rolled up. He had a short graying beard and his glasses were thick enough to be called Coke bottles.

"Mr. Puller?"

"That's me."

"Please come in."

They settled in Mason's office, which was comfortably furnished in leather and soft, dark woods. A bookshelf held a staggering number of weighty legal tomes, and file folders were stacked against walls and also covered his desk, where there was also a computer.

Puller said, "Business looks good."

"Frankly, a trusts and estates lawyer in Florida is a no-brainer from a business point of view. You don't have to be a brilliant attorney. You just have to be competent and have a pulse. The average age of my clientele is seventy-six. And they keep coming. I've had to turn business away even after hiring an associate two years ago. I might have to hire a second lawyer if things keep going that way."

"Nice problem to have. Now, about my aunt?"

"Just as a legal technicality, could I see some ID please?"

Puller pulled out his cred pack and showed Mason, who smiled and said, "Your aunt spoke very highly of you."

"I hadn't seen her in a while." As soon

as he finished the statement he felt a pang of guilt.

"Well, it didn't diminish one iota her admiration for you and what you've accomplished."

"I'm just an Army grunt. There are lots of us."

"Don't be modest, Agent Puller. I was never in the military but my father was. World War II. Your aunt told me about the medals you've earned. Quite impressive."

Puller wondered who had told his aunt about this. He didn't think it was his father. The old man just wasn't that into his sons' lives.

"I tried to phone her when my father received a letter from her," said Puller. "No one answered. Then I discovered what had happened. I understand that my aunt had a caregiver. A Jane Ryon?"

"I know Ms. Ryon. She's a very capable young woman. She has lots of clients in town."

"I look forward to meeting her." Puller paused. "It was quite a shock to hear my aunt was dead."

"I know. It was very shocking to me

as well. She had some physical problems, but she seemed very strong mentally. I thought she would live to be a hundred." He moved some papers around on his desk. "You say she wrote a letter to your father? Is that why you came down?"

"Yes. I thought it was time to pay her a visit." Puller was not going to reveal to him what was in the letter. "Did she have a will?"

"Yes, she did. And I can tell you the contents. I refreshed my memory on them after I got your call."

"What are they?"

"With the exception of a few minor bequests, she left everything to you."

Puller stared at the man. This was not something he had ever expected.

"To me? And not my father?"

"Not unless your father is Chief Warrant Officer John Puller Jr."

"No, he's a three-star, retired. I'm the CWO."

"Then you get it all." He paused. "You seem surprised?"

"I am. Like I said, we hadn't been in contact for many years. I didn't even know she knew my current rank. It was very recent."

"She had no children. And her husband had passed on. And as I said, she thought very highly of you. Was quite proud. Called you the son she wished she'd had."

This statement hit Puller like a sucker punch to his kidneys. "Okay," he said slowly, for he could think of nothing else to say.

"She had various investments and her home. The real estate will need to go through probate. There are numerous legal steps that must be gone through before you will receive the property. It could take up to a year, I'm afraid."

"That's not a problem. I don't need the money."

"I have inventory lists of her personal possessions. I do that for all my clients. That way you'll know exactly what you'll be getting. I can give you a copy now if you'd like."

Puller shrugged but nodded and Mason produced several sheets of paper stapled together, which he handed to Puller.

"They're very recent," said Mason. "We had just gone over her estate about a month ago."

"Did she give any reason why?"

"No. But we usually met about once a year to make sure everything was up to date and that she didn't want to make any changes in her estate planning."

"I see."

Puller ran his gaze over the pages. There were things like books, pictures, jewelry, some Hummel collectibles and the like on there. He didn't really want any of it.

Mason said, "I'll take your contact info from you and keep you posted as we progress through the stages. Once the house is titled in your name you can do with it what you want. Live in it, rent it, or sell it."

"Fine, whatever."

"And her stock, bank, and bond portfolios were fairly substantial. She made some good investments over the years. I have records on all of that as well."

"Okay."

Mason studied him. "But then you don't strike me as the sort to whom any of that much matters."

"I've never owned a home. And I'm not sure I know what a stock or bond looks like."

Mason smiled. "That's actually refreshing. Most heirs I deal with want it all and the sooner the better."

"When was the last time you talked to my aunt?"

Mason sat back and clasped his hands behind his head, revealing sweat patches under his arms although the room was cool. "Let me think. Thursday of last week, I suppose. She called me."

"How did she sound?"

"Sound? She sounded normal."

"What was the call about?"

"Just routine matters. She had a capital gains question she needed an answer for."

"So nothing that was bothering her?"

Mason lowered his arms. "Not that I was aware of."

Puller had interviewed thousands of people over the years. Some were telling the truth, most had been lying. Liars gave telltale signs. Breathing sped up just a bit. Eye contact was lost. Arms retreated to the torso and clenched, like the formation of a little cocoon to hide the false statement, or at least the bearer thereof. A good interviewer could spot the liar nearly ninety percent of the time.

Based on that, Puller was pretty sure that Mason had just lied to him, but he didn't know to what degree.

Puller said nothing. He was waiting for Mason to ask the question that he should have already asked if he had been telling the truth.

Mason said, "Do you think your aunt was worried about something?"

Puller didn't answer right away. He was thinking about one of his aunt's statements:

People not being what they seemed.

He wondered if Griffin Mason fit into that category.

And he wished he had not shared

the contents of his aunt's letter with the police. But he couldn't change that now.

"I don't know. Like I said, I hadn't really communicated with her over the years."

Mason studied him closely and then shrugged. "Accidents happen, I know. But it doesn't make it any easier to accept someone passing. But you can take some solace in the fact that Betsy thought so highly of you that she would leave you all her property."

"Would you happen to have a key to her house? And a copy of the will for me to take?"

"Actually, I do. Betsy entrusted a set of keys to me when she had surgery a while back. I tried to give them back, but she insisted that I keep them."

Mason opened a drawer, took out a silver lockbox, opened it, rummaged through some keys in there, and pulled out a set of two.

"Front door and rear doors. Give me a minute to make a copy of the will."

He ran the pages through a copier that was set against one wall of his office, then handed the still warm pages to Puller.

Puller stood and slipped a card out of his pocket. "Here's my contact info for down the road."

Mason took the card. "Are you going over to the house now?"

"No. In the morning."

"Will you be staying in Paradise long?"

"I don't know," said Puller. "I guess once you get to Paradise it's hard to leave, right?"

He walked out.

CHAPTER

25

Puller parked his Corvette about a block down from the house and walked the rest of the way. Despite what he had told Mason he had decided to check out his aunt's place now. He kept a lookout for police cruisers. Even armed with keys and his aunt's last will and testament, he wouldn't put it past Hooper to bust his balls if he got the slightest chance.

He walked up the driveway and glanced over at Cookie's house. It was dark now and he envisioned the "young'un" partying into the wee hours in Paradise. He thought he heard Sadie yapping from inside the house, but kept walking. The yapping made Puller start missing AWOL, his cat.

He used the key to open his aunt's front door, went inside, and closed the door behind him. The house was dark. He didn't want to arouse suspicion by turning on any interior lights, so he pulled his penlight from his pocket and started moving around. He had the interior of the place pretty much memorized from his earlier visit.

He walked through the kitchen and entered his aunt's bedroom. The bed was made. She had not gone to sleep that night, obviously. She had gone into the backyard, either voluntarily or not, and there her life had ended.

A nightstand next to the bed was filled with books. His aunt had been a reader when Puller had known her all those years ago, and she had obviously kept up that habit. He scanned the titles with his light. Mostly mysteries and thrillers. His aunt did not strike him as the love story type. If she was going to cry, it would be for a legitimate reason as opposed to a manufactured one.

Puller's light skimmed over the top of the nightstand and then came back to it. He risked turning on a light because he wanted to get a clearer view.

With the table lamp turned on he leaned down and saw that his first impression had been right. A small rectangular shape with a slight dust pattern around its edges. He picked up a Robert Crais paperback from the shelf below and laid it on the rectangle. It didn't fit.

Too small.

He tried a Sue Grafton hardback.

Too big.

He opened the drawer and saw a small black journal inside. He lifted it out, opened it. The pages were blank. He placed the journal down on the rectangle. A perfect fit.

There must have been another journal. And it seemed to be missing. And something told Puller that that journal would not have blank pages.

They'd murdered his aunt and taken

her journal because of something that was in it.

Perhaps it would elaborate on what had been in her letter.

People who were not what they seemed.

Mysterious happenings in the night.

Things that just did not seem right.

He put the blank journal back, switched off the light, and left the room.

He took a few minutes to check the bedrooms upstairs but found nothing of interest or help with his investigation. One closet was full of old clothes. Some were men's pants and shirts that had presumably belonged to his uncle Lloyd. The other closets were filled with empty hangers, old vacuums, boxes full of musty sheets and comforters, and the odds and ends that folks collected over a long life.

On a shelf at the back of the closet he found several boxes. One was filled with jewelry that even to Puller's inexperienced eye looked valuable. He went through the box methodically. There was also a collector's book with old coins inserted in it. These looked valuable too. He wondered how long she had had all of this.

He walked back downstairs through the kitchen and into the garage. The Camry sat there looking polished and ready to go, unaware that its owner would not be coming back for another ride. Puller scanned the exterior of the car with his light, looking for damage or unusual marks, but he saw none.

The car looked to be in reasonable shape. He calculated that it was about five or six years old. His aunt might have bought it before she had developed all of the issues with her spine.

He leaned up against the wall and started contemplating things, trying to fill in holes in his aunt's recent actions.

He was primarily thinking that if his aunt had seen something that had caused her death, it was either in the neighborhood or elsewhere. If elsewhere, she had had to get there somehow. And even though Cookie didn't think that Betsy drove anymore, he was often gone at night and wouldn't know if she only took her car out after dark.

He opened the driver's side door and

sat down in the front seat. He noted that, though tight for him, the seat was set back far enough for a tall woman.

Then he saw the special devices that had been fitted onto the car. They were controls set within arm's reach to work both the brake and gas pedal.

So his aunt could have driven this car despite her infirmities.

He noted the sticker on the upper left side of the windshield. It was from a lube shop in Paradise. It listed the next date for service and the mileage the car should reach by that time. The date was from exactly thirty days ago. Puller looked at the mileage listed and then shined his light on the dashboard. He did a quick calculation, and also factored in his aunt's death.

In the roughly twenty-six days she could have driven it the car had gone an average of ten miles per day. He thought rapidly. Could his aunt with all of her back issues have driven hundreds of miles at a stretch? It was doubtful. But could she have driven shorter distances? That was more likely.

What if she had driven the same distance every day? Ten miles a day, in fact. That sounded doable even with her back problems.

So five out and five back. It at least gave Puller something to go on, something to check when there was so much that wasn't clear. He could do that route on all points of the compass and see where he ended up.

The next moment Puller quickly climbed out of the car and softly closed the door. He extinguished his light and pulled his M11.

Someone had just come in the front door of the house.

Puller went through the garage door back into the kitchen, making hardly any noise. The other person in the house was not being nearly as quiet. That could be both good and problematic for him.

He edged around the doorway leading into the family room. He heard squeaks from above. The person had to be upstairs. He wondered briefly if it could be the police, but surely they would have announced themselves. However, if it was Hooper, Puller might shortly find himself in a shootout with the hair-triggered cop. The last thing he needed right now was to be arrested for blowing away a police officer. Yet if anyone was going to get shot tonight he much preferred it not be him.

His hand slipped to his trigger guard. When it moved to the trigger he had to be prepared to fire.

And he would.

And then he saw the person come down the stairs.

And his military cop voice roared, "Down on the floor. Now. Or I will fire my weapon."

The person did not get down on the floor.

She screamed and ran.

CHAPTER

26

She did not make it to the front door before Puller reached her. He wrenched her arm back, pulling her face-to-face with him.

"Omigod, please, don't hurt me. Don't hurt me," she pleaded.

Puller let go of her arm, stepped back, but kept his M11 at a forty-five-degree angle, ready to aim it up at her if the necessity arose. He switched on a table lamp, partially illuminating the room.

"Who the hell are you?" he demanded as he ran his gaze over her.

She was about twenty-five, with blonde hair in a ponytail. She wore faded blue jean shorts cut high up her thighs, a tight-fitting lime green T-shirt, and flip-flops with "Corona" printed on the straps.

"I'm Jane Ryon. Who the hell are you?"

Her tone and words had grown more defiant when it appeared that he was not going to shoot her, but her fearful gaze held on his gun and she still seemed wobbly.

"John Puller." He held out his ID and badge. "CID agent with the Army."

"Good God, you're Betsy's nephew," she exclaimed.

"And you're her caregiver. Or were her caregiver," replied Puller.

"How did you know that?"

"I ask questions. Like I'm doing now. What are you doing here?"

She opened up her bag so he could see inside. "I left some things in an upstairs bedroom. A jacket and some slacks. I thought I'd be back for them when I came to see Betsy again, but of course that didn't happen."

Puller holstered his gun. "I'm sorry if I frightened you."

"It's okay. At least I know my heart is strong now. Otherwise I would've dropped from a coronary."

She was about five-five and in good shape. The definition in her legs and the extreme trimness of her frame made Puller deduce that she was a runner.

"I'm really sorry about your aunt," she said. "She was a nice person. Do they know how she died?"

"How did you find out?"

"I came here on the day they found her body. I was actually coming to visit another client on this street. The police cars were here and then a hearse arrived. I talked to one of the cops. He said Betsy had been found in the backyard dead. That's all I know. I thought maybe she had a heart attack or something."

"Her official cause of death was drowning."

"Drowning? I thought they said she was in the backyard. Did she actually drown in the bathtub?"

"No, in the fountain out back."

"But it's not that deep."

"Apparently she fell, hit her head, and slipped into the water unconscious."

"Oh my God, how awful is that?"

"Well, if she was unconscious she would have felt no pain or panic, but it's still not a pleasant way to go."

"Who found her?"

"Next-door neighbor."

"Cookie?"

"Yeah."

"I'm sure he's really broken up. They were good friends. It was funny to see them together. He's short and she's tall. She reminded me of that lady from *The Golden Girls* TV show. I'd watch it on TV Land when I was a kid."

"Right," said Puller.

"She was her own person, and although sometimes she was hard to get along with, I admired her spunk."

"Yeah, spunk runs in the family," replied Puller. "Cookie told me you help him too?"

"Oh yeah. I've got a lot of clients in Paradise. Keeps me hopping."

"You a native?"

"No. And I don't technically live in

Paradise. I'm in Fort Walton Beach, which is nearby. I came down here about five years ago from New Jersey. The winters are a lot nicer, meaning warmer."

"I bet. How was my aunt before she died?"

"She had the typical aches and pains associated with someone of that age. She was on meds—again, no surprise there. She used a walker. She was tall, a lot taller than me, but her spine was curved. She had her good days and bad ones. Like all of us."

"Yeah, but she recently had a *really* bad day."

"Well, yeah."

"How were her spirits? Did she seem depressed, annoyed, worried?"

"Not more than usual. I've been a caregiver for quite some time now, and I've found that older people's emotions can run the gamut during the day. They tend to be in higher spirits in the morning. As night approaches they start to falter a bit. At least that's been my experience."

"Did she drive? Or did you drive for her?"

"I would run errands. To the store, the pharmacy, stuff like that."

"In her car?"

"No. I'd use my own. The company I work for doesn't allow us to drive our clients' cars. Insurance thing."

"So did she drive, then?"

"Not while I was here."

"Which was how often?"

"Two-three times a week."

"Every week?"

"Usually, yes."

"And did you stay over every time?"

"No, hardly ever. She didn't really require it."

"When would you leave?"

"Around nine."

"So if she went out at night for a drive after you left you wouldn't know about it?"

"No. But why would she go out for a drive? I mean, where would she go?"

"Asking the wrong person. I just got down here. Don't really know the lay of the land yet. But if she did drive around and went, say, five miles out and five miles back, where might that take her?"

Ryon mulled this over for a few moments. "Well, if she went south that would take her right into the Gulf. If she went north, it would take her into Choctawhatchee Bay. This part of the Emerald Coast is fairly long but pretty narrow, with water on both sides. "

"East and west?"

"West, that would come out around the jetty, although it's all back roads there. If she stayed on Highway 98 it would angle northwest and take her to Destin."

"And east?"

"Then you'd be heading toward Santa Rosa Beach, Seaside, and then, way past five miles, Panama City."

"Anything interesting along that way?"

"Lots of beaches. The Emerald Coast stretches for about a hundred miles. You've got Eglin Air Force base to the west, and east of Panama City there's Tyndal Air Force base."

"Lot of military bases around here," commented Puller.

"Right. I guess you'd know that be-ing in the military."

"And there's Pensacola, where all the naval aviators go to learn to fly. And Hurlburt Field, although that's really part of Eglin. Air Force has its special operations command there among other things."

"You obviously know a lot more about that than I do."

"Probably not a lot. I'm Army. The Air Force operates at a higher altitude."

"Well, again, I'm sorry about your aunt."

"And I'm sorry for scaring you. I really appreciate everything you did for Betsy."

He walked her to the door, turned on the outside door light so she could see better, and watched Ryon walk down the driveway to her car, a blue Ford Fi-esta with a large dent in the passenger door.

As she drove off, Puller saw a police cruiser coming down the road. He didn't manage to close the door in time. And he was aware that the exterior door light made him about as visible as a digital billboard.

The cruiser did a hard left into the driveway and the driver hit the rack lights.

Puller stood there watching as Chief Bullock stepped out of the car and headed toward him, one hand on his sidearm, his gaze dead center on Puller.

CHAPTER

27

Bullock stopped when he was within five feet of Puller, who had stepped out onto the front stoop. "You want to tell me what the hell you're doing here? And then try to give me a reason why I shouldn't arrest your ass right now."

Puller held up the keys to the house. "Got these from my aunt's lawyer." He slipped the copy of the will out and held it up for Bullock. "She left me the house. It's all in here. You can call the lawyer if you don't believe me or what the document says."

Bullock lurched forward, snatched

the will out of Puller's hand, and read it under the porch's exterior light. He folded up the will and handed it back to him.

"I'm no lawyer, but it looks like you got yourself a house. Of course if your aunt was killed I guess that gives you a first-class motive to kill her."

"Except that I wasn't in Florida when she died."

"And you can prove that?"

"If I have to. And if I knew I was going to inherit the place, why would I come down here, kill her, and then show up here and get arrested so you'd know I was down here at all?"

"Maybe you're stupid."

"You'll have to take that up with the Army."

"I'll take it up with you anytime I want so long as you're in Paradise."

"Can we call a truce here? If I rubbed you the wrong way, I apologize. It was not my intent."

Bullock rocked back and forth on his heels, let out a loud exhale of air, and said, "Forget it. Much my fault as anybody's. I tend to get the hair on the back of my neck up too quickly."

"No problem. I can understand that."

"You still think your aunt's death wasn't an accident?"

"I don't know. I've talked to the ME and I saw her body. Nothing has jumped out at me."

"But you're still not sure?"

"I guess you can never be sure. Maybe I'm looking for something that just isn't there."

"Folks do that sometimes."

Puller put out his hand. "Look, I know you're busy. Whatever happened on the beach today looked pretty important. I'm going to head back to where I'm staying. Thanks for not arresting me."

Bullock shook the hand and then said, "Yeah, it was pretty bad." He stared at Puller. "What we found on the beach."

Puller took this as an offer from Bullock to talk about the case.

"Drowning?"

"No. Both shot in the head."

"Both?"

"A couple actually. The Storrows.

Nancy and Fred. Like you remembered hearing at the station. Well-known folks around here. Been here longer than me. They took walks on the beach every night. They did the other night and never came back."

"Any witnesses? Clues?"

"Bodies were pretty badly decomposed. Nobody has come forward saying they saw anything."

"Motive? Robbery?"

"Mr. Storrow had twenty dollars in his pants and a gold wedding band on his finger. Mrs. Storrow's diamond ring was still on her finger."

"They have any enemies?"

"Not a one that I know of. They were retired. They grew up together in Fort Walton Beach. High school sweethearts. Moved to Paradise a long time ago. He owned a string of businesses, small stuff, gas station, Subway shop, mobile phone store. He sold all of them quite some time ago and he and the wife were spending their golden years in pretty comfortable style."

"And the couple who reported them

missing and who were at the beach today?" said Puller.

"The Storrows' son, Chuck, and his
wife, Lynn."

"Not making any accusations, but
any motive there?"

Bullock shook his head. "Son is a
banker here in town and makes a great
living. Doesn't need a dime from his
parents. They were very close. Played
golf every weekend. Had parties at
each other's homes. Genuine affection
there."

"So maybe it was a random thing.
Wrong place, wrong time."

"That's what I'm thinking."

"Can you tell from where the bodies
washed ashore where they entered the
water?"

"Having some guys who are good
with the tides and currents around here
doing that for me. Might narrow down
a place to search. We already have a
time frame for when they left the house
for a walk."

"I know I've got no jurisdiction in this,
but if you want another pair of eyes to

look over stuff while I'm down here, I'd be glad to."

"Okay, Puller, depending on how things go I might take you up on that. You have a good evening. Glad we worked things out here."

"Yeah, me too."

Bullock trudged back to his car and Puller closed and locked the front door, then walked to his car and headed off. He drove to the spot where the Storrows' bodies had washed ashore.

Wrong place, wrong time, maybe. Which meant they might have seen something or run into someone and that had cost them their lives.

Mysterious happenings in the night.

He gauged the distance he had driven from his aunt's house.

My house now. And what do I do with it?

The distance was 2.2 miles. This was not where his aunt had driven to. Whether or not that meant the Storrows' murders were unconnected to what had happened to his aunt was not a question he could answer right now.

I don't know enough. I may never know enough.

He was out of his element. He had no powers of investigation down here. His official duffel with all the equipment he typically needed to solve crimes was all the way back in Virginia. Then he had an idea. He picked up his phone and called USACIL, or the United States Army's Criminal Investigation Lab, at Fort Gillem, Georgia. He had a contact there, Kristen Craig, whom he had worked with on many cases. He knew the hour was late, and Georgia was actually an hour ahead of Paradise, but he also knew that Craig often burned the midnight oil.

Tonight proved to be one of those times. She answered on the second ring. He explained to her what he was doing and what he needed.

She said, "I have a shipment going out to Eglin tomorrow morning. I can put the duffel on the plane. You can drive up and get it around noon your time."

"You're a saint, Kristen."

"Just remember to call and tell my boss that around review time."

She gave him the necessary information to retrieve the duffel. Before ending the call she said, "Are you really in a place called Paradise?"

"I really am."

"I take it that the fact that you need your investigative duffel means the town is not living up to its name?"

"Your deductive skills are exceeded only by your ability to work miracles."

"You keep talking sweet to me we might have to get serious." She laughed and clicked off.

Puller slid the phone back into his pocket and put the Corvette in gear.

His work was not over yet tonight.

Not by a long shot.

CHAPTER

28

Puller had already spotted the place before, a Hertz rental outlet that stayed open until eleven. He pulled to the curb and got out. It only took a few minutes before he had turned in the Corvette and driven off in a GMC Tahoe. The man at the counter seemed surprised that Puller would want to trade in the Vette for a glorified truck/van, especially in a beach town, but he smiled and handed him the keys.

"Have a terrific time in Paradise, sir."

"Yeah," said Puller.

He next went to a beach clothing

store and purchased a baseball cap that read "Paradise Is Forever," sunglasses, and sneakers. Flip-flops or sandals were more typical of beach attire, but one could not run in flip-flops or sandals, at least not very far or very fast. He also purchased some T-shirts and cargo shorts with big pockets that could hold big things, like weapons. He changed into the shorts, T-shirt, and sneakers in the dressing room, put the ball cap on, slipped the shades into a pocket along with his M11, and walked out.

He was physically imposing enough that it would be hard to miss him in a crowd, but most people's observation skills were poor. Dressed the way he was now, he could probably walk right past White, Black, and Latino and they wouldn't even look at him twice. At least he had to hope for that.

He parked two blocks from the Sierra, but on the same street. It was well past dark by now but not quiet. There was a lot of activity around here at night, and not just on the beach. Cars gunning up and down streets, people yelling. He heard footsteps running. Whether they were heading to trouble or away from it he didn't know and didn't really care.

Diego had said his *casa* where he lived with his *abuela* was down the street and to the left.

Puller checked his watch and then scanned the street. He figured that White, Black, and Latino had all awoken by now, made sure their brains were still in their heads, to the extent that they had any, and were now on the revenge path. He further speculated that they would have done some recon of their own and found out that he was staying at the Sierra and drove a flashy Corvette. Thus the transfer to the Tahoe. Plus the Tahoe had a lot more space and Puller figured he was going to need it. His investigation duffel would be pretty big and the Vette's trunk wasn't that large. They might have recruited more muscle to help them enact that revenge, seeing as how three of them were not enough. And they were also now spooked and suffering from concussions.

It might come to bullets this time instead of fists.

But before he confronted that, Puller wanted to check something else out.

He walked down the street, slipping past the Sierra, and nearly ran into a boy coming the other way. Puller caught him by the arm to keep him from falling.

"You okay?"

The boy's small face was all bunched up in anger. He cursed at Puller.

"Can you tell me where Diego lives?"

He cursed at Puller again, the expletives coming out in a mishmash of English and Spanish.

Puller slipped a five-dollar bill out of his pocket. "You can either take this or a bar of soap in your mouth."

The boy pointed down the street. "The blue one. On the second floor."

Puller gave the boy the fiver and he ran off.

The blue one meant the little building with the blue awning. It seemed to be a rooming house composed of two stories and what looked to be about eight rooms, four up, four down. There was

"The men they have to eat, right? When they do, I take a rag and wipe the dirt off. Before they come back, I put the dirt back on."

"Describe them to me."

Diego did so.

"Are you sure?"

"Yes."

Puller handed him the twenty bucks.

"Isabel and Mateo. Did someone come here and hurt them?"

Diego shook his head. "Not here or I would have looked like they do too, because I would have tried to stop them."

"Tell me about the men I knocked out. Are they part of a gang?"

"They want to be, but they are so stupid that no one wants them. They run some drugs on their own, but nothing much. Then they hassle people. And get money for that. They are scum."

"Do they have friends?"

"Anyone here has friends, if they have the money to pay for them." As he said this, Diego carefully folded up the twenty and placed it in his pocket.

"Think they're waiting for me back at my place?"

a wraparound deck on the exterior of the building and Puller made his way up the stairs. He knocked on one door but there was no answer. He was about to knock on another one when the door opened and Diego stood there.

He looked up at Puller and right away Puller could tell something was wrong.

"What is it, Diego?"

There was movement over Diego's shoulder and Puller was able to answer his own question.

Isabel was standing there with Mateo next to her. Her face was bruised and so was Mateo's. Someone had used them for punching practice. Mateo was sniffling and coughing. Isabel said nothing. She just stared at Puller with unfriendly eyes.

But Diego said, "Isabel told me what happened. I want to thank you for helping her and Mateo."

"Are they your brother and sister?"

"My cousins."

Isabel stepped forward. "We all live with our grandmother."

"Where is she?"

"Working," said Diego. "At a restaurant on the water. The Clipper. She works in the kitchen."

"As a cook?"

"No, as a cleaner," said Isabel.

Puller motioned to their injured faces. "Who did that?"

"Who do you think?" said Isabel.

"I'm sorry but I had to step in, Isabel. I couldn't just let them do that to you."

"Why not? It's happened before. "

"You're not a *puta*," retorted Diego. Mateo began to cry.

"Maybe I *am* a *puta*," said Isabel.

"No, you're not," said Puller. "It's not a road you want to go down."

"Oh, right. I'll just go to college and become a doctor or something."

"Why not?" asked Puller.

She looked at him pityingly. "What planet do you live on?"

"You are not a *puta*," Diego said again and she looked away, gently stroking Mateo's head to make him stop crying.

Puller refocused on Diego. "Did you see the car?"

Diego looked over at Isabel, who was

watching them closely. He stepped side and closed the door.

"What happened to your and Isabe parents?" Puller asked.

Diego shrugged. "One day they we here and then the next day they weren' They might have gone back to El Sa vador. I do not know."

"Doesn't your grandmother know what happened?"

"She does not say if she does."

"And your parents would just leave you all here?"

"They must think this is better than to go back there. They wanted the best for us. Now I am the man of the house. I will take care of things."

"Okay, I like your guts, but you're still just a kid."

"Maybe I am a kid, but I found your car." He paused. "And you said there would be more money."

"Did I?" But Puller had already pulled out a twenty. "Give me the details."

Diego gave him the license plate number first.

"How'd you get that? It was covered up."

Diego shrugged. "I think you must be very careful."

"Thanks for your help."

"I just do it for the money."

"I admire your honesty."

"Don't trust anyone in Paradise, mister, including me."

"At some point, Diego, you have to trust someone. You need any help, you can come to me."

"If you are still alive, mister. We will see."

"You can just call me Puller."

"Okay, Puller. *Buena suerte*."

"Yeah, you too."

Puller walked off. Part of him was thinking about having to deal with the three stooges again, and possibly their paid help. But part of him was thinking about the descriptions that Diego had just given him of the two men in the Chrysler.

Lean, fit, buzz cuts. They fit the description of men who had the same employer he did.

The United States military.

CHAPTER

29

Puller walked to the Tahoe, climbed into the back, stretched out, and thought about what he had just learned.

If the guys in the Chrysler were former military, then that changed the balance of things. They might very well see through his disguise and change rides. They might be able to fire at him faster than he could fire back.

And if they were still in the military he wondered why they would be here following him.

If they *weren't* in the service he wondered the very same thing.

After what had happened to him in West Virginia it was possible that the military had put a tail on him. He decided to see if that theory held any water. He called Kristen Craig back.

She must've recognized his number because instead of hello she said, "Miss me already?"

"Always."

"Seriously, don't you ever sleep?"

"Look who's talking."

"Yeah, but I heard what happened in West Virginia. Not the official story, because there is no official story. But just scuttlebutt, stuff between the lines. I think you could probably write your own ticket right now. Even take a vacation if you wanted to."

"I'm *on* vacation. Well, sort of."

"I have my iPad ready to take down your next assignment, boss."

Puller chuckled to himself. He got a kick out of the lady, he really did. If she weren't married, he might have even asked her out.

"I need a license plate run down."

"Okay. Not usually something I do, but I know people."

"Do you know people who can get it done sooner rather than later?"

"You know the drill. Somewhere in the world there are DoD personnel awake and on the job."

"And there are two of them on this call."

"I'll turn it around as fast as I can. Now, can you tell me a little of what you're involved in?"

"Why?"

"Just in case you get killed and I have to explain my billable hours. Is it even related to the military?"

"Five minutes ago I didn't think so. Now I'm not so sure. It all started when my aunt sent a letter saying things were not quite right in Paradise, Florida. Then the next thing I knew, she was dead under suspicious circumstances."

"Jesus, Puller, I'm sorry."

"Yeah, me too. Anyway, I got down here and things got even funkier."

"And the license plate?"

"Two guys making my business their business by following me. And from their descriptions they sound a lot like dudes who either wear or wore the uniform."

"I don't like the sound of this."

Her voice had clearly changed. Gone was the playfulness, replaced with legitimate concern.

"Me either."

"Do you have any backup?"

"Like I said, I'm on vacation."

"You need to stop taking vacations, then, and get back to work. Seriously, Puller, get somebody to watch your back."

"Good advice. I'll start looking. In the meantime, get me what you can. I'll pick up the duffel tomorrow as planned."

"Just make sure you get to tomorrow."

"I'll do my best."

He clicked off, set his internal clock to wake in two hours, and closed his eyes. His hand gripped the butt of his M11 and he knew it would take him three seconds to wake, aim, and fire at anyone trying to do him harm. If that wasn't fast enough then he was dead. That's just how it went.

At the end of two hours he woke in

the backseat of the Tahoe, refreshed and ready to go. It was one a.m. now and he believed that the time was right for things to happen. Both military and cops liked to strike at night. Targets were tired, in their beds, with weapons often conveniently out of reach.

Yet even stupid criminals could grasp the concept of coming for you in the dark.

Ten minutes later Puller's theory turned into a fact.

White, Black, Latino, and three of their best friends were heading down the street, marching with purpose. It seemed like they had worked out the optimal ratio at six to one. To Puller, their math was a little fuzzy, but maybe his standards were higher. Actually, there was no maybe about it, his standards *were* higher.

All the men's features were grim. White was perhaps the most grim-looking of all, largely because it seemed his mouth was wired shut.

I must have hit him even harder than I thought I did.

They passed the Tahoe without even

a glance. On the battlefield this negligence would have resulted in their immediate deaths. But this was Florida and not Afghanistan, so Puller refrained from drilling them all in the back with rounds from his M11.

He could see gun bumps under their shirts, front and rear. Two of them carried baseball bats and another was clasping a metal bar. They were loaded for bear. Geared for war. Ready to kill.

Of course probably none of them knew what being in actual combat was like.

Puller did.

And for those who had experienced combat, they never wanted to experience it again. It was not really a situation sane people tended to embrace. But Puller, who was sane, had embraced it countless times, because he had signed up for the job. It had changed him completely and irreversibly. It had made him a killing machine. He could slaughter people in ways unimaginable to most folks.

He debated whether to let the night pass without this encounter, but then decided it was best to get it over with. Otherwise he would always be looking over his shoulder. And he didn't have time for that.

He did make one phone call, relayed certain information to the person on the other end of the line, and clicked off. He waited ten minutes and then got out of the Tahoe.

It was time to go to work.

CHAPTER

30

The stretch of beach was isolated and thus deserted. That was why he was here tonight. He had ridden a small scooter over. With his great size he looked slightly ridiculous on the little machine. But he didn't care. It beat walking and the helmet hid his face.

He stood near a dune and behind a palm tree and observed the sandy rim with a pair of night-vision optics that had been in the welcome package he had received on arriving in Paradise. The ocean was vast and black, nearly impossible to distinguish from the sky above. The conditions were hazy and the featureless horizon blended with the water to seem like one solid mass.

The sea captured his interest for a good reason. What was coming tonight would definitely be arriving by water.

He checked his watch. He had been given parameters of time, and that's all they were, parameters. But his patience was nearly infinite. He had spent years of his life waiting for relatively insignificant events to occur. Those were lessons that never left you. They were mental scars carved on your brain and your soul.

He drew in a breath and scrunched up his face. The smell was foul and it apparently always was here. He looked at the sand with his optics.

The Emerald Coast did not live up to its name here. The sand was marred by black rocks jutting out everywhere, like soft skin pulled back to reveal the hard, charred bone underneath.

There would be no sun worshippers here during the day.

And no one at night for any length of time unless they wore a gas mask.

Forty minutes later his patience was rewarded. It was a wink of white light, nothing more. He saw no red and no green. The boat was not using its running lights, which was highly illegal and highly dangerous under all nighttime marine conditions.

But he could understand their reluctance to announce themselves in such a way. He knew it was not the same boat that had carried him to the abandoned oil platform. He had heard the gunfire. He had seen the men riddled with bullets, their bodies hurtling violently into the water.

But it was another boat, though probably far larger than the one he had been on. It was one in a long string of such vessels carrying precious cargo from one place to another. And this place, this landing, this beach tonight was just one more stop in that string. The ride forward from here would be by land, in a vehicle that was not built for the comfort of its passengers. Nothing about the trip was built for their comfort. But the trip itself would be far more humane than what would happen to them at the end of it.

The boat would not come all the way in to shore, of that he was certain. They would offload onto a smaller, more versatile platform for the final approach.

He turned his attention to the road behind him as he crouched farther down in the native foliage that grew next to the dune. He heard the application of brakes and then doors opening and clunking closed. An overhead door was pulled up.

He crouched still lower, moved to his left, and then lay flat in the sand as he eyed the large box truck and two SUVs that were parked on a small section of asphalt off the roadway. Three men stood next to the truck, its rear door open. Two other men were striding down the path leading to the beach. He assumed they were armed and prepared to use their weapons. He followed their movements down to the edge of the water.

One of the men signaled with a flashlight. A return signal could be seen from farther out on the water. A few minutes passed and then the sound of a small boat engine could be heard. As it drew closer to shore the outline of the vessel became clearer. It was a thirty-foot-long RIB, or rigid hull inflatable boat, which military special forces often used during their missions. It was painted black and was nearly invisible as it made its approach.

It came to within several feet of the beach and the pilot cut the engine, allowing the RIB to gently glide until the bow hit the sand.

The men on the beach hustled forward and started grabbing people off the RIB, one by one until twenty were assembled on the beach. They were tied together and their mouths were taped shut. Even from this distance he could see that many of them were children.

Some had on blue shirts, some red, some green. This was not by accident. The colors designated the purpose and ultimate destination of the prisoners. There were more green shirts than the other colors. He was privy to the meanings the colors represented; thus he

was not surprised by this. The choice
of green had not been by happenstance
either.

To be sure, there was strong cash
flow in blue and red, but green was
where the real money was.

Two of the men on the beach took
the line of captives and led them up the
boardwalk, where they were quickly
loaded into the box truck.

The RIB's pilot put his boat in reverse
and pulled away from the beach, then
turned and headed back out to sea. At
the same time another RIB pulled in,
cut the engine, drifted to shore, and the
same transfer of captives took place.
This happened twice more. After the
other two RIBs departed and the last
group of captives was herded into the
truck, the rear door was closed and
locked, the men jumped into the cab,
and the box truck pulled away with the
SUVs following.

He sat alone on the beach watching
the vehicles for a few seconds until they
disappeared into the darkness, heading west. Then he looked out to sea.
He could barely hear the whine of the

last RIB; a few seconds later, it was gone too.

He counted in his head. Four boats with a total of eighty captives. The entire transfer had taken less than ten minutes. Ten minutes for eighty human beings to be pushed from point A to point B. Forty green, the rest split roughly equally between red and blue.

He had just seen potentially millions of dollars of illegal commerce march across those sands.

He had no idea where the truck was taking them. He knew that the RIBs would go back to the larger ship lurking out there like some great white shark, be loaded on, and then the ship would power its way back to base. Tomorrow night the process would likely start all over again. This was a business, after all. A big one. And like most businesses, the primary motivation was profit. And to be profitable you had to sell product, as quickly and efficiently as possible, getting good prices and making and thereby keeping happy customers.

The purposes for which the prisoners were being used were all insidious, but the fact was that much of the world simply didn't care enough to do anything about it.

Well, he wasn't "much of the world." He was simply one man. And he did care.

Tonight had been merely a scheduled run for the sellers of human beings. For him it had been a dry run to learn valuable intelligence. Soon there would come a time when the valuable intelligence would be translated into action. He wished it could have been tonight. But that most likely would have ended up with him killing all of the guards, freeing the captives, but destroying any chance he had of achieving his larger goal. Or else with his being gunned down and thrown into the ocean.

He walked a mile down the beach, retrieved his scooter, and headed back to the Sierra. He would sleep for a bit, but he doubted his sleep would be restful. He would keep the images of the captives in his thoughts for tonight, and then for far longer. They deserved to have someone care about them. He did care. But he wanted to do more than care.

He wanted to stop it.

He wanted to stop it all.

But most of all he wanted to find someone.

CHAPTER

31

Puller did not enter the Sierra through the front or back door. He hustled up the fire escape and made his way down from the roof via an access doorway used, in part, for maintenance of the HVAC system housed on top of the building. He had scoped out this detail earlier. He liked multiple entry and exit points from every place he occupied. Three floors down he stepped out and onto the third floor. The hall was dark and unoccupied. One overhead light flickered and pulsed like erratic arcs of lightning, but that was all. Puller's room was the next to the last one on the left around the corner. He crouched in the darkness, but he also had a distinct advantage—night-vision goggles he'd bought from a store in downtown Paradise that sold police-level gear. They certainly weren't the best night optics he'd ever used, but they were serviceable. He slipped them down over his eyes and dark turned to light, as fuzzy details were transformed into high-def.

He figured they would be converging on their target about now. Six on one, overwhelming force, or so they thought. Puller was a first-rate, superbly trained close-quarters fighter.

But he was not Superman.

This was not a movie where he could Matrix his way to victory. It would be fearful men fighting, making mistakes but certainly landing some blows.

Puller tipped the scales at well over two hundred pounds. The men he would be facing tonight collectively weighed about a thousand pounds. They had twelve fists and a dozen legs to his two and two.

Six against one, hand-to-hand, no

matter how good you were or how in-
ept the six were, would likely result in
defeat. Puller could take out three or
four rather quickly. But the remaining
two or three men would probably get in
a lucky shot and possibly knock him
down. And then it would be over. Bats
and bars would rain down on him and
then a gunshot would end it all.

If one had a choice—and sometimes
one did—a truly superb close-quarters
fighter only fought when the conditions
favored him.

He didn't have much time, because
they would quickly determine that he
was not in the room. Then they would
do one of two things: leave and come
back, or set a trap and wait for him.
And a trap would involve a perimeter.
At least he was counting on that, because a perimeter meant that the six
men would have to divide their forces.

Then six became four, or three, two,
or even one.

Divide and conquer.

That was the condition on the ground
that Puller needed in order to win. And
it would be even better if his adversar-

ies tonight provided it for him. Something told him they would.

A well-thought-out perimeter could defeat most plans to pierce it. A few moments later he could see that this perimeter was not well thought out. And so it would be pierced rather easily.

The two men were standing in the middle of the hall. They had taken no measures to conceal their presence. One had a bat, the other a gun. They were talking in low tones, looking smug, confident. The man holding the bat spun it like a baton. The man with the gun held it loosely, pointed down. Four fingers were clasped around the butt of the weapon, his index finger not even near the trigger guard.

In other words, the weapons were useless.

The men didn't react until the bat was taken from the first man. A blow to his stomach from the head of the bat sent him pitching to the floor. The second man raised his gun, but did not fire it because he was no longer holding it.

Puller, holding the pistol by the muzzle, brought the butt of the weapon around and crushed it against the man's temple. He went down to join his buddy on the ragged carpet covered in puke stains. A tap from the bat on the writhing first man's head was all that was needed to stop the writhing.

The attack had taken all of five seconds. Puller had swung the bat at almost the same time he had stripped the gun from the other man. The only sounds had come from bodies falling to the floor.

Puller crouched there, the bat in one hand, his other hand around his M11. He had dropped the other pistol after removing the mag and clearing the chamber of the loaded round. He did not like firing other people's weapons. A badly maintained gun could be more dangerous to the one firing it than to the one being fired on.

He counted off a few seconds in his head. Two down, four to go. His room was around the corner. These jackasses had been the front line. He figured perhaps one man at another barrier and then three at ground zero to finish the job.

He crab-walked to the corner, did a turkey peek, and drew back. Here the darkness was near total because someone had removed the overhead lights.

Nice tactic, he thought. But with his goggles darkness was preferable.

Halfway down the hall, in a shadow that was deeper than the surrounding darkness, was stationed the third man. He was crouched in a narrow alcove. Gun, bat, or metal bar would be his weapon. Puller had several options. He could bull-rush and reach the man before he could react. Or he could approach with stealth, take the man down quietly, and move on.

He opted for the latter.

Slithering on his belly like he had through Florida swamps and Iraqi sands in his career as a Ranger, Puller moved forward. He knew the crouching man would be looking at a point parallel to his eye level and then upward. It was just human nature. Only trained personnel would finish off the imaginary vertical line from floor to ceiling, know-

ing full well that an experienced attacker could come at you from virtually
any angle. And the most obvious angle
was never the most popular.

He drew within a foot of the other
man. Puller was looking up, the other
man still swiveling his gaze in an uneven arc. When he looked away from
Puller the bat came up and the man
went down, blood running from his
head. The scalp bled like a bitch. And
the accompanying headache, when the
man awoke, would be one he would
never forget.

He had not hit any of the three men
tonight hard enough to kill them. Puller
knew how much force was required to
crack skulls. He had not minded applying that force to men who raped women
in front of their little brothers. But these
men tonight were just the revenge crew.
They might actually be as bad as or
worse than the ones Puller had already
beaten up. But he would cut them a
little slack. They would live to spread
the message that to leave him alone
was the smart money.

This man had held the metal bar. Puller retrieved it and kept going.

Three down and three to go. The odds were much better. In fact, they had returned to the same ones he had dealt with in the stairwell. And the three men he had disabled were the members of the revenge crew, which meant the men up ahead were the rapist crew. The same ones who had no doubt come back and beaten up Isabel and little Mateo.

Puller decided to up the level of force he was about to bring.

He moved quickly down the hall. The door to his room was slightly ajar. He shook his head at the tactics employed by the opposition. A partially open door was like waving a red flag and screaming, "We're in here waiting for you."

So you wouldn't go in. You would move to the room next door and try to surprise them through the connecting portal. But of course the surprise would be all yours as they blew you away.

He envisioned them grouped around the connecting door, but he doubted their attention would be all that focused.

For Puller to get that far their perimeter would have to have been defeated almost soundlessly. They would imagine this could never happen. They had chosen to be the rear guard tonight because they had hoped that Puller would never make it this far. They did not want another encounter with him. What sane person would, after the beating they had endured?

For all he knew they would be playing cards, or banging back beers to get up their courage, or smoking cigarettes, or peering out the lone window. Anything but being professional.

He hit the door to his room so hard that it broke off the hinges. There were two shapes directly in front of him. As he had thought, they were clustered around the connecting door. The metal bar took out both with one swing. White dropped onto the bed. This time he might very well be dead. Black was flung through the window, shattering the glass, and dangled there, half in and half out.

Now Latino was the only one left.

He was in the far corner of the room,

looking ready to shit his pants. He had his gun out. He was at most six feet from Puller. In the dark and with his adrenaline spiking and turning fine motor skills to zero, it might as well have been six miles.

He fired once and missed by five feet.

He did not get a chance to fire a second time.

The first blow knocked the gun from his hand.

The second blow knocked him off his feet.

The third blow left no doubt that the fight was done.

As Puller rose, his breath already starting to relax, he sensed it.

Light.

Body heat.

Sweat.

Eyes on him.

From the connecting doorway.

He looked.

Two small men there. Both Latinos. Armed. Both pointing compact nines right at his head. Two guns could not miss at this distance.

The rear guard he had not accounted for.

Eight men had come tonight.

Not six.

He had screwed up in an unforgivable way.

The penalty for that was crystal clear.

He was dead.

CHAPTER

32

It was the first time Puller had seen men fly without benefit of an aircraft.

Or so it seemed.

Their feet left the floor like they were attached to piano wire and someone had just hit a switch, lifting them sky-ward.

The next moment their heads col-lided. The sound was like a pair of can-taloupes smacking against one another. Puller could see the sensation of the violent collision spread to their eyes and mouths. The eyes winced, rolled in their heads, and then closed. The

mouths opened wide, cries of pain
came out of them, and then they closed,
like the eyes. But unlike the eyes they
closed only for a moment. Then they
sagged open, even as their bodies became dead weight and they dropped
to the floor. They hit it hard, guns skid-
ding away. Blood pooled from their
open mouths where teeth had cut
deeply into tongues.

Standing behind the two small men
was the giant, the man Puller had seen
twice before. It seemed that the rear
guard had done the unforgivable. They
had used the giant's room as their staging area without his permission. That
was the only reason Puller could fathom
for the man doing what he had done.

He straightened and stared at the giant. Puller's M11 twitched in his hand.
The giant was unarmed but still looked
uncomfortably lethal and completely
unafraid as he stood there, staring back
at Puller.

Puller said, "Thanks."

The giant said nothing. He glanced
once at Puller's sidearm, as though
gauging whether this was a threat that

needed to be dealt with now. Then he put one enormous boot on the torso of the first man and pushed. The man's body slid into the room Puller was in. A moment later another push sent the other man sliding into the room.

The giant looked at Puller.

Puller looked at the giant.

"I'll try to keep things more quiet," said Puller.

Puller thought he saw a hint of a smile before the giant closed the door to his room. A few moments later Puller could hear the screech of sagging bedsprings. The giant was apparently going to sleep after this minor interruption.

Puller holstered his weapon but pulled it again in an instant, found his target, and prepared to fire.

"It's me! It's me!"

Cheryl Landry held her gun up in a surrender position.

Puller slowly lowered his M11 and lifted up his goggles.

"Sorry."

She gazed around at the mess of

humanity that lay sprawled around his room.

"Shit, Puller. What the hell did you do? There are three more laid out in the hall."

"I just take them on as they come." He holstered his gun.

"You were smart to call me. Sorry I didn't get here in time."

"I could've waited, but that was my call. Nothing you could have done."

"Why didn't you wait," she said, pouncing on this admission, "until I got here?"

"My fight. No need for you to get involved except in the cleanup."

"Do I translate that as meaning you didn't think I could hold my own?"

"You're a cop, Landry. If we had fought these clowns together you'd be doing paperwork the rest of your life to explain the whys and hows. And then your career would still be in the toilet. But for that I would have no problem with you backing me up. And believe me, I don't make such a statement lightly."

She seemed both put off and mollified by this statement. She slid her weapon into her belt holster. She was not in uniform. She had on jeans, black-soled tennis shoes, and a gray hoodie with a sliver of black T-shirt revealed underneath.

He watched as she counted off in her head.

Five here, three in the hall, he interpreted.

She looked up at him incredulously.

"You took out eight guys all by yourself?" She noted the guns, bats, and metal bar. "And they were armed?"

Puller's gaze shifted for one millisecond to the sounds of snoring coming from the next room. The giant had dropped off fast. But something told him the man could awaken and kill any attacker within a pair of seconds. He decided it would be much too complicated to bring him into the discussion with Landry.

He said, "They were eight *stupid* guys. Armed has nothing to do with it, if you don't give yourself a chance to use your weapons."

"You said it was three guys who were attacking the girl earlier?"

Puller nodded and pointed to White, Black, and Latino. "These three idiots here. The girl is too scared to press charges. But I'll be glad to. They weren't here to welcome me back to my room. Attempted murder at least." He paused. "And I doubt they have permits for those guns. You know any of them?"

Landry pulled a small but powerful light from her hoodie pocket and shined it on each of the fallen men.

She nodded. "These two, yeah," she said, indicating Black and White. "They don't belong to any gangs that I'm aware of. But they've got a rap sheet with us."

"I heard they were too dumb and unreliable to be of any use to a gang."

"Where did you hear that from?"

"Confidential source."

"You've been here a little over twelve hours. Where do you get confidential sources that fast?"

"You work at it."

"I'm going to call for transport on this."

"Okay."

"Paperwork to fill out."

"I bet."

"It can wait until morning."

"Appreciate that."

"You got another place to stay?"

Puller thought about this. His aunt's house was an option. But right now he considered it an unprocessed crime scene. His moving in there, even for a night, could potentially foul up some important evidence. He couldn't bring himself to do that, even if it was more convenient for him personally.

"My car."

"The Vette?"

"No. Another set of wheels. Figured the Vette was too conspicuous."

"I'd agree with that."

"So I can sleep in my vehicle."

"On the street?"

"Why, don't you keep them safe?"

"Puller, you just beat the crap out of eight guys who live in Paradise. I'm sure all eight have friends and family who might want a little revenge. They'll be looking for you, whether you're in a car or in another cheap motel."

"Well, I can rent a blanket and lie out on the beach."

"You're not getting my point. They could come and kill you."

"You got any suggestions, then? I'm fresh out of ideas."

Landry looked uncertain, and then she looked uncomfortable. Her changing features piqued Puller's interest. He wondered what she would say.

"Look, you can stay at my place. Just for tonight," she added quickly.

"You in Paradise?"

"Just next door in Destin."

"You don't care to live in Paradise?"

"I like the view in Destin better. Besides, it's only fifteen minutes away. But it's an important fifteen minutes. For you. I doubt the friends and family will find you there."

"You don't have to put me up."

"I know I don't. I wouldn't have offered if I didn't want to."

"You don't really know me."

"I told you my brother's in the Army. He checked you out for me. Said there's not an enlisted with a better record in the service. The only knock against you is why you didn't go to West Point. And my brother said your father was like Patton and Schwarzkopf rolled into one."

"I wouldn't disagree with that. Although he probably rotates closer to Patton, at least in his bedside manner."

"So you'll stay at my place?"

"Okay, just for the night."

"Just for the night," she repeated and then slipped her phone out and called for police and medical transport for eight men who'd had the shit kicked out of them.

After she finished and put her phone away she said, "Bullock will want to see you about this."

"I bet he will. In fact, I've already seen him tonight."

"Did he bite your head off?"

"I think we've reached an understanding, actually."

"Okay. But I wouldn't count on that holding after this."

"Right."

"You've sort of set a record for mayhem in Paradise."

"I can see that."

"You going to be here much longer?"

"Wish I could tell you for sure, but I can't."

"Your aunt?"

"My aunt."

"You just don't let go, do you?"

"Never saw the point," replied Puller.

CHAPTER

33

Puller was following Landry over to her place. She was ahead of him in a dark blue, white-topped Toyota FJ four-by-four Cruiser. It looked rugged and durable and ready to roll on asphalt or sand, which was probably why she had purchased it. Puller had pegged her as particularly no-nonsense. He also could tell this by her keeping exactly to the speed limit as they headed west to Destin.

On the way he phoned his brother at USDB. The call had been scheduled in advance, as required, and although he was late phoning in, he was put through a few seconds later.

Robert Puller had been awaiting his younger brother's call and picked up immediately.

"Sorry for the late call," said Puller. "I got sidetracked."

"That's okay. I was going to go out tonight, but decided to just stay here and wait for you to ring up."

"Nice to hear you've retained your sense of humor."

"Most important thing I've got, actually. Maybe the only thing I've got."

"I can see that."

"Now, when you get sidetracked it usually means someone is lying all bloody in a ditch."

"They're not in a ditch," said Puller. "They're in a holding cell."

"Talk to me."

Puller conveyed most of what had happened in Paradise over the last dozen hours or so. When he recounted it, he was amazed that he had packed so much into so little time.

"You've been busy," said Robert.

"Wasn't really by choice."

"So a journal is missing from Betsy's house?"

"Looks to be."

"And a ten-mile drive at night?"

"That was just a guess. I'll have to confirm it."

"And the guys following you?"

"Got a contact at USACIL working on that. Hopefully I'll hear something soon."

"Sorry you had to see Aunt Betsy like that."

"How much of the summers we spent with her and Uncle Lloyd do you remember?"

"Pretty much every second. She was an unforgettable lady. Sort of like the Old Man but with compassion and a heart."

Puller nodded. That would have been his articulated assessment as well. "Some of the best times we ever had," he noted.

"Sometimes I think we're the way we are because of her more than the Old Man," said Robert.

"I haven't really thought about it," replied Puller. "But the older I get the more I think I'm like the Old Man too much."

"Stop thinking that, it'll drive you crazy."

"Maybe it already has."

"You're the sanest man I know. And that's saying something."

"Maybe, Bobby. But maybe not."

"So what do you think? Was she murdered?"

"Factor in the journal missing, if that's what it was, the folks tailing me, the fact that I think the lawyer is lying to me, and what was in Aunt Betsy's note—yeah, I think she was murdered."

"But the police don't see it that way?"

"Not now they don't. That could change."

"So who're in the holding cells?"

"Just some folks I had a disagreement with. Not connected to what I'm down here for."

"You really can't be sure about that."

"You're right, I can't be. But it's just my gut."

"What are your next steps?"

"Get some sleep. I'm running on empty right now."

"Anything else?"

Puller hesitated, then decided to say it. "There's a guy down here. Bigger than me. Stronger than me. Probably can kick my ass."

"That qualifies as remarkable. What's the connection to you?"

"Don't know that there is any. Could just be wrong place, wrong time."

"You could just shoot him."

"He actually helped me out tonight. I don't think he did it because he was a Good Samaritan. I think he was just pissed that somebody was disturbing his sleep."

"Okay. I think I follow that, but not really."

"How are things on your end?"

"The views haven't changed."

Puller cracked a grin, but then it faded. "Yeah."

"So after you get some sleep, what then?"

"Run the ten miles Betsy might have done. Work on the lawyer angle. Follow up with USACIL. I'm getting my duffel of goodies tomorrow at Eglin AFB. Then

I can start acting like a real investigator again."

"Sounds like a plan. But watch your back, John. You're there solo and you don't really know who to trust. And it sounds like you have reason to distrust quite a few people right now."

"Good advice, Bobby."

"So how's the house?"

"What?"

"Aunt Betsy's house, how is it?"

"It's nice. Near the water."

"You gonna be moving down there now that it's yours?"

"I doubt it."

"Come on, lots of people move to Florida."

"Honestly, Paradise is turning out to be way too dangerous for my tastes."

Puller clicked off and kept driving.

CHAPTER

34

Landry's condo was on the tenth floor of a twenty-story building a few steps from the beach. Actually, the front yard of the place *was* the beach. He followed her into a covered parking garage and pulled in close to her vehicle. They got out and he followed her to a bank of elevators, his small duffel containing his clothes slung over his shoulder.

"Looks like a nice place," he said.

"I like it. Good mix of folks. Young to old."

"And the beach a few steps away. Not a coincidence?"

"I'm into water sports."

"So what else do you do for fun?"

The elevator dinged and the doors slid open.

"Target shooting. Catching bad guys."

They stepped inside the elevator car.

Puller asked, "Are those things mutually exclusive?"

The doors closed.

"I hope not," said Landry.

They stepped out on the tenth floor and he followed her down an interior hall with marble flooring done in a dizzying array of colors. She stopped at Condo 1017 and put her key in.

They stepped inside and Puller closed the door behind him.

"I've got a guest bedroom," said Landry, pointing to the left. "It's got its own bathroom. Kitchen's over there. Fridge is stocked. I'm not much into cooking, but help yourself. Patio is over there with spectacular views of the Gulf. I've got a laundry room too if you need any stuff done."

"I'm good on that," said Puller. He went to his room, dropped the duffel on the bed, and came back out. He looked around. The furnishings all looked relatively new and in good taste. He wasn't much into decorating. His apartment back in Quantico was neat and spare, but in all other respects indistinguishable from a college dorm room.

He slid open the door to the small patio and stepped out. The breeze was strong up here and it carried the full weight of the briny smells from the ocean.

There was a chaise sling chair, a small charcoal grill, and a round outdoor table stacked with books. Standing up against one wall was a surfboard and an even longer paddleboard with the paddle next to it.

Slung over the rail and kept there with clothesline clips were several bikinis. Puller gazed at them for a few moments and then switched his observations to the ocean when Landry stepped out and discreetly collected her bathing suits, carrying them back inside before rejoining him.

Puller leaned against the railing and eyed the boards.

"So you really are into water sports?"

"Pretty stupid to live here and not be."

"You from Destin?"

"Miami. Moved here about five years ago."

"How come? I understand Miami is a fun place for young people."

"It can be. For some young people. It just wasn't right for me. Besides, I'd grown up there. I'd seen and done it all. Nothing new. And it got to be too crowded. Too crazy. The Emerald Coast is a better fit. Or the Redneck Riviera, as some call it."

"And becoming a cop?"

"What I wanted. My father was a detective in Miami. I grew up with cops around all the time. Liked what I saw. So I joined the ranks in Miami. I think my father thought my brother would follow in his footsteps too, but the Army was his dream."

"Your father sorry you left Miami to come here?"

"He probably would be if he were

alive. Psycho freaked on PCP took care of that."

"I'm sorry. But detectives don't usually go down that way. They come in after the fact."

"He wasn't detecting. He was a citizen sitting in a bar having a drink when the PCP dude went apeshit. My dad tried to stop him. It didn't work."

"How about your mom?"

She looked up at Puller. "I think I've told you enough about me."

"Not prying. Just making conversation."

"No need. I get along just fine with silence."

"Me too, actually."

"I'm beat. I'm hitting the sheets. You're on your own for breakfast. I get up early, do some beach stuff before hitting the gym downstairs. You can join me if you want. Then I head to work."

"I'll let you get to it, then."

She left him and he heard her bedroom door close a few moments later.

Puller continued to stare out over the

ocean. From his high perch it was like
he could see the whole world from up
here. All he wanted to see, however,
was the truth behind his aunt's death.

He heard a shower start running and
figured Landry was rinsing off before
"hitting the sheets." She was one who
kept things close to the vest. An interesting person. But then again Puller
had been here a little over twelve hours
and he had met a whole host of "interesting persons."

The running water stopped and he
heard the shower door open. He
counted the seconds in his head, giving her time to towel off and go to bed.
A few moments after that he heard her
bed squeak slightly.

He checked his watch. It was really
late. Later, actually, for him since he'd
lost an hour based on his internal clock.

He went back inside. The AC was on
but it somehow felt hotter in here than
it had out there.

He walked to his room, closed the
door, shed his clothes down to his
green Army boxers, and climbed into

bed. The sheets felt cool against his skin. He put his M11 under his pillow, a ritual of his that he figured he would keep until his death. Serving all those tours in the Middle East just did that to a guy.

Over there you were never really certain who was your friend and who was your foe. Depending on the day, it could be one or another. And the next day those roles could reverse. When you were talking about matters of life and death, such confusion was not welcome.

His thoughts turned to the giant. A friend tonight. But what about tomorrow? There was no reason to believe the man had any connection to why Puller was down here. But Puller knew that could change. When he had been in West Virginia recently, many people had turned out to be not who they claimed to be. And connections that seemed absurd before had turned out to be very much real.

He popped his neck, stretched a kink out of his long legs, closed his eyes, and went to sleep. He figured if he

dreamt, it would have absolutely nothing to do with being in Paradise.

He, like Landry, preferred the view
from here.

CHAPTER

35

Cheryl Landry stirred at six a.m.

At six-ten she was outfitted in board shorts and a bikini top over which she wore a short-sleeved T-shirt. With flip-flops on her feet and a large beach towel under her arm she opened the door to her bedroom and saw Puller sitting at the small round kitchen table drinking a cup of coffee and reading the morning paper. He was dressed in workout clothes: black shorts, Army green T-shirt, and sneakers.

He looked up and saw her staring at him. He held up the cup.

"You want some java before you hit the water?"

"No, thanks. I'm trying to cut down." She walked across to the patio and retrieved her paddleboard.

"I'm actually thinking of taking up herbal tea instead," said Puller as she stepped back inside.

"Seriously?"

"Caffeine blows your aim. That's reason enough for the military to ban it, although they never will. It's too ingrained in the DoD's psyche." He held up the paper. "Hope you don't mind. It was at the front door."

"No problem. The only reason I get the paper is that it's free. I read online for the most part."

Puller looked down at the first page of the paper. A large photo of the deceased Mr. and Mrs. Storrow dominated it.

"The Storrow murders are all over it."

She nodded. "I wouldn't put it past some folks in neighboring towns to play that up big just to take tourists away from Paradise."

"Is it that cutthroat down here?"

"When it comes to tourist dollars it is."

Puller rose, rinsed out his cup, and put it in the dishwasher.

"You coming to the beach?" she asked.

"I figure I'll run while you do whatever it is you do with that," he said, indicating the long red paddleboard.

"It's a paddleboard," she said, seeming surprised he wasn't aware of that.

"Okay."

"You stand up and paddle on it."

"Right," said Puller. "Figured something like that."

"They've been around a while. You don't get to the beach much I guess."

"I guess I don't."

"It's not as easy as it looks."

"It doesn't look easy to me. I'm not even sure that thing would support my weight."

As they set off down the hall she said, "How far do you run?"

"How long do you paddle?"

"About forty-five minutes."

"That's how long I'll run, then," he replied.

"I'm going to work out afterwards in the gym."

"Okay."

"You too?"

He said, "Me too. I haven't done much lately. Need to get back into it."

"You look like you're in great shape."

He held the elevator door open for her as she eased the long paddleboard inside the car.

"Looks can be deceiving."

Puller found a swath of hard-packed sand and began his run. He had watched as Landry shed her T-shirt and walked into the water with her board past the breakers. She lay flat on the board and paddled out farther to where the ocean was calm and flat. She hoisted herself up on the board and began paddling, alternating sides.

She paddled parallel to the beach in the same direction Puller was running, so he could keep an eye on her. It was early enough that there weren't many folks out yet. A few older fishermen with their poles mounted in PVC pipe wedged in the sand were talking and sipping coffee from thermoses. An older woman walked along, head down but swinging her arms in elliptical motions as she did so. To Puller it looked like she was performing some sort of physical therapy. Maybe she'd blown out both rotators.

A couple jogged along with a sleek Irish setter keeping pace. Seagulls soared and dove, looking for breakfast in the green waters.

He checked his watch, turned, and headed back the way he had come. He looked out and saw Landry make her turn and do the same thing.

Nearly twenty-five minutes into his run Puller felt nicely warmed up. His lungs were operating fully, his legs felt juiced, his arms kept pumping. He had run literally thousands of miles training to become an Army Ranger. Special Forces was mostly about weapons training and endurance. Yeah, they all pumped weights. Yeah, they were all strong as bears. But it was the stamina that really was the difference between living and dying.

At the end of forty-five minutes he stood in the sand at the spot where he had begun, moving his arms and legs, keeping his heart rate up, but allowing his body to cool down slowly.

Landry paddled back in, hit the breakers, stood, and worked her way through them before arriving back on the sand. She snagged her T-shirt and towel from the beach and carried her board over to Puller.

"I need to do a quick change," she said. "How was the run?"

"It was a run," replied Puller. "They're all the same."

"You don't look out of breath for having just run all that way."

"It wasn't that far. How was the paddling?"

"Enlightening."

"Really?" he said, looking at her skeptically.

"It gives you time to think. Just you and the paddle and the water." She paused and looked up at him as they walked back to the condo building. "Did you do any thinking while you were running?"

"Now that you mention it, I suppose I did."

"And?"

"And I need to do some more of it."

She toweled off before going into the building and then they rode the elevator up to her condo.

She took five minutes to rinse the saltwater off and change, and came back out in black tights that ended above her knees, a tight T-shirt with a sports bra underneath, and sneakers with ankle socks. Her wet hair was tied back with a green scrunchy.

The condo gym was large and efficiently laid out. There were Universal machines, free weights, squat racks, dumbbells, a cardio section with treadmills, elliptical machines, stair climbers, and an open floor space where exercise classes were apparently conducted.

Landry hit the Universal circuit while Puller stretched and then did pull-ups and push-ups, calisthenics, and a lot of leg exercises, pushing his lower body hard.

Finished, they toweled off, grabbed some waters from a small fridge next to the exit door, and headed back to the elevator.

She said, "You do a lot of leg work. Most guys focus on the biceps."

"I've never been able to run on my hands."

She laughed.

"You do this every morning?" asked Puller.

"Every morning that I can, yeah."

"Then you'll live forever."

She smiled and then became serious. "Unless I go down in the line of duty."

"There's always that."

"I guess for you too." She eyed his calf and his forearm where his combat scars were prominent.

She pointed to them. "Iraq? Afghanistan?"

He took a swallow of water and said, "Both."

"My brother's still over there."

"Hope he comes home soon and safe."

"Me too."

"Will he come here?"

"Doubtful. He plans to stay in for the full ride."

"The Army's a good employer. He'll do just fine."

"But you're a little biased, aren't you?"

"Actually, I'm a lot biased."

"So what's on your agenda for today?"

"I'm going back to my aunt's house, check some things out."

She put a hand on his arm. "Puller, you heard what Chief Bullock said."

"That's all worked out. Remember I told you I saw him last night. It was at the house. My aunt left it to me. Legal docs prove it and the lawyer gave me the key."

She removed her hand. "Oh. Hey, that's great." She paused and added, "So do you really think her death was more than an accident?"

"When I know for sure, you'll be one of the first people I tell."

They got back to the condo, showered, and changed.

Puller made some fresh coffee, and when Landry came out in her uniform he poured her a cup. They drank it out on the patio, watching the sun continue its rise. The beach below was starting to get more crowded as families jockeyed for the best pieces of sand.

"You see yourself staying here long-term?" he asked.

"I haven't really thought about it. What about you? I guess you're in for the full ride too with Uncle Sam."

"I guess I am."

"And after that? You'll still be a young guy."

"Who knows?"

"You could become a cop."

"Maybe."

She smiled again. "You always so loquacious?"

"Compared to other times, I'm being downright gregarious."

His phone buzzed. He looked at the readout.

It was Kristen Craig from USACIL. Hopefully she had an answer on the men following him.

Landry looked at the phone.

"Back to work?" she asked, looking a little disappointed.

"Back to work," he answered.

CHAPTER

36

Landry and Puller parted company as Puller answered the phone.

"Hey, Christine."

But it wasn't Christine. It was a man's voice.

"Agent John Puller?"

"Who wants to know?"

"Colonel Peter Walmsey, that's who, soldier."

"Yes, sir," said Puller, automatically snapping to attention even though he was only on the phone. "What can I do for you, sir?"

"I want to know why you're calling

USACIL to perform work on things un-
related to your duties at CID. That's
what I want to *damn* well know. Do you
view the Army's premier forensics lab
as your personal playpen?"

Puller licked his lips and pondered
how to respond to this. "Would you be
referring to my phone call to Ms. Craig?"

"I *would* be referring to that, specifically your request that she run down a
license plate number for you. And also
why a duffel full of investigative equipment owned by this man's army is on
its way to you at Eglin Air Force Base
to be used on a matter not involving
CID."

Shit.

"I apologize for the misunderstanding, sir."

"So you're saying it was a misunderstanding? Why don't you explain that
one in a way that doesn't make me
want to prefer official charges against
you, Puller?"

"I observed two men who looked like
soldiers following me in Florida, Colonel Walmsey. I requested that Ms. Craig
attempt to use reasonable means at

her disposal to determine if the men were members of the service. The most expeditious way of doing that seemed to be tracking their vehicle. I acquired the license plate information and communicated that to Ms. Craig."

"Why would Army personnel be following you, Puller?"

"If I had the answer to that, sir, I would not have involved Ms. Craig."

"And the duffel?"

"Connected to the same matter, sir. I came down here on a family matter. I didn't bring any equipment with me. If it became necessary for me to initiate an investigation I wanted to be properly outfitted to do so."

"When exactly were you going to inform your superior officer of all this?"

"Once I determined that I had something to report, sir, that involved other military members. But I want to make it clear that I accept full responsibility for this. Ms. Craig was under the impression that I was engaged in authorized work. None of this should reflect on her record, sir."

"You cover for your friends well,

Puller, I'll give you that. But for your information Ms. Craig has been relieved of duty pending completion of an inquiry on this matter."

Shit again, thought Puller.

"I'm sorry to hear that, sir."

"Not as sorry as she was. Now let's talk about you."

"Yes, sir."

"I understand from CID that you're on authorized leave right now."

"Yes, sir."

"And that you successfully carried out a commission in West Virginia that saved this country an enormous headache."

Puller said nothing.

"So I'm basically being told that you need to get a pass on this. I don't like that one bit, Puller. Every soldier should be held to the same standard, don't you agree?"

"Yes I do, sir."

"And what is that standard?"

Puller thought he was back in boot camp. "The highest possible standard, sir," he replied automatically.

"But that apparently is not how it's

going down in this case. Sounds like bullshit to me, Puller."

"Yes, sir, it does."

"But you can man up and do something about it. Get your ass up here and take the heat."

Puller admired the skill with which the colonel had maneuvered him into a corner.

"Sir, I would be glad to do that as soon as I have completed my task down here."

"What the hell task is that?" said Walmsey, who had apparently not reckoned on this response.

"My aunt."

"Your aunt? What the hell is going on with your aunt?"

"That's what I'm trying to find out, sir."

"Can't you ask her?"

"I would, sir, but somebody killed her."

"Someone killed your aunt?" Walmsey said skeptically. "Is that why you want your duffel? Is your aunt in the Army?"

"No, sir."

"Then I'm apparently not getting through to you, Puller. What you're planning to do is an unauthorized—"

It was at this moment that Puller ran out of patience. It was contrary to his nature in speaking with a superior officer, but perhaps his brief time away from the Army had dulled those professional instincts. He would just assume that was the case.

"Sir, if I may elaborate. My aunt sent my father a letter at the VA hospital where he's currently staying. The letter stated she was afraid, that things were happening down here that she thought were suspicious. My father asked me to investigate. I came here to do so. I found my aunt dead. Naturally my suspicions were aroused."

When Walmsey next spoke his tone was far less confrontational. "Your father? At the VA hospital?"

"Yes, sir. He's not that well, but he's hanging in there. Even though sometimes he thinks he's still commanding the 101st."

There was a long stretch of silence

and then Walmsey said, "Fighting John Puller is your father?"

"Yes, sir. I'm John Puller Jr."

"That was not included in my briefing on this. I can't imagine why the hell not."

Puller could see a certain aide to Colonel Walmsey getting his or her ass reamed over that one.

"But my father being who he is should not impact this matter at all."

"No, it shouldn't," said Walmsey in a halting voice.

"It's just that my aunt was my father's only sibling. He took it hard. He was her younger brother. You have siblings, sir?"

"Two older sisters. Special relationship, big sisters and little brothers."

"Yes, sir, so I've heard."

There was another long pause.

"Why don't you carry on down there and we'll revisit this issue later, Agent Puller."

"Yes, sir, thank you, sir. And Ms. Craig?"

"Don't worry about her. I'll take you at your word that she wasn't involved in anything that was unauthorized. She'll be back on duty today."

"Appreciate it, sir."

"You tell your father I said hello and convey my best wishes for a speedy recovery."

"I will do that, Colonel. Thank you. Uh, any chance on running that license plate down, sir?"

But the line went dead.

It didn't look like the Army was going to be much help with this.

Puller headed to the Tahoe.

He needed to get his investigation duffel.

CHAPTER

37

The sweat trickled down his neck.

At eight in the morning he'd already been hard at work for an hour. It was eighty-two degrees with a projected high of nearly a hundred today.

He was at the same house. He had been told that the grounds here were so extensive that they required a landscaping crew every day. He had taken steps to make sure that he would get the assignment. It had involved payments and promises to people who didn't give a damn why he wanted to be here. For them it was just an ex-

change of something for something
else. And when you were dealing with
folks who had little money, bartering
became a way of life. For all they knew
he was trying to case the mansion in
hopes of robbing it. They did not care
about folks stealing from the rich. The
rich had everything. They would just
print more money.

He was simply one man working for
others. He was paid a wage that could
barely keep him alive. And he was one
injury away from being homeless.

As he looked around at the workers
next to him, he was actually describing
their state of affairs, not his. Money
meant nothing to him. He was here for
his own purposes and no other. When
he was done he would leave.

Unless he was dead. Then he would
stay in Paradise for eternity.

He rubbed the sweat from his eyes
and commenced clipping a hedge for
owners who demanded a precisely
trimmed bush. But he also focused on
what he had seen the previous night on
the beach.

Those people were lost forever. As

soon as they had been taken, it was
over. On the boat. On the truck. It didn't
matter. Nothing could break the long
chain of ownership, for that's what it
was.

Chattel.

The sixteenth century or the twenty-
first century, it didn't really matter. People with power and means would always take advantage of those without
them.

He clipped and thought about his
next move.

He ran his eye along the top of the
hedge and at the same time skirted his
gaze along the perimeter of the mansion. The same Maserati was parked in
the front cobblestone circular drive. He
assumed that the young couple had
stayed over. Why leave this place if one
didn't have to? He had learned, by asking subtle questions of a house servant
who had come out to retrieve the mail,
that the interior staff consisted of ten
people. These included maids, a chef,
someone playing the role of a butler,
and various others who worked cheap
and were able to live in the servants'

quarters of the grandest home on the Emerald Coast.

The family who lived here consisted of four people:

The cash machine husband.

The pampered second wife.

The even more pampered son.

The mother-in-law.

The cash machine was in his mid-forties, relatively young for having amassed such great wealth. He had not asked the maid how the money had been made.

He already knew.

The second wife used to be a runway model, was in her early thirties, and spent most of her time shopping.

The cash machine's son—the second wife's stepson—was seventeen and attended a private boarding school in Connecticut. He had already been accepted at an Ivy League school based more on his father's largesse to the university than his academic performance. He was now home for the summer playing polo, driving his Porsche, and sowing his wild oats among the available local young women, who were unabashedly competing to one day live in grand houses filled with servants. This he had also found out before coming here.

The second wife's mother lived in the lavish guesthouse and was, at least by most accounts, a bitch of massive proportions.

As he watched, the same woman he had seen by the pool the day before strolled out of the mansion's rear French doors. She had on a white skirt that showed off her bare, tanned legs, a light blue shirt, and spike backless heels. Her hair fell around her shoulders. Her appearance was quite dressy for this early in the morning. Perhaps she had an appointment.

He watched as she crossed over to the guesthouse and went inside, perhaps to pay her respects to the resident mother-in-law.

The rear door to the mansion opened once more and a man stepped out.

He studied him. About five-eleven, trim, fit, dressed in white shorts that showed off his tanned, muscular calves. He had on leather loafers that looked expensive and no doubt were, and a pale blue patterned long-sleeved Bugatchi shirt. He had left the shirt untucked, no doubt to show that despite his immense wealth he was a casual yet hip man. His hair was brown and wavy with just a touch of gray around the temples.

The man crossed the grounds and entered the guesthouse.

He knew who the man was. He was the cash machine. The man owned this estate and everything in it.

His name was Peter J. Lampert.

He'd made and lost most of a multi-billion-dollar fortune as a hedge fund manager, along with most of the money entrusted to him by his clients. Then he had made another enormous fortune to pay for this place and other assorted toys of the rich. But he had not bothered to recoup his clients' money.

That was what bankruptcy was for, he'd responded, when someone asked him if he felt remorse at all for destroying the lives of so many people.

Lampert, he knew, also had his own private jet, a Dassault Falcon 900LX that was parked at a private airport about thirty minutes from here. Its maximum cabin height was six feet two inches, which meant Lampert could stand up straight inside it, but he couldn't. Yet he never expected to be on it. Private jets were not meant for the hired help.

At the end of the estate's main dock, one hundred feet out to sea in deep water, sat Lampert's mega-yacht, named *Lady Lucky*. Lampert had named that after his second wife, whose name was Lucille, but whom everyone called Lucky, because she apparently had been as the second wife of Peter J. Lampert.

Lucky was currently away, he had been told by the same maid. A shopping trip to Paris and London. Well, the rich had to spend their money on something.

As he thought about it, it was quite likely that her mother was traveling with her too. If so there would be no reason for anyone to visit the guesthouse.

Except perhaps for one.

He worked his way over to the left

side of the structure. There were bushes there that required trimming. He managed to look like he was clipping but actually made no noise with his tool. He edged closer to the window. The drapes were partially up. He heard it before he saw them.

Moans and groans.

He looked around for security. They did not seem to be in this sector.

He grew closer to the window, squatting down, trying to shrink his great height.

He took a peek through the window.

The woman was now wearing only her shirt. Her skirt was on the bed along with her spike heels. Her panties were down around her bare feet. On her tiptoes, she gripped one of the bed's four posters, her body bent forward at a forty-five-degree angle.

Lampert was behind her. He had not bothered to take off his clothes. Apparently he could only be bothered to slide his zipper down. She arched her neck back and was making suitable noises designed to urge on her lover.

Lampert pushed into her violently,

grunted heavily one last time, and then bent forward, supporting himself on her back, totally spent. Panting, he freed himself from her and zipped up his shorts. She turned and kissed him. He fondled and then slapped her bare buttocks.

Lampert said something that he couldn't hear, but the woman laughed. A few moments later Lampert was gone. He apparently had other appointments.

He watched as the woman lay back on the bed, slipped a pill bottle from her shirt pocket, tongued a capsule, and swallowed it. She took off her shirt, walked naked into the bathroom, and emerged about a minute later, her face looking scrubbed.

He continued observing as she quickly dressed, smoothing out her shirt and zipping up her skirt before slipping on her heels. When she left the room, he came around the corner of the building, stooped down, and started to weed the lawn.

She stepped from the guesthouse, looked to the right and saw him there.

Her features grew brighter when she saw him. She smiled. The smell of sex was all over her. He wondered if she realized that, despite her freshening up. He wondered what the young man she had driven up with in the Maserati would say if he detected evidence of the morning tryst.

"Hello," she said.

He nodded at her, keeping his gaze partially downcast but still watching her.

"You were here yesterday. What's your name?" she asked.

"Mecho."

"Mecho? I've never heard that name before."

"In my country it means 'bear.' I am as big as one, you see. I was a big baby, you see, so my father decided to make it official." He stopped and smiled shyly.

His English was much better than that, and he was not by nature a shy man, but he did not want her to know that. Mecho was not his given name, but it *had* been his nickname, precisely because of his great size.

"What is your country?" she asked.

"Far away from here. But I like this place. My country is often too cold."

She smiled and waved away a fly with her hand. Her smile was radiant, her cheeks slightly reddened.

Sex agreed with her, he thought.

"It's always warm in Paradise," she said.

"Hey!"

They both looked over to see a burly security guard heading their way. Mecho hastily stood and moved away from her.

"Hey!" the guard said again as he came up to Mecho. It was the same guard as yesterday. "You're really try-ing my patience, bud."

The woman said, "I was talking to him. He was doing his work. I asked him a question."

The guard looked at her like she was on drugs. "*You* asked *him* a question. Why?"

"Because I wanted to hear his an-swer," she said, scowling. "So you can just leave him alone."

The man was about to say something, but seemed to think better of it. "Right, Ms. Murdoch. I was just making sure everything was okay. Just doing my job."

"Everything is very okay," she said sternly.

After the guard retreated Murdoch said, "My name is Christina, Mecho. My friends call me Chrissy. It was nice talking to you."

As she walked away he watched her. She glanced back once, saw him, and smiled again, tacking on a little wave.

In that knowing smile he saw something interesting. He was almost certain that she knew he had been watching Lampert and her have sex. And she didn't seem concerned by it in the least. In fact, she seemed uplifted by it.

A singularly remarkable woman of great beauty.

A part of him hoped he would not have to kill her.

CHAPTER

38

The trip to Eglin Air Force Base took about thirty minutes. The duffel was where it was supposed to be and Puller signed the necessary paperwork, loaded it into his rental, and drove back to Paradise. Along the way he passed through Destin and eyed Landry's high-rise.

That made him remember he needed a new place to stay.

He arrived back in Paradise around noon.

He hadn't missed it for even a minute.

He made a stop at Bailey's Funeral Home, where he needed to see his aunt's body again.

After he was finished there, he drove directly to his aunt's house. The sun was high, the day was hot, and the humidity had crept so high that simply walking produced rivulets of sweat. But Puller had spent many years of his life in heat even worse than this and it had little effect on him.

He reentered his aunt's house using the key that the lawyer Mason had given him. Now that he had his duffel he could make a proper investigation.

He unpacked his duffel and spent the next five hours going over the interior room by room.

The only remarkable thing he found was nothing.

The only fingerprints were his aunt's. That was why he had stopped by the funeral home, to take a set of elimination prints from Betsy Simon.

There was no sign of forced entry, no indication of a struggle.

He found a box of photo albums stuffed in a closet next to the small laundry room. He looked through a few of them and then stuck the box into his duffel. He would look at them later.

He moved his investigation out to the backyard, where he followed his aunt's presumed path from the house to the fountain area. He got down on his knees and examined the stone surround, the disturbed stones under the water, the holes in the lawn made from the walker. If his aunt's body had still been here he might have seen something that was not right, but it wasn't and thus he couldn't.

He sensed someone watching him and turned and saw Cookie peering over the fence.

"Did you grow?" Puller asked.

"I'm standing on a box. What are you doing?" asked Cookie.

"Just satisfying my curiosity."

"You really think she was murdered, don't you?"

"What do you think?"

Cookie seemed alarmed by the question. "I don't have an opinion. I thought it was an accident, but I wouldn't know what to look for."

"Well, I do know what to look for and I'm not finding much."

"Did you speak to Mason?"

Puller rose and went over to the fence. On the box Cookie and he were close to eye to eye.

"I did. He was helpful. What do you know about him?"

"Like I said, good lawyer. He's handling my estate too. He does the same for lots of people."

"You know him beyond that?"

"Some. But we're not really friends socially."

"Did you hear about the bodies washing up on the beach?"

Cookie nodded sadly. "The Storrows. I knew them. Nice people. I wonder what the hell happened."

"The police are checking it out."

"The paper wasn't very full of details. Do you know anything?"

"If I did, I wouldn't be at liberty to say."

"Are you working with the police?" asked Cookie.

"No. I tend to work solo. But I'm just

naturally tight-lipped with details like that."

Cookie glanced over his shoulder at the fountain. "Still gives me the creeps, thinking of her dying there."

Puller said, "I guess I need to arrange for the funeral service and all." He didn't have a clue as to what this entailed.

"Betsy told me that she wanted to be cremated. It should be in her will."

"Mason didn't mention that."

"Did he give you a copy of the will?"

"Yes."

"You should read it. Betsy was very particular about her funeral arrangements. I'm sure she spelled them out to the letter."

"Thanks. I guess I should have already done that."

"You're young. You don't think about wills and funeral arrangements."

"I'm also a soldier. We tend to think about them more than most people."

Puller left Cookie, went back inside, and packed up his equipment. He took one last look around and hauled his duffel out to the Tahoe. He sat in the driver's seat and pulled out his aunt's last will and testament. After skimming over most of the legalese, including the part leaving the house to him, he arrived at the provisions about her final arrangements.

Betsy Simon did indeed want to be cremated. She had prefunded the service with Bailey's Funeral Home. That included an urn for the ashes and a request that they be spread over the Pennsylvania countryside where she had grown up.

He tucked the will back into his pocket. He would speak with Bailey's about this. He figured they were probably very experienced with cremating folks down here.

He was starving and he had no place to stay. He would take care of the food first, the lodgings next. He also had to check in at the police department. He figured Landry would soon require his sworn allegations to process the eight idiots who had come after him last night.

He checked his phone and was surprised that there was no text from her.

Or Bullock.

He wondered if the moron Hooper
had stopped puking yet.

And then he stopped wondering
about Hooper.

He put the keys in the ignition, pulled
his M11, and hit the gas, pointing the
Tahoe straight at the car.

Sometimes the direct way was the
best.

CHAPTER

39

Puller slid the nose of his Tahoe to within an inch of the passenger door of the other car. The man seated there stared at him in surprise. The driver was trying to back the car up. Puller eased the nose forward until his hood was touching the car's passenger door. If the driver backed up any more, he was going to seriously damage his vehicle.

Puller watched both men for any sudden movements. He raised his gun into view, rolled his window down, and motioned the passenger to do the same.

The man did so. "What the hell are you doing?" he barked.

"Not what I wanted to hear," replied Puller as he climbed out of the Tahoe and came around to stand next to the car, the M11 held at an angle that would allow him to shoot at his target within a millisecond and not miss.

"What I wanted to hear was why you've been tailing me. And I would follow that up by asking who the hell are you."

All three men turned their heads when they heard the screech of tires, followed by the whoop of a siren. A police cruiser had turned down the street and was advancing on them.

Puller saw the driver first and his heart sank.

It was Hooper.

Next to him was Landry.

Hooper looked excited.

Landry seemed uncertain.

Puller slipped his M11 back into its belt holster as the two cops got out of their car. Hooper had his gun pulled.

Of course you do, thought Puller.

Landry kept her gun holstered, but placed her hand on top of its butt.

Hooper advanced, swiveling his gun back and forth until he finally kept it pointed at Puller. "You just can't keep out of trouble, buckaroo," he said gleefully.

"I wasn't aware I was in trouble," replied Puller.

Hooper looked at the proximity of the Tahoe to the other car and said, "So you always park this close to other vehicles?"

"If I want to have a private conversation with somebody, yeah," said Puller.

This comment made Landry snort and Hooper scowl.

"You keep up with the bullshit your ass will be in a lockup so fast you'll get a nosebleed," he snapped.

Puller said nothing to this inane comment because there was really nothing to say.

Even the guys in the car looked like they wanted to laugh, and probably would have except Hooper was now pointing his gun at them.

Puller said to Landry, "Can you ask

your partner to holster? His finger is past the trigger guard. To me that means you're going to fire."

"Hoop," said Landry in an admonishing tone. "No more accidents, okay?"

More accidents? thought Puller.

"We know he's armed," said Hooper, indicating Puller.

"I am armed because I'm required to be by the United States government," pointed out Puller. "You can take it up with the Pentagon if you want, but I think federal trumps state, at least in this instance."

He pointed at the two men in the car. "But now they might be armed too. I don't know for sure."

Landry's gaze flicked to the car's occupants. She stepped forward, her hand still gripping the butt of her sidearm. "Will you gentlemen please step out of the car with your hands where we can see them?"

"I can't open my door," said the guy on the passenger side. "His truck is blocking it."

"Then slide across and out the driver's side," said Landry sharply.

With Hooper keeping his aim on them and now ignoring Puller, the two men slid out of the car, their hands held out in front of them.

"Are you armed?" asked Landry again.

Each man looked at the other.

The driver said, "We are not armed."

"Open your jackets," said Landry.

The men did so and there was nothing to see except shirts and belts.

Puller said, "Why have you been following me?"

The driver looked at him. He was about six feet tall, broad shoulders tapering to a slim, hard waist. His companion was likewise built. Their buzz cuts matched too. Up close they looked even more military.

"Who says we've been following you?"

"I do," said Puller. "This is the fourth time I've seen you. Twice on this street."

"It's a small town," said the man.

Landry said, "Let us see some ID."

The men pulled out their wallets and handed over driver's licenses. Landry wrote the info down in her notebook while Puller tried but failed to see the names and addresses on the licenses.

She handed them back.

The first man said, "Unless you have some reason for holding us, I'm assuming we can go now?"

Landry glanced at Puller and then back at the men and said, "Can you tell me what you're doing in Paradise?"

"Just down here on vacation," replied the man.

"Have you been following this gentleman?" asked Landry.

"No. I'm thinking about buying a place on this street, actually. Even contacted a Realtor about it." He flicked out a card to her. "This is her name and contact info. She'll vouch for me. We were sitting here going over what places we were going to check out when this guy came flying at us. Seems to me that instead of questioning us, you should be arresting him. I thought he was going to ram us with his truck."

Landry glanced down at the card and then frowned as she glanced once more at Puller Puller could read all the doubts in that look.

She handed the card back to the man. "Thank you for your cooperation. I'm sorry for any inconvenience."

Hooper said, "Do you want to press charges against him?" He indicated Puller.

The man eyed Puller, as though trying to absorb every detail of his face.

"Nah. He doesn't seem worth the trouble." He smiled at Puller while his friend let out a snort of laughter. "So just move your truck and we'll be on our way." He drew closer to Puller. "But you try something like that again, I won't be as accommodating."

Landry stepped between them. Perhaps she had caught the look from Puller that indicated he was about a millisecond from breaking the man in half.

"That's enough of that," she said, pushing them apart. "Puller, move your vehicle. Now. Gentlemen, you have a good day."

Puller climbed into his truck and backed it up just enough to allow the other car to creep past. Then the driver accelerated, turned the corner, and was gone.

Puller got back out of the truck. "What were their names?" he asked.

"That is none of your damn business," snapped Hooper.

Puller looked at Landry inquiringly.

She shook her head. "It is none of your business, Puller. And just be glad he didn't press charges. Now from here on, just stay away from them."

"Me staying away from them isn't the problem. They're following me."

"So you say," barked Hooper. "Doesn't make it true."

Landry said, "Puller, their story does sound logical. If they're looking for a house on this street." She gazed up and down it. "And I see three for-sale signs."

Puller knew this was bullshit. The guys had their cover story. But Diego had seen them near the Sierra. He didn't think there was any real estate in that area that would interest the two men. But he kept that to himself.

"Okay," he said. "You're probably right."

Landry clearly didn't believe him, and Hooper clearly still wanted to arrest him.

He turned to climb back into the Tahoe.

Hooper said, "How do you know we're done with you yet?"

Puller turned and stared at him expectantly. "Okay. Are you done with me?"

Hooper looked surprised by the question and glanced at Landry. She said, "Hoop, finish the patrol on this street. I want to have a word with Mr. Puller."

Hooper climbed into the cruiser and hit the rack lights and engaged the crowd control button. The blasting noise caught Landry completely off guard.

"Damn it, Hoop, just go," she snapped.

He sped off faster than he should have on a residential street.

"How do you stand working with that idiot?" asked Puller.

She ignored the comment and said, "What is going on with you?"

"Come again?"

"Are you getting paranoid?"

"I'm not paranoid. Those guys are following me."

"You have proof of that?"

"I'll get it."

"What you need to get, Puller, is to just leave it alone. Those guys didn't look like the types to be messed with."

"And you think I do?"

She looked over his shoulder, her arms folded across her chest.

He said, "I know I need to come down to the station and press charges against the guys from last night."

"You might not want to do that."

"Why not?"

"They want to press charges against you."

"Come again?"

"They said you attacked them."

"I did. Before they attacked me."

"You might not want to go around admitting that."

"They were in my room, waiting to ambush me. Little hard to spin that."

"They've already been released on their own recognizance."

"Things work that fast in Paradise?"

"I don't know what to tell you."

"I was told those guys didn't have gang connections. But someone is apparently pulling strings behind the scene."

"I'm just a beat cop, Puller. I don't get into stuff like that."

"So they're out on the street waiting to come after me again?"

"I don't think you have to worry about that."

"Why?"

"Because I told them you were a super special forces homicidal maniac who could kill them in more ways than they could even imagine. I told them that the next time you would kill all of them and then get your Army buddies to come down here and help kill their families for good measure."

Puller cracked a smile. "You actually told them that?"

"That was the gist of it. And for the Latinos I said it all in Spanish so they would get the point without having to translate. I said if they left you alone, I could guarantee their safety. Otherwise all bets were off. They all looked scared shitless when they left. And I really don't think they're going to press charges. They're too afraid of you."

Puller said, "Okay, I appreciate the assist."

"You're welcome. Now you can focus on what happened to your aunt."

Puller smiled. "I wish every local cop I worked with was as cooperative as you."

"You treat me with respect, I reciprocate. The moment you stop doing that, so do I."

"I've got no problem with that." He paused, wondering whether he should even venture there. But it would be a good way to ask more questions. And he found he was enjoying Landry's company. She could be a good asset for him on this case if it turned out his aunt's death wasn't an accident.

"You free for dinner?"

She looked surprised and, Puller thought, a bit pleased by the invitation.

"You let me stay at your place rent-free," he said in a joking manner. "I'd like to do something for you."

She thought about this for a few seconds. Part of Puller thought she was going to say no.

"I get off duty in two hours. Where do you want to go?"

"Your town. I'll defer to you."

"There's a place called Darby's on the main drag."

"Okay. I've seen it."

"Say about eight o'clock?"

"Sounds good."

He climbed into his truck and drove off. But he was no longer thinking about dinner with Landry.

Tweedledum and Tweedledee in the sedan. He needed to know who they were and whether they were connected just to him somehow or to what had happened to his aunt.

And maybe he had a way to do that.

He picked up his phone.

CHAPTER

40

"Well, well, I was wondering when the hell I was going to hear from you."

"Just been a little busy, General Carson," said Puller.

"General Carson? I thought we had moved to Julie."

"It's still working hours, ma'am. Wasn't sure how you felt about that."

Julie Carson was a one-star stationed at the Pentagon in the J2's office. The J2 was a two-star who gave the Chairman of the Joint Chiefs the daily briefing. Carson was the vice chair and gave the briefing when the J2 was unavailable. She had helped Puller during his time in West Virginia.

She was forty-one, very attractive, as fit as a triathlete, and as tough as Puller. They had had a rocky start, but things had turned around after they'd found some common ground.

"What I feel is that you can call me Julie."

"Okay. I need a favor, Julie."

"What, no dinner first?"

"It's always a question of timing."

He heard her sigh. "Okay, what do you need?"

Puller briefly outlined his dilemma to her in succinct, military-crisp sentences that gave her the minimum amount she needed to follow along. The habit was so ingrained in him that he didn't even realize he was doing it.

"Damn, Puller. I heard you were out on R and R. What the hell are you doing in Florida in the middle of something else? Do you plan to work your way across all fifty states getting into murder and mayhem?"

"Believe me, this is not by choice. If

my aunt weren't involved, I wouldn't be down here."

"I'm sorry for your loss," she said quickly. "So you think it's foul play?"

"It's looking more like it, though I don't have a shred of proof."

"And the two guys in the car. You really think they're military?"

"Were or are. I need to find out which."

"I can run the plate for you today. But it might just be a rental."

"It probably is. But if so, they had to put some name down for it and show a driver's license. That might give us enough to go on."

"I'll get to work on it ASAP."

"I appreciate it, Julie."

"Now that's what I like to hear."

"How are things at J2?"

"Actually, I'm fairly bored with the routine."

"Thinking of a transfer?"

"The rest of my military career will be a series of transfers, the choices of which will largely be dictated by other people. That's how it goes when you're chasing more stars."

"Yeah, I got a taste of that with my dad. Probably one reason I opted for the enlisted side. Too much thinking goes on with the stars and bars side of things."

"You're an enlisted and *enlightened* man, Puller." She paused, and when she next spoke Puller heard a subtle change in her voice, like she was going from Pentagon mode to something more human.

"So what are your long-range plans?"

He said, "Finish up down here and get my butt back to Quantico. I'm sure CID will find things for me to do."

"I'm sure they will. Military crime never takes a holiday, Puller. Not when you have hundreds of thousands of mostly young men around the world trying to act all macho. Add to that billions of dollars of taxpayer money flying around and things get complicated. Hands go into cookie jars."

"And around other people's throats."

"So you see yourself being a military cop all the way?"

"I haven't thought that far down the road, quite frankly."

"You really need to start doing that. You're not getting any younger."

For a second Puller thought she was going to say, "*We're* not getting any younger."

"Sound advice."

"Only if you take it. I'll call you as soon as I know anything on the plate. In the meantime try not to get killed down there. I'm just starting to like you."

"I'll do my best."

"So you said your aunt left you the house?"

"What the lawyer told me."

"A house in Paradise?"

"Guess so."

"I might have to come down and check it out."

"Why's that?" he said.

"Hell, isn't it obvious? I've never been to Paradise before. Like to see if it lives up to its billing."

"Well, it hasn't so far."

Puller clicked off and pondered what to do next. He looked at his watch. Now that he didn't have to go down to the police station and press charges he had a little free time before his dinner with Landry.

He had some items on his to-do list. Check out the lawyer Griffin Mason. Check on Diego and his cousins.

Duplicate the ten-mile there-and-back trip his aunt might have taken.

He made up his mind quickly: check on Diego and his cousins.

Just in case.

CHAPTER

41

"He is gone."

Puller stood in the doorway of Diego's small apartment and looked down at Isabel. Little Mateo was behind her, his thumb stuck in his mouth.

"Is that unusual?" asked Puller. "Him not being here? It seemed to me that he spent a lot of time on the streets."

"He comes back for lunch. But he did not. He always comes by six, but he did not," said Isabel.

"Do you have a phone?"

She shook her head.

"When did he leave?"

"This morning. I worked late at the restaurant with *mi abuela*. Diego was here looking after Mateo. He left before I got up. *Mi abuela* did not hear him leave either. I am very worried."

"Did he say last night what he might be doing today?"

She shook her head again. "He usually goes down to the beach. He sells things to the tourists. Sometimes he works for the hotels."

"He's too young for that, isn't he?"

She looked at him like he was crazy.

Puller said, "Okay, I'll keep an eye out for him."

Puller looked at the bruises both had received from the gang of three. "Have any of those punks come around here, Isabel?"

"I have seen none of them. I hear that you beat them up again. And their friends."

"Who did you hear that from?"

"I just hear it."

Puller nodded. "I'm going to get you a disposable phone and leave you my contact info. That way you can reach me and I can get in touch with you, okay?"

She nodded.

It took Puller about half an hour, but he dropped the phone off and then climbed into his Tahoe and drove off.

As much as he didn't like it, Diego would have to wait. He hoped the boy was okay. But something was telling him that wasn't the case.

Twenty minutes later he pulled onto the street where Griffin Mason had his law office. The same Infiniti was in the drive-way.

Yet he didn't pull into Mason's drive-way. He spotted another little house down the street with a sign out front and pulled in there. He got out and knocked on the door. An attractive blonde-haired woman in her forties an-swered the door. She was short and curvy and wearing a short black skirt, black hose, and a matching jacket. Her white blouse was open enough at the top to show a slice of cleavage from her ample bosom. Since it was still about ninety degrees outside, Puller assumed that in all that black plus stockings she was probably sweating just by being at the door.

"Can I help you?" she asked.

"My name is John Puller. I was out here yesterday meeting with Griffin Mason over an estate issue. He's not my lawyer. He represented my aunt, who recently passed away. He said to check references before I decided to keep him on with the estate work."

She blanched. "Grif gave me as a reference?"

"That's right, Ms. Dowdy. You seem surprised."

Puller had gotten her name from the sign outside that had her picture and also helpfully included the fact that she was fluent in Spanish.

"That's because I am. And I don't really have time to talk."

She started to close the door, but Puller held out his Army creds. "I came down here yesterday from D.C. My aunt died unexpectedly. I don't know a soul in town. I'm just trying to come up to speed fast and doing my proper due diligence. The military way. Any help

you can give me would be appreciated."

"My son's in the Navy."

"Navy's given me a ride many a time."
He stared at her expectantly.

She glanced down the street toward
Mason's office. "I've got a dinner meeting to go to in about twenty minutes,
but I can answer questions for you until then. Come on in."

A minute later they were seated in
her office, which was far neater than
Mason's.

"So, as I explained Ms. Dowdy . . ."

"Just make it Sheila," she said. She
pulled out a cigarette. "Don't worry, it's
an electronic one. Damn thing really
works. Smoked for twenty years and
then went cold turkey with this a year
ago. Hope my lungs can regenerate."

Puller watched as water vapor rose
from the device, and then refocused on
her.

"As I said, Sheila, I'm just checking
references on Mason. I assume you
know him?"

"Oh, I know Grif all right."

"So would you recommend him?"

"I'm a lawyer. I say anything negative then somebody can sue me. And Grif certainly would."

"Well, that in itself is sort of a negative answer," pointed out Puller.

"But nothing actionable," she replied promptly.

"So you wouldn't recommend him?"

She sat back, studied him. "Who was your aunt?"

"Betsy Simon."

"Didn't know her. But if she has Grif handling her estate, it's probably most cost-efficient to let him keep going. But a piece of advice, watch the financial accounts like a hawk."

"Is that sometimes a problem with Mason?"

"I wouldn't use the word 'sometimes.'"

"Then why would people use him?"

"He must hide his tracks well."

"But you must know differently. How?"

"Let me put it this way. I've been practicing law down here pretty much as long as he has. Our client list is very similar. We handle the same sorts of cases. Trusts and estates lawyers are not like the Wall Street M and A guys. We don't get rich doing this. I sure as hell haven't, and I work my ass off, excuse the language."

"But Mason *has* gotten rich?"

"Don't let the crummy office in the old house fool you. I live in East Paradise, two blocks off the water because that's all I can afford. I drive an eight-year-old Toyota Camry. Mason has a one-acre waterfront spread that is definitely well into the seven-figure range. In addition to that Infiniti he drives a Porsche and an Aston Martin. And he takes trips all over the world—Africa, Asia, the Middle East, South America. Doesn't take a genius. The clients are not footing all that. At least not knowingly."

"So he's stealing client funds? Again, how come no one has wised up to it? You can't be the only one who's become suspicious because of the house and cars."

"You have to prove it. You have to want to prove it, and apparently no one has. His clients are old and then they're dead. The heirs usually are out of town. I see it because I live here and I'm in the same profession."

"Anything else?"

She tapped her cigarette on the desk. "You didn't hear it from me, but besides the money there's also something else going on with that guy that gives me the creeps."

"What's that?"

"He seems to like children. He seems to like children way too much, if you know what I mean."

"Why do you think that?"

"I was with him at a legal function one time. After it was over he got drunk as a skunk in the hotel bar. I was just about to leave when he pulled me back to the table. I thought he wanted to rent a room and get a quickie on with me, as if I'd even consider something like that with him."

"So he's tried to come on to you before?"

"Let's put it this way. He always tries to look down my shirt and feel up my ass any chance he gets. But then he started showing me all these pictures in his wallet." She paused and pursed her lips in disgust. "They were all of young boys and girls."

"Did he explain why he had them?"

"He said they were his kids." She laughed. "He must've been drunk out of his mind. Probably doesn't even remember showing them to me."

"Are you sure they weren't his kids?"

She smiled and took a puff on her cigarette.

"Well, considering the fact that he's a fair-haired Irishman and the kids in the photos were black and Asian, no, I'm pretty sure they weren't related."

CHAPTER

42

Another hot day on the job had left his fellow workers soaked in sweat and craving cold beers found among air-conditioned bars.

Mecho left them to their bottles and returned to his room. He did not interact with them at work and did not care to be with them while away from work. They seemed fine with that. It would not have mattered to him if they had not been fine with that.

He was not sure what the altercation had been about next door the night before, and he really didn't care.

He had, however, seen the other man fight. He was good. Excellent, in fact.

But he had allowed himself to be outflanked. He would have died if Mecho had not helped him.

And maybe I should have let him die.

This was not a flippant thought on Mecho's part. The other man did not belong here. And people who did not belong somewhere usually had a good reason for being where they didn't belong.

The man had had a gun.

A Sig P228. But it had been slightly altered. He could tell that even from a distance and in poor light.

The other man's fitness, close-shaven hair, close-quarter combat skills, and the weapon were telling.

He was military. American military, judging by how he had spoken to Mecho last night.

There were many military bases around here. Which prompted the question of why the military man was staying in a place like the Sierra. And what had he done to anger the street punks.

Maybe nothing.

Mecho had done nothing to piss off the ones who had come after him that night on the streets. They were like hyenas looking for prey in all the right places, and occasionally running into someone who fought back. Then the hyenas would run away. They always did.

As he sat on his bed he forgot about Puller and reflected on the additional information gathered on the Lampert estate today.

After his brief conversation with Chrissy Murdoch he had continued to work the grounds. Over near a stand of trees he had seen one of the maids talking with the pool man. He had drifted over and listened. When the maid was done with her conversation, Mecho had edged still closer to her.

When she saw him she looked startled. But he spoke to her in Spanish and his smile was disarming. As he worked the lawn he spoke with her. Her reticence diminished. Her answers grew longer.

Her name was Beatriz. She was very beautiful. Her skin was light brown and

smooth. Her hair was dark and luxurious and smelled of coconuts. It was
clear that she took good care of her
hair. She had not worked much out-
doors, he could tell, from the condition
of her skin and the smoothness of her
hands. She was from El Salvador, she
told him. She had been working here
for two years. She looked healthy and
well fed. Her uniform was spotless. She
had not arrived on one of the boats, at
least he didn't think so. But he couldn't
be sure.

He asked her in Spanish about her
coming here.

Then he had his answer.

She looked away and hurried off.

He wondered if she knew what her
name represented in Spanish.

Voyager.

She had not come very far, geo-
graphically. But she had traveled the
equivalent of a trip to the moon, he
knew.

But now she lived in the big house
and wore the spotless uniform and had
enough to eat. Back in her native country he doubted this had been the case.

So she should be happy.

Only he knew she wasn't.

One could not be happy when one was a slave, no matter how well you were treated.

You were still a slave.

He had knelt down and started collecting twigs and scraps of leaves. The Lamperts, he had been told, demanded a perfect lawn, with every blemish needing to be removed. They paid well for this. They probably spent more on landscaping services in a week than most people would earn in a year.

And perhaps Lampert wanted no blemishes on his fancy lawn to compensate for the ugly wounds he inflicted on others. Or perhaps he was not that complicated a man and gave no thought to this issue.

Mecho rose and put the debris in a trash bag he had carried with him.

He knew that security had been watching him more closely, but apparently talking to a mere maid for a bit did not amount to an actionable offense, as it had with one of the ladies of the manor.

He felt a presence nearby and turned to see Chrissy Murdoch come out of the main house with the man who had been with her in the Maserati.

The man had on a seersucker suit, white shirt, and a red bow tie with loafers and no socks. He looked like an ad in one of those magazines where everyone looked perfect and led perfect lives.

Is your life perfect, sir? Would you like a little imperfection in it? Would you like me to take your smug, perfect face and rip it in half?

Chrissy had on a long, flowing white cotton dress with a scalloped front. The harsh light made it pretty much transparent, allowing Mecho a long titillating look at her legs. A wide-brimmed hat protected her from the blazing sun. Her slender, tanned feet were encased in sandals that showed off her pink toenails.

Chrissy spotted him and actually waved. Mecho looked around to see if there was anyone else she could be possibly waving at, but there was no one. The man did not take note of this.

He was apparently lost in his own little world to such a degree that he was unaware his woman was being screwed by Peter J. Lampert.

Mecho began to grow suspicious now. It was not natural that someone like her would pay attention to someone like him. There had to be another reason. He did not wave back but instead returned to his work.

They drove off in the Maserati and Mecho wondered if Chrissy had showered to remove the scent of sex, of Peter J. Lampert, from her body. Maybe she didn't care. Maybe her man didn't care.

Life was perfect, after all.

He had walked through the front gate and busied himself in the bushes. Positioning himself where no one could see, he had snapped some pictures of the gate and surveillance apparatus with his cell phone. He was confident that he could find in the dark the exact positioning of the power and data transmission line. He had better be able to.

And then the long day had finally

ended and now here he was in his
room.

As he sat on his bed he thought back
to Chrissy Murdoch. Something was
definitely off there. But he couldn't put
his finger on it. He would have to reflect on it some more. There were many
things that could go wrong, and some
would. But there were certain things he
could keep from going wrong. Chrissy
Murdoch might be one of them.

He lay back on his bed in the swel-
tering heat. It didn't bother him. He had
trained his mind to ignore such physical discomforts. And when the mind
did not pay attention to such things,
neither did the body. The mind controlled pain. And the mind could make
pain go away. He had survived much
agony with that simple philosophy.

Tonight would be busy. He had two
things to do.

The first surely would be problematic.

The second might be catastrophic.

But he had come here to take risks,
not to avoid them.

CHAPTER

43

Cheryl Landry was not in uniform. She wore light blue capri pants, a yellow sleeveless blouse, and white sandals. Her hair, unconstrained by a police cap, was down around her shoulders.

Puller rose from the table at Darby's as she approached.

He had taken a shower at a local YMCA for a daily fee and changed into fresh clothes—khaki pants, short-sleeved shirt, and loafers.

As she sat down, she looked, he thought, a little self-conscious, as though she preferred the uniform and clunky shoes to what she had on.

The waitress brought menus and Puller glanced over his while also checking out the folks at the other tables.

She caught him doing this.

"Scoping the place?" she asked.

"Always good to have alternate exits, just in case."

"One behind the bar. Another left of the kitchen."

"I take it you like scoping too."

"Comes in handy."

"What's good on here?" he asked, indicating the menu.

"Scallops, swordfish, mussels. And the New York strip, if you're into cows."

They ordered drinks and their meals. Puller had opted for the swordfish over the cow.

They sat back and Landry finally seemed to focus on him.

"Something you want to say?" asked Puller.

"I don't know. Should there be?"

"We could run that one in circles for days."

"You invited me to dinner, not the other way around."

"Fair enough."

"But you do make people nervous, Puller."

"I've been told that before."

"I'm sure you have. Eight guys beaten up. Nearly ramming another car. Doing your own investigation. And we found out you got a set of elimination prints from your aunt's body. The chief was not happy about that."

"No law against me visiting my aunt's remains."

"But there is a law against obstructing a police investigation."

"I was under the impression that you weren't conducting one, so what exactly am I obstructing?"

"It's not that simple and you know it."

"I do?"

Their drinks and appetizers came and they both plunged into them, perhaps as a way to avoid more conversation, at least until it became absolutely necessary. They didn't return to the topic until their entrees were nearly done.

Landry took a sip of her Riesling and glanced at him.

"Ready to resume the War of the Roses?" he asked.

"Oh, I haven't started to fight."

"I think we should be on the same side. A house-divided thing, you know."

"I'm in one kind of uniform. You're in another."

"Not that much of a difference, really."

"Look, I'm not saying that your aunt wasn't murdered."

"And I'm not necessarily saying that she was. That's why people investigate. So I'm really not seeing the problem."

"You come here, do your thing, and let's say you find out she was killed."

"Okay."

"Then what do you do?"

"Find the killer."

"Wrong. That's for the police to do. That's my job."

"So you want me to do all the grunt work and then hand off the arrest to you?"

"I don't need you to help me look good," she said heatedly.

"Never said you did. So where does that leave us?'

"I don't know."

"You could work with me."

She glanced sharply at him.

"I usually work solo," he added. "So it's a remarkable offer. Shows I have great confidence in you."

"And exactly how would that work? I do it on my off time, the little I have of it?"

"Yeah."

"And then what? We crack the case and shove my boss's face in it? How does that advance my career in law enforcement?"

"I'm not saying it does. And if that's your only goal then your answer to my offer should be no."

"What other goal should I have?" she asked.

"Bringing to justice somebody who killed an old lady." He leaned forward, his look growing as dark as he suddenly felt right now. "I hoped that might be why you put on the badge in the first place."

"Don't read me the riot act. I don't deserve that."

"Twenty seconds ago I would have agreed with you."

"Do you really want to go down that road? I can make your life miserable."

"I think the police department has already done a good job of that."

"Yeah, well I'm a lot more subtle than Hooper."

"I'm not looking to make enemies, Cheryl. I'm just trying to find out the truth. If this had happened to your family I have to believe you wouldn't just walk away."

This comment seemed to pierce whatever wall Landry had built up during this exchange. She looked away and then down, all the classic signs of capitulation, Puller knew, from interviewing so many suspects.

She said, "I get how you're feeling. I really do."

"Okay. Then I guess it's just a matter of where we go from here. But just to be up-front, I'm going to keep looking into this. It's just how I'm built."

He paused, searching Landry's face for her reaction to this. When she said nothing, he continued. "If I find something substantial, I will bring it to you. Then we can determine what to do from there. Does that seem workable?"

"What do you define as substantial? If it's a suspect or a body, I think that might be too late."

"I will work really hard to keep you in the loop the whole way, how about that?"

"How about if I work with you on my own time?"

He studied her. "Is that what you want?"

"I think so, yeah. It's what you originally suggested, isn't it?"

"I guess so. I just never really expected you to bite on it. So why are you?"

"I don't like people dying when they didn't have to."

"Then I think we have a deal."

As they were leaving the restaurant Puller's phone buzzed. It was a text from General Carson. She had run down the plate.

When Puller saw the information his eyes widened.

This case had just gone to a whole new level.

CHAPTER

44

"You want to come back to my place and talk about this some more?" Landry asked as they walked out of Darby's.

Puller wasn't paying attention to her. He was staring down at the phone in his hand. More specifically, he was staring at the text on his phone's screen.

"I'm sorry if I'm boring you," Landry said crossly as she eyed the device in his hand.

He put it away in his pocket. "Sorry, something just came up. What were you saying?"

"My place, talk some more? We could

walk on the beach. It's up to you. No skin off my nose if you decline. Just trying to be friendly." She added, "And keeping you off the streets and out of trouble."

Puller thought about this. He still didn't have a place to stay, but he didn't think it was a good idea to crash at Landry's place again. And even though he had finished processing his aunt's home he still didn't feel comfortable staying there. She had left it to him, of course, so he had every right to be there if he wanted. But what it really came down to was that until he figured out what had happened to her, Puller didn't think he *deserved* to stay in the woman's house. Not after all those years of not contacting her, letting her tumble from his life like an insignificant piece of debris.

"You know of any places I can bed down in Paradise?" He paused and smiled. "If you think it's safe enough for me."

"Why not stay at your aunt's?"

"If those guys in the Chrysler are tailing me it would be too easy for them to keep tabs on me."

"You really think they're following you?"

"Don't know one way or another. Until I do I'm not taking chances."

"There's a place called the Gull Coast. It's on Gulfstream Avenue. Two blocks south of the Sierra. It's a little bit more money because it is closer to the beach, but you probably won't have to worry about being murdered while you're brushing your teeth."

"Sounds right up my alley. Thanks."

"So you want to hook up later? I usually take a walk on the beach at night around my condo building."

"I'll meet you there in an hour. That'll give me time to check into the Gull Coast."

"Okay. See you in an hour."

She walked to her car and Puller to his. He punched in the numbers on the phone as he pulled out of the parking lot.

"Wondered what took you so long," said Carson on the other end of the phone. "I figured you'd call me the second after you got my text."

"Just got a little backed up down here. But tell me something. How can the Pentagon be told to stand down for running a lousy license plate?"

"We did trace it, you know. To a big cloud somewhere over the Indian Ocean. Not really, but it might as well have been. Total dead end. I was as surprised as you. Figured it would turn out to be a private company. Then we got the call to knock it off."

"Call from who?"

"The official source apparently did not wish to identify itself to a lowly one-star. I got the word from higher up the chain of command."

"So are you in trouble?"

"I don't think so. But I might be wrong about that."

"I had a friend at USACIL try to run the plate for me. I got called by a Colonel Walmsey. He tried to shame me into coming back and cleaning the mess up, but then he figured out who my father was and backed off. I wonder if he got warned off too."

"I don't know about that. But we sure did. And J2 is not used to having its hand slapped, I can tell you that."

"Who has the horsepower to do that?"

"It's not a long list. What the higher-ups want to keep secret, they do keep secret, right or wrong."

"As a soldier, I get that. As a taxpayer I'm more than a little pissed."

"So be pissed. It is what it is."

"The two guys?"

"Anyone's guess. What did they look like?"

"They looked like me, only smaller."

"So former military, like you said on our last call."

"I don't know for sure, General."

"General?"

"We're back on the clock."

"Okay," she said in an amused tone.

"Maybe they're still on our side. In fact, since you got called off maybe they are on our side."

"Maybe. But it prompts the question of what the hell you've gotten yourself into, Puller."

"Blowback from West Virginia?"

"That's what I was thinking. It touched a lot of very hot wires. It looked like things turned out great and you were the hero, but you know D.C. Things could have changed. Maybe they're looking for a scapegoat for a reason unknown to either of us. Wouldn't be the first time something like that has happened."

"Meaning me as the scapegoat?"

"And I was involved too, if you recall."

"So why would they be down here tracking me—"

He gripped the phone so hard he thought he felt the shell begin to cave in.

"Puller?"

"I'll call you back."

"What is it?"

"I'll call you back."

Puller clicked off and hit a hard right.

Because the Chrysler guys kept showing up where he was, he had simply assumed that they had to be after him.

That had been an assumption he had no business making.

While it was true that the guys had taken up a tail on him—they had been seen around the Sierra after all—they had to have picked him up from some point.

And he knew what that point might have been.

My aunt's house.

They might not have been following him. This might have nothing to do with blowback from what had happened in West Virginia. They might have been checking out Betsy Simon's home.

And it wasn't a huge stretch to their having killed her. He didn't care if they were from the Pentagon or if someone high up was trying to call the dogs off. If they had killed his aunt they were going to pay for it.

He punched the gas and the Tahoe sped off into the darkness.

CHAPTER

45

Puller parked two blocks over and walked the rest of the way to his aunt's home.

He did it by a very circuitous route. If people who could call off the Pentagon *were* involved in this, then Puller had to raise the level of his game accordingly.

He stopped near a fenceline and studied the terrain ahead. It was ten o'clock, dark even on the Emerald Coast, where the sun purportedly never stopped shining. It was quiet on Orion Street. A slight cooling breeze was blowing in from off the water. A car started up somewhere, its ignition shattering the silence.

Puller hunkered down and took cover behind a bush to remove himself from the possibility of headlights reflecting off him. The car drove past. It wasn't the sedan with the two men inside.

But Puller still recognized it.

It was Jane Ryon driving past in her blue Ford Fiesta, the dent in the side door looming large in the wash of streetlights.

What the hell was she doing here? She had already gotten her things from his aunt's house.

There was no way he could follow her. The Fiesta was nearly out of sight as it turned the corner. By the time he hustled back to his vehicle and took up the chase she would be long gone.

He slipped out into the open and continued down the sidewalk, his gaze moving like radar. He reached his aunt's house and opted for entry through the rear door. The lights in Cookie's house next door were on. Apparently the retired baker was in for the night. Or perhaps he had not yet gone out.

As he was walking through his aunt's backyard Puller heard a little yap. He trotted to the fence and peered over.

Sadie looked up at him and yapped again.

Puller eyed the dog and then glanced over at Cookie's house. Then he eyed the dog again.

What had Cookie said to him? He knew the Storrows, the couple found dead on the beach. They were friends. He was stunned by their deaths. Just like he had been stunned by his friend Betsy's death. There was nothing surprising there. But there was one unanswered question.

Had Betsy Simon known the Storrows?

He looked down at Sadie barking. The little dog seemed sad. And lonely. And, if it was possible, her little features seemed confused.

Cookie said he would usually let Sadie out late in the morning to do her business. Puller had seen multiple leashes hanging on a hook by the back door when he had visited the house previously. And he had seen Cookie walking Sadie.

But Florida had snakes and gators and other types of nocturnal predators. Why let your little dog out alone at night even in a fenced backyard?

Puller jumped the fence and landed near Sadie, who jumped back in surprise and started yapping again. Puller scooped the little dog up in one arm and pulled his M11 with his right hand. Sadie, perhaps sensing that something was amiss, stopped yapping. Her tongue gently licked Puller's arm.

Puller kept his gaze on the house. He reached the back steps and slipped quietly up them. The door was unlocked. He passed through, checking out all possible ambush angles before venturing farther in.

He cleared one room after another, keeping low and to the side and giving limited opportunity for anyone hiding inside to get a clean shot at him.

His search ended in the upstairs bathroom.

He put Sadie down and the little dog started licking at the water.

Puller put his gun away and stared down at Cookie.

He was naked and in the bathtub.

More precisely, he was resting at the bottom of the tub.

Puller made no move to pull him out and attempt to resuscitate him. It would have been for naught.

The eyes stared up at Puller.

The eyes of a dead man.

Drowning, he was certain, would be the official cause of death.

Just like his aunt next door.

Folks found submerged in water usually died because water was in their lungs, where water should not be.

The question then became, how did the person become submerged?

Three possible scenarios presented themselves.

Cookie could have had some medical crisis, a heart attack, a stroke, a seizure, or a drug reaction that had rendered him unconscious. He then would have slipped under the water and died.

Or he could have hit his head, knocked himself out, and gone under.

Or someone could have held him under the water.

Puller did not think the fourth possibility, suicide, was realistic. The body had its own emergency reaction to attempted suicide by drowning. It fought for air. You could kill yourself out in the ocean by drowning because you gave yourself no opportunity to get back to land.

But not in a bathtub.

Puller spotted the bottles of medication on the sink next to the tub. He didn't touch any of them, but did read the labels.

Blood pressure pills. Fluid retention capsules. Arthritis. Vascular. Beta blockers. Pills presumably to counteract the interaction of the other medications. The bottles went on and on.

Welcome to being old in America, the land of the blissfully overly medicated.

Puller looked around once more, taking in tiny details that might have great significance. Seeing nothing else, he decided he had intruded enough on

what was now no longer a suburban
residence, but a potential crime scene.
He pulled out his phone and hit 911.
It was shaping up to be a long night.

CHAPTER

46

The long night did not start off well.

The police cruiser skidded to a stop at the curb with its rack lights turning and its siren blaring, crushing the quiet of the night.

Officer Hooper climbed out and pulled his gun as soon as Puller stepped clear of the house. The other cop with him was a man who looked similar enough in appearance to be Hooper's brother. He had his gun out too.

"I can't freaking believe this," said Hooper as he eyed Puller.

Puller said, "Landry's off duty. Why are you still working?"

"None of your business," snapped Hooper. He turned to his partner. "Boyd, this is the jerk-off I was telling you about."

Puller said, "Body's in the upstairs bathroom."

"If you screwed with the crime scene you are in serious shit trouble," said Hooper, keeping his gun pointed in Puller's direction.

"Hoop," said Boyd. "Who's to say he's not our guy?"

"I called it in," said Puller. "I waited here for you to arrive. Why would I do that if I'm 'the guy'?"

Hooper said condescendingly, "Well, that way we wouldn't suspect you. Shit, you Army guys all that stupid?"

"And the motive?" asked Puller.

"Not our problem," said Hooper. "That's your problem."

"Actually, our criminal justice system adheres to the 'innocent until proven guilty beyond a reasonable doubt' philosophy," said Puller. "So it is *your* problem."

Another cruiser pulled up with an ambulance in tow. Chief Bullock climbed out. He was dressed in civilian clothes, so Puller assumed he'd gotten the call at home.

He walked straight past Hooper and Boyd and up to Puller.

"What do we got?"

"Dead man in the bath. No signs of a struggle. Could be he had a medical crisis and went unconscious. Post will tell us a lot more. I saw a car driving away from here a few minutes before I found the body. Blue Ford Fiesta with a big dent in the passenger door."

"Know who was in it?"

"Woman named Jane Ryon. She was a caregiver to my aunt. And she knew the deceased as well. I don't know if she was coming from this house or not. If so, she has a lot of explaining to do."

Hooper and Boyd just stood there openmouthed as Bullock and Puller talked.

Finally Bullock looked over and said, "Hey, Hoop, what the hell you waiting for? Secure the damn area. We have a potential crime scene here. You too, Boyd."

Hooper and Boyd holstered their guns and hurried to do this.

Bullock turned back to Puller. "Some days I don't know why I bother, with the likes of those people constituting my police force."

"You've got Landry."

"If I had all Landrys you'd never hear me complain one second."

He looked up at the house. "If this turns out to be a homicide, that'll be four in just a few days. I don't like that. Way out of proportion to the population down here. Scare the tourists away. Town council won't like that."

"Any leads on the Storrows' murders?"

"Not a one. No one saw anything. No one heard anything. But they were murdered, no doubt of that."

"Cookie, the man in the tub, knew the Storrows."

"How the hell do you know that?"

"He told me so."

"That's a link."

"Yes, it is."

"My tech will be here any minute. In the meantime I better go see for myself."

"You better."

He started off. Puller didn't move.

"You coming?"

"In a minute. Got something to check first."

Bullock went into the house and Puller hustled to his truck, passing by first Hooper and then Boyd as they were stringing up yellow police tape. Both cops gave him dirty looks, which he ignored.

He popped the rear door on the Tahoe and dug through his duffel. He found the photos he'd taken from his aunt's house. He rifled quickly through them.

It took him all of two minutes before he found it. He held it up, letting the interior truck light fall fully on the photo.

In the picture was his aunt.

And Mr. and Mrs. Storrow bracketing her. He recognized their faces from the newspaper story that morning.

Apparently, like Cookie, she'd been friends with them too.

And now they were all dead.

He looked at Cookie's house and then at his aunt's house.

If this kept up there might not be anyone left alive on Orion Street.

CHAPTER

47

Puller called Landry and told her what had happened.

"I won't make it there in an hour," he told her. "Sorry."

"Does Chief Bullock need me to come in?"

"No, I think they've got it covered. Just processing the scene. Your buddy Hooper is working the graveyard shift."

"I think it's punishment from Bullock for being such a jerk."

"I'm starting to like your boss more and more. I'll see you when I see you. Okay if it's late?"

"I'll postpone my walk. But only if you fill me in on the details as soon as you get here."

"Deal."

He clicked off and went back into the house. Bullock was upstairs with his tech guy.

Cookie was still dead. Still at the bottom of the tub.

Bullock was looking around. "No fingerprints in the water."

Puller said, "But most of these surfaces are great for prints. If they left a trace behind, great. If there's no trace behind, that tells us a lot too. Means it's been scrubbed. Which means he was killed." He pointed to the floor. "Dry, but damp. Could be from water sloshing around, which would be the case if someone were holding him under."

Bullock looked at his tech guy. "Get to it."

They both stared down at Cookie's diminutive frame at the bottom of the water.

"Hell of a way to go," Bullock noted.

"Anytime someone other than the

man upstairs decides when you die it's
a hell of a way to go."

"So you do think that's what it is?
Murder?"

"I'll wait for the post. But yeah, I
wouldn't be stunned if somebody killed
him."

"Looking a lot like your aunt's situation."

"Yeah, it is."

"I've got a car going to check on this
Ryon woman."

"That's good."

"You think she might have done it?"

"Cookie was old and small. She's
young and bigger and stronger. So,
yeah, she could have done it."

"And her motive?"

"No way to tell just yet." Puller debated and then decided to share it. "My
aunt also knew the Storrows."

"You really think that's significant?"

"Anytime you can tie murder victims
together in some way it's significant. Or
at least it could be."

"I guess."

"I'm going to go check into a room
at the Gull Coast."

"About those men in your room last night?"

"What about them?"

"We couldn't hold them."

"So Landry told me."

"For what it's worth, I believe you. Eight against one sort of explains itself."

"Yeah, it should."

"Watch your back."

"I always have."

On the way to his SUV, Puller scooped up Sadie along with some of her food and a leash. The tiny dog looked up at him mournfully as she sat in Puller's big hand.

"Yeah, I know, Sadie," said Puller. "But it'll be okay."

CHAPTER

48

The first thing was to make them fearful.

Well, to make *him* fearful.

Fearful people often took steps to stop that fear.

That is, they often made mistakes when they reacted fearfully.

Mistakes were good, when the other side was committing them.

Mecho looked up at the grand estate in the darkness. It looked different in the moonlight. But he knew exactly where everything was.

Tonight would not be the main assault. Tonight was just the opener.

He did not approach the main gate. The use of that gathered intelligence would come later.

There were six security agents roaming the grounds. They did not use guard dogs. Good for him, because his scent would have already reached them. Dogs were much better guards than humans in that regard. But humans were more dangerous.

Dogs only had teeth and claws.

Humans carried guns. And killed with malice, the only species that did.

He had approached from the ocean side, slithering up a dune and then across a stretch of high grass to the fence. The fence did not have electronic monitors or surveillance cameras like the front gate did. It was also not electrified. But there were motion sensors tethered to bright lights. Trip one and you revealed your position. However, Mecho had scoped out where all of them were when he was here working. The lights would not trip him up, but he still had to be careful.

The defensive philosophy here was a simple but effective one. Put up reasonable outer-perimeter measures, like fences and gates. If one got through them, the real defenses, clustered in an inner hardened circle around the target, would kick in and stop you.

At least that was the theory.

He clambered over the fence and dropped silently to the ground. He looked to the east and then to the west. The guards staggered their rounds. He had seen it from prior observation. He had also gained this intelligence from some well-placed questions to other members of the hired help he had encountered while working here. They obviously had no love for their employer.

Perhaps they thought Mecho was simply a burglar looking to steal from the rich.

What did they care about that? Someone who had everything losing a little piece of it?

More power to him, they probably thought.

But he thought there was another reason for their helpfulness. And it was

the most disquieting one of all. It made
the anger boil in his chest. It made him
want to lash out and crush someone.

But those feelings would keep. He
would not crush anyone tonight.

Not unless he had to.

He zigzagged across the lawn, avoid-
ing the motion sensors in the trees. He
waited by a clump of bushes as one of
the perimeter guards made his rounds.
When the man was just past him,
Mecho struck.

The guard crumpled to the ground
unconscious, blood running from the
head wound. It was not fatal, Mecho
knew that. He had calibrated his blow
to wound, not kill. And he was a man
who knew exactly how to do this.

He also had the man's weapons. A
Smith and Wesson .44 semiautomatic
and an MP5. Overkill, perhaps, for a
security patrol around a residence,
however rich the occupants might be.
And you had to multiply that by six, for
the other guards were similarly
equipped. Florida had very liberal gun
ownership laws.

As Mecho looked down at the fallen

man, he had to smile. The fellow apparently was pulling double duty, because it was the same man who had yelled at Mecho during the day for speaking to Chrissy Murdoch.

Well, he would have a nice long sleep tonight.

Mecho moved on, drawing closer to the house.

There was a vintage Bentley convertible parked in the courtyard. A noise from another building drew his attention.

The guesthouse again.

He looked at his watch.

Could it be?

He crept closer. A small light illuminated the front of the building.

Mecho could see another guard posted by the front door of the guesthouse. His .44 was holstered, and the MP5 hung loosely by its strap across his chest. He looked bored. He was smoking a cigarette.

By this Mecho knew he was not a true professional. People who knew what they were doing never smoked on duty. Smelling your opponent before he could attack was sometimes the difference between life and death. As was the split second it would take you to drop the cigarette and close your hand around your weapon.

By then you were dead.

Killed by someone more professional than you.

Three seconds later the man lay prostrate on the brick walk in front of the guesthouse. Mecho stripped out the ammo clips from both weapons and pocketed them. Then he slid the man behind a bush and crept to the door.

The sounds coming from inside were the same ones he'd heard that morning.

He opened the door and slipped in. This was not part of the plan tonight, but he took shortcuts when they presented themselves.

The house was dark and he felt his way along. The bedroom was at the end of the hall on the right. He reached it about five seconds later. The door was partially open. With the guard outside they no doubt did not expect to be interrupted.

He peered in. With the moonlight pouring in through the window, the room was illuminated well enough for him to see what was happening.

Peter J. Lampert was on bottom this time.

But it was not Chrissy Murdoch with him.

It was Beatriz, the young maid whom Mecho had spoken with that morning.

She no longer wore her crisp uniform.

She no longer wore anything.

If Mecho had been curious as to whether her body was as beautiful as the rest of her, he had his answer. She was exquisitely lovely.

She straddled her employer. His hands were around her waist and he was smashing her down on him with what Mecho could see was far too much force. Peter J. Lampert seemed to get a kick out of being overly physical with women.

Beatriz was not moaning as Chrissy Murdoch had been. At least not moaning in pleasure. She was moaning in pain. Her small breasts bounced up and down and Mecho could see her butt cheeks wrinkling with each hard collision against Lampert's thighs.

Mecho tensed, every instinct he had telling him to attack.

But instead he pulled back, moved swiftly down the hall, and reached the living room. He looked around and decided this was as good a place as any.

He did what he had come to do and then left.

Outside he gave the guard behind the bush a kick in the head, pretending he was Peter J. Lampert.

It felt good.

He did one more thing before he left. The package was placed twenty meters away from the house and next to the Bentley convertible that had a license plate reading "The Man."

As he crawled over the fence he counted the seconds off in his head.

He reached the beach and kept counting.

Fifty seconds later, when he was back on firm ground, the explosion occurred, lifting the pristine old Bentley five feet up in the air. When it came back down it hardly looked vintage anymore.

The blast lit up the night over Paradise.

Mecho didn't look up to watch it as he started his scooter.

But he did smile.

Good night, Peter J. Lampert.

The Man.

CHAPTER

49

Puller drove to the Gull Coast and checked in. The front-desk person was young and sleepy, or maybe just bored.

He put his gear away in his room and debated what to do next. He called Landry and told her he was on his way. He hopped into the Tahoe and twenty minutes later pulled into the garage in Destin.

It was a humid night with little breeze.

Landry met him at the garage elevator. She had changed into shorts and a tank top with sandals. She held up two bottles of beer and then eyed Sadie.

"You have a dog?"

"By default." He explained about Sadie being Cookie's pet.

"I can't take her, if that's what you're thinking. My building is no pets."

"No problem. I just didn't want to leave her alone tonight."

"Let's do the beach walk. It's cooler down by the water and you can fill me in on the latest." She glanced at Sadie. "And you can walk your new dog."

They trudged across the sand, the breakers rolling over with a growing intensity.

"Surf always this rough at night?" he asked.

"Don't you watch the news?"

"Not lately, no."

"Tropical storm Danielle formed in the Atlantic and entered the Gulf. Don't think it'll strengthen much, but it's roiling up the waters. It'll make landfall around here at some point. They're not exactly sure when."

The beach was mostly empty except for several young men stumbling along, beer cans in hand.

Puller spent a few minutes filling

Landry in on the details of Cookie's
death as Sadie walked dutifully next to
him, occasionally looking up. The ani-
mal must have been confused as hell,
thought Puller, because it had a far longer way to look up than it had with
Cookie.

"What the hell do you think is going
on, Puller?" asked Landry after he'd
finished.

He shrugged. "If people knew something they're being silenced quite efficiently."

"If they knew *what*?"

He shrugged again. "If I knew that I'd
know it all."

He glanced at her as they walked
along sipping their beers.

Sadie tugged and jerked on the leash,
but she was so small that Puller barely
noticed. It was like walking a cricket.

The cold beer made Puller feel warm,
warmer than the air around him. The
waves crashing with tidal regularity
made him more relaxed than he normally would have been, particularly after what had happened to Cookie.

He caught her gazing at him. "You want to go back up to my apartment?" she asked.

"Why?"

She looked down. "I . . . We . . ."

Interpreting her unease Puller said, "I'd really like to, but I can't."

"Okay, I understand. I know I'm not a girly girl, and I carry a gun at work, but I am a woman. I do like guys."

"And I'm sure guys like you."

"I've been hit on by every man under sixty who lives around here, or at least it seems like it. And then the young punks come in from out of town and think they're so hot, but they're just idiots."

"Lots of guys are idiots. I've been accused of being an idiot."

She looked up at him, touched his arm. "But not with women."

He looked down at her. "No, not with women."

"So that makes you different. And attractive."

He was very hot now, far hotter than the air. Sweat was on his forehead. He could feel the heat pouring from Landry too. They could have been inside an oven.

He said, "We're working a case together."

"But you're not on the police force. I wouldn't sleep with you if you were."

"I don't think you're Hooper's type."

"He doesn't quite get that. Never stops trying."

"I'm sure."

"But we're not talking about Hooper, are we?" she said.

"We have no idea where this will lead us, Cheryl. Mixing business and pleasure is never a good idea. You're a very attractive woman and under other circumstances my answer might be different. But the conditions on the ground are what they are. I hope you can understand that."

She sighed. "I can. Look, I'm sorry I brought it up. It wasn't professional of me."

"We can't be professional all of the time."

She smiled resignedly and they resumed walking.

Puller was about to say something when the phone rang.

Landry's, not Puller's.

And nothing was really the same after that.

CHAPTER

50

Puller followed Landry. Her Toyota flew down the road, and Puller had to keep the Tahoe's pedal nearly rammed to the floor to keep up. Landry was definitely not following the speed limit tonight. Sadie lay next to Puller in the front seat. He kept Landry's brake lights, to the extent that she braked at all, in sight.

Landry had taken the call on the beach, the phone mashed to the side of her head. She listened, said almost nothing, and then clicked off and turned to Puller.

"That was Chief Bullock. There's

been an explosion at the Lampert estate."

Puller had checked his watch. Onesixteen. As good a time as any to have an explosion, he had thought.

"Lampert estate? What the hell is that?" he asked.

"It's owned by Peter Lampert. The richest man in Paradise—hell, probably the entire Emerald Coast, maybe all of Florida. I don't know for sure, but he's loaded."

Puller had waited in her apartment while Landry hurriedly changed into her uniform. Then he had picked up Sadie, run to his truck, climbed in, and they were off.

He felt that Landry was experiencing extreme guilt. She had not gone back in to work after Cookie's murder. There was no reason for her to. There was plenty of manpower to work the scene. But then she had been with Puller when the explosion had occurred. Again, no reason to feel guilty, but he knew Landry was the sort of cop who would.

They arrived in Paradise in record time and he continued to follow Landry

through town until they reached the
eastern edge. She turned off on a private road and Puller followed. The Toyota skidded to a stop in front of a pair
of impressive steel gates that looked
strong enough to withstand an Abrams
tank assault.

Landry jumped out of her truck. She
looked back at Puller as he hurried up
to her. He'd left Sadie in the truck with
the windows lowered and a full bowl of
water.

"You want me to go in with you?" he
said.

She looked uncertain. She had asked
him to follow her here. But now her dilemma was obvious, he knew.

It was about two in the morning. Why
would the pair of them be together?

"I can tell Bullock I heard the explosion, saw you racing through town, and
just decided to follow," he said.

"Thanks, Puller, I appreciate that."

Boyd was at the front gate. Puller
figured Hooper was probably back at
Cookie's house securing that scene. It
was good that Bullock had called
Landry in. He would need the man-

power. Puller doubted the Paradise Police Department was very big.

Boyd looked at Landry the way a man does a woman after he's been rejected by her. Puller assumed that this was indeed the reason for the look. Landry had said that Hooper and all the other cops had been trying to get her into bed. And it was clear in Boyd's look that the rejection had not gone down well. When he saw Puller right behind her, his features became darker.

"What the hell is he doing here with you?" he barked.

Before Puller could launch into his cover story, Landry snapped, "He's here to help us work the scene, Boyd. Take it up with the chief if you've got a problem."

Before he could say anything she bulled right past him with Puller riding her wake.

They first saw the remains of the Bentley. The chrome radiator—now blackened and bent—was the only part left relatively intact to show the model of the car.

Bullock was standing next to it. His

crime scene tech was walking the perimeter of the blast site, apparently
making some calculations.

When Bullock saw Landry and Puller
he waved them over. Unlike Boyd, he
didn't bother to ask why they were here
together, so Puller did not need to use
his bogus explanation.

"Got here as fast as I could, Chief,"
Landry said quickly.

"Looks like the bomb was right under the car," said Bullock. "Blew out
some windows in the house too."

"This Lampert guy have enemies?"
asked Puller.

"Well, it appears likely he has at least
one," replied Bullock.

"What do you know about him?"

"Came here from South Beach about
five years ago. Built this place. Well, he
was building it before he came here.
Took the better part of three years to
finish the sucker."

"How'd he make his money?"

"Finance guy or something. Who the
hell knows how those guys make
money? They rob Peter to pay Paul."

"I take it no one was in the car?" asked Puller.

"No."

"Anything else?"

"Isn't a car bombing enough?" said Landry.

Bullock said, "Two guards were attacked. One near the rear fence, the other over near the guesthouse." He pointed in the direction of the building. "Found them both unconscious. They were pretty burly guys. Whoever took them out was a force to be reckoned with. They finally came to. We questioned both, but they never saw who attacked them."

Puller gazed over at the guesthouse. "Anyone staying there currently?"

"No," replied Bullock.

"Is it okay if I take a walk around the grounds?"

"Looking for what?" asked Bullock.

"I usually know it when I see it."

He left them and walked around the edge of the property. He could see men in black shirts with sidearms and MP5s lurking here and there. Security. Who got their asses kicked tonight. And

Lampert would probably kick them again.

But why blow up the car? A message? Was it a message enough?

He looked at the main house ablaze in light.

Then his gaze ventured to the darkened guesthouse. Why one would require a guesthouse when you lived in a mansion bigger than the White House was beyond him. But he supposed at that income bracket, there were no items of necessity, only items of desire.

But then certain possibilities occurred to him. Why have security at the guesthouse if no one was currently there?

He ventured to one of the windows of the structure and hit the flowerbed with his penlight.

Nothing.

He moved around the house, checking the dirt.

Nothing.

Until the third try.

Footprints. Big ones. He held his own foot over one of the prints and came up short by a lot. He estimated a size sixteen. A big man. He took a picture of it with his cell phone.

Maybe just a yard worker cleaning the flower beds.

He looked through the window. Clean shot into what appeared to be a bedroom.

Okay, maybe it wasn't as simple as a yard worker. And the print was on the house side of the flower bed. Why get so close to the building?

The footprint didn't look particularly recent. It was hard to say, but they must have irrigation here. So he doubted it had been here longer than a day. Otherwise the water would have dissolved the print.

Now he needed to see what it was the person was looking at.

CHAPTER

51

The door was unlocked. The interior was dark. Puller used his penlight to see where he was going.

Technically he probably wasn't supposed to be in here, and he didn't want to call attention to the fact that he was. In his mind he figured out what room that window looked into.

A few moments later he stepped into the room.

Now he had confirmation that it was indeed a bedroom. If this had been a hotel room it would have been one Puller could never have afforded.

He eyed the bed. It was made, but Puller was used to the military precision of square corners and a bed tight enough to bounce a quarter off. This bed was not to that level. And it had a discernible imperfection.

There was a slight bump near the footboard. In the light it would have been hard to make out. In the dark, it was pretty much invisible. But not to Puller.

He carefully lifted up the bedcovers and shined his light under it.

It was a pair of women's panties. He snapped a picture with his cell phone camera. Someone had made the bed in haste and forgotten this item.

He put the bedcovers back down and glanced at the window. Perfect sightline to here.

He noted the two glass ring marks on the nightstand and sniffed them. Some of the liquid had spilled.

Not a big drinker, Puller still knew what it was by the smell.

Scotch.

It had been a favorite of his old man's.

He next scrutinized the bedposts and

saw the scratches on one of them. *Fingernails maybe?* He went into the adjacent bathroom, checked out the trash can, vanity, toiletries, shower, and toilet.

All of these things together were telling Puller a lot about what had happened in here.

When he went back out he saw it in the front room. He shined his penlight over it.

Someone had written on the wall in magic marker: *Your time is almost up, Pete.*

Puller glanced back at the bedroom door and then his gaze returned to the writing. He took a picture of it with his cell phone camera.

Now there was a message that was even more direct than blowing up your super-expensive car.

He had no doubt that the message had been seen. And he was certain it would have been erased in time. Bullock had made no mention of this, so obviously Lampert, if he had been in here, didn't want the police to know about it. And there was no reason for the police to come into the guesthouse.

And they hadn't.

Just Puller had.

He slipped out of the space and made his way back to the wreckage of the Bentley, where Landry was talking to Bullock.

He walked over to the tech, who was poking around the car's remains.

"Find the source of the explosion yet?"

"Pieces of it." He held up a baggie with a twisted fragment of scorched metal inside. "I think this is the detonator. At least part of it."

Puller took the bag and looked at it. He had seen debris like this before. In fact, he had seen enough IEDs in the Middle East to last him a lifetime. He had also analyzed the remains of many exploded IEDs. Most bombs had common components: explosive element, detonator, timer, and power source. But different bombers had different techniques for creating their stuff; the bomb signature, it was called. Puller had gotten to where he could tell at a glance which local bomber had constructed a certain IED.

This detonator debris, however, was not from the Middle East. At least it was not any that he recognized, and he was pretty confident he would have. So, other things being equal, the bomber had not come from that part of the world. It would have been a stretch anyway. A jihadist in Paradise, Florida? The irony was a little much.

Bullock and Landry joined him. Bullock pointed at the evidence baggie and said, "Anything strike you about that bomb fragment?"

"Well, I'm no ATF expert, but I've seen lots of Middle East bombs and this isn't one of them. If I had to guess I'd say it was more Russian than anything else."

"Russian!" Bullock looked stricken by this. "We got Russians blowing up cars in the Panhandle?"

"Not necessarily. The bomb might be Russian-made, but whoever set it off doesn't have to be. The Russians sell to whoever is willing to pay."

He handed the baggie back to the

tech and looked up at the main house. It was the biggest home he had ever seen. The guesthouse had been about four thousand square feet. He couldn't tell how many square feet this was. Perhaps they didn't use square feet when measuring it. Perhaps they used acres. And there were about forty-four thousand square feet in an acre.

Peter Lampert must do quite well for himself.

But his time was coming, at least according to the writing left in the guesthouse. He had already decided not to tell Bullock and Landry about it. He shouldn't have gone in the guesthouse, and by telling them he would have to admit to what he'd done.

Puller pointed at the house. "You questioned them yet?"

"Was just going to," said Bullock. "You want to sit in?"

Puller stared at him for a moment, suddenly disquieted by how nice the chief was being to him. Even Landry raised her eyebrows at this offer.

"I'll just be part of the peanut gallery."

"Suit yourself. But if something occurs to you, speak up. With all the crap that's happening I'm thinking I need all the help I can get. Otherwise I'm going to be the *former* police chief of Paradise."

They walked inside to question Peter J. Lampert and company.

CHAPTER

52

The first thing Puller noticed was that Peter Lampert was fully dressed. White slacks, dark shirt, and sandals. But his hair was slightly damp, so the guy had showered.

Showered at this hour of the night?

Maybe after having sex?

He wondered who else had showered.

Lampert was sipping a drink from a bar that spanned one entire wall of a room that seemed as big as an airplane hangar but was decorated to look like Buckingham Palace.

He came forward and held out his hand to Bullock. "Nice of you to come personally, Chief," he said in a pleasant voice.

Bullock nodded and shook his hand. "Sure thing, Mr. Lampert."

Lampert's gaze flitted across Landry and then came to rest on Puller. He gazed up at him as he jiggled the ice in his cut crystal glass. "And who do we have here?"

"John Puller," said Puller. "Army CID."

Bullock said quickly, "He's just here observing, Mr. Lampert."

Lampert kept his gaze on Puller for another few seconds and then smiled and finished off his drink.

"You're very calm for someone who just had his car blown up," said Puller, who had decided to step out of the peanut gallery.

Lampert held up the empty glass. "That's what thirty-year-old Macallan is for. Replenishes the spine in no time."

Scotch, thought Puller. Like in the guesthouse. Then it just came down to who did the underwear belong to?

Two more people came into the room,

a man and a woman. They looked like models for Ralph Lauren, all-American with nary a flaw. The man was in shorts and a T-shirt. The woman had on a light blue thigh-length silk robe. They apparently had been in bed when it had happened. Guy threw on whatever was handy. Lady stepped into her robe.

The woman's hair wasn't damp.

"James Winthrop and Christine Murdoch," Lampert said by way of introduction. "James works with me and Chrissy is his, uh, significant other." He gave Murdoch a little smile and then turned his attention back to Puller.

Puller checked out both of them closely. Winthrop looked scared, Murdoch simply intrigued. That was miles apart on the emotional barometer, and Puller wondered why the man and his "significant other" would be so dissimilar in their reactions to tonight's events. After all, a bomb was a bomb.

"Ofcourse we heard the explosion," said Murdoch.

"What time was that?" asked Bullock.

"I looked at my watch when I jumped

out of bed," she replied. "It was nearly a quarter past one."

Landry wrote this down in her notebook.

Bullock asked, "Did either of you see or hear anything unusual before or after the explosion?"

They both shook their heads.

Bullock gazed over at Lampert. "Where were you when it happened?" he said.

"I was in my room. My wife is out of town. I was reading a book and then all hell broke loose. Before that I didn't see or hear anything unusual."

Puller didn't know if Landry and Bullock had noticed the man's wet hair. Or wondered why Lampert was, unlike his guests, fully dressed.

"Did your security personnel see anyone?" asked Bullock.

"Not a thing, apparently. I thought they were the best in the business. Right now I feel like firing all of them and starting over."

He glanced at Puller. "Army CID?"

Puller nodded.

"And before that?"

"Ranger."

"Then you could be a first-rate security person. Whatever Uncle Sam's paying you, I'll double it."

Puller had no idea if the guy was being serious or not, but he said, "Sorry, doesn't work that way."

"Anything works, if you want it badly enough."

"Yeah," said Puller. "You have any idea who could have done this?"

"I've had a business career filled with ups and downs. I've made enemies."

"Screwing someone in business usually leads to a lawsuit, not a bombing," replied Puller.

"Who says I screwed anyone?" Lampert said, dropping his friendly demeanor.

Murdoch broke in. "I think he was just speaking in generalities, Peter."

Lampert kept his gaze on Puller. "Is that what it was? Generalities?"

"Let's assume it was. Anyone on that list who would blow up your car?"

"There might be."

Bullock said, "We'll need those names."

"Okay."

To Puller, Lampert looked uninterested by the whole thing. Most people who had had a bomb go off in their front yard would have been a little more stressed out. Lampert was either really stupid or there was a lot more to all of this. And Lampert didn't seem stupid.

"Anything else?" asked Lampert. "I need to get some sleep."

"We'll continue our investigation outside," said Bullock. "And we'll follow up tomorrow."

"Sounds good," Lampert replied.

Bullock and Landry turned to leave through the front door.

Murdoch and Winthrop turned to go back to their rooms.

Puller stood right where he was.

The light blue robe was quite tight. From behind Puller could see the outline of Murdoch's underwear. And the panties in the guesthouse seemed a little small to be hers. Not conclusive of course, but interesting nonetheless.

He glanced over and saw Lampert staring at him, like he had just read Puller's mind.

"You have any other guests staying with you, Mr. Lampert?" he asked.

A thin smile spread across Lampert's face. "Nope. Just the hired help."

Bullock and Landry had turned back when this exchange started. They both stared with puzzled looks at Puller.

"Just the hired help? Thanks, Mr. Lampert, that's all I needed to know."

Lampert smiled and held up his glass. "I'm sure it is, Mr. CID. I'm sure it is."

Puller walked out.

CHAPTER

53

Another eighty had been delivered to-night.

Just like clockwork.

Four boats' worth.

They looked just like the last shipment.

Destroyed.

Mecho watched from a different spot tonight. He did not like patterns. Patterns could get you killed. He had no reason to believe that anyone suspected he was here. But he had no reason to think they didn't either. He imagined these men lived their lives full of suspicion.

Just as he did.

After the bomb went off at Lampert's house they would have to proceed with caution. Calling off tonight's shipment might have been tempting for them, but apparently the allure of a mountain of dollars was too much. And the boat was probably already on its way when the Bentley had been blown up.

So the show went on.

These folks wore the color-coded clothing of the previous group. As he observed them Mecho concluded that tonight was heavy on drug mules and prostitutes, by far the most profitable. The simple laborers, the ones who silently mowed grass in nice southern suburbs or mutely hefted cartons in warehouses in the Midwest, brought the least amount of money.

But the profit margins were still excellent, just not off the scale like those associated with the drugs-and-hookers revenue streams.

The fourth RIB turned and headed back out to the mother ship.

Mecho turned his attention to the truck in which the eighty people had been placed. The rear door came down and was bolted shut. The back of the truck would be soundproofed, of course. No screams would be heard, though Mecho imagined the prisoners were probably too terrified to utter a sound.

He hustled to his scooter and climbed aboard. When the truck started off with its two-SUV motorcade, Mecho fell in behind it, keeping about eight hundred yards back. He did not worry about losing the vehicles. He had placed a tracking device on the underbelly of the truck while the first shipment of passengers was arriving on the beach. The guards had made the mistake of moving away from the vehicles to draw nearer to the beach, never thinking that leaving their rear flank exposed would be a problem.

Yet it was a problem, a big one. But one man's problem was another man's opportunity.

They traveled east for four miles, their

route gradually leading away from the Gulf as they did so.

The destination was not surprising: a warehouse in the middle of a decrepit industrial park. This was far away from the tourist traps and nowhere near the pristine white beaches or the emerald green waters.

This had the look and stench of the real world. A world where people toiled away for crap wages doing shit work and wondering when their ship was going to come in.

Mecho understood that very well. He had wondered that very same thing. Only far away from here. A universe away from here, in fact.

Where is my damn ship?

Well, maybe it was a RIB with human cattle on it.

After the truck drove through the open overhead door of the warehouse the door rattled down behind it. One SUV had driven in with the truck. The other had stayed outside. Mecho had a good idea what was happening inside the warehouse.

It was like U.S. Customs' processing

in a way, and in a way the farthest thing
from it. The folks in the truck were being led off, dressed in different clothes,
and given certain documentation, a bit
to eat, a few ounces of water to drink.
They were being told things. Things
that would further demoralize their spirits.

Such as, "You will do exactly as we
say."

And if you don't, not only will you die,
but your entire family, back in the little
village or town or city where we took
you from, will die too. No exceptions.
Ever.

The instructions would be given.
They would be able to sleep for a bit.
They would be segregated according
to their ultimate function. The future
prostitutes would be given the best ac-
commodations and rations. Their looks
and overall health mattered, at least for
now; later, they wouldn't. And then they
would be discarded, most drugged beyond rehab, and they'd shuffle away
and die alone.

The drug mules would be given things
too, things that would allow their in-

nards to receive more bags of drugs than they would have thought possible. Ten percent of them would suffer ruptures of these bags while they were still inside them. All ten percent would die from it. Heroin or coke pouring into one's bloodstream in such profound doses is not something the body was built to endure, because nowhere in the evolutionary chain did humans have to adapt to such treatment.

That was good for humanity, bad for the ten percent.

The ten percent was known, in the industry, as a reasonable and acceptable cost of business. Indeed, like credit card companies that jack up interest rates to cover losses from hackers and deadbeats, the slavers upped their chattel rates to cover these losses.

Businesses always passed the costs along, whether they were selling hammers or humans.

Again, there was nothing Mecho could do to help the eighty people in the warehouse tonight. That was not why he was here.

He sat on his scooter just outside the

gate of the fence that surrounded this industrial park and waited.

He took a photo out of his pocket. While it was dark and he had killed his scooter light before approaching the warehouse area, Mecho could see, in his mind's eye, the image of the young woman in the picture he held.

She looked a lot like Mecho. There was a reason for that.

Family was family.

Her name was Rada. In his language her name meant "joyfulness."

And she had once possessed it in abundance.

But no longer. That he knew without knowing it for certain.

Sometimes Mecho wished that Rada were dead.

Being alive and doing what she was doing must be worse than being dead.

He had no idea where in the world she was.

He had come here to get an idea.

But that was not all.

There were other pictures in his jacket pocket. All women. All young.

These women were not related to him.

But that did not matter. There was another connection, a strong one. That was enough for him.

He had no idea where in the world any of them were.

And it was a big world.

He needed help.

Tonight would begin his attempts to find such help.

An hour went by and the overhead door opened. The SUV zipped out and the door closed once more.

The second SUV stayed where it was while the first SUV approached the gates. They automatically opened and the SUV sped through them.

Mecho knew there were four men in the SUV.

As he started up his scooter to follow them it didn't matter to him which one of the four would provide the assistance.

He would work through them all until he got it. To him, they were no longer human. Just like they treated the people in the truck.

They were there for him to use, in any way he chose, to achieve his goals.

In a way he was a businessman too.

Only his incentive, his profit, was not measured in money.

It was measured in justice.

It was calculated in revenge.

And in Mecho's case, those two things were exactly the same.

CHAPTER

54

The hotel was far nicer than the Sierra. And it was right on the water.

The SUV was parked in the hotel's garage. The four men had ridden the elevator to the lobby and then gone on to their rooms. They each had their own, a perk of this job. Money obviously was no limitation.

The man who had ridden shotgun in the SUV reached his room on the fifteenth floor and opened the door with his key card. He slipped off his jacket, revealing his holstered Glock nine. He made a beeline for the minibar and mixed a gin and tonic, then went to the window and gazed out over the Gulf. He took a long breath and slipped a cigarette from his pocket and lit up.

It was a nonsmoking room but he apparently didn't care.

Thirty minutes later there was a knock at the door. Not his hotel room door, but the one connecting the room next to his. One of the other men was staying in that room.

He walked over to it. "Donny?"

"Yep."

"What's up?"

"Call from the boss, we got to roll," replied Donny.

"Shit."

"Got something for you," said Donny.

He opened the door.

The blow hit him so hard it lifted him off his feet and he flew backward and landed on the soft bed, his nose broken and his consciousness gone.

Donny stood there with a gun barrel held against his right temple. Mecho was behind him.

"Please, man, don't kill me," moaned Donny.

Mecho shoved him into the room and closed the door behind him. A ferocious blow to Donny's head dropped him to the floor.

When he awoke later he was tied to the bed along with his colleague, who was now awake as well. The two men looked at each other.

Mecho stood over them looking down. He duct-taped their mouths, pulled their pants and underwear down, and held the knife pointed at their privates.

When he cut him there, Donny screamed, but it was a nearly soundless one with the duct tape across his mouth.

The next instant Mecho slammed the knife straight into his chest so hard that the point came out the man's back and stuck into the mattress.

Donny's mouth sagged open as he died.

The other man looked in panic at his dead colleague.

Mecho took off the other man's duct tape.

The man braced for the strike of the knife, but Mecho just looked at him.

The man glanced at dead Donny. "Why did you kill him? He'd tell you anything you wanted to know."

"I killed him," said Mecho, "because I could."

"What do you want to know?" the other man said, his voice panicky.

Mecho sat on the bed next to him. "What is your name?" he asked quietly.

"Joe."

"Where are you from, Joe?"

"New Jersey."

"What is this New Jersey?"

"It's a state. Of the United States."

"Do you have a family?"

Joe hesitated, but Mecho pointed his blade at his chest and Joe said, "Wife and two little girls."

"In New Jersey?"

Joe nodded, his eyes filling with tears.

"And you want to see them again?"

"Yes," Joe gasped. "More than any-thing."

"And the people from the boats?"

Joe's chest heaved more and he sobbed. "It's just a job."

"They have family too."

"I just do it for the money, I swear to sweet Jesus. It's the only reason. I got nothing against those people."

"They have people they love and who love them."

"Just a damn job. That's all," moaned Joe.

Mecho took out the photo of Rada and held it in front of Joe. "Do you recognize this person? Her name is Rada."

Joe's eyes were so filled with tears that he could barely see.

"I . . . I don't know."

Mecho gripped him around the neck and jerked him upward as he thrust the picture closer. "Do you know her?"

"I . . . I'm not sure. Maybe."

"Her name is Rada."

"I don't know any of their names. We don't get names."

"She is a beautiful woman. About a month ago she came through here. Were you here then?"

Joe started to nod, sensing perhaps that if he had valuable intelligence it would keep him alive. "Wait a minute, yeah, I think I do remember her. Right, a month ago. Yeah, Rada."

"Rada," repeated Mecho. "One month ago."

"You want to find her, right? Maybe I can help."

"One month ago," said Mecho again. "Rada. She is beautiful."

"Absolutely," said Joe. "A real looker. I can help you. If you untie me—"

Mecho slammed the blade into Joe's chest and drove it in up to the hilt. Joe gave a shudder and joined Donny in the land of the dead.

Mecho stared down at him. "Rada has been gone for one year." He fingered the photo. "And this is not a picture of Rada."

He looked at dead Donny.

"And your friend already told me all I needed to know back in his room."

He pulled his knife free and some pent-up arterial blood squirted from the wound. With the heart no longer beating and zero blood pressure, there would not be any more significant blood loss.

Mecho said, "So you can see that I have no further need of your assistance. I perhaps forgot to mention that. Forgive me, Joe. I'm sure your family in this New Jersey place will mourn you."

He stood, wiped the blade off on the sheets, and stared down at the two men.

For the money. Just for the money.

They did not know the names. They never knew the names.

But I know their names.

I know them all.

CHAPTER

55

Puller sat in his room at the Gull Coast staring at the wall. Sadie was curled up at the end of his bed. The dog had drunk so much water that she had peed in the Tahoe. Puller had cleaned that up and then walked her before coming up to his room.

It was four a.m. and he had not yet been to sleep.

There were many items swirling through his mind.

At four-thirty he closed his eyes and willed himself to rest for three hours.

When he woke at half past seven

he felt like he'd slept for a full eight hours.

He showered and dressed, walked Sadie, and then fed her with food he had taken from Cookie's. He walked the dog again to let her do her business and then went out to eat breakfast, leaving Sadie back in the thankfully air-conditioned room. He knew he would have to make other arrangements for the dog, but that was not at the top of his priority list right now.

He walked two blocks to the waterfront and found a small diner with a fifties retro interior and ordered the biggest breakfast it offered. In deference to the heat outside—the temperature was already in the eighties—he had water with ice in lieu of coffee.

Fully fueled, he left the diner and walked down the street.

"Did you get enough to eat?"

He turned and saw her standing by a mailbox.

Julie Carson was not in uniform. She had on jeans, sandals, and a green sleeveless blouse.

She didn't look like the one-star that

she was. She looked like a tourist. A very fit, attractive tourist.

Puller walked over to her.

"I'm more than a little surprised, General," he said.

"I'll take that as a compliment since I know it's very difficult to surprise you, Agent Puller. And you can make it Julie. No uniform today."

"And you can make it John. When did you get in?"

"Grabbed a free seat on a cargo plane into Eglin. Little perks we generals get. Got in around midnight last night."

"And you found me how?"

"How many guys that look like you are in Paradise?"

He watched her, awaiting her real answer.

"Okay, I ran your credit card activity. Saw you checked into the Gull Coast."

"Then you should have had breakfast with me."

"I overslept. I knew you'd be up early to get chow. That diner seemed to be your sort of place. I was about to walk in when you walked out."

"And you're here why?"

"Had a week of leave I never took. Found out J2 could get along without me for a few days. Your description of Paradise sounded so inviting it was an easy decision."

"It might not meet your expectations."

"Let a girl decide that for herself, John."

"I take it you want to be updated on my investigation even though you're here on R and R?"

"I crave information. So why don't we go back into the diner and I can eat and you can have a gallon of water to keep hydrated and we can have ourselves a nice conversation?"

And they did exactly that.

Puller saw that Carson had an appetite. She put away eggs, pancakes, bacon, and grits, and while she drank three glasses of water, she also had two cups of coffee.

While she worked through her meal Puller brought her up to speed on all events, including the explosion at the Lampert mansion the night before.

Carson took one last sip of water and set her glass down. "You've been busy."

"I've been reactive, actually. Not an ideal situation."

"Eight guys. I'm impressed."

"I only took out six. If the big man hadn't been there we wouldn't be having this conversation."

"So if I've got this right, you're investigating your aunt's suspicious death. And her neighbor's murder. You also have the disappearance of this kid Diego. There are two guys down here following you who are so well connected the Pentagon gets stonewalled. And some rich prick gets his Bentley blown sky-high. And I almost forgot the murders on the beach."

"The two guys might not have been following me. They could have picked up my tail from when I visited my aunt."

"Meaning their focus was her not you, which lends credence to the theory that she was murdered."

"That's how I see it," said Puller.

"Which prompts the question of what the hell she was involved in that would get her that kind of attention. You sure she wasn't some retired spy with a dark past?"

"If she was, she was damn good at keeping her cover. No, I think she found out something down here and that's what got her killed. I wish she had been more specific in her letter, but she wasn't."

"You mentioned mileage on her car."

"Right. Five miles out and five back. At least that's my speculation. Jane Ryon said that five miles east seemed the best bet. But I'm not sure about her now, considering what happened to Cookie."

"Have the police found her?"

"Don't know. By now they should have, I guess."

"She might be able to clear some things up if she is involved."

"Maybe."

"So what's the next move?"

"You really sure about this, Julie? I mean, you don't have to do this."

"I've been covering enlisted men's backs most of my career. It's why I'm beloved by the rank and file. Besides, my last few vacations have followed similar patterns and have been pretty boring. And my J2 assignment, while necessary for my career path, is pretty damn uninteresting at times. I need some excitement."

Puller looked across the table at her. "Well, I think you came to the right place. But keep in mind that at least four people have died so far."

"I can take care of myself."

"I thought the same thing about me, and I almost bought it. The punks I dealt with are nothing special. I just messed up but got lucky. I can't count on being lucky again."

She looked across at him, her amused features turning more serious. "So we treat this just like combat?"

"Just like combat," he replied.

"So the next move?"

"The most obvious. We find out if the police have picked up Jane Ryon."

"And if they haven't?"

"Then we find her, before someone else does."

"You really think she killed this Cookie person?"

"I have no idea. But if she did, she also might have killed my aunt."

"And all the other stuff that's been happening down here, you think it's all connected?"

Puller thought about this for several long seconds while the sounds of traffic picked up out on the street as Paradise came to life.

"I don't believe in coincidences."

"Meaning what exactly?"

"Meaning exactly that I don't believe in coincidences."

CHAPTER

56

When they came out of the diner a police car was zipping past. It screeched to a stop and Cheryl Landry leaned her head out.

"You're not going to believe this," she began, before her gaze came to rest on Carson.

Puller noted this and said, "General Julie Carson, Officer Cheryl Landry."

As Puller's gaze swiveled between the two women he felt a pang of guilt. He had been out twice with Carson, though the first time was not a real date. However, he sensed the general was interested in something deeper than mere friendship. Landry clearly wanted a relationship with him. Thus having the two women together was deeply discomforting.

Carson nodded and said, "Nice to meet you, Officer Landry."

"I've never met a general before."

"Well, now you have, and we don't look any different from anyone else," said Carson.

"I won't believe what?" said Puller.

"Two more murders. At the Plaza Hotel two blocks down. Two guys in a bedroom stabbed to death, it appears."

"Two guys," said Puller quickly.

Landry nodded. "I know what you're thinking. I don't know if it's the same two who you think have been following you."

"You want us to come?" asked Puller.

Landry glanced at Carson and then at Puller.

Puller, sensing her indecision, said, "Make the offer to Bullock. He can make the call if he wants."

"Thanks."

"Did you pick up Jane Ryon?"

But Landry had already hit the gas and the car had sped off.

Puller looked at Carson. "Two more dead."

"Who knew Paradise could be so damn bloody," said Carson. "And of course it can't be a coincidence," she added, raising her eyebrows at him.

"Don't think so."

"So we wait until we get the okay from this Bullock guy? And what about Ryon?"

"We can check her out. But while we're here I want to find out something else."

She followed him down the street and away from the beach. The sun seemed to be fighting its way to the top of the sky with astonishing speed. Carson wiped a bead of sweat off her brow and picked up her pace so she was walking next to Puller.

"What's this place we're heading to?"

"Diego's."

They passed the Sierra and Puller arrived at the building with the blue awning. He marched up to the second

the other day. They might
you."

they tell me." Then her face
d and her shoulders started to
Puller put a hand under her arm
p the woman from slumping to
oor.

Vhat's wrong?" he asked her.

Los niños, they no here."

"Where are they?" asked Puller.

"*Donde están los niños*?" amended
Carson.

"*No sé. Desaparecido.*"

Puller looked at Carson. "They vanished?"

Carson nodded. "That's what she
said."

Puller said, "Have you called the police? *He llamado a la policía?*"

She shook her head. "*No policía.
Nunca la policía.*"

Carson said, "Doesn't sound as
though she likes the police very much."

"She could be undocumented. And
the kids too."

"Right."

Puller looked at the sobbing woman
and said to Carson, "it could be the

THE FORGOTTEN

story and knocke— on the —
came.

He knocke—

And then—

He heard —
slightly as Carso— locked —
tantly.

The door opened. —
it would be one of two—
or Isabel. Well, maybe —
counted little Mateo.

It was none of them.

The woman standing there w—
her sixties, short and plump with br—
hair streaked heavily with silver. He—
face was thickly lined and a prominent
mole had grown in the crevice between
her cheek and nose. She was dressed
in sweatpants, cheap sneakers, and a
dark top. She looked curiously from
Puller to Carson.

"*Sí?*"

So this was the *abuela*, thought
Puller, the grandmother.

"*Habla inglés, señora*?" asked Puller.

"Yes. *Poquito.*"

"My name is John Puller. I know Diego and Isabel and Mateo. I helped guys I beat up. But something feel me it's not. But Diego did help me track down the two guys."

"So the two guys made them disappear?"

"I guess that's the most likely answer. Diego was following them. Maybe they spotted him and Isabel and Mateo were with him." Puller felt sudden guilt for involving Diego in this.

"Unless the two guys are lying dead at the Plaza."

"Still could have been them. Diego and his cousins might have escaped from them."

"After killing the two guys?" Carson said skeptically.

Puller looked at the woman again. *"Lo siento. Podemos ayudar de alguna manera?"*

The woman shook her head and told Puller that only God could help her now. She shut the door and Puller stood staring off over Carson's shoulder.

"Should we report it?" she asked.

"We might do more harm than good if the kids are okay. They might end up getting deported."

"Better than being dead, John."

"Yeah, I know."

"We can ask around. Maybe someone has seen them."

"That's a good idea. Diego has some friends around here. They might know something."

It took them twenty minutes to locate two of Diego's friends. The first had not seen Diego for two days. The second one had seen him yesterday.

"Was he with anyone?" asked Puller.

The boy held out his hand.

Puller put a five-dollar bill in it.

"Yes."

"Who?" asked Carson.

The boy held out his hand again.

Carson put a dollar bill in it. The boy said nothing.

Puller said, "You tell us something useful there'll be more. Otherwise, the ATM is shut down for the day."

The boy looked around and said, "He is with the *dueños de la calle*."

"The street kings?" said Puller.

"Yes. The street kings."

"What is he doing with them?"

The boy held out his hand and Carson put another dollar bill in it.

"I think he is trying to join. If he is, he is stupid. They are a very bad gang."

"What about Isabel and Mateo?" Puller asked.

The boy withdrew his hand and put the cash in his pocket. He shrugged. "I do not know about them."

"Where do we find the street kings?" asked Puller.

"You do not want to find the street kings, *señor*," said the boy.

"Actually, yes, I do. Where?"

Puller held out a twenty. *"Ahora!"*

The boy gave them an address and then ran off.

Puller looked at Carson. "You don't have to go with me."

"The hell I don't. This is just getting interesting."

"You have any weapons?"

"You're asking a one-star if she has any weapons? Other women might like shoes and nail polish. I grew up on Winchesters and Colts on a farm in Oklahoma. So I brought some goodies with me."

"Okay. So we might want to gun up for this."

"Hell, John, I don't think there's any 'might' about it."

CHAPTER

57

The small shack sat behind an aban-
doned-looking building ten blocks off
the water. It was in an area that would
be discreetly described as in a transi-
tional stage, meaning don't go there at
night and also try to avoid it during the
day. The place looked dead and wasted
and nothing like Paradise and its emerald beaches relatively close by. It
seemed that the town's beauty was
only skin deep. A few layers under the
surface it became quite ugly.

Three young men were standing outside the building and taking turns toss-

ing knives at tin cans set atop a Dumpster. They were good enough that each one consistently knocked the cans over from a distance of ten feet.

"Decent aim."

The men whirled, their hands dipping to the guns in their waistbands.

And then they stopped reaching for their guns.

Puller stood there holding an MP5 set on two-shot bursts. Carson had not been kidding about weapons. And flying on military transport had allowed her to bring whatever guns she wanted.

"Wise decision," said Puller, coming forward and lifting his gaze past them and to the windows of the shack. They were covered and he saw no one trying to peek through to get a sightline on him with a weapon.

"Got a question."

The men looked at him warily. Puller could tell they were trying to think of some way to turn his tactical advantage into a disadvantage.

But he wasn't worried because the MP5 at close quarters was a difficult nut to crack.

"His name is Diego. He has two cousins. Isabel and Mateo. Where are they?"

The men said nothing.

Puller moved closer. "Diego, Isabel, and Mateo, where are they?"

The men remained silent.

Puller moved a foot closer. With one sweep of the MP he could lay all three down for eternity.

He shifted the fire selector on the MP to full auto. "I'll ask one more time and then I won't ask again."

"We don't know where they are," said one of the men, staring at the muzzle of the MP.

"But you did know, right?"

The three men looked at one another. The man who had spoken shrugged. "Hard to say."

"No, it's really not. You just have to say it."

Puller moved another foot closer.

The men smiled.

Puller thought he knew why.

"I wouldn't," said Puller. "I'm not the only one here."

The men stopped smiling.

It was in the corner of Puller's eye. A fourth man.

He'd come around the building's east side. He had a slim compact pistol aimed at Puller's head.

"Check your chest," said Puller.

The man flinched, looked nervous, but didn't look down, obviously suspecting a trick.

The other men glanced over. The one who had spoken swore under his breath as he saw the red dot squarely over the man's heart.

He said something in Spanish. The man with the gun looked down, saw the dot. He swore too, lowered his gun.

Puller pointed his MP at him. "Why don't you lose the gun and join the discussion group."

It wasn't a question.

The man dropped his gun and walked over to the others, the red dot following him the whole way.

"Diego and his cousins," said Puller. "They were here and now they're not. So where did they go?"

The four men glanced nervously at one another.

"Glancing and not talking tends to make me very angry," said Puller. "And when I get angry I do unpredictable things."

He put the fire selector back on two-shot bursts and fired some rounds above their heads. They all instinctively dropped to the dirt.

Puller eased his finger off the trigger and said, "Where?"

The men rose on trembling legs. One of them said, "They took them."

One of the other men glared at him and looked ready to punch his colleague.

The speaker sensed this but hurried on. "They were taken last night. The man paid one thousand dollars for them both."

"Both? Which both?"

"*Los niños. Diego y Mateo.*"

"Who paid one thousand dollars?" Puller said sharply.

"Like I said, *un hombre.*"

Two of the other men hissed, but the speaker looked defiantly back at them.

Puller said, "What was his name? What did he look like?"

Before the other man could answer there was a roaring sound. Puller looked to his left and saw the pickup trucks coming. In the truck beds were men standing and holding a lot of firepower and looking ominously in Puller's direction.

In Puller's earwig Carson's voice crackled. "I think retreat is the order of the day," she said.

Puller grabbed the man who had answered him and they ran off.

The trucks veered off to give chase, but several shots rang out and both trucks ground to a halt with flattened tires. Two men fell out of one truck bed as it screeched to a stop.

Puller turned the corner with the man in tow and saw the Tahoe up ahead. He double-timed it and saw Carson coming down from her high perch on another building carrying her scoped rifle. She jumped into the passenger seat. Puller threw the man into the rear seat and leapt into the driver's seat as he heard feet pounding down the road and men yelling in Spanish.

He hit the gas and the Tahoe sped

off, turned a corner, and disappeared in the maze of streets.

Carson had her rifle pointed at the man in the backseat. She studied him calmly. "What man took the boys?"

Puller glanced at her.

She said, "I heard over your earwig."

She looked at the man in the backseat. "We need some details."

The man shook his head.

"You've come this far," said Carson. "In for a dime, in for a dollar."

The man looked at Puller. "You are big. Like the other guy."

Puller glanced at him in the rearview. "What other guy?"

"The big guy. Bigger than you. He can fight."

"Is he staying at the Sierra?" asked Puller.

The man nodded. "He picked up one of our guys like he was nothing. Threw a knife twenty feet point-first into a wall. *El Diablo.*"

Puller glanced at Carson. "The same guy who saved my butt the other night."

Carson looked at the man. "*El Diablo* have a real name?"

The man shrugged. *"No sé."*

"Is he the one who took *los niños*?"

"No."

"Who did, then?"

"No sé."

Carson moved her finger closer to the trigger of her rifle.

A smile crept across the man's face. "You won't shoot me."

"Why?"

"Because you are military. A general."

Carson looked down at the one-star ring she had on.

The man said, "I was in the military once. Not yours. From my country."

"Sorry to see you've fallen so low," snapped Carson.

Puller said, "We want to help Diego and Mateo. That's all. Help us do that. They're just kids."

"They are beyond help."

"You don't know that."

"I know that. And I don't care. They're not my problem."

Carson looked at Puller and shrugged. "Open the door," she said.

The man said, "What?"

"Open your door and jump."

"What?"

"Jump!"

She pointed her gun at his crotch. "General or not, you jump now or you'll be missing some very vital parts."

The man kicked open the door and leapt out, tumbling along the road and then coming to a stop. They watched as he picked himself up and slowly limped off.

Puller said, "I like your style."

Carson eyed him with a stern gaze.

"What?" he said.

"Next time you go on R and R, pick a safer place than Paradise."

His phone buzzed. He answered it and listened for a bit before saying, "Okay." Then he clicked off.

Carson said, "Talk to me."

"I've been officially invited to join the murder investigation."

CHAPTER

58

Mecho studied the police officers.

He was bagging yard debris and the police officers were bagging the remains of a very expensive automobile.

Mecho wondered if they had found the bits of the license plate with "The Man" on it. He hoped not. He hoped it had been blown into the water and swallowed by a shark.

As he used a rake to collect some dead branches that had fallen to the ground, he watched the maid Beatriz walk across the lawn with a tray of lemonade and snacks. She was headed to the pool where Lampert and James Winthrop and Chrissy Murdoch were lounging. Her eyes were puffy and she kept her gaze downcast as she served the drinks and food. He watched Lampert eye her as she walked back across the lawn.

As she neared the house and was out of sight of the others, Mecho hoisted the bag of debris and used his long legs to reach a spot that would cross her path. She pulled up when she saw him. He was well over a foot taller than her and more than twice her weight.

He spoke to her in Spanish, asking her if everything was okay.

She mumbled that it was and kept walking. He kept pace beside her.

He asked more questions, and finally queried Beatriz about her employer. Her features hardened.

Mecho pounced on this vulnerability.

"I understand that your boss is leaving the country soon."

She looked sharply at him. "How do you know that?"

"One of his guys told me. Asia?"

"And Africa. At least that's what I overheard."

"When does he leave?"

"Why do you want to know?" she asked suspiciously.

"I was thinking of asking you out. It would probably be easier if he weren't around."

Whether she understood the significance of his words or not it was impossible to tell from her features.

"You want to ask me out?" she said slowly.

"I wasn't always a laborer," said Mecho truthfully. "I treat women with respect and courtesy."

"It is impossible."

"I understand."

She put a hand on his arm. "No, you do not understand. I am not allowed to leave the premises."

"You cannot leave here?"

She shook her head and said in a low voice, "It is not permitted. I should not even be talking to you."

"I am a nobody. They do not care about nobodies."

She glanced up at him. "I think you are somebody," she said hopefully.

"Is it the guards that keep you in here?"

"Not just the guards." She glanced over her shoulder in the direction of the pool.

"You could call the police."

She shook her head. "No."

"Why not?"

"It is not just me."

"I don't understand."

"There are others."

"Your family?"

She nodded, tears trickling from her eyes. She picked up her pace and hurried across the lawn and into the house.

Mecho slowed his walk and ambled over to the truck with his load of debris. He dumped it in the vehicle's rear bed and watched as Lampert walked down to the gate that led to the pier and unlocked the gate. The walls back here were wrought iron, six feet high. Lampert obviously didn't worry too much about prying eyes from the water. There was enough foliage to block the main house and guesthouse from observers on boats.

Mecho continued to watch as Lampert walked down the pier, climbed on board the yacht, and disappeared belowdecks.

I could kill him. And maybe I should.

But Mecho didn't move toward the boat. Part of it was practical. He counted five security men within his sightline.

He had no way to easily get through the gate. And he also had no weapon. Each time they had come here every man on the landscape crew had to walk through a magnetometer and then was wanded by the security detail. Lampert was a careful man. Before he even got to the big boat they would have shot him, and what would that have accomplished?

No, better to let the plan play out the way he had envisioned.

As he continued to work under a hot sun he thought about what the man Donny had told him last night at the hotel.

The shipments came nearly every

night. The last platform used as a staging area was twenty miles off the coast and to the west. Mecho believed that was the one he'd been on.

Mecho had also been told that the plan was to start smuggling even more people in beginning next month. This would include people from Asia and Africa. That made sense if Lampert were planning to travel to those continents.

How soon he would be leaving could be problematic. If things were not in place and he left before Mecho could act?

I will not let that happen. Even if I have to somehow shoot his plane out of the sky. He will not get away again.

Never again.

Mecho sensed someone watching him and turned to see Chrissy Murdoch staring at him from just off the pool deck. She had on a bikini with a short terrycloth cover-up over it.

He continued to work away as she walked over to him.

He knelt down and pulled at some

weeds around a flowerbed. He saw her painted toes stop a few inches from him. He looked up.

"Mecho?"

"Yes?"

"You work very hard."

He shrugged as he threw the weeds into a sack he had taken from the truck. "The only way I know. Hard."

She smiled at this as though the comment had amused her somehow. "Did you hear what happened last night?"

Mecho didn't look up. It was beyond odd that she was talking to him at all, and particularly about bombs exploding in the darkness.

"I saw the car," he said in a low voice.

"And you saw me too, didn't you?"

He looked up at her, shaded the glare of the sun with the width of his hand. "I do not understand."

"At the window of the guesthouse yesterday morning. You were looking. I saw your reflection in the mirror hanging on the wall."

Shit! thought Mecho.

"It's okay. I'm not upset or anything. Did you like what you saw?"

Was she playing with him? Yet for some reason he thought she really wanted to hear the answer.

"Did you like what you were doing?" he shot back.

She seemed to mull this. "It's complicated."

"Complex things are actually simple."

"Oh, you think so?"

"Don't you?"

"Maybe. What do you think? Did I like it?"

"No. But then again, it's none of my business."

She looked over his shoulder at the yacht. "He has the best of everything," she said. "Houses, planes, yachts."

"And you? Are you one of his bests?"

"You don't seem like a typical member of a landscaping crew."

"I came here for a better life. I have yet to find it. In my country I had a good job. I used my brains. Here, I just use my back."

"So why come here, then?"

"I had to."

"Were things bad in your country?"

"Things were bad," he said curtly.

"I see."

"Do you really see?"

She looked at him with a bemused expression. "Why do I think you're talking more about me than you?"

"Does the other man know?"

"James? James is lock, stock, and barrel with Peter."

"This is a phrase I don't understand."

"Peter owns James. So, no, he doesn't care."

"Then James is less than a man."

"A fact I know perfectly well."

"Why do you bother to talk to me? Because I saw?"

"I trust my gut on people. And you passed that test."

"That doesn't matter. People like you do not talk to people like me."

"Is that the rule?"

"Yes."

"I like to smash rules, Mecho. I always have."

He shrugged and went back to weeding.

"Will you be here much longer?" she asked.

"Will you?"

"I don't know. It's up to Peter."

The same for me, thought Mecho.

CHAPTER

59

The Plaza Hotel did not look like the far more famous one in New York City on the edge of Central Park. Its exterior was the usual beige stucco, its roof the usual terra-cotta tiles, and each balcony overlooking the water had columns shaped like palm trees.

Puller did not focus on the architecture of the building as he and Carson walked inside. He was thinking about Diego. And how to get him and Mateo back in something other than body bags. And he still had no clue where Isabel was.

"Do we tell the police about what just happened?" asked Carson as they hurried through the ornate lobby that had as its centerpiece a fountain with King Neptune in the center on a pedestal with dolphins and mermaids leaping around him. If it weren't so garish it might have actually been funny.

"Yes, we do. They need to get an APB out on the kids right now."

Landry met them at the elevator banks and they rode a car up to the floor where the murders had occurred. On the way Puller told her about Diego and Mateo and their run-in with the street kings.

"You're lucky to still be walking around. Those guys are real animals."

"They wouldn't last a minute in Afghanistan," said Puller.

"Amen to that," added Carson.

Landry called in this information. "I'll let you know as soon as we hear anything," she said after she got off the phone.

As they climbed off the elevator Puller caught Landry and Carson checking each other out in a way only women could do and most men would never even notice. But Puller noticed and, again, it made him uncomfortable.

The hotel room was empty except for Bullock and the two dead bodies. Other than that there was no visible sign that anything had been processed.

Bullock came over to them, and as if in answer to his thoughts he said, "Called in some support from the state police. And I'm trying to think of a way to engage the FBI. This is getting out of control. But I've heard nothing back yet. Florida's slashed its budget like every other state. Not sure we're going to be getting any help."

Puller was only half listening. His attention was on the bed where the two men lay. He drew closer, Carson right next to him.

"Who called it in?" asked Puller.

"Hotel. Room service came up here with a breakfast order one of the guys had put in the night before. No one answered. She opened the door and, to put it delicately, tossed her cookies along with the breakfast tray. Luckily someone cleaned that up before we got here."

"Those wounds look deep," said Carson.

"They are," replied Landry. "The knife blade came out the other side on both men."

"Long blade and strong killer," said Puller. He focused more on the faces. He had already seen that the two men were not the same pair that had been following him.

When Carson asked him about this, he shook his head. "No. Different guys. Never seen them before."

He looked at Landry. "Time of death?"

"The ME came in and did a quick look-see and pronounced death. She said between two and four last night."

Puller ran his gaze over the bodies. "Tied up." He looked closer at their faces. "Were their mouths taped? I see some residue."

"Apparently so, but the killer took the tape with him. And there's this."

Landry edged down the pants and underwear of one of the men.

"The killer cut his groin?" said Carson.

Landry nodded. "We saw the blood on the pants and the ME had a look."

Puller said, "Torture? Getting them to talk?"

"I guess that technique would work on most guys," observed Landry dryly.

"Who are these two?" asked Puller.

"Joe Watson is the guy on the right. This was his room. Stiff on the left is Donald Taggert. He was in the room next door."

"What else do we know about them?"

"Not much. They came down here about two weeks ago. They're both from New Jersey. We're checking into their backgrounds now. Next of kin being notified, all the standard stuff."

"Two weeks here," said Puller. "Pretty expensive."

"It can be, yes," said Landry.

"Nice suits," said Carson, edging up Watson's jacket to see the label. "Hands manicured, expensive shoes. There's money here for sure."

Bullock came over to join them. "And

a bombing at Lampert's place. Murders on the beach. Gangs attacking folks. I don't know what the hell is going on. Just last week this place was as peaceful as a small town in the middle of Kansas."

"Even small towns have problems," said Puller, thinking of his recent escapade in rural West Virginia.

"Well, right now I'll switch with any of them," replied Bullock. He looked inquiringly at Carson, and Puller quickly introduced her.

"A general?" said Bullock. "That's pretty impressive."

"Not really. The Army has a lot of one-stars."

"Not many who are women, I bet," said Bullock.

"The Army could definitely do better in that regard," agreed Carson.

Puller said, "Any leave-behinds from the killer?"

"Not much so far. No one saw anything. And unfortunately the hotel doesn't have security cameras in the corridors."

"Why not?' asked Carson.

"What happens in Paradise stays in Paradise," replied Bullock.

"Vegas has tons of surveillance cameras," she pointed out.

"In the casinos. And I guess we're a little more forgiving here."

"Not very forgiving to those two," said Puller, pointing at the dead men.

"How's the investigation coming with your aunt?" asked Landry.

"It's coming. Did you ever find Jane Ryon?"

"She wasn't at her home. We left messages on her phone for her to contact us."

"How about an APB?"

"We don't have enough cause to issue an APB. You just saw her driving down the street. She could have been coming from anyone's home, or just passing through the neighborhood. We learned she has other clients on that street. And the ME has not issued her report yet. We don't even know if it was a murder."

"So you're just going to wait to hear from her?" said Puller. "And if you don't? If she's already fled the country?"

Carson said, "You can put markers in the system for passport, credit card, and cell phone usage. She can be tracked that way."

Bullock looked doubtful. "I'd need a court order for that. Let's just try to work the case a bit more. I don't want to get my butt sued in case she's just off on vacation or something. And now I've got all this to deal with. *This*, we know, was a murder."

Puller turned back to the bodies on the bed. "What do you want me to do?"

"You're a trained investigator. Look around and tell me if you see anything that strikes you."

"I've got my evidence duffel in my car. If I'm going to look around I'd rather do it my way and professionally."

Bullock exclaimed, "Hell, have at it. I'm not too proud to admit I'm out of my depth here."

Puller left to get his duffel.

CHAPTER

60

Four hours later Puller rose off one knee and bagged one more piece of evidence. He gave all the bags to Landry and slipped off his latex gloves and booties.

Carson, Landry, and Bullock had watched Puller methodically work the crime scene, taking photos, measuring, dusting for prints, and generally scrubbing the room for any clues to the killer's identity. He had done both this room and the one next door.

"Army trained you well, John," said

Carson, looking impressed as he tossed his gloves and booties into his duffel.

"Yes, they did, *John*," Landry added hastily.

Puller tried not to think about the increasingly complex situation with the two women as he packed his tools away.

Bullock was sitting on the edge of a credenza. While Puller had worked away, Landry went for sandwiches and waters. They had eaten outside the room, at Puller's insistence, so as not to contaminate the crime scene.

"Any conclusions?" Bullock asked.

"Got a partial footprint near the edge of the bed in the other room. Dirt pattern that was probably carried in from outside. No obvious smells. Killer probably wasn't wearing any type of strong cologne that might have lingered. I did elimination prints on the dead guys. Those are most of the prints I found in the rooms. I would assume some others match hotel personnel. For elimination purposes, we'll need to print any of them who came up here."

"Unless it was someone working at

the hotel who killed them," Carson pointed out.

"Right," said Puller. "Then we'll need to print all of them."

Bullock said, "We'll get right on that." He nodded at Landry, who walked out to get it done.

Puller swept his gaze around the room. "Anything else?" asked Carson.

"Not forensically. I think we'll know more when we find out about the dead guys' backgrounds." He looked at Bullock. "These aren't street bangers. But you have drug problems here, right?"

"What city doesn't have drug problems?" he said stiffly.

"Any other issues here we should know about?"

Carson looked at Puller and then at Bullock.

The police chief stared back at the CID agent. "Like what?"

"I don't know. That's why I'm asking you. You know this town better than I do."

"There's nothing special about Paradise in the crime department. In fact, before this last wave of violence we were pretty clean."

Puller glanced at Carson.

Bullock caught his look and said, "You know something I don't?"

"People disappear here?" asked Puller.

"Disappear? What the hell do you mean? Spontaneous combustion?"

"Do they live here one day and then they're gone the next?"

"Missing persons? No. We don't get much of that."

"How many folks here are undocumented illegals?" asked Carson.

"This is a beach town on the Gulf. Unprotected border. Tourist destination. Cheap labor is important."

"Meaning you have a lot of undocumented," said Puller.

"I wouldn't say a lot."

"But if they went missing you wouldn't necessarily hear about it. I mean, folks might not report it."

"I guess they might not. But what are you getting at?"

"When I find out I'll let you know."

Landry said, "I'll fill you in, Chief.

Some kids are missing. We have an APB out on them."

Before Bullock could react to this, Puller hefted his duffel over his shoulder and looked at Carson. "You ready?"

"Let's go."

"You just gonna leave it at that?" said Bullock.

"I came down here to find out why my aunt died. I intend to finish that mission."

"And all the other stuff that's going on?"

"If it's connected to what happened to my aunt, then that too." He motioned with his hand to the bed. "You might want to get them out of here. The smell is only going to get more unpleasant, especially in this heat."

Carson followed him out as Bullock stood in the middle of the room looking at the dead men.

Puller loaded his duffel into the Tahoe and climbed into the driver's side while Carson got in the passenger seat. Landry hurried up to them.

"Are you heading out?" she asked.

"For now, yeah. You getting the elimination prints done?"

"Organizing it right now."

"Let me know when you find out anything about the two stiffs. They weren't down here for a vacation."

"I will."

Landry glanced at Carson and then back at Puller. "You have time to get together later?"

Puller licked his lips and felt the heat rise to his face. "That's a possibility. I'll give you a call."

Landry looked like she'd been slapped and she glanced once more at Carson. "Are you at the Gull Coast?"

At first Puller thought she was asking him, but then it became clear she wasn't.

Carson said, "Yes. Just checked in."

"I assume you're down here on vacation."

"I am."

"Then you might want to try a place closer to the beach. The Gull is a long walk. And you don't want to miss any rays."

"Thanks for the advice."

"You're welcome," she said curtly and then turned and stalked off.

Carson said, "Am I interrupting something?"

Puller put the Tahoe in gear and backed out of the space. "No," he said.

"Okay. Where are we going?"

"You want to hit the beach?"

"Is that what you want to do?" she asked, looking surprised.

"No. But I'm here working. You're not."

"I'm not a sun worshipper. And I'm here because you're here, so let's get to work."

"All right."

"So where to?"

"Where it all started. My aunt's house."

CHAPTER

61

"What are you looking for?"

Carson was staring at Puller, who was searching through his aunt's closet.

"Things that aren't here."

He went back outside, dug through his duffel, and pulled out the stapled pieces of paper, rifling through them. He counted down the items on the list and nodded his head.

"Breakthrough?" asked Carson.

"You could say that."

Puller slid the papers into his pocket and stared over at Cookie's house. Yellow police tape was still up, but there was no police cruiser parked out front. They were probably over at the new crime scene at the Plaza.

"John, what's going on?"

"Just trying to piece something together."

"About the murders?"

"Maybe. Maybe not."

She followed as he walked over to Cookie's house and through the gate into the backyard.

The house was dark.

The door was locked.

Ten seconds later the door was no longer locked.

"Army teach you that?" whispered Carson over his shoulder as he eased the door open.

"Army taught me a lot of things. Most of them useful."

She followed him inside.

"While I'm here I might as well get some stuff for the dog," he commented.

He opened some cabinets in the kitchen, found the doggie supplies, and piled them in a plastic bag he pulled from the recycling bin next to the pantry door.

"So you just came for the dog stuff?" asked Carson.

Puller didn't answer. He went over to the cabinet housing Cookie's watch collection. He counted off again.

"This is getting to be a little tiresome, Puller," Carson said, a bite in her tone.

"Just trying to add up the pieces before arriving at a course of action."

She looked at the watches. "And those figure in all this somehow?"

"They figure in something. But we've got one more place to check." He looked at his watch. "It's still too early yet. We've got some time to kill. Let's take a drive."

"Where?"

"Not where, really. More like how far. Five miles."

They left Cookie's house and climbed back into the Tahoe. Puller checked the rearview.

"See the two guys anywhere?"

"No, but I didn't expect to, really." He looked at his odometer. "Okay, five miles out, five miles back. We're going to head east. At least that seems to be the direction based on what Jane Ryon told me."

They left Orion Street and then the community of Sunset by the Sea. Three miles out they left any semblance of civilization behind. Four miles out it was only them, the sand, and the ocean.

Five miles out Puller stopped the truck and looked around. They were on the main street. To the north looked busier, with some buildings visible in the distance. To the south was a row of palm trees.

"The ocean has to be on the other side of those trees," said Puller.

"Provides a natural screen from the road," observed Carson.

They pulled down a side road and quickly found that beyond the trees was a section of thick brush, more trees, and some surface roads running through them.

And then the sand.

And then the ocean.

Puller swung the Tahoe to a stop on an asphalt park-off and they climbed out. He looked in all directions except toward the ocean.

"Pretty isolated here," he said. "No people."

"I wonder why?" asked Carson. "The beach looks pretty enough."

They walked toward it and quickly found out why the beach was not very popular. The sand was gritty, the beach was covered with sharp rocks, and then there was the smell.

Carson covered her nose. "Sulfur."

"Must be some geological quirk around here that makes this stretch of beach the way it is. And then there's that." He pointed at the large sign erected on a dune.

It read, *Warning. Strong riptide. No swimming allowed.*

"So not all of Paradise is a paradise," said Carson.

"I think we might have left Paradise about a half mile ago. Not sure what this place is called. Maybe it's nothing."

"It's a wonder that sulfur smell doesn't foul up the other beaches."

"Wind probably doesn't carry it that far," said Puller. "Or there might be some sort of meteorological reason. I didn't smell the sulfur until we got near the beach."

"Me either, come to think of it. But why in the world would your aunt come here?"

"I don't know. She was old, disabled. Used a walker."

"So walking on a beach like this would be problematic. I've almost fallen twice."

They stopped and looked around.

Puller fixed his gaze directly out at the ocean. "Any shipping channels out there?" he asked.

"I don't know. It's the Gulf of Mexico. I would imagine there are lots of ships coming and going. And then there's all the oil drilling platforms."

"Right. Like the one that popped and kept spewing oil for a long time."

"I remember when the BP well burst open. J2 was tracking it for security reasons. And we did some background on the area. There are thousands of oil platforms out there. Most of them are concentrated off the coasts of Louisiana, Mississippi, and Texas. But some extend over into the Panhandle."

"Oil is king."

"At least for now, yeah." Carson bent down, picked up a chunk of rock, and tossed it into the waves. "Can we go? I'm about to puke with this smell. And I'll need a shower to get the stink off."

"A lot of smells more gross than this in the military," said Puller dryly.

"True. But that doesn't mean I have to endure them when I'm on vacation."

They walked back to the Tahoe. Before they got in Puller stopped and knelt down.

Carson said, "What is it?"

"The king."

"Excuse me?"

She walked around to join him.

He ran his finger over the asphalt and it turned black. He lifted his finger to his nose and looked up at her.

"Oil. Not from a platform. From a vehicle."

CHAPTER

62

Mecho walked the lawnmower up the ramp of the truck and positioned it next to two other pieces of motorized equipment. He turned and stared back out across the Lampert estate. He didn't know how much the man spent on landscaping, but it must be a lot. They had come every day and worked all day. When one part was done it was time to move on to another. When the cycle was complete it started over again.

When he had asked the foreman about it the man had just shaken his head and muttered, "He spends more on grass than I'll make in my entire life. What's fair about that?"

"Life is not meant to be fair," Mecho had told him.

"You got that right," the man said. "Life is meant to suck. Unless you're rich."

"There are things other than money," Mecho said. "To bring happiness."

The foreman smirked. "Keep telling yourself that. You might actually start believing it."

"I do believe it," Mecho had said after the man walked off.

Mecho climbed down and washed the back of his neck with cold water from a bucket carried on the truck. He glanced toward the yacht. Lampert had never come back off it. He had been on there most of the day. But then again, when you had a yacht like that why would you get off?

Then Mecho wondered if he were there by himself. He doubted it.

He knew that Chrissy Murdoch was not there. He had seen her go into the house.

The maid Beatriz had not gone out there either.

But there were other women here. And one could have arrived directly at the yacht from the waterside via a tender and Mecho would not have been able to see it. The yacht blocked the water view along its full length.

Mecho looked back over at the guesthouse and then at the remains of the Bentley. The police had finally left, apparently having exhausted the evidence remaining at the crime scene.

Actually, they would not find any, because he had not left any. If they were looking for a bomb signature they would not find one. He had gone totally generic on that. It would provide them with a thousand possible paths to go down with nary a viable prosecution case at the end of any of them.

He looked up in time to see the sun reflecting off something in an upstairs room of the main house. He immediately walked in the opposite direction, took cover behind a tree, and knelt down, ostensibly to look for weeds to pull or mulch to tidy up.

From the partial cover provided by the tree canopy he looked up, shielding the sun's glare with one of his huge hands. He counted windows. Third floor, second window from the left. Southwestern side of the house.

He squinted to see if he could tell who was holding the optics. But he couldn't make out the person.

He ran a sightline from the window to what the person was looking at.

It was a simple process and yielded a simple answer.

The yacht.

With decent optics and from that height the person could probably make out quite a few details on the boat. Which also meant the person was well ahead of Mecho when it came to recon.

He saw Beatriz come out again.

Mecho moved swiftly enough to intersect her path. He walked along with her for a few paces. He asked the question that he needed answered.

She didn't seem to want to, perhaps thinking he was casing the place for a later burglary. But finally she did tell him.

Mecho thanked her and said that he would try to help her.

"How?" she immediately asked him.

"I can get you out, perhaps."

"You cannot do that," she replied, her face turning as pale as her almond skin would allow. "My family."

"I know," he said. "It's complicated."

"It is not complicated," she whispered back. "Do not do anything to help me. I am beyond help."

She turned and rushed off.

Mecho looked around to see if this conversation had engaged the interest of anyone, security types or otherwise.

He could see no one paying them any attention.

They were merely servants conversing. Perhaps it was expected.

Class to class.

It was only when you tried to mingle outside your class—steerage passengers emerging on the main decks during daylight hours—that people became upset.

But she had told him what he needed to know.

The room with the optics belonged to Christine Murdoch.

She was the one spying on Lampert and his yacht.

And Mecho wondered why that was so.

CHAPTER

63

Peter Lampert sat back in the leather chair that was located in his private office on *Lady Lucky*. He was surrounded by only the best here. The best boat, the best equipment, the best crew, the best wine, the best views, and the best ass money could buy.

It had been a long slog for him, though. South Beach was a rough place to survive, much less build a successful business. Lampert had tried the legitimate side for a long time. But ultimately he found it too stifling with all its rules and regulations and laws that could trip you up. He did not like regulatory agencies looking over his shoulder. He didn't know of one businessman who did.

After his hedge fund had imploded he had decided to build a different business model. Thus he had taken his talents to another line of work. He had installed proven business systems in a field that often existed on crude violence and sketchy accounting.

Now he had built an incredibly profitable empire by charging fees tied to profitability, like royalties on a book. He charged a standard fee up front to find and transport product to the end user. If the product hit certain benchmarks once deployed in the field, additional monies started to flow back to him.

If a prostitute reaped over six figures then monies started to come back to him. If a drug mule successfully completed ten missions, monies started to flow back to him. The lowest-level product, the common laborer, typically had a more modest threshold to meet because their initial cost was the least. But the profits generated by them

added up because there were so many
of them deployed in the field. Volume
was volume.

Slave labor in civilized countries was
one of the fastest-growing segments of
the criminal world. Not that he ever saw
anything remotely criminal about it. To
Lampert he was doing these poor folks
a favor. As slaves they were fed and
housed and lived a decent life, despite
the fact that they were not free.

He had often had these people taken
from worlds where there was never
enough to eat, never a roof over their
heads, and where wages were something one dreamt about but never actually received.

Freedom was vastly overrated in his
mind.

He had accountants placed in stra-
tegic areas with full access to the books
of his business associates. These associates, often not the most cooperative of men, had fallen in line with his
demands solely because he had made
the business far more lucrative and
stable than it ever had been before.
And he guaranteed a steady stream of

product across all service lines. That was the most critical factor in his business and it demanded constant foraging for bodies in some of the most remote places on earth. There was no margin of error in this segment of the business.

As a result a boat that was late with product was a boat that would not be sitting above the water much longer, along with its captain and crew.

He looked out the starboard window and checked his watch. Then he glanced back at the computer screen over which a stream of business data poured over secure networks.

He played hard, but he also worked hard. It was not easy building what he had. Most people would not have the nerve or stomach for it. He had been born with a silver spoon in his mouth on the shores of Lake Michigan. His father had been CEO of a Fortune 500 company. His mother was a beautiful socialite who entertained often and lavishly at their multiple homes. They had lived the life that most Americans dreamed of.

He had gone to the most elite univer-
sities and set up shop on Wall Street
along with a gaggle of his classmates.
Many were now titans of industry and
preferred to keep the money and influ-
ence that came with it in tightly controlled circles of people who were just
like them. Upward mobility was nice to
talk about to the masses, but not something that people at his level ever really
took seriously. The pie was only so big.
Why share it with folks who did not
share your values?

Your vision for the future?

Your fraternity affiliation?

What most people didn't understand
was that it was the risk-takers who
made America great. It was said that
the rich had captured nearly all the
wealth and all of the income generated
over the last decade or so. Well, Lampert thought, they should. It was right
and just. The only thing wrong with income inequality was that it wasn't un-
equal enough.

The 99.9 percenters were sheep and
stuck right where they should be. They
were the players to be named later.

There were billions and billions of them and they looked exactly the same. The 0.1 percenters deserved everything because they were the elites. They were special. They moved the world to new heights.

And it didn't deter Lampert in the least that he was acting on the wrong side of the law. People wanted whores and drugs and slave laborers. Thus there was a need.

He was simply fulfilling that need. Nothing more, nothing less. Like cigarette manufacturers, porn sites, fast food outlets, and casinos fed people's desires and addictions. That simple model had driven business success for all of recorded history.

Find a need and fill it as hard as you can.

Ten minutes later he checked his watch again and looked out the window. It was growing dark. That was good.

An hour later he heard the *thump-thump*.

He rose and looked out the window. The lights of the chopper were drawing

closer, coming in from the Gulf where a
boat larger than the one Lampert was
on lay at anchor.

A few minutes later he felt the wheels
of the bird come to rest on the helipad
at the aft of the yacht. The chopper
powered down and he could envision
but not hear over the sounds of the engine the doors of the aircraft opening
and then thunking closed.

He sat back down in his chair, put
his fingers together, and waited, counting off the seconds in his head.

The door to his office opened and
the person came in, escorted by a
member of Lampert's security team.

With a curt nod Lampert dismissed
the guard, who closed the door behind
him.

The visitor was around five-eight and
strongly built, with a head that was too
large by half for even his muscular
frame.

There was a lot contained in that
overly big head, Lampert knew.

The man was dressed all in black.
His shoes had blocky heels to push his
height up as much as possible.

It was enlightening, thought Lampert, that a man that powerful still felt compelled to artificially inflate his stature.

He nodded at Lampert and sat down across from him.

"Good trip?" asked Lampert.

The man flicked a cigarette from his shirt pocket and lit up without asking whether it was permitted or not.

Lampert would not have questioned the man's decision to smoke on his floating palace.

Peter Lampert did not fear many people.

The man sitting across from him was one whom he did fear.

"A trip that ends safely at one's destination is, de facto, a good trip," said the other man in an accent that showed that English was not his primary language.

"Things are going well," said Lampert.

"Things could be better," said the man as he exhaled smoke and watched it float toward the elaborately carved ceiling.

"Things could always be better," replied Lampert, leaning forward a bit in his chair.

The other man tapped his cigarette ash against the arm of his chair, letting it fall to the carpet.

Lampert did not object or even react to this.

"Things could be better," said the man again. "For example, there have been a number of killings in Paradise. The police are investigating. Your car was bombed. Again, the police are investigating." He stopped talking and stared across the width of the desk.

Lampert's expression didn't change. "Steps had to be taken. The fallout is what it is. The investigations will lead nowhere." He might be afraid of the man, but he could not show that fear. And Lampert could debate a point with the best of them.

"*Your* opinion that the investigation will not go anywhere," said the man, studying him closely as he bent the fired match between his two fingers.

"My *educated* opinion based on conditions on the ground."

"And if you're wrong?"

"I don't believe that I am."

"But if you are?"

"There will be consequences."

"Of course there will be. For *you*."

"Then I have every incentive to make sure I'm right."

The man eased a bit to the left, making the leather seat squeak. "Moving on. It's getting more difficult to acquire product. The price has to go up. You'll send this down the line."

"How much?"

"Ten percent for now. As a base. Add five percent for each category above base."

"Meaning a twenty percent increase for the top tier?"

"Yes."

"That's steep."

"It could be more. But I'm a reasonable man."

"I'll have to eat some of that."

The man looked around at the luxurious interior of the yacht. "I think you'll be just fine."

"I'm sure I will."

"So long as your educated opinion

turns out to be right. Money isn't everything."

Lampert smiled. "I would disagree
with you there. Money *is* everything,
because it leads to everything else of
value."

"Would you like to visit my boat? I
have a new submarine. It can hold over
thirty people. The marine life here is
quite fascinating."

"I would like to, but demands here
will prevent me."

Lampert was thinking, *I don't actually want to become part of the marine
life.*

The man rose. "Someone who blows
up Bentleys and disappears like a wisp
of smoke is someone who is formidable. It was a message."

"Yes, it was. Perhaps more directly
than you know."

"And you have the answer?"

"Working on it as we speak."

"A small measure of advice?"

Lampert looked up at him expectantly. "I'd love to hear it."

"Smoke often evidences a large fire
that can burn out of control." He paused

and put out his cigarette on the surface of Lampert's forty-thousand-dollar custom-built desk. "So work faster."

The next moment he was gone.

Like a wisp of smoke blown out to sea.

CHAPTER

64

Mecho lifted his head slightly out of the water and watched the chopper lift off from the helipad and head south out to sea.

He turned on his back and used small strokes of his hands to propel him closer to the boat.

There was security on the main deck and two men on the pier holding MP5s. However, they had no one in the water. That was a large breach in security. But then again the sharks would be out now.

And while Lampert paid well, he apparently didn't pay *that* well.

Mecho drew close enough to the boat to touch its hull on the starboard side. He looked out to sea where the lights of the chopper were still visible.

From land and with the aid of binoculars he had caught a glimpse of the man who had first climbed off and then climbed back on the bird.

Mecho had known instantly who he was.

Stiven Rojas.

Police around the world would pale at the name.

There had never been a successful prosecution of Rojas, though many had been attempted. But when witnesses, prosecutors, and even judges are slain during the course of a trial, convictions are exceedingly rare. He had given a whole new definition to the term "ruthless" and would make some of the world's worst terrorists look innocuous by comparison.

He had started as an orphan on the streets of Cali and built himself into a cartel chief of near mythic proportions.

Despite his modest stature, men twice his size would drop to their knees at his approach. He would kill without warning or provocation. He was not simply a sociopath who happened to be a global criminal.

He was *the* sociopath who happened to be a global criminal.

But something had come along that even Rojas had not anticipated.

Rojas had watched his hemisphere's drug pipeline into America move from his native Colombia to Mexico. But then he had adapted to a new business line. He would provide the mules to move the drugs throughout the United States. And along with that he would move other valuable product, namely prostitutes and slaves. Slaves in particular were the new growth market. Forget illegal immigrants. They expected to be free, and paid at least something. Slaves expected nothing. They just hoped not to die. Everything after that was a positive for them—not that there was much that was positive.

Rojas and Lampert were partners in

the largest slave ring in the world. And they were poised to make it even larger.

Unless they were stopped.

Still in the water, Mecho moved down the starboard side of the ship. There was a line of portholes low enough for him to see in. He gripped one and pulled himself partially out of the water.

The room he was looking into was dark. And empty. He lowered himself back into the water and moved to the next window.

It was on the fourth porthole that he found something other than dark and empty.

Beatriz was still dressed in her maid's uniform. She stood in one corner while Lampert sat at a table and ate his dinner. He ate slowly, chewing his food methodically. When he glanced at the bottle of wine within a few inches of his arm, Beatriz shot forward and refilled his glass.

As she bent slightly forward to do so Lampert's hand slipped to her bottom and grabbed. She didn't jerk or drop the bottle. She was apparently used to this treatment. She finished pouring the wine and retreated to the corner, her gaze downcast.

A minute later Lampert glanced at the basket of rolls.

Beatriz shot forward again, picked up one roll, broke it open, and used a small knife to butter it.

While she did this Lampert cupped her left breast with his hand and snaked his other hand under her skirt. As she buttered the roll Mecho could see her face. Bubbling just below the surface was anguish, coupled with a hatred that Mecho, in all his life, had rarely seen. He saw her hand tremble ever so slightly with the knife in it. He knew what she wanted to do. Even as Lampert stroked her she wanted to take the blade and stick it into his chest.

Mecho wondered why she didn't do so.

Just do it, Beatriz!

Then he looked to the right and saw why she didn't.

A man stood there with a gun pointed straight at Beatriz's head.

She finished buttering the roll, placed it on Lampert's bread plate, set the knife down, and once more retreated to the corner.

The man with the gun relaxed his stance and holstered his weapon.

Mecho sank back into the water.

Peter J. Lampert was not a man who took chances.

Mecho let the current pull him away from the yacht. When he was far enough away he struck out with long, powerful strokes.

And with every stroke he imagined plunging a knife into Lampert's chest.

CHAPTER

65

Puller was driving fast.

Carson eyed him from the passenger seat.

"So where are we going now?"

"I need to see my lawyer," Puller answered cryptically.

When they reached the street on which Griffin Mason had his law office, Puller parked the Tahoe at the curb about a hundred yards down from it. He reached into his duffel and pulled out his pair of night-vision optics and put them to his eyes. He trained them on Mason's office.

Carson followed his gaze.

"Your lawyer?"

"Actually, my aunt's lawyer. He's handling her estate."

"And how is Mason doing handling her estate?"

"Not so good."

Puller eyed the other buildings on the street. They were all dark.

There was no car in Mason's driveway. No lights on in the office.

"How do you feel about a little breaking and entering?" he asked.

"It's a felony. That's how I feel about it."

"Then you can wait here. I'll be back shortly."

She grabbed his arm. "Puller, think about this. You don't want to piss away your military career, do you?"

"What I want is to do right by my aunt. And that includes taking a hard whack at a creep who's screwing her. And others."

Carson sighed. "I'll come. I can keep lookout."

"It wasn't fair to ask you. You have a lot bigger career to lose than I do."

"So don't get caught. And if you do I'll disavow all knowledge."

"And I'll back that statement up one hundred percent."

"You're damn right you will, soldier."

A few moments later they were walking down the street. When they got to Mason's place, Puller hooked a left and entered the man's backyard. At the fence he told Carson to wait and keep watch.

"This shouldn't take too long," he said.

"Make sure it doesn't."

Mason had a security system, but one glance through the back-door window told Puller that it was not armed. The green light on the panel was lit.

Puller was surprised by this. Why have a security system if you didn't use it?

The door lock was a deadbolt that took Puller only a few seconds to defeat using a pick gun from his duffel.

He opened the door and penlighted his way to the lawyer's interior office.

It took him about thirty minutes to find what he was looking for.

Mason was meticulous in his record-keeping.

A little too meticulous.

Puller looked at the pages he had brought with him, the inventory list Mason had given him about his aunt's personal items. He checked it against the inventory list Mason had in the files.

It matched down to the last item.

He next searched for and found the inventory list for Cookie's estate. He ran his gaze down it.

Puller saw what he knew he would see.

He put Cookie's inventory list in his pocket along with his aunt's. He shut the file drawer and looked around.

He thought about what the other estates attorney, Sheila Dowdy, had said.

Mason's other car was an Aston Martin. He took expensive vacations. He had a big house.

It was all adding up, the pieces falling into place faster and easier than was normally the case.

The next moment his phone vibrated.

He looked at the text.

Bogie on our six, the text from Carson said.

Someone had just pulled into the driveway of Mason's office.

Now Puller could understand why the security system had not been engaged.

This also told him that it probably wasn't Mason coming back to work. He would have armed and then disarmed the system. This was someone whom Mason did not want to give his passcode to.

And maybe the person wasn't supposed to be here at all.

He thumbed a text back to Carson.

Description?

Blue subcompact. Young slender woman with blonde hair.

As Puller read the text he knew they didn't have to look for Jane Ryon any longer.

She had come to them.

CHAPTER

66

"Taking something or bringing something?"

Jane Ryon screamed and jumped backward as the light came on.

Puller stood there staring directly at her.

When Ryon turned to run, she pitched headlong into Carson, who stepped into the other doorway.

Ryon bounced off Carson, but before she could move again, Puller had her wrist clamped with his hand. She didn't even try to tug herself free, understanding that that was impossible.

"What are you doing here?" asked Puller.

"I could ask you the same thing," she said defiantly. "I have permission to be here." She held up a key. "Mr. Mason gave me this."

"And why would Mason give you a key to his office?" asked Carson.

Ryon looked at her. "Why is that any of your business?"

"I saw you leaving Cookie's house last night, Jane," said Puller. "And then I found Cookie lying in the bottom of his bathtub."

Puller watched her intently for any reaction to this.

"Cookie's dead?"

He shook his head sadly. "You're not a very good poker player, Jane. You knew he was dead," said Puller. "And the police are looking for you. Where have you been hiding out?"

"I haven't been hiding. Why would I hide? Why would I hurt Cookie? I liked him."

With his free hand Puller slipped the stapled pieces of paper from his pocket.

"Inventory list of my aunt's personal

possessions. Mason gave it to me. The only problem is it doesn't list all of my aunt's jewelry. There are two rings, three sets of earrings, and a necklace missing. All looked pretty valuable. And a dozen old gold coins are also missing from a coin book she had."

"I wouldn't know anything about that," said Ryon.

"Actually, you know everything about it. Those pieces were in your bag when I ran into you at my aunt's house. I had told Mason that I was going to my aunt's house in the morning, but then I changed my mind and went that night. He had sent you to the house to get the jewelry and coins before I would have a chance to go through her things. You had already inventoried the items and then Mason had decided which ones he wanted you to rip off and changed the real inventory list to reflect those subtractions. But you had to get them out before I saw them. Or so he thought. The fact is I had already seen my aunt's jewelry and coins before you got to the house, only he didn't know that. When I went back to check later those items were gone. You took them. You did the same thing to Cookie. You took some of his watches. I found the inventory list for Cookie's property in the file here. It didn't list the watches that were missing. And I know they were missing because Cookie showed me his collection.

"You and Mason have a nice scam going. You get inside the houses of elderly people that Mason represents and find out what their valuables are. Then when they die, you take them and Mason alters the inventory list accordingly, fences the items, and the poor heirs aren't any the wiser. Then Mason can afford his Aston Martin and trips around the world, and I'm betting you're damn well paid for your part."

Ryon's face had been growing paler with each word spoken by Puller.

Carson added, "And maybe you help your targets into the hereafter. You kill Cookie and that way you get his property faster."

"I didn't kill Cookie."

"But you were in his house."

Puller stared at her bag. "Open it."

"What?"

"Open your bag."

"You have no right to—"

Puller grabbed the bag and opened it. Wrapped in a silk scarf were four of Cookie's watches.

Puller stared down at her. "Say good-bye to your life, Jane."

Ryon was crying. "I didn't kill him. I swear to God I didn't."

"Tell the police that. You just walked into his house, took his property that you could only take after he was dead, and he was coincidentally dead upstairs in the bath. It might give the jury a nice laugh before they sentence you to prison for the rest of your life."

"Mason told me to go there and get the watches. So I did."

"He told you to do that?"

"Yes!" she exclaimed.

"Didn't you wonder how that was possible with Cookie still being alive?"

She took a shuddering breath. "Okay, look. He . . . he told me that Cookie was . . . was dead," she said in a trembling voice.

"And how did he know that?"

"I don't know."

Carson looked at Puller. "Mason kills him for some reason, then orders her up to get the stuff."

"Why wouldn't Grif just snag the watches if he was already there?" asked Ryon.

"So it's Grif now and not Mr. Mason?" Puller looked at her and shook his head wearily. "And the answer is because he wanted you to take the stuff, not him. That would put you at the scene of the crime. As soon as you found out Cookie was dead, you'd get suspicious. But you're not going to say anything because you were in the house too. He set you up."

"That little son of a bitch," snarled Ryon, who was no longer crying.

"But why would he kill Cookie?" asked Carson.

Puller put his hand on Ryon's shoulder and gripped. "Any ideas on that?"

"No. He never mentioned anything to me about it. He would have no reason to kill Cookie."

"When did he call you to go over to Cookie's?" asked Puller.

"Last night. I was in the area, so it only took me a few minutes to get there."

"Would Mason have been at Cookie's?"

"I don't know. Maybe he went over for a drink. Or to get some baked goodies," she said callously.

Puller shook her. "An old man is dead. Did you have anything to do with my aunt's death?"

"I swear I didn't."

"Why don't I believe you?" said Puller.

"I'm telling the truth," exclaimed Ryon.

"Well, a jury will determine that. Now, where is the little son of a bitch?" asked Puller.

"I don't know."

He shook her again. "Not good enough. Try again."

"Is he at his home?" asked Carson.

"No, I don't think so."

"Why not?" asked Puller.

"He has another place he goes to. It's more isolated."

"Why does he want isolation?" asked Puller.

"He just does sometimes."

"Does it have to do with the photos of kids he has in his wallet?"

Ryon looked up at him, stunned. "What are you talking about?"

"The guy's a pedophile?" snapped Carson.

"Where is this place?" asked Puller sharply.

"It's north of here, up near the bay. Nothing else really around it."

"You have the address?"

"Yes."

"Why, do you like kids too?"

"No, of course not," shouted Ryon, and she started to cry again.

Puller squeezed her shoulder once more and cupped her chin and directed her gaze right at him.

"We're going to give you a chance to make amends, Jane. But you only get one shot. You blow this, it's all over. Do you understand?"

She looked back at him, the fear etched on her face.

"I understand."

CHAPTER

67

Mecho put his phone away after making the call.

It was the longest he ever had been on the phone. The man on the other end was critical to the success of Mecho's task. The man knew this and Mecho knew this.

It was give-and-take. What the man wanted Mecho would have to give him, if he wanted to succeed. And he had never wanted anything more in his life.

"You will have to prove that to me, Mecho," the man had said. "Words are available to anyone with a mouth and half a brain."

"It will be done," Mecho had told him. Now he just had to figure out how.

He left his room at the Sierra and walked to a diner nearby. He ate lightly for such a massive person. He had never eaten very much for the simple reason that he had never had much available to eat. Over the years one's stomach and appetite withered.

But it was partly the hunger that drove him, kept him on edge. Complacency and comfort were not words that he accepted or even understood.

He drank copious amounts of water, though. The physical ordeal of swimming through the Gulf still lingered. He felt like he would never get enough liquid inside him.

He paid for the meal with some of the dollars he'd earned keeping Peter Lampert's property pristine.

He considered it blood money. Anything that helped the man was blood money in Mecho's mind.

He looked around the small diner and was not unduly surprised to see two uniformed police officers eating their meals. They sat near the door. A man and a woman.

The male was short and burly with a shaved head. The woman was taller with an athletic build and blonde hair. They were having an intense discussion. The man looked upset, the woman looked consoling.

It seemed to be a woman's lot in life to ease the ridiculous anger of men, thought Mecho.

As he rose to leave, both officers' gazes rose to meet his.

He nodded, attempted a smile, and walked out.

He did not much care for the police. For him they were as much an adversary as his actual one. They were bound to uphold the law.

There was no law that would ever touch Peter Lampert or Stiven Rojas. They were too clever and too dangerous by half for anything as impotent as laws to bother them. They had to be punished in other, more straightforward ways.

He walked down the street, trickles

of sweat winding down his shoulders and broad back. He opted to take a stroll on the beach, to attempt to catch an ocean breeze before he headed back to the little oven that was his room.

He trudged across the sand, oblivious to the other beachcombers, but his antennae were still on high alert.

Or so he thought.

"Mecho?"

He turned but he already knew who the speaker was.

Chrissy Murdoch stood there, sandals in hand. She had on a white sundress and the wind whipped it around her long legs.

Mecho simply stood there, neither advancing nor retreating.

She walked toward him, looked up at him.

"Why are you here?" he asked.

"I was just walking on the beach and saw you."

"Mr. Lampert has a private beach nicer than this one."

"I suppose he does. I'm surprised you know that, though."

"Enjoy your walk."

He turned to walk back to the Sierra. Every warning bell he possessed was clanging so hard he felt almost deafened.

"Mecho?"

He stopped but did not turn back around.

He felt her hand on his arm.

Still he didn't look at her.

"I understand that you were asking about the whereabouts of my bedroom," she said.

This question was not the one he had been expecting.

She stood in front of him.

"Was there a reason for your inquiry?" she asked. "Beyond the obvious one?"

"What is the obvious one?"

She smiled disarmingly. "Sex, of course."

He did not smile back. He had no reason to smile. She was playing an odd sort of game with him. But of course it wasn't a game at all. It was never a game when people died.

"I doubt that the guards would let me into the main house."

"Well, we're not at the main house right now, are we? Where are you staying?"

He turned and trudged off down the sand.

She followed, her feet making springy steps over the sand.

He stopped so abruptly that she almost bumped into him. He turned, looked down at her.

"So what is the non-obvious reason?" he asked.

She didn't seem surprised by the question.

"Since it's not obvious, I'm not really sure."

"You treat everything so casually?" he asked.

"Your English is much better in town."

"I learn quickly."

"About my bedroom?"

"Who told you I was making inquiries?"

"I like being on the top floor. It gives one some interesting perspectives."

"On what?"

"Lots of things."

"Why are you at Lampert's?"

"I'm staying with Mr. Winthrop."

"The man who doesn't care if another man screws you?"

"There are lots of men like that, Mecho."

"I am not like that."

"No, I would imagine you wouldn't be." She slipped her sandals back on. "The sand is so hot even at this hour. So where are you staying?"

"Why do you want to know?"

"I like to know things."

He turned and walked off.

"I can find out, you know. On my own."

He stopped and turned back as she drew closer.

"What do you want?" he asked.

"Maybe the same thing you want."

"How would you know what I want?"

"Perhaps you're not as subtle as you think you are."

Mecho stared right through her.

"The thing is, Mecho, I'm not sure we can both get what we want. Only one of us can."

"Only one of us can," he repeated.

He turned and walked off. This time

she did not follow and he did not look back.

Mecho was thinking only one thing. *I will have to kill her after all.*

CHAPTER

68

"Jane, what the hell are you doing here?"

Griffin Mason stared back at Ryon as she stood on the front stoop of his cottage near Choctawhatchee Bay. He was dressed in a robe and his hair was disheveled.

"Actually, it's a threesome," said Puller as he appeared on the right of Ryon while Carson appeared on the left of the woman.

Mason paled as he looked at the pair.

Puller said, "We need to come in and talk."

He glanced nervously over his shoulder. "This isn't a good time."

Before he could look back he was being propelled into the house by a hard shove from Puller. His robe flew open, revealing his naked body.

"I didn't say it was a request," said Puller as he stood over Mason, who had ended up on his back on the floor.

"Where are they?" Puller demanded.

"Where is who?" yelled Mason.

Puller grabbed him by the shoulders and jerked him to his feet. "The kids," he barked. "Where are they?"

"What kids?"

"Diego and Mateo."

Carson glanced sharply at him.

Puller eyed her. "It occurred to me on the way over. This jerk-off can afford a thousand bucks to buy a kid."

They all heard a noise from the next room. Puller raced to the door and threw it open.

Mason shouted, "Damn it, you can't go in there."

"The hell I can't," said Puller.

He froze in the doorway as the others joined him.

They all stared into the room.

A bedroom.

Someone was on the bed.

It was not Diego. Or Mateo.

It was Isabel.

And she was naked.

She barely had time to lift the sheet to cover her body.

"Isabel?" said Puller.

She stared back at him, her face a ball of anger. "What the hell is going on, Grif?" she exclaimed, looking over at Mason.

Mason grabbed Puller by the arm and tried to jerk him around, but Puller was so big and strong that Mason merely ended up knocking himself off balance and falling to the floor.

He jumped back up and screamed, "I am going to sue your ass off."

Puller turned to him. "What is she doing up here?"

"That is none of your damn business," yelled an apoplectic Mason.

"It is my business," said Puller. He looked at Isabel. "Are you here voluntarily?"

"Of course I am."

"Now get your ass out of here," yelled Mason. "And you better damn well lawyer up. I'm going to own your military pension and every other asset you have, including your aunt's house."

"What about the photos of the kids in your wallet?" asked Puller. "The black kid and the Asian?"

"How did you know about them?"

"Who are they?"

"They're my kids," exploded Mason.

"What?"

"My ex and I adopted them years ago. They're both grown now. But I carry their pictures in my wallet from when they were kids. Not that it's any of your damn business."

Carson said, "Isabel, how old are you?"

"Sixteen," she replied automatically.

"Isabel, the truth. It's something we can find out easily, but it'll be better coming from you."

Isabel hesitated and said, "I'm almost sixteen. In a year and a half."

Puller looked at Mason in disgust. "You're in bed with a fourteen-year-old?"

"She told me she was sixteen. Check out her rack. She looks eighteen."

Puller said to Isabel, "How much is he paying you?"

Mason yelled, "I'm not paying her anything. This is not a prostitution thing."

"Right. She's just up here screwing an old fat guy because it's so much cooler than doing the young bucks."

"He just gives me things," said Isabel.

"Like what?" asked Carson.

"Don't say anything, Isabel," demanded Mason. "They're just trying to trick you. I'm calling my lawyer."

"Stat rape is stat rape, Mason," noted Puller. "Not much of a defense to that."

Mason took a step back. "Look, we can work this out. It was just a misunderstanding."

"It doesn't matter. You're going down either way, stat rape or not."

"What?" said Mason, looking confused.

"We busted your scam."

"What scam?"

Puller looked at Ryon and Ryon looked at Mason.

Puller said, "I caught her with the stolen goods. She ratted you out. And now we know how an estates lawyer can afford an Aston Martin. So maybe *you* better lawyer the hell up."

Mason stared at Puller for a few seconds and then lunged at Ryon. "You stupid bitch!" His hands were around her neck and he was squeezing with all his strength.

Puller ripped him off her and threw Mason back against the wall.

Ryon slumped to the floor, gasping for breath and looking terrified.

Puller whipped Mason's hands behind his back and secured them with plasticuffs.

"Okay, we also now have your ass for assault and attempted murder. Thanks for the favor."

"You dumb bitch!" screamed Mason again at the sobbing Ryon.

Carson said, "Yeah, we got it the first time."

Puller grabbed Mason by the neck. "And maybe you help your targets into the grave a little faster so you can cash in, Grif?"

Mason looked at him blankly. "What?"

"Cookie? Floating in a bathtub. You were there. You told Ryon to get over there and take his most valuable watches. Only way that works is if he's dead."

"I didn't kill him."

"Yeah, right. And what about my aunt? You make her do a header into the fountain? Hold her under?"

"I swear to God I didn't."

"We know you were at Cookie's house," roared Puller.

"Okay, okay, I was there. For a meeting. I found him dead."

"Bullshit."

"He was. That's why I told Jane to get her ass over there. I wanted to get the watches out before anyone came to the house. Do you know how much they're worth?"

"Save it for your trial."

Puller looked back at Isabel. "Get dressed. I'm taking you home. By the way, your *abuela* has been worried sick."

"I have a life to lead."

"Where are Diego and Mateo?"

"I don't know."

"Did you know they were missing?"

She stared at him defiantly and then shrugged. "They'll probably come back."

"Get dressed," he said quietly and shut the door.

As they hauled Mason and Ryon outside, Puller's phone buzzed. He looked at the text that had just come across. His jaw plunged.

"Son of a bitch."

"What is it?" asked Carson as they loaded Ryon and Mason into the back of the Tahoe and slammed the doors shut.

Puller stared across at her.

"ME finished the post on Cookie. He wasn't murdered. He died from a popped aneurysm."

Carson said, "So Mason's not a killer?"

"And he's not a pedophile."

"He's just a scum who steals from old people and beds underage girls."

Puller sighed and leaned on the top

of the Tahoe. "So we're back to square one."

"With Diego and Mateo too," added Carson.

"With everything, actually," said Puller quietly. He glanced at his watch. It was a quarter past one. As he looked at the time something clicked in his brain. It had always been there, he supposed, but until this moment it had not registered.

Carson said, "Puller, what is it?"

Puller didn't hear her. Part of him couldn't believe it. Part of him could. But he would have to make sure. He would have to make calls. He would have to dig. He would have to once more become the investigator.

It was about time, he thought. It was about damn time.

CHAPTER

69

Mason and Ryon were in custody with the Paradise Police Department. Puller had given a full report to Bullock, who was burning the midnight oil. It had taken hours to fill him in on everything and then hours more to complete the paperwork. Justice, it seemed, was obsessed with paper.

Bullock did not seem pleased to have one more thing added to his plate, but he had his people fill out the necessary reports and ordered Ryon and Mason into holding cells. Mason was screaming about suing the entire city of Paradise, but Ryon had signed a confession and it was confirmed that Isabel was only fourteen, so the stat rape charge seemed solid.

Isabel was released into her grandmother's care after confirming in writing the account of what had happened.

Puller had also filled out a missing persons report on Diego and Mateo. He had told Bullock about the allegation that a man had paid a thousand dollars for them.

Bullock's features had turned darker while he listened to this.

Carson, who had been hovering in the background, said, "Do you have a problem with things like this in Paradise?"

Bullock glanced sharply up at her. "What do you mean?"

"With people being bought like that," said Puller.

Bullock frowned. "Look, we have a large population of undocumented down here, even with the reverse immigration because of the bad economy. If people are here illegally it's hard to know if anyone's disappeared. Folks come and go."

"These are two little kids," countered Puller. "They lived with their grand-mother."

"I get that, Puller. But I don't have the manpower to put on every case of folks disappearing. Not even the big-city departments can do that anymore. It's just the way things are."

"Then things suck," Puller said.

"Okay, they suck. What do you want me to do about it?"

"You're putting a lot of resources on the Lampert case."

"A bomb exploded there."

"But no one was hurt."

"It's different."

"It's only different because he has the biggest estate in Paradise."

Bullock rifled through some papers and didn't respond.

"Any leads on the bomber?" asked Carson.

"No," replied Bullock, still rifling.

"What about Cookie?" asked Puller.

"Not a homicide. You know that. An-eurysm popped. So if you were thinking there was a homicidal lunatic loose on Orion Street and that person killed your aunt too, well, stop thinking it."

"Just because Cookie's death was from natural causes doesn't mean my aunt wasn't murdered."

"Puller, I appreciate you bagging Mason and Ryon, I really do. If the case holds against them they're scum who deserve to go away to prison. But what I will not appreciate is you running around town playing detective."

"I offered my services before and you told me you might take me up on it."

"I said might. And I've decided not to. You're not part of this department. You're in the military. You have no authority here and I have no authority over you. Things would get tricky real fast."

"Okay, I guess I understand that."

"Thanks. Now if you'll excuse me, I've got to process the paperwork on Mason and Ryon."

Puller and Carson left and walked out into a new day with the sun already well up into the sky and the heat and humidity feeling like a pitcher of warm beer poured on them.

Carson stretched and worked a kink from her neck. "Well, I'm officially tired."

"Yeah, not going to bed at night does that to a person." He looked at his watch. "It's already ten hundred."

"We should catch some bunk time, John. Otherwise we'll be no good for anything."

Back in his room with Sadie bedded down on a large beach towel in the corner, Puller showered. He toweled off, slipped on a pair of boxers, and toppled backward on his bed. He wanted to go to sleep, but he couldn't. Not yet. He rose and spent the next two hours burning up cell minutes. He found out a great deal of interesting information. All of it dovetailed nicely with what he had been thinking. And if he hadn't looked at his watch last night, he never would have thought of it. Sometimes the mind did work in mysterious ways. He had more calls to make and more digging to do, but now he lay back on the bed and fell instantly asleep.

Hours later the knock on his door surprised him. He rose, snagging his M11 out of its holster.

"Yeah," he said, standing to the left of the door.

"You can stand down. It's just your friendly neighborhood one-star. You decent?"

Puller opened the door and looked at Carson. She had on a clingy light blue sleeveless dress with a V neckline and two-inch heels.

"What time is it?" asked Puller, who had gone from groggy to alert at the sight of her.

"Seventeen hundred."

"Damn, I must have really been asleep. It only felt like an hour of sack time."

"Can I come in?"

He stepped back and let her pass. She smelled of ginger and lilacs. Her skin glowed. Her hair was swept back, highlighted by the sun. The dress stopped about mid-thigh.

She sat on the bed and crossed her long legs as he closed the door.

"I thought we could talk about the

case and then think about dinner. Unless you wanted to hook up with Officer Landry."

She was gazing not at his face, but at a spot lower.

Puller looked down and realized he was still in his boxers.

"You must have a different definition of decent than I do, Puller."

"I don't want to hook up with Officer Landry," he said curtly.

"All I needed to know."

She rose, stepped out of her heels, undid a clasp at the back of her dress, and it fell to the floor.

She had nothing on underneath.

"This must seem very forward of me."

"It actually seems just right."

She rubbed her hand across his cheek. "I've learned from the Army that when you want to take a position you just have to go for it. Hesitation is for losers."

She lay back on the bed and lifted up the covers. "I know you've been asleep a long time, but you want to crawl back in here? You won't be sleeping. That I can guarantee."

They kissed lightly at first and then deeper, their fingers probing. When they drew apart Carson looked unsteady, vulnerable and breathless, her hair askew, her lips parted. Tough one-star now naked, helpless, and literally in his hands. He traced her lips with his finger.

No words necessary.

He lifted her up, her long legs immediately scissoring around his torso. He laid her back on the bed.

There was a rim of sweat on her back that Puller flicked his hands over as he gripped her tightly. He rose up and settled down firmly on top. His hands slid to her buttocks and squeezed the soft flesh. Her hands kept busy too, slipping to his thighs and directing him to where Puller now needed to go.

A familiar motion took over, growing more and more frenetic as the fire inside each of them reached a point of no return.

Her moans were becoming more

rapid. She started to talk. Telling him in his ear precisely what it was she wanted.

A while later Puller gave one last shudder and fell limp over Carson. She was gasping and trying to catch her breath and telling him how pleased she was at his performance. Together they slowly moved down to lie flat on the bed side by side.

"That was truly unbelievable, John," she murmured in his ear.

It was, thought Puller, and he told her so.

She turned, faced him, and kissed him, first on the cheek, then the lips, sliding her fingers up and down one side of his face.

It had been a while for Puller. He worried whether he could bring the necessary level of passion. Apparently he had. And that made him feel both satisfied and relieved as he lay there next to her. He was still breathing hard, like he'd just completed the Army two-mile in record time.

"I don't do this sort of thing lightly, just so you know," she said.

"You don't seem the type."

"I'm not," she said firmly, propping herself up on one elbow and looking at him.

"I'm not either," he said.

"Trust me, I know."

"You've been checking me out?"

"Your record speaks for itself. Not a lot of room in there for personal time."

"You either."

"Simple story, chasing stars." She rubbed his chest. "So where do we go from here, big fellow?"

Puller jerked up and stared at her.

She laughed. "I'm not looking for an engagement ring and a wedding date, Puller. I'm talking about eating. I'm starved."

He smiled. "Then how about we go eat?"

She kissed him, ran her fingers along a part of his anatomy that made him shudder.

She whispered in his ear, "Is that an order, soldier?"

"With all due respect, ma'am, yes, it is."

CHAPTER

70

Their bellies full, Puller and Carson sat back from their empty plates and studied each other.

"You're looking at me as though our relationship has changed somehow," she said.

He cocked his head, studied her even more intently. "Hasn't it?"

They were occupying the back corner of a restaurant. The hour was still early enough that the large dinner crowds had not come in yet. They had the place mostly to themselves.

"Why? Because we've slept together?"

"I can't think of any other reason."

"Was it that important for you?"

"I guess it wasn't for you."

"Don't be offended, John, but it is the twenty-first century. Like guys have for most all of history, girls just sometimes want it for no other reason than they want it."

"Okay," he said slowly.

She suddenly smiled. "Feeling used?"

He looked at her, grinned back. "Turning the tables on the male psyche?"

"About time, wouldn't you say?"

"I'm a poor representative of the typical male."

"That's what I like about you. Take Landry, for instance."

"What about her?"

"She's young and hot. She wants you in the sack, no leap of deduction there. But she's no doubt been hit on by every cop in the department."

"Probably has."

"And you think the DoD is any different?"

"Come again?"

"I've had my ass pinched by my share of one- through four-stars. At West Point it was the same. Instructors and boneheaded plebes. Then out in the field with leafs and clusters thinking it was okay what they said and did to a woman in the ranks. Hell, during my tours of combat in the Middle East sometimes it seemed I was fighting a war on both flanks."

She picked up her iced tea and glanced at him. "Surprise you?"

"The Army answer would be yes, it would surprise me."

"And your answer?"

"You know my answer. It's not the same as the Army's."

"Propositioned, harassed, threatened, even assaulted. Welcome to this 'man's' army, right?"

He sat forward, his hands making fists on top of the table. "There are procedures for that shit, Julie. You don't have to take it. Like you said, it's the twenty-first century."

"Right. And part of this century looks just like all the others. Men are still men, however much more enlightened they may be, or constrained by the threat of lawsuits, courts-martial, wrecked careers, and pissed-off wives. But they still pull that crap because they think they can get away with it. They always think that."

"And so you just took it?"

"I didn't say that." She held up her fist. "Sometimes it was this. Sometimes it was a knee to the nuts. Sometimes it was just a stare. And, yeah, sometimes it was paperwork filed and careers torpedoed. But sometimes I didn't do or say anything. Sometimes I just walked away."

He stared at her. "You don't seem the type to just walk away."

"I had long-term plans, Puller. The Army wasn't just a lark for me. I wanted big things. I wanted to do big things. I wanted the star path. I have one. I want at least two more."

"So go along to get along? Not my idea of leadership."

"Leadership is a funny thing. The parameters keep changing. But one thing you can't compromise on is can you look at yourself in the mirror the next day? I always could. No matter what happened. It wasn't my problem. It was theirs. *They* shouldn't be able to look in the mirror. They're the ones who couldn't control their dicks."

"So where does that leave us?" Puller asked.

"I didn't come down here to get you into bed. Well, maybe a part of me did. Now that we've done that I can focus on what I really came down here for."

"R and R?"

"To help you solve a case. What do we do next?"

"I'm not used to generals asking me for direction."

"The best leaders let their people do what they do best. You're CID. I don't have a clue about investigating criminal acts. So, again, what do we do next?"

"The Storrows."

"The Storrows?"

"The couple murdered on the beach. They knew my aunt."

"You think that's why they were killed?"

"I'm thinking that the Storrows were

out a lot. Sometimes walking, maybe sometimes driving."

"Driving, like five miles out and five back?"

"Maybe so."

"And they told your aunt what they saw?"

"Or thought they saw. Or suspected. She wrote the letter to my old man. But she really wanted me to come down and look into things. She would have been able to tell me more, but she never got the chance."

Puller slipped the letter from his pocket and passed it over to Carson. She ran her gaze down it.

"Mysterious happenings in the night. People not what they seem. Something just not being right. Pretty cryptic stuff."

"My aunt was not given to overstating things. For her those words might as well be screaming murder."

"Well, if you're right about her death, she was entirely justified in thinking so. But if the Storrows are dead, how do we proceed?"

"Son and daughter-in-law. They reported them missing. I'm hoping they can fill in some gaps." He rose. "You ready?"

She smiled up at him and almost purred. "After the sack time? I'm damn well ready for pretty much anything."

CHAPTER

71

Mecho chugged water from a gallon container and stared across at the big house. Everything about it was perfectly designed, perfectly placed. The shell was of amazing beauty. What lay underneath was not so beautiful.

But then that was how the world often worked.

He wiped his mouth, put the jug back on the truck, and picked up a rake. He trudged off to a patch of lawn underneath some trees. In a side lawn a large fountain poured water into a concrete catch basin. The perimeter of this "se-

cret garden" was lined with lush plant-
ings, wooden benches placed in nooks
and crevices with cobblestone pavers
underneath.

Mecho had worked this section of
the estate before. He found it peaceful,
meditative. He suspected this had been
Mrs. Lampert's design. He did not think
that Peter Lampert was capable of contemplating such a place of serenity.

As he rounded the corner and set to
work with his rake he was surprised to
see that one of the garden seats was
occupied.

Chrissy Murdoch held a book in her
hands, but she wasn't looking at it. She
was staring off in the direction of the
water that lay close enough that they
could hear the rolling breakers. She
wore pale green shorts, a white blouse,
and tennis shoes with ankle socks. Her
hair was pulled back and fixed in a tight
braid. The sun filtered across her face
through the branches of nearby trees.

Mecho watched her, momentarily
caught up in both her beauty and her
apparent melancholy.

When she started and looked his

way he returned to his work, raking flowerbeds and settling the mulch back into neat, compact mounds.

"It's a beautiful day, isn't it?" she said.

"Every day in Paradise is beautiful, isn't it?" he replied.

"Don't we both know better than that?"

He looked up, his large fingers gripping the handle of the rake. He said nothing, prompting her to speak again.

"Have you thought about our encounter on the beach last night?"

"Have you?"

"I've thought of nothing but that."

"I've given it little time in my mind. I think you have me confused with someone else."

She rose, closed her book, and drifted over to him.

"So you're simply a common laborer who maintains a rich man's property?"

"I'm holding a rake. My shirt is slick with sweat. I ride in a truck. I live in a hole. Draw your own conclusions."

"But you are educated."

"Educated or not, I have to make a

living. This is not my country. One has to start from the bottom. It is the way with any country."

"Some start from the top."

"Those with connections. Or family wealth. I have neither. Do you?"

"I have my looks. I have a certain grace. I know which fork to hold, small talk to make. I know an Italian wine from a French. A Monet from a Manet. The rest I can fudge if need be."

"Then you have your whole life figured out."

"No."

He leaned on his rake. "This is very dangerous what we do. Talking like this. Eyes and ears everywhere."

"But not here. Not in the secret garden. Mrs. Lampert saw to that."

"She is an accomplished lady?"

"Probably not. But perhaps real to the touch, unlike me."

"You're a fraud, then?"

"Most of us are."

"You gave me an ultimatum on the beach."

"Yes, I did."

"I did not understand it."

"I thought the terms crystal clear."

"You won't believe that I am who I say I am? Where is your proof?"

"Right before my eyes."

"What is your interest in Lampert?"

"He is an interesting man, on many levels."

"You let him inside your body."

"You find that disgusting?"

"Don't you?"

"Perhaps I do."

"Then why allow it?"

"Life is full of trade-offs, she said."

"What are you trading for?"

"On the beach. I thought it was clear."

"What is your grievance?"

"What is yours?" she countered.

He stood erect, his fingers sliding up and down the rake handle.

She said, "The timing is truly remarkable. You and me."

"Remarkable was not the word I was thinking of."

"You were thinking the timing sucked?"

"As you said, it can only be one of us."

"So you admit your intention?"

Now Mecho's face darkened. He had been a fool. She had drawn him in, without seeming to do so.

He looked around. He expected to see Lampert's security team closing in. He looked at her, trying to discern the communication wire under her blouse or her shorts.

As though reading his mind she said, "No, Mecho, it's not that way."

"So you say." He turned to leave.

"Will you stand down?"

He said nothing, but he also didn't move.

"Will you stand down?" she said again.

"Will you?" he asked.

"I guess I have my answer."

"I guess you do."

"It's been a long time for us, Mecho. A long time. And much pain."

"And you think you're alone in that?"

"No. But I have obligations. The end result will be to your liking."

"I have obligations too."

He walked swiftly away from her. Away from the secret garden that held no more secrets.

Everything needed to be sped up now. The schedule, so carefully crafted, was now blown to shit.

But there was something else.

Ultimatums given were usually carried out. Prices had to be paid.

His rear flank had just been exposed. He was now fighting on two sides when only one had been anticipated.

He looked back at her.

Murdoch stood there, book in hand, staring at him.

He saw many things on her features.

Sadness.

Resignation.

But most of all, resolve.

He turned back and kept walking.

He didn't feel sadness, or resignation.

But he did feel resolve.

The war had truly now begun.

CHAPTER

72

Peter Lampert put down his binoculars but continued to watch the big man stride across the lawn and put his rake back in the landscaping truck.

Lampert gauged the man's height.

Six-six, perhaps a bit more.

Weight near three hundred pounds, perhaps, but he wasn't bulky. He was lean but with massive shoulders and legs that revealed corded muscles through the fabric of his too-small pants.

An interesting fellow.

Lampert had seen him talking to the

maid, Beatriz, on several occasions. He had seen Christine Murdoch paying him attention as well. He was not a bad-looking man.

Rugged, the ladies would undoubtedly call him.

And his great size, the women appreciated such things, he knew.

The old adage that big feet meant large appendages everywhere was still popular.

Large feet, thought Lampert.

Perhaps size sixteen.

Perhaps the same feet that had been in the flowerbed outside the window of the guesthouse. He wondered what the man's handwriting was like. Would it match the message left on the wall of his guesthouse?

And Lampert's men had told him of the big man, the giant they called him, who had escaped from the oil platform by diving off into the water. He was presumed dead. What else could they presume after a dive off the platform into a dark ocean? No one could have swum all the way to land from there.

Yet perhaps this man had what it took to do so. Or perhaps he had help.

Lampert was a risk-taker, always had been. It would be nothing to him to risk eliminating the man even if it turned out he posed no threat at all. Collateral damage was something that did not bother him.

He did not know quite what to make of Chrissy Murdoch's talking with him. He knew Winthrop didn't come close to satisfying her sexually. Thus the occasional rendezvous in the guesthouse.

Perhaps she liked her men giant in all respects. Perhaps it was as simple as that.

Again, the question of risk.

He had Stiven Rojas looking over his shoulder. No, breathing down his neck, he corrected.

Such a man did not tolerate mistakes. Lampert had every incentive not to become one of those errors.

He continued to watch the big man as he toiled away under a hot sun.

Lampert had somewhere to go today. It was risky, but he felt he had to.

way, not his wife, not his only child. It was simply how he was wired.

But you could get to a man like Lampert, hit him where it hurt. These spots were few and well hidden, but they existed.

Murdoch intended to smash them all.

She withdrew from the cover of the tree and walked back to the secret garden.

She sat back down on the bench and opened her book.

Her decision was not made yet because she couldn't make up her mind.

Live or die, Mecho?

Live or die?

But there was something in his eyes.

And Murdoch felt her own eyes tear up as she thought about this.

CHAPTER

73

Puller had phoned ahead and Lynn and Chuck Storrow were waiting for them at their house a block off the water. It was a one-story that occupied a large part of their yard. They were ushered in by Chuck Storrow. His wife sat huddled on the couch, a shawl around her shoulders even though it was brutally hot outside.

When she looked up at them the pain of the recent loss of her in-laws was evident on her face.

Puller and Carson both expressed their condolences.

Chuck said, "Please sit. Now, you said you were with the Army?"

Puller and Carson perched opposite the couple on a settee that was barely wide enough to contain them.

"We both are," said Puller. "But I'm down here in connection with the death of my aunt Betsy."

"Omigod, you're John Puller, her nephew, then," said Chuck as Lynn wiped at her eyes with a tissue and looked more interested.

"That's right. I understand that my aunt and the Storrows were friends."

"They were," answered Lynn in a hushed voice. "Very good friends. And we knew Betsy too. A wonderful woman."

"Which makes it odd that all three of them should die so close together and under such suspicious circumstances," said Puller.

Chuck looked confused. "But I thought Betsy's death was an accident."

"The police think that might be the case. I don't."

"Why?" asked Lynn.

Puller slipped the letter from his pocket and handed it across.

The Storrows read it together.

Chuck looked up. "Mysterious happenings?"

"At night," added Lynn.

Puller focused on her. "Right, at night. Betsy died at night. So did your parents, Chuck."

Tears clustered around Lynn's eyes and her husband put an arm around her shoulders.

Chuck said, "I don't see what the connection might be."

"They were friends. Maybe they confided in each other. Maybe they all knew something about what my aunt wrote about in that letter."

"But surely they would have mentioned it to us," said Chuck.

"And they didn't?" asked Carson.

"Of course not. We would have said something."

"Were you here all the time?" asked Puller. "Recently?"

The Storrows looked at each other.

"Well, actually—" began Chuck.

Lynn said, "We were gone for about

three weeks. Africa. A safari. We got back and I phoned my in-laws. They didn't answer. I figured they were doing their usual beach walk. When I called the next day and they didn't answer I started to get worried. That's when we got the police involved."

"But your parents didn't try to contact you when you were out of town?" Puller asked Chuck.

"Neither one liked to use the telephone and they would never call long distance even though I explained to them that calling my cell was not calling long distance. I don't think they ever quite understood that. And they were from a generation that was very frugal. And they were not into emailing or texting."

Lynn gave a little sob. "We should have called *them*."

Chuck shook his head. "Cell reception isn't the best over there. I figured maybe they'd had an accident or something. I never dreamed anyone would have . . ."

"I can see that," said Puller. "Did they still drive?"

She nodded. "Oh yes. They were still quite active physically."

"Would they drive my aunt around?"

"Sometimes, yes. But she could drive too. She had her car fitted out specially with the hand controls."

"Right, I saw that."

Chuck eyed them. "All these questions. And that letter. Do you have any idea what could have happened to them?"

"Not really sure yet. We're just following up any lead that presents itself. Did either of them keep a journal?"

"A journal?" said Lynn. "I don't think so, why?"

"Just asking. There might have been one missing from my aunt's house."

"So maybe if we had been here this wouldn't have happened to them," said Lynn slowly.

"Sweetie, we can't beat ourselves up about that. We'd been planning that safari vacation for years."

"You really can't blame yourselves," said Carson. "It's just not worth it and they wouldn't have wanted you to."

Lynn blew her nose.

Puller said, "Your parents' attorney wasn't Griffin Mason by any chance?"

"No. They used my attorney," answered Chuck.

"Good. I think Mason will be pretty busy from now on."

They rose to leave.

Lynn put a hand on his arm. "If you find out anything, anything at all about who did this?"

"You'll be the first ones I'll tell," replied Puller firmly.

Chuck shook their hands. "Best of luck to you."

"God bless you," added Lynn.

"I think we'll need luck and blessings," muttered Puller under his breath.

Puller sat in the Tahoe but didn't start the engine.

Carson looked over at him. "Are we going to sit here and swelter or are you going to turn this sucker on?"

Puller turned the key and the engine caught. He put it in gear and pulled away.

"So what did that get us?" asked Carson as she put the AC vents full blast on them.

"Information. Even if the Storrows had found something out they might not have told anyone, other than my aunt."

"You said she had put all these miles on her car, right?"

Puller turned to look at her as he hit the main street and sped up. "Right."

"And you think she kept a journal?"

"Yes."

"Well, maybe she found something out and told them, not the other way around. They might have been spotted or overheard. So they all had to die. Your aunt and then the Storrows. Or maybe the other way around. Or maybe simultaneously."

"That makes sense," said Puller.

"We generals sometimes do."

"So the oil spot we found near that sulfur pit?"

"A truck or a car probably. But why there?"

"Good place to do something clandestine," he noted.

"Right, it stinks and you can't use the beach."

"But still, it would seem to be a night-time endeavor."

She nodded. "Yes, it would. So I guess I know what we'll be doing to-night."

"Yes, you do."

"There is something unaccounted for," she said.

"There are lots of things unaccounted for."

"I'm talking about one in particular."

"The two men in the sedan who can make the Pentagon tuck its tail between its legs and run off."

"Exactly," said Carson. "That has me worried."

"All of it has me worried," replied Puller.

CHAPTER

74

He could hear the sounds of large doors being raised. He didn't know exactly what the sounds represented, but they scared him. Everything and everyone here scared him.

He felt a tap on his shoulder and jerked. Then he turned to face him.

Diego stared at Mateo and Mateo stared back at Diego.

They were in a space about twenty feet square and steel bars kept them there. They were more precisely *lying* on the floor of the cage that had been their home for the last two days.

Mateo whispered, "I'm scared, Diego."

Diego nodded and gripped the little boy's hand.

Diego had gone to the *dueños* to see if they would protect him and his cousins from the three men who had beaten Isabel and Mateo. He had taken Mateo with him because there had been no one at his *abuela*'s home to watch the little boy. And plus Diego did not think they would harm him with Mateo there.

He could not have been more wrong.

What had come next had been frighteningly chaotic.

Men had arrived.

Something had been given to Diego and Mateo to drink. The next thing he knew he was in this place. He didn't know where this place was, or how he had gotten here.

He cupped Mateo's ear with his hand and whispered back, "It will be okay."

It was a lie, and from the look on Mateo's face he knew it.

The light here was dim, so dim in fact as to make Diego queasy. Mateo had thrown up once, perhaps as an aftereffect of whatever had been slipped into their drinks.

They were not alone here. There were ten cages like the one they were in. And all of them were full. In Diego's cage were ten other people. All adults, or close to it. They had segregated men from women.

Diego could make out some of these shapes in the weak light.

In his cage the men and teenage boys sat on their haunches, looking at the gap between their knees.

Hopeless. Beaten.

It was exactly how Diego felt.

He didn't know for sure why he and Mateo had been taken.

In the back of his mind, however, he had heard the stories on the streets.

Secuestradores de personas.

Takers of people.

Diego never thought he would be taken.

He looked over at Mateo. He was only five. Little more than a baby. Why would they take Mateo? It made no sense.

A guard came by with a slender jug

of water and a plate of bread and fruit. He passed them through a slot in the bars.

The biggest men in the cage grabbed at the plate and jug. They drank their fill and ate what they wanted and the left-overs were passed down. By the time the plate and jug got to Diego and Ma-teo there was barely a sip of water left, a few crumbs of bread, and a wedge of apple. He gave it all to Mateo, trying to ignore the thirst in his throat and the rumble in his belly.

He sat back up against the bars and stared down the line at the other cages. His gaze flitted to one that contained women. None looked older than thirty. Many were teenagers.

Diego could understand why they had been taken.

Putas, he thought. They would be worth a great deal of money.

His gaze ventured upward to the high ceiling of the place where exposed air ducts and electrical lines were revealed.

This was a warehouse of some kind, Diego had already deduced.

But where it was he had no idea. He

had no idea if he was still in Paradise. Or even still in Florida.

He thought of his *abuela* and his eyes grew heavy with tears. He thought of Isabel wondering where they were and his eyes grew heavier still.

Then he thought of the big man who had asked him to find the two men in the car. He seemed interested in Diego. He had helped Isabel and Mateo. He could beat people up. He was big and strong. He had driven a fancy car. Perhaps he was rich. Maybe he would come and find them.

But Diego maintained this hopeful thought for barely a second. That was crazy, he told himself. The man would not come. No one would come.

He looked around at the other cages again.

This was obviously a big business. They were organized and had lots of money behind them. They took people and sold them all over the place; he just knew this to be true.

He looked at Mateo.

Would they sell them together? Or would Mateo go off alone?

Without me?

He knew Mateo would cry and cry. And maybe the *secuestradores de personas* would get angry and kill him to quiet him.

He reached out and gripped Mateo's arm so tightly that the little boy let out a small gasp.

I will never let you go, Mateo, Diego promised himself.

The lights grew dimmer still. Diego looked around, fear gripping him.

All the other prisoners in the cages were doing the same thing, looking around, but also trying to shrink themselves so as not to draw attention.

They could all sense that something was coming. And that what was coming would not be good for them.

The man slowly came up the metal steps and stopped in front of the line of cages. Peter Lampert's image was not clear enough for Diego to make out who it was. But he had never seen Lampert before, so an identification would not have been possible in any case.

There were other men behind Lampert. One was James Winthrop. The men were dressed elegantly in blazers, white shirts, and slacks that looked professionally tailored to their bodies. Thousand-dollar shoes were on their feet. They could have been investment bankers going to a meeting.

Winthrop held an electronic tablet and was making notes on it as Lampert inspected his product and made certain decisions. He walked up and down in front of the cages pointing to people inside and giving instructions to Winthrop, who dutifully inputted them on the tablet. They could have been inspecting cattle in slaughterhouses or cars rolling off an assembly line. There was a clear air of business being conducted here, even though the product was human and breathing.

Breathing fast.

Two other men came toward them. They carried packages wrapped in plastic. Lampert snapped his fingers and the men hurried forward.

Lampert examined the packages and slit one open with his finger. He pulled out four blue shirts, looked at the list Winthrop had compiled, and pointed at four people in three different cages. The shirts were taken to these people and they were forced to put them on.

Red shirts came out and were given to all men who were larger and more muscular than the others.

Green shirts were pulled out and placed on the younger, good-looking women and some of the younger, angelic-looking men and boys.

All the shirts were given out, except for two in a separate package.

Lampert slit this package open and pulled out two yellow shirts.

He glanced at Winthrop's tablet, running his eye down the list.

Then he turned and looked up and down the row of cages until his surveillance finally came to a stop in front of Diego's cage.

He looked down at the two boys and smiled. He said something to Winthrop that Diego could not completely catch, but it sounded like, "New product line." Then some more words were spoken he could not hear, and then he caught another snatch.

"Family unit. Lower scrutiny. Fetch a good price on the market."

He gave the yellow shirts to another man, who went into the cages and forced Diego and Mateo to put them on.

A few moments later, men, hardened evil-looking men, came through the cages and told each of the prisoners what would happen to them if they uttered one word about where they had come from once they reached their final destination.

"Everyone you love, every family member you have—and we know where they all are, indeed we have many of them in cages like this—will be slaughtered. If you speak one word to anyone we will bring you their heads as a reminder of what you have done."

They had looked down at Diego and Mateo and asked them if they would like to hold the severed head of their *abuela*.

Mateo had started to cry but had instantly stopped when one of the men struck him in the mouth.

Diego had stood between Mateo and the man, but the man had laughed.

"Do you want your *abuela*'s head?" he asked again.

Diego had said nothing but had shaken his head, and the man had moved on.

A similar encounter had happened to all the others, demonstrating that the men had inside information on each of them. Thus there was not one person in any of the cages, even the older, stronger men, who did not believe every word of this. None of them would talk. None of them would even think of trying to tell the truth.

After this was over Lampert came back to Diego's cage. He slipped something from his pocket and held it through the bars of the cage.

As Diego focused on it he saw that it was a necklace of some sort.

"Take it," said Lampert.

Diego did not move.

"Take it. Now."

In Diego's peripheral vision a man
with a gun edged forward, the muzzle
of the weapon pointing at Mateo's head.

Diego reached out and took it. He
looked down at the disc of metal attached to the end of the chain.

Lampert said, "It's a Saint Christopher's medal. You know who Saint
Christopher is, don't you?"

Diego looked up and slowly shook
his head.

Lampert smiled and said, "Saint
Christopher is the saint who protects
children from harm. Put it on. Do it
now."

Diego slipped the necklace over his
head and the medal came to rest on
his chest.

"Now nothing can harm you," said
Lampert, still smiling.

Winthrop snorted with laughter.

Lampert turned and walked off, Winthrop behind still chortling.

Diego stared at their elegant clothes
hanging on their well-nourished, fit phy-
siques. He lifted off the necklace and
let it drop to the floor. Then he stared
at the silver ring on his finger, the one

with the lion's head that his papa had given him.

His courage came flooding back as he looked at the lion.

He looked up, slowly raised his hand, made a gun with his finger, aimed, fired twice, and killed both Lampert and Winthrop over and over.

CHAPTER

75

Mecho was on the phone once more.

It was his "friend."

Details were gone over. The latest encounter with Chrissy Murdoch had convinced Mecho that his schedule had to be sped up.

The "friend" was sympathetic and agreed to be ready. But he reminded Mecho of their deal.

Mecho impatiently answered the man. It would be done.

He clicked off the phone and looked down at the floor of his room at the Sierra.

He stiffened when the paper was slipped under his door. He didn't move for a few seconds, wondering if something or someone was going to follow the paper in.

He reached under the bed and pulled out the pistol from where he had slid it between the springs. He rose, inched toward the door, touched the paper with his foot, and moved it toward him. Keeping his eyes on the door, he knelt and picked up the paper. He moved away from the door and opened the folded page.

Two words. Two meaningful words.

"They're coming."

Mecho folded up the paper and slipped it into his pocket.

He could attempt to follow the person who had given him this warning.

But he chose not to.

They're coming.

Twenty minutes later he didn't hear or see anything coming.

He sensed it with something other than his ears and his eyes. Perhaps it was their smell. The smell of death coming. It could be quite potent.

He reached under the bed, snagged
two more items, rose, opened the door,
and moved to his left with a speed that
was belied by his immense frame.

There was too much light here for
what he wanted. He entered the stairwell and moved down one flight at a
time, pausing at each landing.

Waiting.

Sensing.

He was using faculties that most
people would never discover they had.

But when you had lived as Mecho
had, those faculties rose to the surface.

At least for those who survived.

He left the building at the ground
floor and headed west.

The people were good.

Not because they had found him at
the Sierra. That would take no skill at
all.

No, they were good because they
had followed him from his room down
to here. Even now he could sense their
approach, one set from the left, one set
from the right.

He slipped his gutting knife into his

waistband and then spun the suppressor onto the end of his pistol.

He kept walking, zigzagging his route and moving closer and closer to the water.

These back streets were deserted. Not even the *dueños* were out. He wondered about this. But then he thought perhaps they had been told to stay off the streets tonight.

The *dueños* considered themselves tough until they ran into those who were truly formidable. Then the street toughs melted away into little balls of dough and found places to hide in the darkness, like the mice they were.

Mecho was not and never would be a mouse.

He walked on, instinctively varying his route but heading inevitably to the water, to the Gulf.

It had carried him here from a position of slavery, though the last part of his journey had been as a free man swimming for his life.

He would go back to the sanctity of the water tonight.

It would either be his final resting

place or simply one more bump in a long road of them in his life. Sometimes all a person could do was not good enough. So be it. He had never been one to regret. Not when it came to survival.

He passed some late-night stragglers who were too drunk to see that he was walking along with a pistol. He turned down one more street and the deepness of the ocean stretched ahead of him.

It was secluded.

It was completely dark.

There were no people around who could see or be harmed by what was about to happen.

And the tide was coming in.

Tides were often handy.

He quickened his pace.

In a few more seconds he was on his scooter, which he had hidden behind a trash receptacle, and was flying down the sand.

This had surprised the men following him.

That was his intent. His other intent was to draw them farther down the beach, away from the town, away from any eyes, drunk or not.

Two miles later he was away from all such eyes except for the ones still chasing him. He had not gone fast enough to lose them. Mecho's thinking was simple. He could deal with this now or he could deal with it later.

Might as well get it over with.

Mecho calculated he was facing six men.

They would be trained, armed, cagey, cautious, but with enough close-quarter combat skills to size up the ever-evolving battlefield.

The dunes were up ahead. He left his scooter behind and set out on foot. A minute later he skirted a narrow cleft between two dunes. His front flank was now a funnel his pursuers would have to breach. But it was only wide enough for one man to come through at a time. A classic defensive measure. The same one the Spartans had employed to hold off the far larger Persian army so the Greeks could escape destruction. That same technique had been taught in war colleges ever since.

If your opponent has far larger numbers, make it as difficult as possible for them to employ those numbers to their advantage.

Mecho knew this sort of confrontation might happen, so he had hunted for this sort of tactical advantage shortly after he had arrived in Paradise. And then he had spent time doing something to it that would hopefully work to his advantage.

The dunes were thick enough to stop any ordnance unless they were going to attack him with shoulder-fired missiles, and he doubted that was the case.

Mecho only had two worries now.

His rear flank.

And something coming through that opening other than a man.

His next steps would address both issues at once.

The men after Mecho fanned out in a classic attack formation. With a numerical advantage of six to one it would be successful against just about any foe.

The cleft in the dunes was just ahead.

A funnel. These men had seen that one before.

One way in and one way out.

None of them had any plan or desire to breach that opening with Mecho waiting to pick them off as they came through.

But they had come prepared for just such a scenario.

The first man approached, keeping well back of the cleft. He lifted the fist-shaped metal object from his pocket, engaged it, and tossed it through the opening.

It wasn't a grenade, but it was as good as one.

He turned away from the cleft and used his hands to cover his ears as additional protection over the plugs he wore.

The flash-bang went off.

Blinding light, paralyzing sound.

And a concussive-force kicker.

Anyone in the dune would now be immobilized, easy to kill.

The six men swarmed through the cleft. Sand dislodged by the flash-bang was swirling everywhere. They had guns ready to fire into the paralyzed man who should now be resting on the sandy floor.

He would never know how he died.

The space between the dunes was barely ten by ten. The space had resulted from erosion, wind, and different compactness levels of the sand. The men crowded in, but there was no one lying immobilized on the ground.

What the leader of the squad did see was a now visible knotted rope dangling in the center of the space. He looked up to where the rope was attached to the thick limb of a tree twenty feet up.

None of the men had looked up before coming in here. They had focused on the cleft.

But what was currently up was now coming down.

Mecho landed on two of the men and they broke his fall by breaking their necks.

A third man was gutted by Mecho's knife, the bodies of the first two kills covered with blood from his dissected belly.

Number four caught two rounds in his face from Mecho's pistol.

Number five tried to run.

One big arm around his neck stopped that retreat and the snap of the spine was followed by the man collapsing to the sandy ground.

Number six got lucky, however.

Mecho had stumbled over number five as the man's legs involuntarily kicked out as he went through the last spasms of death.

Six drew his bead on Mecho with his MP5. Shot selector on full auto, thirty rounds fired in a couple seconds, if that.

Not survivable.

Pistol and knife useless against that.

Mecho looked at Six.

Six looked back at Mecho.

A triumphant smile, a finger on the trigger, ready to finish the job.

Mecho had a millisecond left to live and there was absolutely nothing he could do about it.

One shot erupted.

But it didn't come from the MP's muzzle.

A hole opened in number six's forehead. The MP had no chance to do its killing because its owner had just died.

Six fell headlong into the sand, some of his brain splattered along the wall of the dune behind him, because the shot had come from in front of him and behind Mecho.

Mecho whipped around in that direction, pistol and knife up and ready.

Chrissy Murdoch stood there. She was not outfitted in Hermès and Chanel tonight. Nor a bikini.

She wore all black. Dark smudges were under her eyes and over her thin, high cheeks. The eyes looked very different from the pampered ones of the person lounging around the pool at Peter Lampert's estate.

They were hard and dark and cold.

They are like mine, thought Mecho.

She held a pistol. It was pointed at Mecho's heart.

She looked at him and he looked back at her.

She slipped the gun into a belt holster and said, "We have to get rid of the bodies. I have a boat. Let's move."

As she came forward to do just this, Mecho could only stare.

She struggled to lift one of the men. Mecho still hadn't moved.

She glanced sharply at him. "I said, let's go."

"You were the one who warned me?"

"Who else?" she snapped.

He put the pistol and knife away and started to help her.

CHAPTER

76

Puller eased out from behind a tree and did a sweep of the area with his night-vision goggles. He had picked the surveillance spot with the same care he would on a battlefield. It gave him maximum observation coverage with minimal exposure to prying eyes.

Carson sipped on a bottle of water and watched him. It was hot, muggy, and the sulfur smell was nauseating.

It was also two in the morning and they had been here for three hours.

He sat back next to her.

She said quietly, "Anything?"

He shook his head, kept his gaze moving.

"How much longer do we wait?"

He looked at her. "As long as it takes, General. These things don't run on a schedule."

"So all night?"

"Daylight comes, we'll leave. They won't be doing anything in the daytime, even at a place like this."

"What do you think it is?"

Puller shrugged, leaned back against the tree, but remained tensed, ready to move in an instant if need be. "Drugs. Guns. The Colombians have lost the drug pipeline to the Mexicans. But the Gulf is still full of traffickers."

"Then it could get pretty dicey tonight. We might not have enough firepower."

"This is an intelligence-gathering expedition only. No engagement. We take what we find to the proper authorities."

"We might not have a choice about engagement. If we're spotted."

"Risk of the battlefield."

"On U.S. soil no less. Didn't teach us that at the Army War College."

"Maybe they should have."

"Yeah, maybe they should have. I'll speak to the appropriate parties about it. If I survive hanging with you."

They fell silent until Carson said, "Something else on your mind?"

Puller didn't look at her. There *was* something else on his mind. He had continued his investigative work prompted by looking at his watch outside of Grif Mason's hideaway. And everything he had found out only reinforced his suspicions. It didn't sadden him. It angered him. But he would have to productively channel that anger. He looked forward to the opportunity to do so.

"Just a jumble of things," he said.

Carson was about to say something else when Puller put up a hand. "Stay down," he hissed.

A few seconds later Carson heard what Puller's quicker senses had already registered.

The truck crept along the surface road shielded by a line of trees. It turned and puttered down toward the water, easing into the small park-off, where the driver killed the engine. Several men got out even as Puller and Carson hunkered down at their observation post.

Puller held up a finger, indicating to Carson that they would communicate solely via nonverbal signals from now on. She nodded in understanding.

Lying prone in the sand, Puller intensified the power on his night-vision goggles and pointed them at the truck, which sat about a hundred yards away from their position.

At first Puller was thinking that another vehicle would meet the truck, but that didn't make any sense. Truck and truck at a clandestine meeting site was not logical. Moving over the road you'd get a warehouse and do your transfer in privacy.

The only reason to drive down near the water was if you were expecting a delivery from the water.

A minute later Puller's deduction was proved correct.

The whine of the boat wasn't much, but water was a great conductor of sound. The boat was moving fast, and within thirty seconds Puller could see the outline of what he almost immediately recognized as a RIB. It was the same type of amphibious boat the Rangers used.

As the RIB grew closer to shore, Puller could make out many people on board. Too many for the boat's small footprint.

Carson touched his arm. He looked at her, found her pointing back toward land. Puller focused that way and saw the men from the truck coming down to the beach.

Right now he would have given anything for a night camera to record what was about to happen.

People were being pulled off the RIB. When they hit the sand, Puller could see that they were bound and their mouths taped shut.

They also wore different-colored shirts.

Puller flipped up his goggles and saw green, red, and blue.

He felt a gentle squeeze on his arm and turned to see Carson staring over his shoulder. She looked at him. He shook his head and turned back to what was happening on the beach.

The people were herded up the sand and to the truck where two men were posted there to guard them.

Puller turned his attention back to the beach, where the RIB had disappeared, but another one was now approaching the beach. The scenario that had just happened on the beach was repeated with this second group.

A third RIB beached, disgorged passengers, and left.

Then a fourth RIB came and did the same.

After the last RIB left, the truck was locked and three men climbed into the cab.

Carson said, "What do we do now?"

Puller was thinking this very same question.

What do we do?

"We need to call the police, right now," Carson urged.

But Puller shook his head. "No," he said.

She looked at him in bewilderment.

"No? Are you crazy? Those people were prisoners, Puller."

"Yeah, I can see that."

"Then we call the cops."

"Not yet."

"When do you think might be a more suitable time?"

Puller looked at the truck as it started to pull away. "Let's go," he said.

CHAPTER

77

Puller kept back as far as he could from the truck while still keeping it in sight.

It was tricky. Headlights back here at this time of night would no doubt make the guys in the truck dangerously suspicious.

Carson alternated between looking at the taillights of the truck and scowling at Puller.

"I'm still not getting this tactic, Puller. If you don't call the police for something like this, what then?"

He said nothing, but kept his gaze upon the truck as it wound around the curves with thick trees on both sides. They might as well have been in a forest. There was no hint of the nearby ocean except for the occasional whiff of brine.

He finally looked at her. "Well-timed op. Secluded spot, middle of the night. Bring them in by water, truck them out."

"Right, so?"

"How many nights you think they do this?"

"I have no way of knowing that."

"Let's say they do it three or four times a week. Maybe seven days a week."

"Maybe not. Maybe we just got lucky."

"No one is that lucky."

"And your point?"

"Maybe this is what my aunt saw. Or what the Storrows saw."

"Maybe it is."

"My aunt was a good upstanding citizen. The Storrows were, by all indications, pillars of the community."

"Granted, they probably were."

"And you think these elderly solid citizens saw what we saw and didn't tell the police?"

Carson started to say something and then stopped. "So your point is they did tell the police and nothing happened."

"Oh, something happened. They ended up dead. All of them."

"You think the police are in on what we just saw?"

"I don't see how you can run an op like that, even once a week, and trust that the cops are not going to happen upon you. All it would take is one cop on patrol seeing a boat light, or the truck, or just happening to walk down the beach and see what we saw tonight."

"And they couldn't risk that?"

"We just saw four RIBs. They're not long-distance boats. That means there's a larger vessel out there that they launched from. I counted eighty people off the boats, and now they're in the back of that truck. You're talking equipment, money, and manpower. The payoff has to justify that."

"Like you said before. Drugs, guns."

"They were people, General. No guns, no drugs."

"So maybe drug mules?"

"And there were young women. So prostitutes. And bigger, older men. Maybe slave laborers."

"Slave laborers? In America?"

"Why not?"

"I thought we fought the Civil War to take care of that little bit of evil."

"If it's profitable, evil can come back strong, just like a cancer with fresh blood lines to feed off."

"Damn, Puller, do you really think that's what this is about?"

"A pipeline is a pipeline. You can run lots of different things through it."

"And the police?"

"Part of the equation. Paradise is wealthy and a tourist destination and no one wants to rock the boat and maybe the cops are paid to look the other way. Hell, maybe the whole damn town is."

"I can't believe that."

"Maybe not. But if I'm those guys I'm not putting an operation like this together and risking a cop stumbling onto it and blowing it out of the water."

"Something like that has to come from the top. So Bullock?"

"Maybe. I was surprised at how quickly he turned into my friend."

"I wonder who's running the op from the other end."

"My bet is on the guy who got his Bentley blown up."

"What? Lampert? How do you figure that?"

"I checked the guy out. Made and lost a fortune. Then made another one back, obviously. Only I can't find out how. And he screws the hired help. And maybe they're not hired at all. Maybe he's got slaves on his 'plantation.'"

"Okay, let's say he is the guy. Why would someone blow up his car?"

"Maybe a guy with size sixteen shoes has a beef with the man."

"Size sixteen shoes?"

Puller explained about the footprints outside the guesthouse window. "He's the same guy who saved my butt the other night. I don't think he did it out of kindness. And maybe he regrets it now.

But he may be the one after Lampert. He works on a landscaping crew. Why do I want to bet he works the Lampert estate?"

"And his beef with Lampert?"

"No idea. And I may be barking up the wrong tree. But guys that big with skills like he has are rare. And I can't believe he came here to cut grass."

"So with the knowledge in hand, what do we do? Call in the Army? The DEA? The Border Patrol?"

"We need to know more. If we start making noises and they have moles on the inside, we'll never get the evidence we need to put them away. They'll be gone, never to return."

"Well, when we find out where that truck is going we may have all the evidence we need," she said.

Puller suddenly punched the gas and the Tahoe sped up.

"What are you doing?" Carson exclaimed. "They'll see you."

"We've already been seen."

"What?"

"Twin bogies behind us and they're

closing like an Abrams tank brigade on a soft target."

She looked behind her and saw the set of twin beams coming on way too fast.

"Shit!"

Carson lifted her pistol from its holster.

Puller shook his head. "Ineffective at this range and tactical position. Take my rifle. I'll pop the back window. Take up a position in the rear. Use the tailgate to steady the rifle." He eyed the rearview again. "I'm thinking fifty yards. Aim for the windshield and the radiator."

She was already scrambling over the seat. "Roger that."

He popped the window, she took her spot, settled the rifle on the tailgate, but then she paused.

"Puller, what if it's the police or Feds back there?"

A bullet shattered the back glass, covering Carson in shards.

"Don't think so," said Puller. "Fire! Now!"

Carson pumped five rounds from her

rifle into the windshield and radiator of the first vehicle. It swerved and smoke started pouring from the hood.

Carson fired twice more and the windshield shattered completely and then came off in one large chunk. She could see the driver hunched over and then the vehicle flew off the road.

"One bogie down," she called out.

"Don't declare victory yet," barked Puller.

Out of the smoky haze thrown off by the first vehicle the second, an SUV, raced, bearing down on them fast.

These people were taking no chances.

Bullets poured from twin gunmen hanging out the windows.

The Tahoe's left rear wheel shredded.

"Puller," cried out Carson.

"I know."

He fought the wheel, keeping it on the asphalt.

Carson fired back but then stopped.

"Keep shooting," snapped Puller.

"My rifle jammed."

"Shit," barked Puller. He checked the rearview. Bogie coming fast, major firepower. They had one bad wheel and as he checked his fuel gauge he saw it plummeting. One round must have pierced the fuel tank.

"We're losing gas," Carson called out. "I can smell it."

"They hit the tank."

Carson looked back and her eyes widened as the SUV came on hard and fast, its hood nearing the back of the Tahoe. Then it abruptly slowed and fell back.

At first Carson thought they were retreating, but then she saw something that told her otherwise.

"Puller!"

"What?"

"They've got an RPG."

The man on the right side of the SUV was hanging out the side getting a bead on them with a rocket-propelled grenade launcher riding on his shoulder, while another man inside the truck held on to him.

That's why they had fallen back. To avoid the blast from ground zero when rocket and Tahoe plus leaky gas tank erupted in a flame ball.

Carson ducked down as the man fired. It was a good thing she was holding on, because at that very moment Puller, who'd been watching this unfold in the rearview, cut the wheel hard to the left at the exact instant the grenade launched.

The Tahoe shuddered and then responded.

The grenade passed by on the right, hit a bank of trees, and exploded.

Carson tumbled across the rear of the truck's interior as the Tahoe skidded off the road and slid onto the shoulder. The rear door was ripped open and a large hand flew in, grabbed Carson under the arm, and lifted her out of the Tahoe.

The next instant she and Puller were running for their lives.

CHAPTER

78

They had two pistols and a jammed rifle between them.

Puller led Carson to cover behind a dune. It wasn't perfect, but it didn't need to be. They looked at each other as they heard people running toward their general position.

"Tight spot," said Carson.

Puller checked the pistols. "We've both been in tighter. They haven't located us yet. It'll take some time."

"But they will."

"Yes, they will."

"Superior numbers and firepower."

"We're the underdogs, certainly."

"I don't mind that. It'll just take a little figuring to move us to the top of the food chain."

"I like your confidence."

She looked at her phone. "Can't call in the cavalry. No service."

"I know. I already checked mine." He hunkered down, looked around.

He said, "We need higher ground."

"Soldiers always want higher ground."

He looked at her, apparently sizing her up for the question he was about to ask. "You mind taking orders from an enlisted?"

She managed a smile. "Under the circumstances I think I'm going to insist that I do. I've sat behind a desk too long. Your combat boots are fresher than mine are."

He rubbed a bead of sweat from his eye. "You think you can hold this position alone?"

In response she scrambled up to the top of the dune, surveyed the beach, and then rejoined him.

"If they have another RPG round to fire, no. But if it's gun to gun, I can. For about ten minutes if I manage my ammo properly."

"I won't need that long. And I'm leaving both pistols with you." He handed the weapons to her.

"What are you going to do?" she asked.

"Get to higher ground."

"As a sniper? But the rifle jammed on me."

Puller cleared the rifle's breech, checked the firing mechanism, and pronounced it workable.

She said, "You think anyone heard what happened? The guns, the explosion? We're not that far out of town."

"We're too far out. And the breakers make a lot of noise."

"Okay."

"We'll make it, General."

"No doubt. But then every soldier wants to believe that. Good luck."

"It'll be about more than luck."

She touched him on the arm. "Counting on you to come back, John."

"There's only one thing that will stop me."

Carson knew what that was.

Death.

She drew a long breath and nodded. "Okay."

Puller slung the rifle over his shoulder and in a few seconds was gone.

Carson blinked. It was like he had simply vanished. And for a man as big as he was, that took some skill.

But then again, he's a Ranger, she thought. *That's what they do.*

She gripped her Glock, racked the slide, slid her secondary weapon, Puller's M11, into the back of her waistband, and took up her defensive position in a slot she burrowed on top of the dune. She was trying to make herself as invisible as possible. You couldn't kill what you couldn't get a bead on.

Gun on gun she could hold this piece of sand for a time. But after that it would just be inevitable.

She would die.

And if they fired another grenade she would be blown into little bits of organic matter.

She crossed herself, settled in, and took aim.

CHAPTER

79

Puller had sized up the battlefield and chosen his high ground. Now he knew he simply had to get there "fastest with the mostest."

And in that he had pretty much summed up the winning strategy of every military campaign ever fought.

When opposed by superior numbers and firepower it was essential to hit the other side fast and hard and in multiple spots. This would hopefully cause confusion, blunt any momentum they might have, and ideally force a tactical retreat.

Puller would be just fine with confusion. But then he would also be just fine with killing all of them.

He found his spot and shimmied up a tree, coming to rest in the crook formed by the trunk and a sturdy limb. He settled his rifle into place and sighted along the scope, dialing in necessary adjustments to fit the wind, distance to target, and other factors.

There were six men. They came on in two groups of three. They were moving in a V shape, one leader and two followers. From Puller's perch up the tree they looked like two arrowheads moving forward across the sand. They had some military training, he deduced, but not as much as they should have. He scanned behind the men, looking for reinforcements waiting to be deployed. He'd made that mistake at the Sierra; he didn't intend to make the same error again.

No reserves—they were bringing their full force against one they presumed was a weaker foe.

Puller's tactics had already been thought out. He didn't just line up one shot. Like a chess match he was lining up four. Two from each group. That would leave it at two on two, odds he liked much better.

He observed Carson burrowed in on top of the sand dune. He knew she would see the oncoming enemy, but she was holding her fire, awaiting his first strike. Then he knew she would know what to do because she was a soldier just like him. On the battlefield stars, bars, and stripes fell away. You were just two trained fighters using that training to defeat the other side.

He glanced out at the water and saw a curious sight. It looked like a boat coming in. The navigation lights were steady red and green, so it was heading directly to shore.

This might be backup coming from the big boat out there. If so, he had to get this skirmish on the beach over with pronto.

He let out a breath, got his physiological barometer to cold zero, optimal for minimal muscle quiver, and lasered his crosshairs on target number one.

Bang.

Number one went down.

Bang.

Number two hit the sand.

Puller had known what the other four would do when the first two went down.

They scattered. But they scattered in a predictable pattern.

Bang.

Number three went down with one of Puller's 7.62 NATO rounds blowing a large hole in the man's chest.

Bang.

This kill shot came from a Glock.

Number four went down and stayed there.

Carson was emptying the clip from her Glock, spraying fields of fire both left and right, which were the only two directions worth aiming at, because it would also cover fore and aft movements.

She dumped her Glock and aimed the M11 but didn't fire.

The two survivors down there had made it to cover, both from Carson below and Puller above.

But Puller had gotten most of what he had wished for.

It was now two on two.

The only unknown was the boat.

But for that, he would have just played a waiting game, keeping the two pinned down until they lost their patience and made a run for it.

It would have been a short run.

Puller would get one.

Carson would get the other.

But the damn boat was coming on fast, so Puller didn't have the luxury of waiting.

He looked down at the same moment Carson looked up. He didn't know if she could see him without the benefit of the goggles he had on, but she had obviously either seen or heard the boat.

He shimmied down the tree, landing quietly in the sand.

A minute later he had rejoined Carson.

"Two left," he said.

"Right, but reinforcements are coming from the water."

"I know. I saw."

"Now what? Those two are between us and the road."

"So we have to remove the obstacle."

"We don't have time for a standard pincer movement."

He said, "What do you suggest, General?"

"So I'm back in command?"

"Superior rank is never really out of command. You earlier deferred to my judgment. Leadership defaults back to you."

She looked around. "Feint, draw out, and strike. Speed and finality."

He nodded in agreement. "I'll do the feint and draw."

"I was thinking the other way around. You're better with the rifle."

He shook his head. "We're close enough range to do it with pistols. And I know you've kept your certifications up."

"How?"

"You're chasing the second star. You wouldn't let something that simple trip you up."

"I am damn good with a handgun at anything under twenty-five meters."

"Then we're well within your comfort zone."

"But the feint will get shot at."

"That's the hope."

She gazed at him. "Did you so readily volunteer for all the dangerous assignments in Iraq and Afghanistan too?"

"All the assignments over there were dangerous."

Puller checked the water again. The boat was almost there.

"We're out of time."

"Let's do it."

It worked.

Nearly perfectly.

But anything less than perfection under the circumstances was problematic.

Puller took up position fifteen meters off the left flank of the targets, who had committed the tactical blunder of retreating to the same spot. It marshaled their firepower but also left them sitting ducks for the strategy devised by Carson.

Carson had taken up her strike position five meters off Puller's left flank, down in the sand, the M11 positioned on the hard shell of a long-dead sea creature. She had the goggles on now. She had crystal-clear fields of fire.

Now it was up to Puller to do the feinting just right.

And he did, almost.

He sprinted out of seemingly no-where, a nearly six-foot-four blur wide-stepping through the sand running a zigzag route as though traversing a minefield.

The shots rang out almost immedi-ately from the two men.

Puller had chosen his angle well.

It had made the two men step out from cover in order to draw a bead on him.

Carson popped off four shots. They were well placed, compact rounds, de-signed for close-quarter battle and max damage.

Two shots hit one man in the torso. The other two hit the other man in the exact same spots.

Double tapped, they dropped to the sand.

But so did Puller.

CHAPTER

80

"John!"

Carson raced forward through the sand.

She reached him in seconds. He had already risen to one knee.

"Where?" she said automatically.

"Left side. In and out," he said. "I think it was the first guy who fired. He obviously knows how to grid shoot."

"Let's make sure it's out."

She pulled up his shirt, felt around for the entry and exit points, and found them both.

"You're bleeding pretty heavily."

"I'll be okay."

"We need to get you to a hospital."

"I'm not arguing with that. In my duffel in the Tahoe I've got some medical supplies. I'll patch myself up."

"I can patch you up, Puller."

He looked over her shoulder.

"Okay, but right now, keep low, get your gun ready, and turn around."

She flinched, but just for an instant.

"The boat?"

"The boat," he replied.

"Shit."

She turned and saw what he had already seen.

The boat was beached on the shore. There was no one in it.

"Looks like the opposition has already deployed," said Puller.

"It's not a RIB. Maybe fewer people."

"More than two is problematic. We're clearly not at full strength."

"Can you manage?" she asked.

"Not the first time I've been shot."

"I know."

Puller took off his shirt and wound it around his middle to try to stanch the bleeding. He gripped the rifle and stood.

"How many rounds do you have in the M11?" he asked.

"Ten. You?"

"Five and then I'm out."

"How do you want to do this?"

"Seek and destroy. I go left and you right. You see me fire, you fire at whatever I'm targeting. I'll do the same with you."

"Let's manage our ammo carefully."

"We need to kill what we can when we can, General. Hand-to-hand after that if it comes to it."

"They hit you one time on your wound you're going down."

He turned to stare at her and said quietly, "It'll take more than one time."

Her lips parted, she eyed the bloody shirt and said nothing before looking away.

They split up. Carson moved toward the water, Puller the opposite way. Fifteen meters apart they stealthily advanced, their gazes rotating side to side, up and down.

Puller stopped when he smelled it.

Sulfur.

It was coming from his right, meaning Carson's left. They were up ahead. The stench on the clothes of whoever was out there was being driven into his nostrils by the breeze.

And then Puller realized what that entailed. He and Carson carried the exact same stink. The wind changed, carrying their smell the other way.

"Down," he roared as shots flew overhead.

He sank into the sand but did not return fire. He had no clear target and with only five rounds left he had none to waste.

He just hoped that Carson had heard his warning in time.

He waited, his heartbeat hammering in his ears.

He wanted to call out to Carson, but that would do neither of them any good. He had already told the other side there was more than one of them by calling out to her.

He gazed ahead, sweeping the area in grids. Carson had the goggles. She would be able to see things he couldn't.

He decided to play off whatever she did.

He looked over and saw Carson on her belly gliding forward. The sound of the breakers covered this movement.

He did the same. Her movements became faster and Puller, shot up as he was, was hard pressed to keep up with her. Then it occurred to him that she wanted to get there first, to absorb the attack or counterattack before he would be in harm's way.

"Screw that," he muttered and redoubled his efforts.

It all came to an end several seconds later. Carson jumped to her feet and aimed.

Puller got there a millisecond later and did the same, his rifle finding and fixing on the target.

One gun was pointed at Carson.

One gun was pointed at Puller.

Mecho faced Puller.

Chrissy Murdoch confronted Carson.

Mecho and Puller recognized each other at the same instant.

Carson and Murdoch did not have the same advantage.

Puller said, "Who the hell are you?"

Mecho looked back at him, his finger

a bare millimeter from the trigger of his weapon.

Murdoch kept her gaze dead on Carson. The women's gun muzzles were barely six feet apart.

Murdoch said, "Who the hell are you?"

"Brigadier General Julie Carson, United States Army."

Puller said, "Special Agent John Puller, Criminal Investigation Division, United States Army."

Mecho did not take his gaze off Puller.

Puller did not take his gaze off Mecho. He said, "Now who the hell are you?"

Mecho again said nothing. Puller eyed Murdoch. "The last time I saw you, you were in your bathrobe at Lampert's estate and your name was Christine Murdoch."

"That is my cover name. I'm actually Lieutenant Claudia Diaz with the Colombian National Police. I'm assigned to a joint task force between my country and yours."

"For what purpose?" asked Puller.

"Antislavery efforts. It has been authorized by your State Department."

"And him?" asked Puller, motioning at Mecho.

"He's assisting me."

"He doesn't look Colombian to me."

"That is because I am not Colombian," snapped Mecho.

"But you saved my butt the other night," said Puller. "Why?"

"I didn't like the odds. Too many against one."

"Did you know who I was?"

Mecho shook his head.

"Why are you helping her?" Puller asked.

"That is my business," replied Mecho.

"Can we all show some creds?" said Carson.

Puller, Carson, and Diaz pulled out their badges.

Mecho pulled nothing.

"Where are you from?" asked Puller.

"Not from here," said Mecho.

"You're making this a lot harder than it has to be."

"That is not my problem."

Diaz said, "We were attacked by a half dozen of the slavers."

"Seems to be going around," said Carson. "So were we."

"And you obviously survived," said Diaz.

"As did you," replied Carson.

"We carried the bodies out to the ocean. I would recommend we do the same for you," said Diaz.

"Why?"

"To cover our tracks. So the big fish do not get away."

"I'm afraid they already have," said Puller. "The truck with the people got away."

"Damn," said Diaz, and she was the first to holster her weapon.

Carson followed suit.

The two men did not budge; their guns remained pointed at one another.

Diaz said to Mecho, "Stand down, Mecho. They're obviously not with the slavers."

"Puller, lower your weapon," said Carson.

"Screw that! Him first."

"The same," snarled Mecho.

Carson and Diaz looked at each other with exasperated expressions.

"Men," said Diaz. "They have too much—"

"Testosterone," finished Carson. "Shall we?" she added, and Diaz nodded.

The women walked over and stood between the men's pointed weapons.

"Stand down," they said in unison.

With their targets obstructed, Puller and Mecho slowly lowered their weapons.

Diaz looked at Puller. "You've been shot!"

"Yeah, that one I had figured out. You two have some filling in to do."

Diaz said, "But we also don't have much time. If the truck got away, they know what's happened. They will pull out of all their operations. And we'll lose any evidence we might have."

Puller glowered at Mecho. "Then we don't have any time to lose, do we? And I hope you can change a tire, big guy."

CHAPTER

81

Mecho changed the tire on the Tahoe and plugged the gas tank hole while Carson and Diaz patched Puller's wound.

"You still need to get real medical treatment, Puller," said Carson.

"She's right," added Diaz.

Puller put his shirt back on and stared at each of them. "Okay, first we get the bad guys and then I go get stitched up. Deal?" He glanced over at Mecho. "You done yet?"

Mecho gave the last tire lug one final

turn and then rose holding the tire iron in one big hand.

"I'll drive."

"No, I'll drive," said Puller. "You just tell me where."

The women rode in the back and cleaned and reloaded all of their weapons.

Mecho sat next to Puller and gave him directions to the warehouse.

"Can you fight with your wound?" Mecho asked Puller without looking at him.

There was no sympathy in the question. Puller neither expected nor wanted any. Mecho simply wanted to know the physical status of his comrades in arms. He wanted to know if he could count on Puller or rather have to compensate for him.

Puller would have wanted to know the exact same thing.

"They gave me a painkiller I had in my duffel. I can shoot and I can fight and I can take punishment. So don't worry about me. I'll handle my end. You cover yours."

"What about your woman?" asked Mecho. "Can she hold her own?"

"What about your woman?" asked Puller. "Can she?"

"Are you always this cooperative?"

"I don't even know who you are, so yeah, this is about as cooperative as it gets from me."

"Diaz will be fine."

"So will Carson."

They rode for another minute in silence. The only noise was the sounds from the women readying the weapons.

Finally Mecho said, "My name is Gavril. That is my given name. My surname would mean nothing to you. But people call me Mecho."

"You're Bulgarian," said Puller.

Mecho glanced at him. "How did you know?"

"I fought with them in Iraq way back. They were great fighters and could drink any other nationality under the table. Even the Russians."

Mecho smiled. "The Russians think vodka is gold. It is merely water with perfume. It does not even put hair on the chest."

"Were you military?"

Mecho's smile faded. "I used to be. Then things changed."

"What things?"

Neither man noticed that Carson and Diaz had finished their work and were listening intently to this exchange.

"Bulgaria was no longer part of the Soviet Union, of course. But some things don't change. I love my country. It is a place of beauty. The people there are good. They like to work hard. They love their freedoms. But that does not mean that every leader we have is a good one who deserves the respect of the people. So sometimes when you do not follow along blindly things happen to you."

"Were you imprisoned?"

Mecho glanced at him sharply. "Why do you say that?"

"Because the Soviets were big on that, that's why. And Bulgaria was part of that world for a long time."

"For a time," Mecho said. "Perhaps

a longer time than I care to remember."

"How did you end up here going after slavers?"

"I come from a small village in the southwest part of my country. The Rila range, it is called. It is remote. The people there work hard. There are few if any outsiders who come there. My family still lives there."

Puller said, "But outsiders did come?"

Mecho nodded and glanced out the window so as not to show the tears forming in his eyes.

"Men came and promised things, a better life for our young people. Education, jobs, all good things. They took about thirty of them." He paused. "Including my youngest sister. We are a large family. She is far younger than me. She was only sixteen when she left." He paused again. "No, not when she left, when she was *taken*."

"They were slavers," said Puller.

Mecho nodded. "Who thought that a little village on a mountain in Bulgaria would never be able to strike back for the evil that was done. I was not there at the time, or I would have not allowed this to happen. I have seen a lot of the world. The people in my village have not. They are trusting, too trusting. When I came back and found out what had happened, I started to look for my sister. And the others."

"What's her name?" This question came from Carson, who had put a hand on Mecho's big shoulder, gripping it.

"Rada. This is she."

Mecho took out the photo and held it out to Carson. She took it and looked at it.

"She's very beautiful," said Carson, and Diaz nodded in agreement.

"Not like the rest of the family," said Mecho matter-of-factly. "They look more like me. Big and ugly."

"You are not ugly, Mecho," said Diaz fiercely. "You are a man trying to do the right thing. There is nothing more handsome than that."

"And you tracked her down to Lampert?" asked Puller.

Diaz answered while Mecho took the photograph of Rada back from Carson and stared down silently at it. "We have talked," she said. "He actually worked the connection from the other way. Through Stiven Rojas."

"Rojas," exclaimed Carson. "He's on our most wanted list. He's even been deemed a national security risk. He's involved in this?"

"He collects the product, the people, and then they are transported to this country," said Diaz. "Lampert takes over from there. He has established buyers everywhere. He gets the people to them. They are separated into three main categories. Prostitutes are the most valuable. Next are drug mules. Then common laborers."

Mecho added, "They wear different-colored clothing that shows which category they fall into. I have seen this."

Diaz nodded.

Puller said, "We saw it tonight."

"And you said he has buyers in the U.S.? For slaves?" said Carson.

"The slave trade has never been more lucrative," said Diaz. "As governments crack down on drugs and guns, it is becoming more and more popular.

You need people to carry drugs. You need hookers to score tricks. And you need people to work the fields and the factories. If you don't have to pay them or pay them very much it is good for the bottom line."

"But it's not like you can keep those people locked up. Prostitutes, drug runners, laborers. Why don't they just escape? America is a big country," said Puller. "And there's always a policeman nearby."

"Because they tell them that if they do try to escape, or tell the police, their families will be killed," said Mecho.

"How do you know this?" asked Diaz, looking at him curiously.

"I had a talk with two of Lampert's men. They told me. And his house-keeper, I could tell from the little she told me that she is a slave. She is afraid for her family. Lampert also uses her for sex."

Mecho's eyes drifted toward Diaz's when he said this last part, but she quickly looked away, her face redden-ing.

Puller said, "You had a talk with two

of Lampert's men? Would they be the same pair that were staying at the Plaza?"

Mecho did not answer, which to Puller was answer enough.

"So you killed them?"

"They were not human. Not any longer. They were like rabid dogs."

"You still murdered them."

"You have not killed before?"

"I have not *murdered* before."

Diaz said, "That can be dealt with later."

Puller said, "Mecho, do you know anything about the death of an old lady and an old couple?"

Mecho said, "I saw an old couple killed on the beach when I first came here."

Puller glanced sharply at him. "On the beach? Did you see who killed them?"

Mecho shook his head. "But it was one person. Shots to the head. Then their bodies were dragged into the water. The tide took them out."

"And you just let it happen?" said Puller.

"There was nothing I could do. It happened too fast."

Carson said, "Okay, their bodies were dragged out to the water. So probably a man. Big, small, white, black?"

"Not that tall. I could not see the color of the skin clearly but I think white. And slender, but obviously strong."

"And you blew up Lampert's Bentley," said Puller.

Mecho looked at him, puzzled. "How did you know that?"

"You have big feet."

Diaz said, "This can all keep. We need to be prepared for what is coming up in the next few minutes."

Mecho nodded. "The warehouse. It is where they keep the slaves. That is where the trucks go."

"Then we should call in the police," said Carson.

"No," said Diaz. "Lampert and Rojas have assets everywhere. We can't trust the police."

"Then the U.S. military. Eglin is right up the road."

"By the time they can send anyone it'll be too late," argued Diaz.

Puller had a sudden thought. "You said this was a joint operation with the U.S. Did you happen to be working with military-looking guys in a Chrysler?"

"Yes," said Diaz. "They told me of their interaction with Americans. I guess that was you."

"Guess it was. Were they tracking me or Betsy Simon?"

"They had spotted a car belonging to Simon near the transfer spot one night. They traced it to her. Then she was killed. They started watching."

"Where are they now?" asked Puller.

"After their encounter with you, they were reassigned. No one has replaced them yet."

"Great," muttered Puller.

"Okay, give us the layout of the warehouse," said Carson. "If they're still there we'll have to hit it hard and fast."

"We *will* hit it hard and fast," said Mecho. "And we will kill who we have to kill." He looked at Puller. "Unless you have a problem with murdering slavers."

"No problem at all," said Puller. "If they're trying to murder me."

"That I think you can count on," said Mecho.

CHAPTER

82

There were four sides to the warehouse and they covered all of them. They had to split their forces in quarters to accomplish this, but allowing a hole for anyone to escape was deemed not acceptable.

Puller took the rear.

Mecho the front.

Carson the left side.

Diaz the right.

They were prepared for a war.

They did not find one.

They did not find anyone at all.

The warehouse was empty.

The makeshift prison cells held no one.

They searched the space in ten minutes and then regrouped in the center of it.

Puller said, "They move fast, I'll give them that."

"But where have they gone?" asked Carson. "We can get APBs out. They have to be using trucks to transport."

"Lot of trucks going up and down the highway," pointed out Puller. "Can't stop and search them all."

He glanced over her shoulder and stiffened. He raced past Carson and over to a spot against the wall. He knelt and picked it up.

The others joined him.

"What is it, Puller?" asked Carson.

Puller held it up.

It was a ring. A small silver ring with a lion on it.

"This belongs to my friend Diego."

"Who is this Diego?" asked Mecho.

"A kid. About twelve years old. His cousin is Mateo. He's five. They were probably both here. Diego probably left this as a clue. He's a pretty smart kid."

"A five-year-old," said Diaz. "Why would they have taken twelve- and five-year-old boys?"

"Prostitution?" said Puller. "Sick bastards out there."

"No. Rojas is a criminal. And a truly evil man. But he has never taken anyone that young before."

"Diego didn't come through the normal pipeline. He lived in Paradise. He was snatched from right here. Along with Mateo."

Diaz looked worried.

"What is it?" asked Carson.

"Then it was Lampert who ordered this. Not Rojas."

Puller rose and pocketed the ring. "So what exactly does that mean?"

"It could mean that Lampert is expanding his product line, without Rojas's approval or even knowledge."

"Expand it where?"

"Terrorists."

"What?" exclaimed Carson.

"You build mock families to divert suspicion. A mother. A father. With young children. If you travel with little ones security is instinctively lessened.

It is against human nature to take your own children into harm's way."

"Not in the Middle East," said Puller. "Happened all the time."

"Yes, they were used as shields and sometimes bombs, I understand this," said Diaz. "But this is not the Middle East. And the people who used children as shields and bombs were not their parents."

Puller said, "So you're saying it's great cover to travel with small kids. To avoid detection or at least heightened scrutiny."

"Maybe getting in and out of the country," added Carson.

"Yes, that is what I'm thinking," said Diaz.

Puller looked at Carson. He said, "I should have shot Lampert the night I met him."

Diaz said urgently, "We need to find them."

"They had to have trucked them out of here," said Puller. He looked at Mecho. "Any idea how many people might have been held here?"

Mecho looked around at the empty

cells. "I watched the beach for two nights. Each time eighty prisoners were brought in."

"So a lot of people to move," said Puller.

"They are probably heading toward the interstate highways as we speak," said Diaz.

Puller mulled this thought over as Carson stared at him. "I'm not too sure about that," he said.

"Where else?" asked Diaz. "They have product to move. They have buyers."

"If I'm Lampert and I know my pipeline was compromised, then I'm not going to deliver the product to my buyers. He couldn't be sure it wouldn't be followed. That blows his pipeline sky-high. And that also wins him a death sentence from Rojas."

"What, then?" asked Carson. "What do you think he's doing with them?"

Puller stared in the direction of the Gulf. "I think he's returning them to sender."

"Back to Colombia?" said Diaz.

"Back to wherever they came from," said Puller. He looked at Mecho.

"How did you get here?"

"I swam mostly," said Mecho, but Puller could tell by his face that the man was leaping ahead to the ultimate conclusion of Puller's question.

"I was one of the taken," he said. "It sidetracked me for a bit. But I escaped. The crew who brought me was not so lucky. They were late and it cost them their lives."

Diaz said, "Where did you escape from?"

"An oil platform off the coast. No longer used, of course. They dock at a series of them going from Mexico to Florida. That is how they move the product."

Diaz said, "But I didn't think there were any oil platforms off the coast of Florida."

Carson spoke up. "That's mostly true. The vast majority are off the coasts of Louisiana and Texas. And some off Alabama. There are no oil platforms on the Atlantic side of Florida. And pretty much all the oil wells dug in Florida state waters in the Gulf over the years came up dry."

"Okay," said Puller. "But Mecho is saying there is one out there and that he was on it. How does that make sense?"

Carson continued, "Some energy companies made natural gas discoveries in the mid-eighties to mid-nineties. About twenty-five miles off the coast. But the state of Florida objected to the gas being mined and the Feds put the kibosh on it in the early 2000s. But there were some platforms built out there in anticipation of the gas being brought up. Energy companies usually have to dismantle the platforms within a certain amount of time. But I think there was litigation involved with those platforms. Nothing moves fast when the lawyers get involved."

Puller stared at her. "How do you know so much about it?"

"I did a white paper on it for the DoD. I told you that we were looking into things like that for national security purposes. They were worried about terrorists using the abandoned platforms to enter this country. So I mapped pretty much every platform in the Gulf. And there are thousands of them that are abandoned and in the process of being either dismantled or turned into reefs for marine life. Those are basically the two options for them."

"Did the DoD act on your paper?" asked Puller.

"No. It went into the black hole where most white papers go. But we never thought about slavers using them."

"It's sort of like the opposite of the Underground Railroad during the Civil War," noted Puller. "Ferrying people to slavery instead of freedom."

Diaz said, "We never thought of slavers using the oil platforms either."

"Why should you?" asked Mecho. "People like Rojas and Lampert spend every minute of their lives trying to stay one step ahead. Money. That is all they care about."

"So the last oil platform before here," began Puller. "Do you know how to get back there?"

"I believe so, yes," said Mecho. "I tried as best I could to fix its position in my mind."

"We can call in the Coast Guard," said Carson. "They can send a cutter right at these guys. There's no way they can match that sort of firepower, I don't care how badass Rojas and Lampert are."

"A cutter is a big ship," countered Mecho. "They will see it coming from miles away. They will kill all the prisoners and be gone before the cutter even gets close. The same for aircraft."

"Well, we have to do something," said Carson. "We can't just let these people get away."

"A small force. Stealth. At night," said Puller. "That's our only shot."

"There're only four of us," Diaz reminded him.

"A small force, like he said," observed Mecho. "Small in number, big in fight."

"But can't we at least call in some help from the locals?" said Carson.

Diaz said firmly, "I do not trust anyone."

"Neither do I really," said Puller. "But

"People disappear."

"Come on, Puller."

"And Paradise is part of a pipeline for slaves being brought into the U.S."

Landry froze and blurted out, "What?"

"Right down the road from here. At the beach that smells like sulfur."

"I know that stretch of sand. No one goes there."

"You're wrong. People do go there."

"No one from Paradise, I meant."

"So the police don't patrol there?"

"It's not part of the town. It's a no-man's-land between Paradise and the next municipality over."

"That makes it perfect for a pipeline, then."

"And you have proof of this? Then let's call in the Feds. Right now."

"We don't have proof. The proof is getting away as we speak."

"So what are you doing here, then?"

"We need another gun."

Landry once more looked at the SUV. "Who the hell is in there?"

"Carson. The big guy who saved my life at the Sierra. And one other person who I can vouch for. Are you with us?"

"I'm on duty. I'm on patrol. I can't just up and leave on some wild-goose chase with you."

"It's not a wild-goose chase. And you can get someone else to relieve you."

"Puller, I can't."

"Can't or won't? Look, Landry, we nail this group you can write your own future in law enforcement."

"I like it just fine here."

"Then you'll be helping us catch some really bad people. It's why you carry the badge, right?"

"Does this have to do with your aunt? And the Storrows?"

"I think it does, yes."

"Slavers killed them?"

"Yes. Because they found out what was going on."

Landry drew a deep breath.

"Come on, Landry. We need you to get this done. You're the only one here I'd ask."

"Let me make some calls, see if I can get someone to cover for me."

"Why don't you call Hooper and Bull-ock?"

"Why them?"

"Because I'm betting they don't pick up."

"Why wouldn't they?"

"Just call them."

She did so and there was no answer on either phone.

Landry put her cell away. "Both went to voice mail. But they could be asleep."

"Doubtful."

"Why?"

"Just don't think so."

"You're not implying that they're somehow involved in all this."

"We don't have time for explanations. Are you coming or not?"

Landry drew another long breath.

Puller said, "I think the town can get along without you for a few hours."

"If this costs me my job?"

"Then you can kick my ass. And I'll help you get another job."

Landry smiled resignedly. "And your friend the general?"

"She'll help you too."

"Right, like I believe that. I don't see us being best friends."

"You might be surprised. Let's go."

"Where exactly?"

Puller pointed toward the Gulf.

"Out there."

CHAPTER

84

The boat was not large, and the seas were rough. Water continually washed over the sides of the boat.

Puller had everyone put their weapons in a watertight compartment. Mecho had given up his gun reluctantly.

Puller could hardly blame him. He did not like to be without a weapon either.

Puller had the wheel of the twenty-two-foot bow rider that Diaz had led them to. It was the same one they had used to dispose of the bodies of the men they killed. There was still some blood on one of the gunwales.

When Landry saw this she looked startled, but on a glance from Puller she said nothing. However, there was wariness in her eyes after that as she stood next to him at the helm holding on as the boat bounced over the waters.

Mecho had given Puller general directions to follow to the oil platform. In the darkness he was navigating by compass and the GPS plotter.

"Are you sure about these directions?" asked Puller. Mecho nodded, though he didn't look all that confident.

Carson came to stand next to him. She held up her smartphone.

"Before we left land I had my office forward me the locations of every platform within fifty miles of Florida. There is one that is far closer to the coast than any other. Here are the coordinates."

Puller looked at the numbers on her phone and then checked his plotter. He shot Mecho a glance. "Your memory is good. It's pretty much right where you said it was."

A wave hit them and Puller had to execute a sharp turn.

Puller looked at Landry, who was watching the rising seas with caution.

"Why so rough out here?" he asked.

"Remember Tropical Storm Danielle? It's heading this way. Might get up to a Cat One. We're catching the front edge of it."

"Great, love the timing," said Puller.

"You want me to pilot?"

"I got it."

Landry looked over at Diaz. "That's the woman from Lampert's place. Murdoch, right?"

"Right."

"What's she doing here?"

"Her name isn't Murdoch."

"What is it then?"

"Diaz. She's a cop."

"A Fed?"

"You could say that. She was planted at Lampert's."

"Lampert? He's involved in this?"

"Apparently his source of wealth is selling people."

"Jesus! And his car being blown up?"

"A not so subtle warning that someone was on his track."

Landry pointed at Diaz. "Her?"

"No, the big guy over there."

"Why him? Is he a cop too?"

"No. I think this is more personal with
him."

Mecho sat in one of the stern seats
and stared straight ahead. The pitching
and rolling of the boat seemed to have
no effect on him.

However, Carson and Diaz were leaning over the sides of the boat and looking green.

Landry observed this and said, "They
don't have their sea legs."

"Carson is Army. She's used to firm
land under her feet. Diaz, I don't know."

The boat caught a large wave the
wrong way and nearly capsized. They
were all drenched.

Puller regained control and focused
on the seas ahead. "Take a seat, Landry,
and hold on."

Puller turned and called out to the
others, "Everybody get life jackets on,

now. This is going to get worse before it gets better."

They all pulled on life jackets, although Mecho's was far too small. It wouldn't even stretch across his chest so he just held on to it.

Puller looked up ahead. The sky was jet black even though the dawn wasn't all that far off. While light would be welcome so he could see the approaching waves better, he preferred the dark. Attacking something in broad daylight was never a good idea even with superior numbers.

And they would not have superior numbers.

They would in fact probably be vastly outnumbered, with prisoners who could instantly be turned into hostages. It would take perfection to actually pull this off. And one almost never achieved perfection on the battlefield.

The VHF radio mounted underneath the helm squawked. Diaz must have programmed it to sound off when there were weather alerts available. Puller picked it up, listened to the taped announcement. He put the handheld back in its slot and looked grim.

Carson crab-walked over to him as the boat rolled and pitched in waves that were far higher than it.

"What is it?" she asked.

"Small craft warning was just issued. Ordered to get to shore."

"Well, we're going the other way," said Carson.

"You okay on the water?"

"If I were I would've joined the Navy."

"I'd take you back to shore if I could."

"I wouldn't let you. Army, Navy, Marines, Air Force. We all go where the battle will be fought. Get there however we can."

"With that attitude you'll get at least three stars, General."

"General?"

"Back on the clock."

She looked up ahead. "Any idea how much farther? Even with the storm the skies are lightening."

"I know. And in this weather the trip time is hard to judge."

A moment later there was a huge bolt of lighting that briefly turned night to day. It was followed by an enormous crack of thunder that seemed to shake the bow rider to its fiberglass core.

"This boat was not built to take a beating like this," said Carson.

"Neither were people."

"If we go down we'll never survive in these seas."

"Some R and R for you, huh?"

She touched him on the shoulder. "Like I'd have it any other way."

"Okay, you have my vote for four stars."

"And so what's the plan when we get there?"

"The plan is we beat the bad guys and rescue the prisoners."

"That concept I got. I mean how do we do it?"

"I don't think we can tactically battle-plan this one, General. It's all about conditions when we get there. It's an oil platform. We get to the base and work our way up. With the head start they had they're already there. And with the storm like it is they'll have to move to an enclosed space. I doubt they'll have perimeter security set up. They wouldn't expect anyone to hit them tonight. When the storm has passed they'll head back out, retracing the way they got here, taking all the evidence with them."

"And then?"

"And then they'll set up a pipeline somewhere else. These guys are bacteria. They keep mutating to keep one step ahead of the antibiotics."

"So we're penicillin?"

"Something a lot stronger, I hope."

"If they're higher up in an enclosed space?"

"It gives us a chance. Stealth plus ability plus luck. That combo has equaled victory on more battlefields than you and I can count."

"Let's hope we can add one more to the pile."

"Do my best."

"I know that, Ranger. And if you were wrong and they didn't come back out here?"

Puller didn't answer. He was looking up ahead.

"Go sit down, General."

"What?" She looked up ahead, but couldn't make out what he could.

"Julie, go sit down. Now! And hold on. Tell the others. Quick."

Carson scurried to do this.

She had just heard something in Puller's voice she thought she never would.

Fear.

CHAPTER

85

It was not a giant wave heading at them.

Maybe it would have been better if it were.

It was a boat. No, boats were small.

This was not small. This was a ship. An ocean-going vessel of immense proportions.

A horn sounded from somewhere, deep and penetrating.

Puller did not even bother hitting his horn. It would not have been heard over the sounds of the storm or the engine noise from the approaching vessel.

Puller had an immediate problem. He

had to keep taking the approaching waves at roughly a forty-five-degree angle. As even sailors with limited experience knew, hitting waves at that angle cut their power sharply and also lessened the height the water would send a boat to.

Head-on at ninety degrees would ensure that you would receive every ounce of kinetic energy the oncoming liquid hammer could provide.

And you might very well climb a wave only to find yourself capsizing when a vertical point of no return was reached. Once your bow was straight up in the air, you were done. Flipping over backwards was pretty much inevitable. And for the passengers on board, you'd either be crushed by the boat or thrown out into the water to drown.

The problem was that for Puller to veer away from the path of the oncoming ship, he would have to hit the waves nearly directly on. The oncoming vessel was big enough, and with a deep V hull made of steel, it was strong enough to take the waves head-on. In fact, the ship was creating vast banks of rolling seas as it churned through the water at about twelve knots, pushing millions of gallons of already frothing Gulf water ahead and to the sides of it like a shovel does snow.

At the last possible instant, with the ship's horns ringing in his ears, Puller cut the wheel sharply to the left. He not only had to avoid the ship, he had to avoid its wake, which could easily capsize the bow rider.

In order to achieve that he had to cut a wide arc around the ship and move away quickly.

To do that he had to increase his speed.

That was not easily accomplished in seas like this. In fact it was nearly impossible. Half the time his prop was completely out of the water, spinning uselessly in the open air with no water around it for traction.

He did not entirely achieve his goal.

Puller yelled, "Everybody hold on."

They didn't hit the ship. But they did hit something else.

The leading edges of the ship's wake broadsided them. The boat's port side tipped down and the starboard side lurched up, probably far beyond the manufacturer's recommendation.

Carson and Landry slid across the deck and hit the port gunwale.

Carson would have gone into the water except that Mecho, one big hand wrapped around a handrail inside the boat, grabbed her leg in a crushing grip.

Landry managed to hold on to the gunwale, but her legs were dangling over the side before she regained her equilibrium and fell back inside the boat.

Diaz had slid back to front and ended up entangled with Puller's legs. One hand firmly on the wheel, Puller grabbed her with the other and lifted her up.

Unfortunately, the wall of water thrown off from the trailing edge of the ship's wake hit them just as the boat righted itself.

Gagging on saltwater, Puller managed to call out, "We're getting swamped."

They all grabbed buckets that Mecho found under a seat and started bailing.

The drains on the boat helped, but they were overwhelmed with the volume of seawater.

Puller watched as the sides of the boat started lowering into the ocean.

Using two buckets, Mecho bailed like a machine with inexhaustible fuel. Puller gave the wheel to Diaz and grabbed a bucket.

Soon, as first Landry and then Carson grew exhausted and slumped down into the water collected inside the boat, it was just the two men standing nearly side by side in the boat throwing water out a little quicker than it was coming in. Puller's painkiller was wearing off and his wound began to throb. But he didn't stop.

"We're coming back up," shouted Diaz. "Keep bailing."

Renewed by this, Carson and Landry jumped back in and started to bail simply using their hands. The tide began to turn in earnest.

Forty minutes later, the drains and bilge pump took over and the interior of the boat became relatively dry.

It was only then that Carson and

Landry hung their heads over the side of the boat and threw up the seawater that had collected in their stomachs.

Puller upchucked over the side as well and then took over the wheel from Diaz and continued his fight through the leading edge of Danielle.

Mecho dropped the buckets and stood there, soaked, his big arms at his side, breathing hard and looking up ahead.

It was if he could sense something coming.

At the helm Puller eyed the fuel gauge. He had filled the tank before they had left from cans that Diaz had had on board. But the pounding waters had caused the engine to suck a lot more fuel than normal to keep its forward progress.

Puller performed a quick calculation in his head.

The answer was unmistakable. And deeply disturbing.

We're not going to have enough gas to get back.

He looked over at Mecho, who still stood, braced against the stern seats.

Mecho was watching him. It seemed the big man had read Puller's mind as he had studied the dials in front of him.

Then he looked over Puller's shoulder and slowly pointed up ahead.

Puller turned back and looked at where he was pointing.

A huge structure suddenly became visible in the middle of the storm's fury.

Neptune's Seat was dead ahead.

They had reached the battlefield, exhausted and nearly drowned.

And now the real fight was about to begin.

CHAPTER

86

Nearly two hundred people were clustered in cages meant to hold half that number.

Diego and Mateo crouched in a corner of one cage. Both were seasick from the journey out here. There were many others who were in the same condition. Pools of vomit lay everywhere. The stench made more people sick to their stomachs, which only added to the vileness of the cages.

Diego gripped Mateo's hand and looked around.

The guards were everywhere but they didn't look as confident now.

Perhaps it was because there were far more prisoners than normal.

Perhaps it was because they all could feel the battering effects of the angry ocean against the steel frame of the oil platform. The room they were in shook with every wave.

Mateo's eyes were big as he watched the ceiling, and his fingers tightened around Diego's every time a wave slammed into them.

Diego dipped his lips to Mateo's ear. "It will be okay, Mateo. We'll be okay."

Mateo said nothing. He just kept looking at the ceiling, kept tightening his grip.

Diego looked down at his finger. Where the ring had been.

He had dropped it at the place where they had been held. He hoped someone would find it. Someone other than these people.

He kept a brave face for Mateo. But their odds of getting out of this were dwindling. If the storm did not kill them,

Diego had no idea what would happen to them or where they would end up.

With this thought, a feeling of terror seized him and he tightened his grip around Mateo's hand.

Perhaps sensing this, Mateo put his mouth to Diego's ear and whispered, "It'll be okay, Diego. We'll be okay."

Puller eased off the throttle and slipped his night-vision goggles over his eyes for a better look.

He studied the structure that had risen up from the midst of the storm. It seemed to tower right up to the top of the sky. Waves were crashing over its lower platform. Its steel legs shuddered with the pounding from millions of tons of water hitting it, driven by the fierce winds propelling Danielle landward.

Puller was looking for sentries first.

Entry points second.

Overall weaknesses third.

Mecho joined him at the helm.

"Docking will be a problem," said Puller as he watched the floating platform pitching and rolling with the waves.

"I don't think we can dock. It will crush the boat."

"Well, we can't exactly jump in and swim for it. The wind is heading away from the platform and right at us. We'll be swept out in seconds."

Puller ran his gaze over the platform once more.

"I'm thinking that in a storm like this they're not expecting any visitors. They're probably inside trying to stay warm and dry."

"Probably."

"I mean, someone would have to be batshit crazy to be out here attacking this place in the middle of a tropical storm."

"Batshit crazy," agreed Mecho.

"And they have no way of knowing that we could find our way to this platform." Puller had a sudden terrifying thought, despite the coordinates Carson's people had sent. "You're sure it's the right platform? There are a lot of them out here."

"It's the one I was on. I jumped from that deck."

Puller looked up about forty feet. "And then you swam to shore?"

"Yes. With help from some fishermen."

"No perimeter security. Wind coming from the south. Floating platform over there."

"What's your plan?"

"All timing."

Puller told the others what he was thinking.

Carson shook her head as she surveyed the rough seas and the approaching storm.

"No margin of error, Puller," she said.

"No, it's slight, but it's there."

Landry said, "Is this the only way?"

"Only one I can think of, and if we wait much longer that plan won't work."

Mecho said, "We need to try it."

Diaz nodded. "Okay, and let's break out the weapons. We're going to need them."

"I'll take care of it," said Puller.

"And once we're on the platform?" said Diaz.

Mecho pointed up at the enclosed structure. "They'll be in there. There are multiple entry and exit points. Prisoners and guards. The guards are not that well trained but they have heavy firepower. More than what we have."

"So we have to hit them hard and fast and take them by surprise," said Carson as a large wave pummeled the boat, forcing everyone to grab something to hold on to. "That will negate their superior numbers and ordnance."

She looked at Puller. "So how are you going to get us there?"

"Two at a time," he replied.

"What exactly does that mean?" asked Landry.

"It means, exactly, that you're going to have to jump. Two at a time."

CHAPTER

87

Puller aimed the bow of the boat directly at the floating platform. The bow rider fought through the waves and against the wind.

At the last possible instant he swerved, missing the bucking platform by only half a foot.

"Now," shouted Puller.

Mecho and Diaz, standing on the starboard side, leapt off the gunwale and landed, sprawled, on the platform.

Puller pulled the boat away from the platform and had Landry take the wheel while he unlocked a storage compart-

ment on the boat and opened the watertight compartment inside where he
had stored their weapons. He organized their arsenal as Landry focused
on keeping the boat within striking distance of the platform.

Finished with the weapons, Puller put
them in a collapsible, watertight duffel,
zipped it shut, and handed it to Carson.

He retook the wheel from Landry and
swung the boat back around.

He looked at Carson and then down
at the duffel she held. "That's not exactly light." He glanced at Landry. "I
think it'll be a team effort."

Landry gripped one end of the duffel. "We'll get it there," she said.

He hit the throttle and once more
steered the bow rider right at the platform, veering off at the last second
again.

It was then that Landry and Carson
collectively tossed the duffel toward the
platform. It sailed over the raging waters and Mecho caught it.

Puller brought the boat back around
again.

He roared toward the platform, fighting through the pitching, rolling seas.

Now, Landry looked green and Carson not much better.

Puller said, "You ready or do you want me to come back around?"

Carson waved this offer off. "I just want to get off this damn boat."

Landry nodded in agreement.

At the last second Puller steered to port again.

"Now," yelled Puller.

Both women launched themselves off the gunwale.

Landry touched down on the platform, rolled, and came up to a sitting position.

Carson wasn't so fortunate. Her foot slipped on the slick gunwale as she jumped. She came up short, landing half on the platform and half in the water.

As she started to lose her grip and fall fully into the Gulf, Mecho snagged her arm and lifted her completely out of the water and onto the platform.

Carson looked up at him, stunned by his strength.

"Thank God they grow them big and strong in Bulgaria," she said.

Mecho passed out the weapons and they crouched down. When Diaz's and Landry's hands closed around their weapons, they both smiled.

Carson caught their looks and smiled too as she gripped her rifle. "Guns can be a girl's best friend," she said.

No shots had come from the enclosed space. No one seemed to know they were even there. The storm had obviously drowned out the noise of the boat. And their landing on the platform was nothing compared to the pounding the ocean was giving the massive structure.

They turned and looked out to sea where Puller was maneuvering the boat for the last pass.

Landry said, "I still don't get how he's going to get on the platform. He can't jump and pilot at the same time."

"We'll find out," said Carson.

In the boat Puller was lining up the last run. He waved to the others on the platform to clear away. They moved well back.

Puller eyed the waves, analyzed the wind direction, gauged the troughs and peaks of the water. A bolt of lightning crashed down so close by that the hairs on the back of his neck went vertical.

It was now or never.

He pushed the throttle forward and aimed the boat right at the platform.

Two hundred yards.

One hundred yards.

Fifty yards.

Every image on the platform came into sharp focus despite the raging storm because Puller was totally focused.

Lining up a bead on a target with his sniper rifle.

Figuring out how to put down six guys in a few seconds without receiving a mortal blow in the process.

Working out how to get off this boat and land on that platform at forty miles per hour.

It was all the same. It required complete focus. Special skills.

And luck.

Puller said a silent prayer and gunned it.

Ten yards away.

Five.

He ripped the wheel to port and rammed the throttle into neutral at the exact same time he jumped.

The forward momentum of the boat carried with him even as the boat turned and its hard rubber fenders—which Puller had put on before attempting this maneuver—slammed against the platform.

Puller was in the air. He looked down and saw frothing water.

He looked up and saw a dark sky full of muscle and potentially catastrophic damage.

He looked down and saw steel.

He landed, rolled, and came up in time to see Mecho starting to tie off the boat to the platform.

The platform had rubberized sides to prevent the metal from smashing the boat, and along with the fenders, the bow rider did not appear to have sustained serious damage. Still, with the seas as high and frenetic as they were, there might not be a boat left much longer.

Carson tossed Puller his M11 and an MP5.

No time to wonder how he'd made it. No time to thank God for the assist.

Puller led them up the metal steps.

Zero hour was here.

CHAPTER

88

Enclosed space.

High up.

Inside the enclosed space there would be perimeter security.

Puller wanted very much to see what it looked like.

Surveillance was tricky under most conditions, particularly so under these.

But Puller found a gap.

One metal shutter was improperly closed, leaving a significant gap. He spotted this weakness and motioned Mecho over.

Diaz, Carson, and Landry had set up perimeter points around the structure.

The rain pounded down and the wind was so fierce it was hard to stand upright.

Puller glanced into the right side of the shutter and Mecho did the same from the left.

The first thing they both saw was that the space was big and open.

That was problematic on a number of levels.

The second thing they saw was that there were jury-rigged cages full of people in the middle of the space.

That was also problematic but not unexpected.

There were some good points.

The guards were deployed in regularly spaced clusters. They were not alert, weapons held loosely. Some were smoking, chugging from gallon water jugs and beer cans, and others were sitting, their guns holstered and their focus wavering.

There were also few places to hide. But some discreet shooting positions. Firing down into the massed sentries they could do a lot of damage in a very short time with minimal exposure to counterfire.

Puller looked at Mecho and could see from his expression that he had just gone through the same analysis and arrived at a similar conclusion.

"Do you think Lampert or Rojas are here?" Puller asked.

Mecho shook his head. "Big fish don't swim with the small."

"Yeah, what I was thinking too. So assuming we can get past the perimeter?"

"The guards will be instructed to kill the prisoners."

"Like burning the evidence?"

"That may have been their plan all along. Kill them, dump their bodies in the ocean, let the sharks do their job."

"But the storm put the kibosh on that."

Mecho nodded.

Puller glanced over at the women. Carson looked determined, focused. Landry the same. However, Diaz looked apprehensive, unsure.

"Your partner isn't looking too good," said Puller.

"She will be fine."

"You know her well?"

"I don't know her at all."

"So what, then?"

"You learn a lot about a person when she saves your life."

Puller nodded. "I agree with you." He glanced back through the gap in the shutter and then looked at Mecho.

"We can fire from up here. I count twenty guards. We have eight weapons among us, including an MP5."

"We'll miss some of them."

"I just want to cut down on their numbers as quick as we can."

Puller looked back through the gap and saw something he hadn't picked up on before. Diego and Mateo sat in a corner of one of the crowded cages. A guard stood directly in front of them.

Puller told himself that that guard would be the first one he killed.

"So, fire through the gap or do we try to get in?" he asked.

Mecho shrugged. "If we had more than one gap, with multiple fire lines, then I would say yes to the gap, but we don't."

"So how about we shoot from the gap and we also break in and attack from down there?"

Mecho nodded approvingly. "I like that plan better."

Puller said, "I say you, me, and Landry form the penetration team. Diaz and Carson provide cover from up here. We'll do the ingress through that doorway over there." Puller pointed to his left. "Once we breach as stealthily as we can, we form a triangle attack. I'm point, you're left, Landry right. We clear each section and keep moving. Any guards shooting into the cages get priority fire."

Mecho nodded at this plan. "I like it. I think it will work. And after we have killed all the guards?"

"Not all. We need a couple to testify."

"They will know nothing about Rojas or Lampert."

"Still, on the off chance they do."

"And the prisoners?"

"We'll get them out as previously discussed."

Mecho checked his weapon. Puller handed him his M11.

"Fires straight and true," he said.

"I will count on that," said Mecho.

Puller hefted the MP5 and put it on two-shot bursts. He wasn't going to do full auto. He had to manage his ammo carefully. And taking the time to switch out clips was problematic in the middle of what would undoubtedly turn into chaos. For luck, and a combat ritual of his, he tapped the Ranger Ka-Bar knife in its leather holster three times. It felt both odd and exhilarating to do it.

He saw that Mecho also had a knife stuck in his waistband. He assumed the man knew how to use it with maximum lethalness.

Puller called the women over and explained the plan to them.

"I'd prefer to go in the penetration team with you," said Carson.

"You have the sniper rifle, General. I'm counting on you making good use of it."

Puller looked at Diaz. She still looked nervous. "You going to be okay?"

She nodded but her features were not in agreement. "Still seasick," she replied in a hollow tone.

Mecho put a big hand on her shoulder and looked directly at her. "No time for sick. Time to fight."

She nodded.

Carson said, "Good luck."

Puller glanced back at her. It might be the last time they saw each other; he didn't know.

She said, "I know, it won't be about luck."

"Actually, this time it'll be a lot about luck."

He looked at Landry. "Round chambered?"

"Always."

He glanced at Mecho. "Good to go."

He nodded.

The three headed down the metal stairs to the breach point.

CHAPTER

89

The opening assault went according to plan.

The breach door was not locked.

Carson and Diaz had been instructed to lay down fire as soon as the door opened.

It did open, and they opened fire a millisecond later.

The guards were stunned by the attack, jumping to their feet, dropping cigarettes and beer cans and snatching up weapons.

By then of course it was too late.

Carson and Diaz took out five of them with the opening salvo.

Then Mecho and Puller hit them like an Abrams tank at full throttle.

They used their guns, their knives, their fists, and their legs.

Guard after guard dropped under their overwhelming attack.

They were an army of two.

Puller killed and moved on to the next target, a seamless flow of compartmentalized savagery.

Next to him Mecho was doing exactly the same thing, perhaps with a bit more savagery.

Precise gunfire rained down from above as Carson aimed and shot, aimed and shot, dropping guard after guard.

From below Mecho and Puller hammered the enemy relentlessly, shooting, stabbing, killing to such an extent that the superior force of guards was quickly turned into an inferior force through sheer terror.

That's when things started to go wrong.

A round fired by a guard hit a vapor-filled fifty-gallon fuel tank and it ignited into a flame ball. Oxygen-fed, it flared to twenty feet high. Thick, toxic smoke engulfed the room.

The remaining guards, giving up all hope of defeating the invaders, started pumping rounds into the cages, dropping prisoner after prisoner.

Puller and Mecho did their best to shoot them down, but the smoke was making it difficult to find the right targets. The last thing Puller wanted to do was kill any of the prisoners.

Diaz and Carson's vantage point from above was quickly turned to a disadvantage because of the smoke. They could no longer fire because they couldn't see what they were firing at.

Mecho and Puller kept low and moved through the smoke and haze.

They killed what they could.

Puller reached the first cage, shot the lock off, and the prisoners started streaming out after Puller motioned to them to keep low.

Mecho did the same with another cage.

Puller next reached the cage where Diego and Mateo were.

Diego saw him and shouted, "Behind you!"

Without looking Puller whirled with his Ka-Bar in hand.

The guard fell forward with his throat cut, jugular to carotid.

Mateo saw this and started screaming.

Diego grabbed him and pulled him through the opening.

Puller snagged Diego by the arm. "Nice work on leaving your ring behind."

"It was the only thing I could think to do."

"You both okay?"

"Yes."

"Go out the door we came through. Take the steps up. There are people up there who'll help you."

Diego nodded and he and Mateo fled.

Puller shouted at the others in every language he knew to follow the boys to safety.

All the prisoners still alive were free now and escaping the room through the door.

Meanwhile, Mecho gutted one guard

while he shot another. A pistol round tore through his left forearm, but he kept fighting with his right.

Puller was slashed on the leg by another guard's knife an instant before he put a bullet in the man's head.

The two men looked around and saw no more opponents.

Mecho grabbed blankets and attempted to beat the flames down. Puller snagged a fire extinguisher off the wall and hit it from the other side. Smoke poured out of the now dying fire.

Puller dropped the empty extinguisher, turned, and stopped.

Landry stood there with smoke misting around her. She looked like the sole survivor appearing from an apocalypse.

Puller noted that her gun was pointed directly at him.

He said, "I wondered where you had gotten to."

"Sorry about this," she said.

"Like hell," said Puller.

She pulled the trigger two quick times.

The gun fired just as it was supposed to.

Yet Puller still stood there, unharmed.

She pulled the trigger two more times.

Again, her pistol fired twice.

And again Puller simply stood there.

"No body armor," he said. "You can take a head shot if you want."

She did, right between the eyes.

Nothing.

She turned when she sensed him behind her.

Mecho ripped the gun from her hand and bent her arm behind her back. She cried out in pain as he drove her elbow to an angle it was not designed to go.

Puller took the gun from Mecho and slid out the clip.

"I carry blanks in my duffel, as a means to fire warning shots without doing any damage. I substituted them for your live rounds when I was getting the weapons ready. And if you got your hands on another gun and tried to kill us, Diaz up there had orders to take you out. It was probably why she was nervous, killing a cop and all. Goes against her instincts, I guess. Even when the cop is dirty."

They all looked up to see Diaz pointing her weapon directly at Landry's head with a determined look on her features.

Landry gasped, "If you knew, why did you ask me to come out here?"

"Simple. Friends close and enemies closer."

"I don't understand how you could have known."

"It's all a matter of timing, really, Cheryl. Just timing."

"What do you mean?"

"I'd explain now, but we've got a few more things on our to-do list. And you're going to help us cross them off."

"I'm not helping you."

"Yes you are."

"Go to hell."

It only took a second, but Landry whipped her body around and slammed a knee into Mecho's crotch. He doubled over. She grabbed the knife from his belt and was about to deliver a killing strike to the back of his neck when the blade was knocked from her hand.

She turned in time to see Puller's fist coming at her.

That was the last thought she had before Puller slammed his fist into her jaw.

She fell to the floor, unconscious.

Puller stood over her.

"Yes you are," he said quietly.

CHAPTER

90

They had refueled the boat and were racing back to land.

The freed captives were still on the oil platform, but a Coast Guard cutter was—despite the storm—powering toward them as fast as it could. It had enough space to take them all on board and to safety on the mainland.

Diego and Mateo had wanted to come back on the boat with them, but Puller had refused. "You'll be much safer on a Coast Guard cutter," he explained. "I'm not even sure we can get this tub back to Florida."

However, the tropical storm had made landfall and quickly lost much of its energy. The ride back was bad, but not nearly as bad as the ride out had been.

On the way Puller had gotten a cell signal and managed to make one more call. Carson had gotten on the phone when the conversation started to go downhill. Puller had watched in admiration as the one-star didn't ask the man on the other end of the line what she would like him to do. She told him what he was *going* to do.

"This is a national security issue, Lieutenant. And the United States Army takes those very seriously. You have your orders and I expect they will be carried out with all the dispatch and professionalism that the uniform demands. Are we clear?"

"Yes, ma'am," came the immediate reply from the lieutenant, who was probably trying hard not to allow his voice to crack.

Carson clicked off and handed the phone back to Puller.

He smiled.

She said, "What's so funny?"

"I guess I just like seeing you being a general."

Halfway to shore, Landry had regained consciousness. Carson piloted the boat while Puller and Mecho focused on their new prisoner. Landry's face was bruised by Puller's blow and she looked angry and unrepentant.

"How?" she demanded of Puller.

"Like I said, timing."

"That means nothing to me."

"Lampert's car blew up."

"So what? I didn't do it."

"It blew up, according to Diaz, at one-fifteen. At one-sixteen you got a phone call while I was with you on the beach. You said it was from Bullock. But there was no way it could have been. Lampert would have had to find out what the hell was going on, call the police, and track Bullock down. He'd have to hear what happened and then Bullock might start phoning people. But you weren't on duty. You wouldn't have been the first person he'd call. All of that would take a lot longer than a minute. And just to be sure, I checked with Bullock by phone last night. He said you'd called him that night on the drive over to Lampert's. Not the other way around. He said you'd heard something on the news about an explosion. The call you got was from Lampert."

Landry shook her head. "That's not enough, Puller. There's no way you'd make a decision like this on something so skimpy."

"I didn't. I started to connect the dots. Lampert is from Miami. So are you. You both arrived here around the same time. After I started thinking about the timing of the call you got, I went into detective mode and started making a lot of phone calls. Your father. You said a guy on PCP shot him down at a bar."

"That's what happened."

"I know. But I talked to your former police sergeant. What I found out was from that moment forward you were a changed person. You didn't seem to care so much about doing the right thing. It seems that instead of wanting to get the scum even more badly after your father was killed, you went the other way. You ended up just not giving a shit. And then you got into business with Lampert and things really took off." He paused. "I also checked on your condo. Four hundred thousand. And your mortgage is less than fifty thousand. Cops don't make that kind of money. At least honest ones. Maybe that's why you wanted to live in Destin. I take it you never had anybody from the police force over for drinks. It was stupid of you to have me over, Landry. It made me start thinking."

He looked at Mecho. "The Storrows were killed by someone on the beach. Mecho was there. He saw it. More to the point, he saw *you*. You pumped rounds into their heads and dragged them out to the surf. You're plenty strong enough to do that, Cheryl. All that paddleboarding you do, it would have been easy. Two old people, they weighed nothing to you."

Landry said nothing but she looked at Mecho with hatred.

Puller continued, "And that's why no one answered when you called Bullock and Hooper. They were under orders from me not to. I didn't want you to think I was suspicious about you. Just them. Bullock didn't want to believe that you were a bad cop, but when I told him what I'd found out, he really couldn't defend you."

"So you say."

Puller kept looking at her. "That stretch of beach with the sulfur. It *is* part of Paradise. I checked with Bullock on that too. It's not regularly patrolled because nothing ever happens there. But he did tell me that one of his officers volunteered to check on it from time to time. Care to guess who that volunteer was?"

Landry still remained silent.

Puller drew closer to her. "And on that 'patrol' one night when you were really checking on the flow of slaves, you saw my aunt sitting in her Camry with a journal, observing and writing notes. She could barely walk anymore but she still wanted her independence. And she got it by driving in her specially equipped car late at night when it wasn't so hot and humid. And she saw something one night. And she told her friends, the Storrows. They probably drove out there too and saw what my aunt had. And they came to you, Officer Landry. You patrolled their neighborhoods. They respected you. They told you what they had seen. And you pretended to take a report and then you shit-canned it."

He drew even closer to Landry and slipped his Ka-Bar knife out of its sheath. "So you went down to the beach where you knew the Storrows liked to take late-night walks and you popped them in the head and dragged their bodies out into the water so the tide would carry them away."

He drew still closer and held his knife up so the point was an inch from Landry's throat. Diaz looked on nervously while Carson drove the boat but kept glancing over her shoulder while this scene played out.

Mecho sat there stoically holding his injured forearm and staring at Landry.

"But I think my aunt suspected you. You know, 'people not being who they seemed'? She was very good at seeing through bullshit. And maybe you realized she suspected you. And so you went to my aunt's house, stole her journal, and then took her outside and stuck her head in that pool of water until she was dead."

"You can't prove any of that," snapped Landry.

Puller eased the knife blade forward at the same time he snagged her hair and jerked her head back. The big veins riding up her neck were fully revealed. He pressed the tip of the Ka-Bar directly against one of them.

"With the seas as bad as they are and how we're pitching all over the place I could easily lose control of this blade. And it could easily sever all the blood vessels going to your brain."

"That's not exactly the way to get proof in a court," Landry said. But she stared at Puller, obviously trying to read the intent on his features.

He stared back at her with deadly calm. He was in another zone right now, even more so than in the killing room back at the oil platform. He was as focused as he had ever been, like he was about to make a kill shot on a Taliban at a thousand meters under a hot sun where the margin of error was nearly zero. The whole world contained just him and Cheryl Landry.

"Who said anything about proof?" he said quietly.

Landry tried to smirk, tried to look like she was still somewhat in control of this situation even though she never had been and never would be. "You're not going to kill me, not with all these witnesses."

Mecho said firmly, "We went out with four and we came back with four."

Diaz shrugged resignedly, and Carson said, "The ocean is a big place, Landry. Things get lost from time to time and never show up again. But scum will eventually sink to the bottom."

Puller added, "As far as anyone knows you're still supposed to be on patrol. You didn't call anybody to say differently and I sure as hell didn't."

Landry looked back at Puller. Now there were tears in her eyes. "Look, maybe we can cut a deal."

"Maybe what you can do is shut up and I'll tell you exactly what you're going to do."

"What incentive is in it for me?"

"You either do what I tell you to do or your ass is going into the ocean."

Landry looked at the raging ocean, the gunwale barely a foot away. "You're in the military. You can't just kill me like that."

"Oh, I kill people like you all the time."

"I'm a cop."

"No, you're the enemy. I judge what you're doing as a crime against this country and what it stands for. That makes you a terrorist in my book. And in my book terrorists have no rights. You don't get to remain silent. You don't get access to a lawyer. And I'm sure as hell not wasting my tax dollars paying for your ass to sit in an American prison. I will dump you right out there and the last image you'll see before the sharks move in will be me."

Landry gasped, sniffled, and coughed and was seemingly trying to look as pitiful and helpless as possible.

Puller didn't respond to any of this.

She was no longer a young, beautiful, sexy woman.

She was repulsive.

She had forfeited her rights when she had helped to enslave others. When she had callously killed three old people who were simply trying to do the right thing. All while wearing the uniform.

Carson added, "You know, if you were in the Army, we'd just shoot you."

Landry, seeing that Puller was not bluffing, stammered, "What do you want me to do?"

CHAPTER

91

Lampert was on his yacht contemplating the implosion of his business empire. The operation on the beach had been compromised. There were at least four of them in on it. Puller, the woman with him. The giant.

And Murdoch, who he knew now was not whom she appeared to be.

He'd had a mole in his midst and didn't even realize it until it was too late.

His associate, Winthrop, had already paid the ultimate price for bringing a spy to them, unaware or not. His dismembered body was sinking into the depths of the Gulf as Lampert sat on his luxury ship.

Lampert didn't know where Puller and the others were. He had hoped that the giant would have been dead by now, but he'd been tipped off.

Murdoch.

He didn't know whether she was a member of a rival criminal enterprise or was with the police, but either scenario was equally problematic.

Ironically enough, the Paradise police didn't concern him. He had aces in the hole there. But he was concerned about Stiven Rojas. The man had given Lampert an ultimatum. And that had been before this enormous screwup.

He had cleared the warehouse and sent the product back out to sea. The storm had interfered with his plan, but only to a limited extent. His intent was to keep the prisoners there until he had located a new landing spot and then he would take up his business once more.

It probably wouldn't be in Florida. His people were right now looking at the logistics of funneling product through Alabama.

The oil platforms were a godsend right now. Oil companies had a certain amount of time after shutting them down to do something with them. Many were cut off below the waterline and towed to other spots to create artificial reefs. This was the cheaper alternative in many cases. Other firms chose to simply dismantle them completely. Other firms, having run out of money or gone bankrupt, simply abandoned them.

There was safety in numbers, and the number of oil platforms no longer in use in the Gulf was in the thousands. And they were spread all over. There was no way the Coast Guard or any-one else could check on them all.

But he couldn't keep the product there forever. He would nail down a new landing spot and then start the shipments once more.

His next problem was obvious. Mur-doch and the others. How much did they know? What would they do with that information?

Should I leave the country now?

Why wait until I'm arrested or have subpoenas served?

But what could they have on him?

There was no trail back.

Even if any of his men talked they had no proof. And he didn't think any of his men would talk. Lampert had friends everywhere, including in the judicial and prison systems. This had been made clear to all people coming to work for him. And if they weren't sufficiently scared of him, they were of Stiven Rojas.

That bastard can get you anywhere. Even in witness protection.

Of course, that means he can get me.

Lampert picked up his phone and communicated with his chief of security. His words were terse. "No one in and no one out. Call me immediately if anyone approaches."

He next called his yacht captain. "I want to be ready to leave in the next hour."

"The seas are still rough," the captain said, obviously surprised by the order.

They had moved the yacht out into open waters to let it ride out the storm on anchor. A tropical storm was not the same thing as a Cat Four. A Cat Four could pick up a yacht and throw it onto land.

The seas were rough, and once or twice Lampert thought he might be sick. But he would take vomiting over someone blowing out his brains. If he did have to make a run for it he would have to leave his wife and son behind. That was okay. He could always get another wife. And his son was growing up to be a real prick. He could fend for himself, with his trust fund.

"Well, that's why I pay you what I do. One hour."

"Yes, sir."

Lampert clicked off and looked around his cabin. The finest materials from around the world and fashioned by immensely talented craftsmen stared back at him.

He had the best of everything. It was his due. He worked very hard. The rank and file had no idea how much hard work it took to build a fortune. And it was even harder work to keep it.

Taxes were too high and regulations were choking off business, but still he persevered. And he employed people too. Created jobs where there had been none before. He had done the same thing on Wall Street. And been vilified for his efforts.

He shook his head. Business was really just picking up too. He had put enormous amounts into infrastructure, training, equipment, manpower. The risks he took were huge. And it was all paying off. His product pipeline was the envy of the world. He moved more product than anyone else by a factor of five. He had brought precision and a business mentality to a formerly dirty, chaotic enterprise.

And unlike oil or natural gas or other resources, the supply of product was infinite. Until the world ran out of poor people he could have his pick. And the world would never run out of impoverished folks if he had any say in the matter. There was only so much room at the top. And he was not relinquishing his space.

Lampert knew that he had always been meant for bigger and better things.

But he had to survive. This was where the risk was greatest. This was why he was making so much money. Because it could cost him everything.

Including his life.

He refocused on the tasks at hand.

Rojas did not know of the latest maneuvers. The storm had forced his boat far out to sea. He doubted the man would chance coptering in when the skies and winds were still too unpredictable. All that gave Lampert something he desperately needed now.

Time.

Time to figure this out. Plan his next moves.

Survive.

The unknown factor, of course, was Puller and his cohorts.

They had followed the truck with the product. They obviously knew what was going on. There had been a gunfight on the beach. He had not heard from his men, so he knew that they had lost.

So what was Puller up to?

He had tried calling out to the platform, but the call had not gone through.

The storm again. The timing truly sucked.

And then, as if in answer to his prayers, his cell phone rang. He looked at the number and smiled.

He clicked on and said, "I was hoping to hear from you."

Cheryl Landry said, "I've got a lot to fill you in on. Can we meet? Now?"

CHAPTER

92

The storm was rapidly dissipating but downpours were still occurring intermittently as Danielle finished expending its energy.

It was daylight now, but Danielle was keeping the skies dark. It could have been the wee hours of the morning.

Someone knocked on the front door.

Lampert answered it himself. He had taken a tender to shore. He had thrown up twice because of the rough seas. Now he was hoping for some good news.

He stared across the threshold at

Landry. She was drenched and her face was bruised.

"What the hell happened to you?" he asked.

"Can I come in first? And can I get a drink?"

He turned and she followed him in. He led her to his private study and closed the door behind them.

"You want a change of clothes?" he asked.

"I'd like that drink. That's what I really want."

He poured her out a scotch from the bar set against one wall.

"I was on the *Lucky Lady* contemplating whether I should make a run for it," said Lampert.

"Trust me, I was contemplating the same thing."

"But on the phone you said you had good news."

She accepted the scotch from him, took a sip, and then sat down in a chair opposite his desk. He sat down too, steepled his fingers, and stared at her expectantly.

"Well?" he said.

She took one more sip from the tumbler and then pressed the glass against her bruise. "The operation was compromised."

"That I know."

"Murdoch is a spy."

"That I know too."

"Her name is Lieutenant Claudia Diaz. She's with the Colombian National Police."

Lampert simply stared at her for a long moment before exclaiming, "Shit!"

Landry smiled at this reaction. "I take it that you didn't know." She held up her glass. "You might want one of these."

"Tell me what happened."

Landry took another sip, sat back, and exhaled a long breath. "What happened is, I saved your ass."

"How?"

"I never trusted Winthrop or Murdoch."

"Smart of you."

"So I watched them. Winthrop was clean. Murdoch wasn't. It was clear she was just letting him get into her panties so she could get close to you."

"I can see that now."

She smiled, cocked her head at him as the rain beat down outside and the thick dark swirling clouds kept the sun at bay. "And did she let you get into her panties?"

"Irrelevant to our discussion, but the answer is yes."

"So you were deceived as well."

"Women are my weakness. And I think I'll have that drink now. But keep talking. I'm very interested in how you saved my ass."

While he poured out a drink she said, "Your hit team against the big guy went awry. Diaz tipped him off."

Lampert sat back down with his scotch. "And why would she do that? Is he working with her?"

"It doesn't matter at this point. They're both dead."

Lampert choked a bit as the scotch went down the wrong pipe. "Dead? How was that managed?"

"Like I said, saved your ass. Puller is dead too."

"What about the other woman? You

told me she was a general. Carson, right?"

"Dead too. They're all dead. It's not like we could allow any of them to survive."

Lampert stared furiously across the desk. "You just ignited a shitstorm, Cheryl. The Pentagon will be all over this."

"And would you have preferred the alternative? They follow the trail right back here to you."

"That would not have happened."

"It *did* happen, Peter."

He said nothing, just stared at her like she was the last thing he would ever see in his life.

"They found out about the warehouse."

"I cleared it. There was nothing to find."

"Well, they found the platform out there," she said, pointing out the window toward the Gulf.

Lampert put down his drink and edged forward in his chair. His face was drained of color. "That is not possible."

"The big guy? His name is Mecho, by the way. He was on that platform. Your people snatched him from Mexico. He escaped. Made it to shore. And then he made it back. Last night."

"I thought that might be the case. I thought he was spying on me. But I didn't know why. I just thought he was trying to steal something."

"He was tracking you, Peter. What he wanted to steal was your whole life and everything you have. And he came really close to accomplishing that goal."

Lampert took his glass and hurled it against the wall. "Son of a bitch!"

Landry watched the scotch drip down the once immaculate wallpaper.

"Get a grip, Peter. Like I said, they're dead."

"How?"

"I'm drenched and my face is smashed up. What does that suggest to you?"

"A fight in the storm."

"To the death. Out on the platform. I won't lie and say we didn't take casualties. We did. They killed nearly all your guys, but in the end, we overwhelmed them with sheer numbers and a little luck."

"How did you come to be there?" he asked, looking at her suspiciously.

"Like I said, I'd been following Diaz. They got on a boat. I got on a boat. They rode out to the platform. So did I."

"In the storm? How is that possible?"

She looked at him incredulously. "I grew up in Florida. I've surfed in the aftermath of hurricanes. I've been piloting boats since I was ten. If it had been a Cat One or Two, maybe not. But a tropical storm, if you know what you're doing, you can manage. And it's lucky for you that I did. I thought that's why you hired me. For my local expertise. And my balls under pressure."

"What happened?"

"I called ahead. At first my phone wasn't working, but I finally caught a signal. I told them they were coming. They were ready for them, but it was still a hell of a fight. Those four were true warriors, I have to give them that. They didn't go down easy."

"And the product?"

"Mostly intact. We took a few casualties there, though."

"And the bodies?"

"In the drink. Diaz and the others will never be found. We cut out the lungs. Bodies will go down and stay down."

"Good thinking. And your work killing the Storrows and that old woman was truly appreciated, Cheryl. They could have ruined everything. The bonus I paid you for doing that probably was inadequate."

He seemed to realize this was not praise enough. "And you've just earned yourself another bonus after last night. An enormous one. And a promotion. We're going to get you out of that uniform and into a suit. You can take over Winthrop's position."

"Won't he have a problem with that?"

"He would, except I had him killed for allowing Diaz to infiltrate us. And we're moving the operation. My logistics guys are crunching the numbers now. I'm thinking Alabama."

"One problem?"

"What's that?"

"Stiven Rojas."

"What about him."

"He's your partner in the slave trade."

"So what?"

"You told me he gave you an ultimatum."

"He did."

"And now with all this, what do you think he's going to do? It's not exactly a clean exit."

"I'm thinking that I've become important enough that Señor Rojas will need to listen to my terms. Pipeline trumps product. I can get product on my own. I already did. Asia and Africa. Lots of poor, stupid people there. But Rojas can't duplicate my pipeline. He doesn't have the requisite connections."

"Still, a dangerous game to play with the man."

"I'm not underestimating him. But when you have an advantage you have to seize it."

"Exactly my thinking."

This comment did not come from Landry.

Puller had kicked open the door and stepped into the study.

Behind him charged Diaz, Carson, and Mecho.

They all had their guns drawn and pointed at Lampert.

Lampert stared first at them and then glanced at Landry in astonishment.

"You set me up?"

"Afraid so."

"Do you realize what you've done, you idiot?"

"I'm not sure you're aware of the full extent of it."

Landry unbuttoned the two top buttons of her shirt and pulled the wire and recorder out. She handed them to Puller. She turned back to Lampert.

"I saw an opportunity and seized it," she said and added in a hollow tone, "but don't feel like I got anything special. Life in prison instead of the needle. Some deal."

"I don't think you're going to get the same deal," Puller said to Lampert.

Lampert said, "How did you get past my security?"

"You should tell them to check the

interior of every vehicle more thoroughly. With Landry at the wheel they just passed us through."

Lampert looked from him to Landry. "You idiot."

"They had me dead to rights, Peter. Sorry."

"I'll have you killed in prison."

"You can try," said Puller. "But I think you'll have more important things to think about."

"I'll hire the best lawyers."

"You're going to need them," said Diaz. "And I'm going to push hard to have you tried in Colombia. The Americans are too soft. Justice is much swifter in my country."

Puller cuffed both Landry and Lampert.

"Now let's go," said Puller. He motioned with his M11. Lampert rose and looked at Landry.

"You're dead. You're *all* dead."

Then he walked out with the others behind him.

They reached the front courtyard, but then Puller stopped abruptly.

"What is it?" asked Carson.

Mecho was looking around warily too.

"Down, now!" yelled Puller.

Right as he said it the guns started firing.

CHAPTER

93

Puller had spotted the shooters' positions a split second before he hit the dirt.

He pulled his M11 and fired in an arc, emptying its mag. It was a defensive measure, solely designed to give him a few seconds to take up a new position and plan a counterattack. He took cover behind a car, gripped his MP5, and surveyed the area in front of him.

"Puller!"

He glanced behind him. It was Carson. She'd taken up position behind a stone column outside the front entrance.

She was pointing to the left.

Puller looked in that direction and his gut tightened.

Diaz was lying facedown in a pool of blood. Even from this distance and in the darkness Puller could tell she was dead.

He looked around for Landry and Lampert.

Landry was cowering behind a tree. She yelled to Puller, "Lampert ran off!"

Puller looked up ahead, to where the shooters were.

He had one person unaccounted for. Mecho.

Puller didn't think the big man had run off. He was wired to fight just like Puller was.

Puller looked back at Carson after a wave of bullets was fired over his position.

With hand motions he communicated to Carson what he intended to do. She nodded and tightened her grip on her gun.

Puller turned back, his gaze flitting over all relevant points.

It was on the second pass when he saw him.

Mecho was directly on the shooters' rear flank, his gun aimed at them.

It had been neatly done, Puller thought.

There were six shooters.

Puller looked around for the vehicles they had come in, but saw none.

Then he thought the shooters were actually Lampert's bodyguards.

A second later he noted the lumps of flesh lying around the ground.

They were the bodyguards.

This was a new force to be reckoned with.

And they hadn't come by car.

Puller considered deliberately the tactical situation.

There were three of them, six on the other side.

In his mind the other side was woefully undermanned. They should have sent more guys.

Puller counted to three, rolled out, and opened fire with the MP5. It was a feint only. Again, he was aiming at nothing. He was drawing attention. A moment later he drew counterfire. They were totally focused on him.

Carson's weapon fired twice. One of the shooters went down. Another clutched at his arm and dropped his weapon. Good as out of the fight.

Two down, four to go.

And that was before Mecho struck from the rear.

The two shooters nearest to the big man went down a second later. One with a bullet to the medulla. The other with a knife strike to the heart.

Even with a wounded arm Mecho had more than enough strength to wield a killing blow with the blade.

Four down, two to go.

The two remaining shooters shifted their attention to Mecho.

Now it was Puller's turn.

He did a zigzag run to the left and then shot back to the right.

He lined up his targets and squeezed off two shots from his M11.

Head shots both.

Kill shots both.

Six down. Zero to go.

But then Puller's mind went back to the hotel room at the Sierra.

In a millisecond his brain worked through the facts.

Six shooters against four. You had to take out Lampert's guards. You had to allow for possible losses in that confrontation even with a surprise attack. All the lumps of flesh were dressed in the uniforms of Lampert's security detail. So no losses there. Six was their full strength.

They had to assume that Puller and company might be here. That meant they would be seriously outgunned when combined with Lampert's detail.

Puller had to assume that the shooters were from Rojas. And Stiven Rojas was a smart guy. Smart guys did not send underwhelming force.

The millisecond over, Puller reacted.

"Second wave coming," he called out.

Carson and Mecho instantly moved to cover and took up new firing positions.

Puller slid back and over to Landry.

She looked up at him pleadingly. "For Chrissakes, Puller, take the cuffs off and give me a gun. I'll help fight."

Puller reloaded and looked over at her. "Don't think so, Landry. You already tried to kill me once. I'm not into second chances."

"I'm defenseless here."

"Nah, you've got me. And I've got every incentive to keep you alive."

"What incentive?" she snapped.

He leaned close as he slapped a fresh clip in his MP5. He whispered in her ear, "To make sure you spend the rest of your life in prison." He set the MP5 on full auto.

"Puller, please," she sobbed.

He ignored her.

The second wave was about to hit the shore.

And it was going to hit a lot harder than Tropical Storm Danielle had.

But then Puller had an ace up his sleeve. At least he hoped he did.

Otherwise, they were dead.

CHAPTER

94

The second wave was far more sophisticated than the first.

That made Puller think that the first wave was just a feint. It had cost them Diaz, reducing their force by twenty-five percent. Losing six guys for that was smart if you had a lot more guys to throw into the battle.

Turns out they did.

Twenty by Puller's quick count. They moved in hard clusters of four each. They wore body armor and had major firepower, far more than Puller's MP5. They took up tactical positions that

were in the form of a classically designed pincers maneuver.

Puller looked at Carson and she
looked back at him.

They both recognized the tactic and
they both clearly understood the inevitable outcome it would produce.

Puller lifted his MP5. There was an
old Army mentality that his father had
taught him.

There is absolutely no shame in going down fighting.

He fired his full thirty-round clip in a
sweep at the two clusters in front of
him. Two of the men dropped and were
not going to rejoin the fight.

Puller reloaded.

He had used thirty rounds to kill two.
There were eighteen foes left. He clearly
didn't have enough ammo to kill them
all.

They were a smart, well-trained unit,
because they deployed their force on
one target and brought to bear overwhelming fire on that target.

The car Puller was taking cover behind was riddled and a number of the
rounds passed right through the thin

metal and nearly took Puller's limbs off. He had no choice but to retreat.

Carson laid down fire to allow him to do this and thus she became the next focal point of the enemy force.

Her position was obliterated by the concentrated firepower. She was not so lucky in her retreat. She went down with wounds to both her leg and arm.

Puller did not rush to her side, because that would have kept the enemy guns on her. He fired back from his new position and the counterfire once more swiveled to him.

He ran farther away from Carson's position, dodging gunfire by running unpredictably. After doing it for years in the Middle East the muscle memory was well established in his limbs. He almost seemed to know where the aim of his opponents was going.

The men confronting him now should have mapped out fire grids and placed rounds in every conceivable path Puller could choose. Then he would be dead.

But they didn't and he wasn't.

He made it to safety before turning and firing back with his MP5.

It was only he and Mecho left now. Two against nearly twenty.

But that was about to change.

Puller's cell phone vibrated. He pulled it out, glanced at the screen.

He thumbed a one-word response.

Now.

General Julie Carson's orders were about to be executed.

All heads turned as though connected by string to the sounds coming from the north of them.

The MH-60L DAP was basically a modified Black Hawk chopper with major firepower added, including Hellfire antitank missiles, rockets, and 7.62 miniguns. Operated by the Army's 160th Special Ops Aviation Regiment, nicknamed the "Night Stalkers," it was a versatile battle platform. Fortunately for Puller, there had been one stationed at Eglin for a joint Army–Air Force exercise. It thundered over the wall and into the Lampert estate. Its 30 mm cannon zeroed in and then lined up on the clusters of men crouched with their weapons waiting to overrun a vastly smaller opponent.

Some of the men pointed their guns at the chopper. When two of them stupidly fired at the aircraft, Puller thought to himself, *Wrong move.*

He lay flat on the ground, his hands over his ears.

The 30 mm cannon opened up. It could lay down compact fields of fire at over six hundred rounds per minute. It created what the Army termed a non-survivable event. In less than ten seconds nearly twenty mostly obliterated men lay on the ground.

The chopper landed and Puller raced to it after laying his MP5 down. The last thing he wanted was a 30 mm cannon pointed at him.

The door of the chopper slid open.

"We need a medic," shouted Puller over the whine of the blades. "Got a one-star with gunshot wounds."

After grabbing bags of equipment a doctor and a medic jumped off the chopper and followed Puller over to where Carson lay.

Her face was white but she was conscious.

Puller knelt down next to her as the

doc and medic prepared their equipment. He gripped Carson's hand as they hooked up bags of blood and saline and stuck IV lines into her.

She opened her eyes and looked up at Puller.

"You're bleeding," she said, reaching out slowly and touching his arm.

"Lot of that going around."

"Am I going to make it?" she asked.

Both slugs were still in her. She'd lost too much blood. She was pale and weak and when Puller glanced at the doctor he looked grim.

But Puller looked at her straight in the eye, squeezed her hand, and said, "You're going to make it."

The human spirit was the strongest medicine on earth. And sometimes all it needed was a little encouragement to pull off a miracle. Puller had seen it countless times on the battlefield, and even been the recipient of such positive words when an IED had nearly ended his life in Iraq.

You're going to make it. Sometimes that was all it took.

She squeezed his hand back and

closed her eyes as the painkiller the doctor administered took effect.

Puller stood and jogged back over to where Landry sat on the ground, her hands still secured behind her.

"Don't forget our deal, Puller," she said. "I delivered you Lampert."

"Yeah. You can console yourself with that fact when you're eighty years old and still in prison. And I don't think they have paddleboards there." He motioned to a soldier heading over to them, and flashed his creds and badge.

Puller said, "Sergeant, this woman is a prisoner of the United States Army until she can be turned over to local authorities."

"Yes, sir."

The sergeant trained his weapon on Landry.

Puller heard a noise.

He turned, at first thinking Lampert had reappeared and was trying to make a getaway.

But it wasn't Lampert. It was Mecho.

He was running hard and already near the dock that led down to the beach.

Puller set off at a dead run.

He knew exactly what the man was going after.

Peter J. Lampert.

And so was Puller.

CHAPTER

95

Lampert had run as hard as he could. It wasn't easy with his cuffed hands behind his back. He was in decent shape, but not combat fit. He'd never fired a weapon in his life. He hired others to do that for him. He had never before had to run for his life.

He was paying for that now.

The sounds of the gunfire had stopped. All Lampert heard now was the breakers on the beach.

His boat was docked about a quarter mile out.

He would live to fight another day.

It just wouldn't be in this country.

That was okay. He was getting tired of living here anyway.

He pressed his forearm against a stitch in his side and kept his feet pointed toward the dock.

His twenty-foot tender was out there.

He could see his yacht from here.

He believed he could manage to pilot the boat out to the yacht. If Landry could make it all the way out to the oil platform in a tropical storm, he could make it out to the yacht in calmer seas.

He had a knife on board that he could use to cut the plasticuffs off. Then it was a straight shot out. The tender was sturdy and the waves were diminishing as the winds died down. Yeah, he could make it.

He was almost at the dock when he saw it.

At first he didn't register what it was.

But then it hit him.

He was looking at the conning tower of a submarine.

Rojas's sub. He had mentioned it during the meeting on his yacht. It could hold lots of people.

So that was how the gunmen had made it to his estate. They had come by sub.

Now taking the boat was problematic. What if they came after him? The seas were still rough. If the sub struck the tender, capsized it, and he went into the drink? He would drown.

He stopped, still pressing at the dull ache in his side. He should have exercised more. The problem was his main form of working out was sex. Somehow it didn't prepare you for long runs over uneven terrain.

He looked around desperately for another way out.

If not the boat, what?

The road out of his estate was not an option. Even now he could hear sirens in the air. He walked slowly along, parallel to the beach, thinking hard.

There had to be some way.

Maybe he should just chance the boat. It would be more maneuverable than a sub, wouldn't it?

The fact was he didn't know. But he couldn't think of a viable alternative.

Then, as he watched, the sub started

to sink into the water. It turned and, its tower still visible, rapidly made its way back out to sea.

Maybe they had heard the sirens too, way out there. Or maybe they just assumed that things had gone badly and they had better retreat.

Whatever the reason, Lampert now had his window of opportunity.

Lady Lucky had a steel hull. It could take the pounding of the ocean. He had crossed the Atlantic in it before. Once he reached international waters he would feel much safer. It would take time for Landry and the others to talk to the police. Warrants would have to be issued. Police would have to be sent out. By that time Lampert could be very far away.

He heard the sounds behind him, turned, and saw what was coming.

Frantic, he started running flat out for his precious boat and the open seas.

Lampert looked as though he had seen Satan himself after him.

And in some ways, he had.

*   *   *

Puller had caught up to Mecho and the two men ran side by side.

Mecho did not look at him or say anything to him. His total focus was on the man up ahead.

Puller and Mecho ran like the combat warriors they were. Not the fleetest in the world, they ran with a practiced motion, a fluidity that got maximum results with a modest output of energy. When you were in combat you often had to run. Mobile targets tended to survive. Stationary targets tended to die.

But when you stopped running you usually had to fight. The latter took a lot more energy than the former. Better not to waste all of it on the running part.

They were still neck and neck as they gained on their quarry. But Puller snaked ahead at the last moment and tackled Lampert.

The man went down, the wind knocked from him.

Mecho reached down and lifted Lampert off the sand with a violent upward jerk of his arms.

Puller slowly rose and watched the two men.

Mecho looked at Lampert and Lampert looked back at him.

Mecho's features were stone.

Lampert's were fear mixed with curiosity.

"What the hell is your beef with me?" he finally shouted.

Mecho threw him back down on the sand, reached into his pocket, and pulled out the photo. He held it in front of Lampert's face.

"Do you remember her?" Mecho asked, his voice strained.

Puller kept watching, and waiting. He wasn't sure what he was going to do if Mecho decided to try to kill Lampert. The man was his prisoner, a potential witness against one of the biggest criminals in the world. Mecho was wounded, but then so was Puller. In a one-on-one all bets were off. Puller knew his skills and his limits and he wasn't sure he could take the bigger man.

But then he might surprise himself.

The thing was, though, Puller didn't want it to come to that.

Mecho was not his enemy.

Lampert stared dully at the photo.

"Uh, am I supposed to know this person?"

"Her name is Rada. You took her from a village in the Rila mountains in Bulgaria. Her and many others. That was *my* village."

Lampert looked at Puller. "Is he serious? You think I'm going to remember someone like that?"

Puller stared stonily back at him. "Wrong answer, Pete."

Mecho again lifted Lampert up off the sand, held him up with one arm, cocked his other arm back, and hit Lampert so hard that several of his teeth exploded out of his mouth. He flew backward five feet and landed in the sand. He hit so hard on his cuffed arms that he popped both shoulders out of their sockets.

Screaming and crying in pain, he tried to wriggle away.

"Shut up," said Mecho.

"Oh God," screamed Lampert. "Oh my God."

"Shut up."

Mecho kicked him in the gut.

"You don't remember her? You don't remember Rada?"

"Oh God." Lampert was spitting chunks of teeth and bloody gums from his mouth and rolling all over the sand.

Puller knelt down next to him, cut his bindings, and with two firm, quick thrusts popped both shoulders back in place.

Lampert lay there crying quietly and gasping for air.

Mecho stared down at him, his hands balling and unballing. His huge chest heaved with every breath.

Puller rose and looked at him. "How is this going to play out?" he asked.

"He is coming back with me."

"He's in my custody. He's wanted for crimes here."

"He is coming back with *me*," Mecho snarled.

"Mecho, we'll make sure this scum never sees the light of day."

"He took everything we had. I made a promise."

Puller drew out his sidearm and pointed it at Mecho. He had no bullets left in it, but Mecho didn't know that.

"The last thing in the world I want to do is hurt you, Mecho. But I've got a job to do and I plan on doing it. This guy was responsible for my aunt being murdered. He's going to pay for that."

Mecho eyed the gun and then turned to look down at Lampert and held up the photo once more. "Tell me where she is. Tell me now."

"I don't know where she is," Lampert sobbed through his broken and bloody mouth. "I swear to Jesus."

Mecho grabbed him, jerked him up. "You do know. You will tell me."

"I don't. I don't know, damn it."

Lampert fell over on his side crying when Mecho let him go.

Mecho looked down at the photo and, as Puller watched, tears slid down the big man's face. His body began to tremble.

Puller looked out to sea, where Lampert's yacht was visible. All that money.

Based simply on misery. Based simply on greed. Based simply on destroying people's lives for cash.

He glanced back at Mecho and holstered his weapon. He gave a long sigh. What he was about to do flouted every rule in the book that had guided him for most of his adult life.

"How were you planning on getting him out of here?" he asked.

Mecho glanced up at him. "Why?"

"Just curious."

"I have a friend. He pilots a cargo ship. He will take us back home. No questions asked."

"Where and when?"

"Tonight. From Port Panama City."

Lampert had stopped crying and was listening intently to this.

Through his busted mouth he stammered, "You . . . you can't be serious. You're not going to let him take me to . . . to Bulgaria."

Puller glanced down at him. "Why not? You've been there. Had a good trip, right? Got everything—correction, everyone—you needed, right?"

"You can't."

"You sure about this friend, Mecho?"

"I am sure."

"What will happen to Lampert back in Bulgaria?"

"We have justice, just like you do here."

"Do you have the death penalty?"

"We have worse."

"Worse? Like what?"

"He'll get to live. In a part of Bulgaria that no one would ever choose to live. He will get to live there for the rest of his life. And he will be busy every minute of every day of every year until he drops from being worked to death. We Bulgarians are relentless when it comes to people who hurt us."

Lampert struggled to sit up, blood pouring from his mouth. "For God's sake, Puller, you can't let this happen. You're a cop. You've got a duty. You can't let this guy take me. He's a foreigner. He'll be kidnapping an American citizen. I'm a taxpayer. I pay your damn salary. You work for me."

Puller ignored this and said, "And your friend is doing this for free? Why?"

"Not exactly for free. I promised him

something, but I don't know how to get it. I'm not even sure what it is."

Mecho described his friend's request. Puller smiled and glanced at Lampert. "That's okay. I know what it is."

Mecho looked surprised but also hopeful. "So you can get this thing?'

"I can get this thing," said Puller.

CHAPTER

96

Panama City, Florida, was known to generations of college students who invaded the town for spring break.

Port Panama City was a port with easy access to the Gulf along a nearly nine-mile-long channel.

Ocean liners disgorged tourists.

Cargo ships brought products to America through here and took American-made products to the rest of the world.

It was a busy place, even at night.

Puller stood on the dock holding a box and eyeing the Cyrillic writing on the side of the steel-hulled cargo ship as cranes lifted metal containers onto the ship, stacking them on top of each other.

As he continued to watch, a large wooden box was carried on board. There were two men carrying one end and one man carrying the other.

The one man was Mecho. He was cleaned up from his fighting, his wounds bandaged and mostly hidden under his clothes.

For those who looked closely, and no one did, the wooden crate had two holes for air drilled in it.

Inside the box was Peter J. Lampert. He was bound, gagged, and drugged.

He would wake up in about six hours.

By then the cargo ship would be well out in the Gulf. It would make its way around the southernmost tip of Florida and then begin the long trek across the Atlantic. The cargo ship would plow along at an average speed of ten knots. Seventy-six hundred nautical miles and a month later it would arrive in Bulgaria.

Once Lampert touched Bulgarian soil he would never leave it.

The crate secured on board, Mecho came back down the gangplank followed by a heavyset man who looked strong as a bull.

His thick-veined neck was the size of an average man's thigh. His sleeves were rolled up and revealed forearms knotted with cords of muscles. He wore a skipper's cap, and a cigar stuck out from his mouth at an angle.

They reached Puller and stopped.

Mecho introduced the man as his friend and the cargo ship's captain.

The captain looked at Puller appraisingly. "Mecho tells me you have something for me."

Puller held out the box. "Ten bottles."

The captain lifted the top of the box and looked inside it.

His smile was wide and immediate.

Puller handed him the box and the captain thanked him and carried it back on board ship.

Mecho looked at Puller.

"So what is this thirty-year Macallan?"

"It's a scotch. Actually a very good scotch."

"And it is thirty years old?"

"So they say."

"Where did you get it?"

"Let's just say that it was another opportunity for Peter Lampert to make restitution."

Mecho's jaw slackened in surprise. "You took it from his house? Weren't the police around?"

"They weren't watching me too closely."

Mecho put out his hand and Puller shook it.

"I thank you for all that you have done."

"I hope you find your sister."

Mecho nodded slowly. "I will never stop looking."

"But you can stop looking for Lampert."

Mecho smiled grimly. "I will always know right where he is."

Mecho turned and walked up the gangplank. Halfway up he turned and waved back at Puller.

Puller returned the wave.

A few moments later Mecho was gone.

An hour after that, the ship was gone too and Lampert had begun his long journey to his final resting place.

"Good riddance," Puller muttered as he walked back to his car.

CHAPTER

97

When Julie Carson opened her eyes the first thing she saw was the bright light overhead. The second thing she saw was Puller sitting next to her hospital bed.

He gripped her hand.

"I made it," she said groggily.

"Never any doubt on my part. Docs say you'll be good as new in no time."

"Never got shot while wearing the uniform. Only while hanging out with you."

"Seems to be an occupational hazard with me."

She sat up a bit. "Don't take this the wrong way, but I don't think I'm going on vacation with you anymore."

"Completely understandable."

"What happened to Landry?"

"In custody. Talking her head off. Bullock was thinking of retiring, but after this big bust he might run for governor."

"So he's getting all the credit?"

"Not something I care about, General."

She squeezed his hand. "Julie. Off the clock now."

"Julie," he said.

"Diaz?"

"Colombians have already picked up her remains. She died a hero. They'll see to that."

"And Mecho."

"He made it through with a few dings, like me."

She focused on his bandaged arm and leg. "Oh, God, John, I just remembered you were wounded too."

"Just a few more scars to add to the package."

"Please tell me they caught Lampert.

The last thing I remember is seeing him running away with his hands cuffed."

Puller hesitated. "If I tell you the truth will you swear that you'll never tell another soul? Even if you're called on to testify?"

She sat up a little more and looked at him squarely. "What?"

"Maybe I should just let it alone. I don't want you to have to perjure yourself."

"What are you talking about?"

Puller looked at the med lines going into a single unit inserted near her collarbone.

"Morph drip for the pain."

"I think so, yes."

"Morph messes with your memory."

"It can. But we were talking about Lampert."

"We were?"

"John!"

"He decided to take a little trip abroad."

"He got away? On his yacht?"

"To Bulgaria. Understand he'll be making it his permanent home."

"How is that possible? Didn't the police arrest him?"

"The police were a little tardy. We took Lampert's tender to an isolated spot down the beach. From there, it was easy to put him in a truck and take him away. As far as the police know he got clean away. At least that's what I told them when they asked."

Carson stared at him for a long moment and then said, "I think I feel the morph erasing my short-term memory."

"I can understand that."

"When can I get out of here?"

"A few days."

"Will you come to visit me?"

"I've been living here," he said, pointing to a chair next to the bed with a pillow and blanket over it.

She smiled tenderly at this. "Diego and Mateo?"

"Back with their *abuela*. And they're living in my aunt's house. The other prisoners are being processed and will be returned to wherever they came from. That includes Lampert's household staff."

"Rojas?"

Puller shook his head. "No. Not today. But his time will come."

Carson looked overly agitated by this and Puller put a calming hand on her arm. A few minutes later the morphine kicked in and her eyes closed.

Puller went outside and called his brother at USDB. He filled Robert Puller in on nearly all that had happened, only leaving out the fate of Lampert in Bulgaria.

"Damn, John," said his brother. "You need another month of R and R to get over the last few days of R and R."

"Actually, I think I'm ready to get back in the rank and file."

"What are you going to tell the Old Man?"

"Not sure yet."

"You going to tell him that his sister is dead?"

Puller thought about that and finally said, "No. I'm not."

"I agree with you."

Puller had given Sadie the dog to Diego and Mateo. The two boys and the little dog had instantly bonded. Puller figured they would be good friends for many years. And he hoped that living in a nicer neighborhood well away from the gangs would be a big plus in their lives. And Bullock had promised to keep an eye on them.

There was a lot of paperwork and face time with Bullock, the state police, and the Feds. They said this would intensify the hunt for Stiven Rojas, but that the man had proven very elusive in the past.

"Keep trying," Puller told them before walking out of the last debrief.

Carson was released from the hospital two days later, bandaged, bruised, and tired.

But alive. Very much alive.

That morning she and Puller flew back home on a private jet sent down by the Army.

"Gulf Five," said Puller. "Never been on wings like this."

"Stick with a rising general and she'll take you places," Carson told him as the steward poured out two glasses of champagne for them.

* * *

Puller drove to his apartment after promising to have dinner with Carson that night at her place. A friend of his had taken care of AWOL while he'd been gone, but he let the cat out for a good long time and then played with him for an even longer time.

The next day he drove to Pennsylvania carrying a small package. He parked near a field of green grass, climbed out, and walked to the middle of the field. He opened the top of the urn and took his time sprinkling his aunt's ashes across the Pennsylvania countryside, just as she had wanted. He closed the empty urn, looked to the sky, and said, "Goodbye, Aunt Betsy. For what it's worth, a long time ago, you meant the world to a little boy. And the man he became will never forget you."

Puller knew what he had to do next. In fact, it was past time to do it.

He drove back to Virginia, showered, put on his dress blues, and headed to the VA hospital.

He walked down the sterile corridors, his frame tall and ramrod straight.

He heard his father before he got close to the room.

The same nurse as before confronted him in the hall.

"He's been a bear the last few days. Been screaming for you nonstop. Thank God you're here."

"Yeah," said Puller. "It actually feels good to be here."

The nurse looked at him oddly as he passed by her and opened the door to his father's room.

Puller Sr. was in his usual blue scrub pants and white T-shirt. He looked both agitated and confused.

When his father caught sight of him, Puller stood as erect as possible and executed a single crisp salute to his father.

"Reporting in, General."

His father's agitated state seemed to melt away and was replaced with a scowl. Puller would take a scowl over confusion from his father any day.

"XO, where the hell you been?"

"In the field executing your orders, sir," Puller said in a loud voice, enunci-

ating his syllables just as the Army ha
taught him.

"And the outcome?"

"Mission accomplished, General. Fair
winds and following seas."

"Damn good work, XO. Damn good.
At ease."

"Yes, sir," said John Puller and he
lowered his hand and sat down next to
his father.

For the moment no longer a solider.

Now only a son.

ACKNOWLEDGMENTS

To Michelle, for keeping it real *and* fun.

To David Young, Jamie Raab, Mitch Hoffman, Emi Battaglia, Tom Maciag, Maja Thomas, Martha Otis, Karen Torres, Anthony Goff, Lindsey Rose, Bob Castillo, Michele McGonigle, and all at Grand Central Publishing, who support me every day.

To Aaron and Arleen Priest, Lucy Childs Baker, Lisa Erbach Vance, Nicole James, Frances Jalet-Miller, and John Richmond, for being the best team a writer could ever have.

To Anthony Forbes Watson, Jeremy

Trevathan, Maria Rejt, Trisha Jackson, Katie James, Aimee Roche, Lee Dibble, Sophie Portas, Stuart Dwyer, Stacey Hamilton, James Long, Anna Bond, Michelle Kirk, and Natasha Harding at Pan Macmillan, for leading me to new heights in the UK.

To Arabella Stein, Sandy Violette, and Caspian Dennis for being great partners across the pond.

To Ron McLarty and Orlagh Cassidy, for continuing to knock the audio performances out of the park.

To Steven Maat at Bruna, for taking me to the top in Holland.

To Bob Schule, for your friendship, enthusiasm, and editorial skills.

To Chuck Betack, for keeping me straight on all things military.

To the families of Jane Ryon, Griffin, and Mason, I hope that you enjoyed the characters.

To my buddy Carl Brown, I hope you enjoyed seeing your name in print.

To Kristen, Natasha, and Erin, because I'd be hopelessly lost without you.

And to Roland Ottewell for another great copyediting job.